Ramblefoot

***

Ken Kaufman

ISBN 978-0-578-09245-4

It is 1917, *somewhere in Wyoming*

...not that it matters much to a wolf.

That Which is Master of the Wolf

No matter what a wolf's status is, whether he is the facet who makes the law or the wandering ramblefoot who follows no wolf's law, there is one master of him, and that master is his stomach. This master rewards him when he is a good servant, and punishes him when he is an unreliable one. This master never sleeps, has no mercy, and you are his slave from the moment life's spark starts your journey till the moment that spark is snuffed out.

Nowhere is this more evident than at hunt's end, just as the prey falls. Killing that prey may have required the selfless teamwork of many wolves, but once the slain animal emits its last gasp of breath, everything changes. Gone is the cooperation of a hard working troupe. Forgotten is the shared risk. Ultimately, each wolf must serve his invisible master above all others.

Thus, the hunting party that works with precision and efficiency and moves and breathes as a single organism dissolves into a melee of hostility, fear, anxiety, jealousy and violent mayhem. Fangs flash. Hackles are raised. There are no brothers and sisters, mothers and daughters, uncles and aunts. There are only wolves, each driven by the lashings of their individual master, the pitiless ogre that is their stomach.

But there is that rare wolf who defies the orders of each and every master, even the dreaded one that claws from within. This wolf despises answering to anything or anyone other than his own will, and since only his law will do, he struggles through life to overthrow his sovereign stomach. And when he finally ascends the mountain where he is king of himself and none are king of him, hunger has no more sway over his destiny than a thorn irritating his foot or a fly orbiting his ear.

There, on this lofty perch, where light and sound are swallowed by the clouds and calmness prevails, this lucky wolf stands, proudly feeling mastery over his stomach, able to hear his own heart thump. And once he hears his heart, with the quietude around him amplifying this organ's pumping into the rush and roar of an overflowing river, the wolf realizes that in the hierarchy of overlords the stomach was a merciful angel compared to his beating heart.

Book I

Cob Ash

Raspail, a wolf of indomitable spirit who would be tested by trial after impossible trial throughout his life, encountered his first challenge before he was born. His mother's womb, which was designed to protect and feed him, had by circumstance become a perilous tangle of twisting cords that was instead trying to starve and kill him.

He kicked and whipped his body in protest. And as he flailed about he knocked into his brothers and sisters, who like him were cut off from the nourishment of their mother. But unlike him these unborn wolves did not fight. There was only himself to slay this enemy, this starvation that was eating him from the inside out.

And so he fought the enemy by thrashing his arms and legs, because the first instinct of all young creatures facing danger and determined to survive is to thrash. In the pup's random flailing he loosened the knotted tubes in the crowded womb, and nourishment again warmly trickled into him.

Two weeks later he was thrust into the world, born to an old wolf named Parsay.

Parsay enjoyed being a respected and powerful wolf since she was young. She had been chosen by the pack's facet wolf to bear children, and she had birthed five or more strong healthy pups every year for five years. Now at the age of eight, her old womb could only sustain one life, so she heaped all the love that would have been divided among five healthy wolves on this one little black survivor.

Parsay gave her favored son Baudry the privilege of seeing the black pup before the others. He licked the black pup joyfully, for no adult wolf can resist tasting a new pup, but as he licked the little creature he thought: *If she does not let this poor runt die--if she selfishly spoils it with attention as she is doing--it will be the end of her reign.*

Baudry's prediction was based on what every wolf knows to be true. A large, healthy litter is an auspicious sign that food will be plentiful enough to fill every stomach in the enlarged pack. But the birth of a dead litter foretells of gloomy times ahead. So when Baudry returned to his brothers and sisters and reported that their mother was determined to care for the sole surviving runt, they all agreed that their mother should abdicate her rank and authority.

Over the next weeks, with anxiety building over how to get rid of the mighty Parsay, each wolf became self-absorbed, secretly worrying how their position in the shuffled hierarchy would be affected, and this turned their sacred social harmony-the harmony they relied on for survival -- into discord.

Beaudry, who had brought less and less meat back for Parsay and her son as the days went on, announced confidently at the start of the day's hunt:

"As of today, no wolf brings meat to Parsay."

They pounced on him joyfully, relieved by his initiative to become facet, and the dark feeling of doom brought on by the dead brood suddenly lightened. Parsay, secluded in her underground den, was oblivious to the relief experienced by her discontented children as Beaudry seized power.

Hearing the pack return from hunting, Parsay crouched low and scrambled through the den's tunnel and emerged into the warm winter sunlight, stretching her muscles while her eyes adjusted to the daylight. In the distance she could see Baudry leading the hunting party home. Something was odd in their demeanor. When Beaudry entered camp, instead of delivering food to her, he walked past her and lay down. The others copied him.

The regal Parsay stared at her family contemptuously.

"Why is there no meat today?" She demanded. "Was there no room in your blood-stained jowls and swollen bellies to carry food for your mother and brother?"

No wolf dared look at her.

Parsay walked desolately back to the mouth of the den where Raspail had blindly wandered and waited, crying for her.

"Look how meat drunk they are!" she said loudly to him, "And yet you starve! Cry, son - cry! Share your misery with them; it will ease your pain! Cry!" she commanded him.

Parsay's plea for him to cry instead turned him silent and well-mannered. Raspail, as we shall see, was not one to obey on command -- his mother or anyone else -- even at this young age.

The next day, Parsay joined the hunting party as they started out of camp. Immediately she felt the coldness of the group.

"If my children will not bring back food, I must at least hunt for myself," she announced haughtily.

Baudry halted and flashed fang at his mother. Parsay's heart swelled with shock and horror as she reeled back from the grotesque mask of her son.

As she watched them continue on without her she finally realized: *So... I am an outcast now.*

***

Parsay's Ramble

A faint whiff of foul air blew from the south. Parsay, lying outside her den, squinted her eyes and tucked in her ears to better savor the familiar sulfurous smell. Pitching her scarred gray muzzle upwards, she breathed in short rapid bursts at these beguiling puzzle pieces.

To the south was Warmpools, a land pitted with boiling cauldrons that spewed thick clouds of steam. These cauldrons, with their putrid fragrance, attracted an abundance of animals. These animals flowed like rivers of meat through the valleys of Warmpools. And this, in turn, attracted a dense population of wolves.

When Parsay was in her youth, the occasional Warmpools air that blew north excited her curiosity. Her aunts would say, "I would rather suffer the lashings of my stomach than eat like a facet in that stench."

But Parsay thought, *They are wrong; It must be so wonderful and plentiful what they are eating that it is worth breathing in that wretched air all day and night.*

It had been years since the smell had aroused feelings of wanderlust in her heart. Her mood lightened at the irony of how at the old age of eight she might yet ramble to the land she had yearned to visit as a child.

Raspail stumbled out of the den. Parsay gazed at him impressed that he'd survived whatever killed his brothers and sisters inside her. She marvelled at this creature, always moving, seeking food in the barren cave, his eyes still unable to open.

She lowered her head and nudged the pup on to his side where she licked his eyelids with her rough tongue. When his eyes finally opened, they groped desperately at blurry smudges of light. The moist orbs bobbled spastically, unable to keep up with his eager mind's curiosity.

Once Parsay watched a tree burn after a lightning storm. The embers burned long and bright, but then they flickered until they faded to cold gray. His eyed were not like the flickering embers. They were like the stars, sharp and intense.

Parsay played hard with the pup, toughening him for their journey. They were long days; she was fatigued by hunger, surviving only on rodents she caught outside the den and shared with her child.

And so on the morning of his fifth day with vision, while the pack was gone hunting, Parsay lifted her son in her soft mouth and quietly made the long walk to the southern border of the province she'd spent her whole life in. At this invisible line, inscribed with the piss of her and those before her, she stopped, let her pup drop into the snow, and considered her next step. She could openly enter hostile realms, act submissively and beg for mercy. Or she could travel the narrow routes between pack provinces, the dark and treacherous alleys where ramblefoots roamed. The ramblefoot, driven scattermad by his isolation, was notoriously desperate and unpredictable.

Neither course gave her confidence.

Raspail was tugging on a branch frozen in the ice when the massive voice of his mother rang out, a powerful vibration that seemed to come from everywhere but her. He dropped flat to his stomach trembling, hoping the roar wasn't some punishment meant for him.

"I am Parsay!" she announced, pausing till her howl stopped echoing. "With your mercy I am passing through! I am with child and pose no threat! I have read your scent posts and respect the boundaries of your province!"

She gathered the pup in her mouth and made her first step into hostile territory.

It took very little time. Raspail's eyes widened in awe as he watched five wolves mysteriously appear as if the dappled sunlight and mist suddenly combined and took physical form. They stood ground twenty lengths from them, scrutinizing Parsay more with curiosity than hostility. To see an esteemed wolf reduced to humility and submission was irresistible entertainment for her neighbors. To kill her would end the spectacle.

Parsay tucked her tail under her rear, bowed her head and declared, "I am not here to poach your elk. I am traveling south, past the mountains, with your mercy." She lowered her head again and said, "Respect."

She waited for a response but none came. She slowly began her terrifying trek through their province while they leisurely followed her from a distance. Three more wolves casually joined her escorts.

She did not look back until she reached the scent posts at their southeastern border. Parsay turned to give grace to her merciful escorts, but they had vanished as mysteriously as they had appeared.

As Parsay lapped water from the stream, she decided they would take this winding thoroughfare the rest of the journey. The sounds and perfumes of the streams and creeks would camouflage their footsteps and scent.

Wolfmother and son made good progress, passing six provinces without incident, and on the seventh day Parsay discovered an abandoned wolf den. She crouched low and entered, walking through the short narrow tunnel to the birthing chamber. There she lowered the pup on a soft bed of dry leaves. The restless pup sprang up, showing no signs of wanting to sleep, so she nuzzled his ear, flattening him into the bedding, and patiently breathed the soft, slow rhythms of sleep that she knew would eventually make his breathing relax in sympathy with.

Once he began snoring, she slipped out of the den and kicked together a barrier of leaves and snow to block the entrance. Satisfied that the wall would keep Raspail inside if he woke, she left the pup alone and went hunting for food.

***

An Uninvited Visitor

The pendulum of hunger, swinging reliably from the painful throbbing of starvation to the merciful dulling of appetite, reflected itself in poor young Raspail's dreams. When the pendulum swung in the direction of numb relief, he dreamed he was in a warm, safe place. And in that wonderful place (that was the faded memory of his mother's womb), his stomach was always full and his sleeping body twitched with joy. Then, as the pendulum swung back towards nagging hunger, the physical pain wended into the fabric of his sleepy imagination. The pup kicked and twitched in protest, trying to beat back the web of tentacles strangling him. He wanted the good place to come back.

He was startled awake by the sound of digging. His mother, he quickly realized, was gone. His fear escalated, first from realizing he was alone, and then from realizing he wasn't going to be alone for very long. The strange wolf entered so fluidly his steps left no sound as they embossed the den's downy floor. He entered like a vapor, his thick smell the only proof of his existence.

The pup, hoping he wouldn't be discovered, held on to his last scraps of courage by thinking of his mother. But it was the thought of his mother, of not knowing where she was amidst this danger, that made him lose control and cry a terrified squeal of helplessness.

The intruding wolf, who had been staring sadly at the pup thinking it was for sure dead, recoiled back, startled.

"Hoy!" the intruder said in surprise. "You know how to scare a wolf!"

Raspail's gaze drifted to the ramblefoot's hind leg which, to the young wolf's amazement, was lacking its foot . He stared in wonder at this amputated limb, then shifted his gaze back to the intruder's cockeyed gaze. His heavy eyelids hung low, as if he were in a permanent state of waking from a good sleep.

"Look at you. Wretched with hunger. Where's your mam? She dead?"

Raspail whimpered hungrily.

"Hungry. Sure, I know. Let's see what the master can spare!" His back arched, his gut pumped, and he retched up some meat for the pup. Raspail could not wait for him to finish before licking up the generous gift.

"Great riches, the endless meal, the river of easy meat, they're all waiting for you, son."

His syrupy words soothed the pup as he licked up the last drops of retch. When he was done, he looked up into the wolf's twinkling eyes and begged for more food.

"Hagi Shahn will take you to a place where your hunger be gone forever. Where the gloom of the past and the cloudiness of the future lift like the morning mountain mist."

There was a flash behind Hagi Shahn as the wolfmother charged into the den. Parsay hooked her fangs into his thigh and dragged the trespasser backwards out of the den. He pleaded for mercy as he was hauled out:

"My good leg!" Mercy, let go!"

Once they were outside the den she released him. He shrieked and squirmed backwards awash in pain. Parsay stood over him with gaping jaws -- the same jaws she delicately carried her pup with -- and prepared to kill him with one massive bite to his throat.

Hagi looked properly intimidated. Parsay, like her northern ancestors before her, was a massive-headed beast with a stature that you could only describe using words associated with such natural wonders as mountains, rivers, and storms -- like *majestic, impassive, formidable.*

She saw his mangled leg, stinking of rotten flesh.

"What animal took your foot!" She roared angrily at him.

"That animal be a wolf, and that wolf be me."

"You were so desperate for meat you ate your own foot?"

"Ha, no!" Hagi laughed, even though he was scared out of his wits. "I was bit by the jaws and they wouldn't let me go."

Hagi tried to get back on his feet. "Stay down!" She snarled. "What jaws bit you?"

"Jaws that's bigger than a bison's . No body. No head. Hard and cold like rock. No way out but to bite through your own leg. They're everywhere, mind the ground."

He's stricken with the scatters, she thought. She swung her head towards the den and saw Raspail sitting there watching, enthralled.

"Mercy then, permit me lick my wound?" Hagi asked.

She looked away and he began licking his wound with fanatical attention. It was as if being one of only three good legs had made it that much more precious to him. He paused to talk.

"Wolfmother, there's paradise meats for you and your son. I can guide you to the *Endless Meal.* Ah, you're right to be dubious, but take a glimpse at where I've been, and you will know I speak the truth, for it's not been two days since I last visited that southern cornucopia and the scent on me is fresh."

"Move and I'll kill you," she warned him.

She circumspectly put her muzzle by his and flared her nostrils. Indeed, exotic smells wafted off the matted fur under his mouth. She closed her eyes and breathed. He talked in seductive tones as the aromatic images swirled in her head:

"Big fat birds, so heavy they can't leave the ground. Bison, only fatter and slower, and with all the fight taken out of them. Hard to fathom, isn't it?"

She moved her head to the pads of his feet and sniffed vigorously at them, the creatures he described coming to life in her mind.

"White tufted beasts -- fat, gorgeous meat clouds, all you can eat as long as you like. *Ahhhh,* the treasures that wait," he moaned just thinking about them "I'll take you to what you smell on me, be your guide. You need my knowledge to survive."

"Go!" She growled at him. But he remained stationary, knowing he had an audience with her stomach.

"Why be satisfied with beaver..." She looked down at the beaver that she hunted and brought back for her son as he continued, "when you can feed your child on the juicy flesh of gorgeous paradise meats!"

"*Zut!* Go -- or I'll take *all* your legs!--" she growled at the crazy ramblefoot, "I'll make you look like the snake you are!"

Hagi rolled submissively in the dirt again.

"Go or I'll take your tail and ass too! I'll turn you into a maggot! *That is my last warning!*"

The three-footed ramblefoot took her at her word and scuttered off. Raspail watched him disappear into the darkness, then walked to his mother and sniffed at the beaver. She opened it's thick pelt just enough that the ravenous pup could peel the rest back on his own.

Watching the pup eat helped slow her racing heart, but her mind kept wandering back to the absurd beasts the mangled wolf described. When Raspail finished eating, Parsay licked the fur around her son's mouth clean. As she licked it she tasted the meat the ramblefoot retched up for him and thought: *"As wretched as he was he stole meat from his stomach to give my hungry son."*

They continued along the edge of the stream with the moon, nearly full, lighting their way.

***

Parsay Unwittingly Becomes an Accomplice

For every hundred lengths Parsay could have rambled, she dared not cover half that, having been whipped into an overly cautious state by the three-footed ramblefoot. The landscape changed so dramatically each day that, even at this slow pace, she couldn't catalogue sights and smells fast enough. The plains of her home were long, drab and flat. Here, she marveled, the worlds of animals and plants were richly layered and complex.

Eventually the creek they'd followed for days terminated in a series of small lakes. Passing these lakes, they emerged from the wooded forest into a wide, snow-covered valley that was very tempting to Parsay. Having trudged for so long at such a slow, cautious pace, Parsay was hungry to run, to run without worrying about where she was or the fate of her son, to bound in long open strides into the inviting meadow before her and chase something, *anything.*

But she couldn't. The scent posts were fresh and pungent here, left at regular intervals on trees and boulders. Their message was simple and clear: *Cross this line and you will be killed by us.*

Without the creek to cover their scent, she chose a path through the timbers to the east and they continued on. They felt the rumbling of an elk herd through their feet, and Parsay made her pup lay low between the trees telling him, "Where you find prey running, you also find predators."

They watched in wide-eyed amazement as the herd of elk, vaster than anything Parsay had ever seen, thundered past them.

When the last elk passed and the din died down, they continued along at their slow pace. She heard the sounds of wolves revelling at their good fortune, then fighting over their hard-earned meat.

As they trudged further, the smell of fresh elk carcass stimulated Parsay's nose. Her mouth grew wet as she fantasized about pulling the still-warm liver out of an elk and swallowing it whole. Finally a voice in her head broke through this dreamy haze and asked, *"Where is Raspail?!"*

She spun around; he was nowhere in sight.

Her heart raced as she retraced her steps -- she dared not call out -- and searched frantically for him. She located where his scent diverged from her path, traced it among the trees and out into the open meadow. There she saw the tiny black wolf, bounding across the stark white field of snow to where five wolves were hovering around their kill. She ran as fast as she'd ever run.

Raspail thought nothing out of the ordinary about following the scent of the elk. All he knew was, *there is food somewhere close by and I want it.* He did not think of what else might be waiting at the end of that scent trail, which in this case was five wolves, all staring at him incredulously.

Suddenly a huge shadow grew around him as Parsay pounced on him. She enveloped him protectively and stared down at the snow, averting the wolves' eyelines.

"This is your territory, mercy. We don't want your food."

Raspail peered out from between his mother's huge legs and saw an elegant looking male with a fancy strut and a disquieting grin. When this wolf -- whose name was Balfort -- stopped in front of Parsay, he fanned out his ruff so they could see the fine markings of his crest.

"You don't want our food?"

"No."

"Hmm. Is there something wrong with our food?"

"Nothing except that, like you say, it is yours and not ours."

Balfort laughed. "Everything is yours, wolfmother, so long as you take it."

"I don't wish to take what isn't mine."

"Ah! The air you breathe is not yours yet I see you have no difficulty taking it."

"There was a time when all was mine," she said, raising her head and uncraning her neck. Balfort stepped back dramatically, taking her size in. "Now, nothing is mine. Only this black pup. He is all I have to protect in this world, and I will protect him with all the fury of a wolfmother."

"Well then, being the good wolfmother you are you must desire to feed him. Look how hungry the wretched pup is. Why he's so hungry, he would even eat with us!" This provoked laughter from the other wolves.

"He is too young to know this is your territory."

"*Our* territory? Balfort chortled, "Did I say this was *our* territory?"

Parsay was baffled. She sniffed at Balfort and compared it with the land around her. This pack was poaching from another's province, and they seemed very bold and carefree about it.

"Wolfmother, *please* -- take as much meat as you can and feed your hungry son." He gestured to the elk carcass where their facet was eating. The facet, a handsome beast with impressive authority and spired markings over his eyes, watched her while he ate, but most of his enmity seemed focused on the fast-talking Balfort and not her.

She watched as the other three wolves casually spread out to block any escape she might attempt. There was no choice but to challenge their facet wolf for food. Why they desired this she could not fathom.

She looked deeply into Raspail's eyes, knowing this might be the last time she did so, then narrowed her eyes, extended her head straight in line with her back, and trotted to the carcass like she was entitled to it and anything else she wished to devour.

The facet wolf's eyes blazed threateningly as she strutted in a circle around him and his kill. He flashed fang and raised his hackles, but it was obvious to her that he did not want to abandon food for fight. Beyond him Parsay saw the four other wolves licking their lips in anticipation of a meal, and suddenly she understood: *They are using me as a distraction to steal food from their facet.*

She sprang forward at the elk's open chest, ripped out a mouthful of flesh and ran off with it. The facet wolf leaped after her. Parsay stopped suddenly, dropped the meat and gnashed at the facet until she was able to clamp her jaw tightly around his lower jaw, locking his mouth open and twisting his neck.

As she'd predicted, the three wolves scuttled quickly in the background, working together to rip apart the elk so they could run off with meat while their leader was occupied.

She wrenched his head, forcing his attention on to Balfort and the others advantageously raiding the carcass. "Watch them eat your meat."

Parsay released him. Immediately the big facet ran to his traitorous comrades to punish them and get back his food. She grabbed her pup and flew out of the meadow, back into the timbers with the sounds of crying wolves getting punished for their trickery fading in the distance.

***

Meatdrunk

They traveled quickly and by day's end encountered a group of fat beasts whose stout torsos were covered with dense white curly fur, and whose legs looked comically unfit for the job of transporting their bulky cargo. She sniffed at their scat -- indeed, it was the smell from the pads of the crazed ramblefoot's feet.

Fat, gorgeous meat clouds, she thought. He wasn't lying afterall.

She watched the sheep graze on remnant patches of grass under the snow. As soon as they sensed her, they froze in a crouched posture. Parsay marveled, *How does this animal survive here without the means to run or fight?*

Raspail jumped excitedly as he watched his mother wedge into the herd and take down a sheep. Parsay peeled back the thick white coils of fur with her teeth and revealed the glistening treasures inside. The pup joined her in the meal, slipping on bloody entrails as he tore at the fatty ribs. Parsay stuffed her stomach till it cried for pity then slowly ambled to a sunny clearing and let her aged body flop in the snow-covered grass. This was where she would raise her pup, she decided, in the land where she could hunt alone.

Her belly was so gorged with meat it ached to breathe. She waited for the great sensation that comes at the end of an epic meal like this, when meat is rammed into the stomach beyond the point of satedness, beyond that even of discomfort. She felt euphoric. Her woes vanished. The past no longer mattered, the future was inconsequential. Parsay was meatdrunk.

She watched Raspail through a hazy screen of falling snow, sitting and gnawing at something on his foot, and beyond him the ravens, jays and magpies squabbling over the remains of her kill. She shut her eyes, flush with a feeling of incredible well-being.

A sudden pain shuddered through her, quickly followed by a shrill snap from far off that echoed in every direction. She smelled her own blood. She quickly searched her body and saw blood spilling from a hole in her side, a hole created as if as if she had been bitten by an invisible, single-fanged predator. She stood up in shock and looked around, unable to locate her attacker. There was nothing to run from, nothing to defend herself against.

She swooped down and gathered Raspail in her mouth. Another loud snap exploded in her ears, but this time there was no bite.

She ran carrying Raspail until she lost all strength and collapsed to the ground where she struggled to breathe. Her side was drenched in blood and Raspail clung to her, whimpering.

With his head pressed against hers she said, "If I don't wake, wait here till the birds come down to eat my flesh. Eat them or you will die."

She did not wake. Raspail watched as his mother, who hadn't moved since uttering her last words hours ago, was rendered more and more unrecognizable by the swarming birds until she no longer reminded him of his brave, loving protector. He sat there whimpering and squealing, wishing that the birds would reverse their course and put his mother back together again. He slept by her side, dreaming she would be alive when he woke.

When he woke, the empty pain in his stomach rivaled that in his heart. Heeding his mother's advice, he attacked a magpie, slicing its wing with his sharp, infant claws. The wounded bird, unable to fly, tried to hop away from its attacker. Raspail picked the bird up in his mouth and shook it back and forth till it stopped flinching, then dragged it off to a tree where he devoured the bird -- feathers, bones and all.

His wolfmother, the great guardian that she was, had managed to feed him even after her life had gone.

Snow began to fall again, covering the blood-soaked tundra with a fresh, pristine layer of white, and soon all physical traces of Parsay were erased. Raspail, unable to restrain his utter despair, wailed a keening howl that was as pathetic and heartbreaking as any sound heard in the wild.

He was startled from this state by a raven squawking and flapping its wings in his face. He recoiled from the raven, fearing for his life as it thrust its massive black beak at him. She chased him like this, further and further away from the site where his mother died, until he was running as fast as he could, deeper into the world of predator and prey.

***

Poitu the Raven (...Earlier That Day)

The snow pinned a soft blanket of pure silence over everything capable of making sound. It must have been in league with the sun, whose bright rays ricocheted off the twisting crystals in every direction, making a blinding field of light that seemed to lull all of Warmpools to sleep.

For the two young ravens who had begun courting a day earlier, love made them immune to the sun's intoxicating effect. They wanted to play.

They glided opposite each other in a circle, the falling snowflakes giving them the sensation of floating upwards. Poitu watched the bird opposite her thinking, *When I move my wings, he moves his the same way. When I sing, he mimics my voice. He is my reflection in the water.*

Then, to test him, she broke the circle and flew at him. And as if in some watery reflection, he flew towards her.

Testing him further, the girl raven tumbled as she flew towards him so that she was gliding on her back -- backwards, no less -- talons first. She soared like this until she felt his talons crash against hers and clutch them. Their bodies, caught in each other's trajectory, stalled in mid-air and went into a gyration powered by their combined momentum. They pushed and pulled on each other, drawing their wings in tightly at the same exact moment, free-falling like some massive black whirling seed pod. They plummeted quickly like this, talons attached, through the haze of snow.

But the lovers, so connected in the moment that nothing else mattered, lost track of how fast they were falling and where the earth's floor was.

Poitu awoke from the impact stunned and confused. She lay in the snow, her talons still clenched tightly on to her lover's. She sensed immediately that he had not survived the fall.

She had devoted two years searching for him. During those years she bustled with enterprise and ambition. Every day had a purpose. She had no idea what to do now or how to nurse her pain. Unlike physical injury, for which there was always a balm (or at least the sense that the pain would heal) the throbbing in her heart felt permanent, life altering.

She flew mindlessly, unaware of time.

Then she heard the song.

It was such a perfect expression of her own anguish it seemed impossible to have been made by any creature other than herself. She headed in the direction of the song; she desperately needed to witness its tormented singer.

The commotion of ravens roosting in a grove of paintbrush trees made him easy to find. There was blood and fur in the snow, and beside it a wolf pup, black as a raven, waiting by the spot where his parent had died. The scavengers that had eaten her were now waiting patiently for him to die as well.

She landed in a tree and listened to the young wolf cry, taking solace in the fact that she was not alone, that some other creature suffered despair equal to if not greater than her own, that she had a comrade in suffering.

She dropped to the ground, hopped closer to the wolf and peered into his eyes. They seemed to be looking through her head and beyond the mountain behind her.

Poitu then had that inscrutable feeling of familiarity all animals have when they first taste warm milk, smell rotten meat, or hear water flowing. Most animals are too young when they awake these ancient memories to ponder the obvious question: *How is it I can remember that smell or taste if I have never experienced it before?*

In that very same way, Poitu recognized the black wolf. But not being an infant, she marveled at the impossibility of it. Before her was a wolf she'd never seen in her two and a half years of life -- the animal couldn't have been older than two months! -- and yet somehow she recognized him.

There was a ruckus in the trees. The mob of ravens, thinking she was stealing their food, threatened to kill her if she didn't leave.

She squawked at the wolf to move, but he didn't hear her.

She opened her wings and terrorized the wolf, charging and pecking hard at his rump and tail, until finally she had his attention. He lurched back. She chased him like this, half flying and half hopping, until seven ravens attacked her, forcing her to abandon the wolf and defend herself. Through the flapping of wings she could see him bounding away, his over-sized feet clumsily kicking up gobs of loose snow behind him.

He will be okay, a reassuring voice inside her said. This wolf has a knack for survival.

***

Hunting for Mice using a Snake

In the two days that passed since the raven chased him from his mother, time, in one of its rare acts of mercy, had begun blurring the horrific details of the tragedy.

Raspail's stomach, no stranger to hunger, showed less pity. He ate snow, which only made his master angrier. He roamed aimlessly between the tall trees looking for meat and by mid-day he smelled something. Poking around under a pile of rocks with his muzzle, he exposed a snake, its coiled body cold and motionless. He swiped his foot at the hibernating snake, then hopped back and watched the reptile writhe spastically. He swatted it again, and this time the snake struck back, nearly sinking its fangs into his muzzle. He reeled back, then patiently followed the snake as it undulated through brush and under rocks trying to evade the wolf and find some food.

Eventually the snake caught a mouse, which Raspail boldly stole out of his jaws. The young wolf kept the snake company all morning, cheating the hard-working creature of two more mice.

The fourth mouse was not so easy to steal. Raspail did his best to yank it out of the snake's mouth, then gave up and lay down, watching the snake slowly ingest the mouse, its head flaring impossibly around the fat rodent. With its mouth engorged by the mouse, the snake had no way to defend itself. Raspail, recognizing the opportunity just given him, circled the snake and grabbed it from behind, whipping it energetically against tree and rock until it stopped moving. He ate the snake, followed by the mouse.

The shrill ache started in his stomach and quickly spread to his limbs as the venom that paralyzed the mouse now got absorbed into his body. His muscles felt like brittle icicles, shattering with every movement, the jagged shards of ice seizing his body's coordination, making it painful to move or breathe. His stomach spasmed and he retched. Then, unable to hold his head up any longer, he heaved a sigh and collapsed as he lost control of his muscles. And that is where Raspail would have died had it not been for the involuntary actions of his bladder.

The smell of infant pee lit a bright beacon around the paralyzed wolf. And not a creature lurking in the vicinity didn't notice and turn its nose in his direction.

***

The Cob Ash Pack (Several Days Earlier) and "That Conversation Which is Impossible for Wolves to Have"

The wolves of Cob-Ash luxuriated in the morning sun, watching clouds of steam float off the snow floor of their spring camp. Food was plentiful, there were five new healthy pups -- three boys and two girls -- and life was generally good. Aratus, Balfort, and Maddocq, the core of the pack, watched the little ones playing in front of the den with Cob Ash, their reigning facet, and Cortess his mate. The new pups were old enough to play and fight, but still young enough that the hierarchy which would one day dominate their lives was not yet imposed on them.

Aratus was a quiet, pensive wolf. He was in spirit, if not in stature, every bit as mighty as his brother Cob Ash. He was clever and quick-witted, had a noble disposition and big heart, and was as confident a hunter as Cob-Ash. What he lacked was the desire to make law and carry it out. So he "led from behind", formulating hunting strategies, guiding Cob Ash's decision-making, and raising the next generation of hunters.

Of these future hunters playing before his critical eye now, none impressed him in the way he had hoped. Abillon, the second largest of the new brood, possessed beauty and stature but lacked confidence. His brother Polwin acted subordinate to Abillon even though he was larger and seemed to have more aggression and ambition. Kileo their sister was confident to a fault, carried herself with authority, yet was also cautious. She had a stunning, complex beauty and a perceptive nature, but she was, alas, not a boy, and thus she could never be Cob Ash's heir.

Aratus sighed, for therein was the source of his despair. He secretly desired to ramble some day, but for him to leave Cob Ash he would first have to groom a successor, someone to take his place in the hunting party and in the life of the pack. Of these new wolves, none truly shined.

Aratus' brother Balfort fastidiously groomed himself, licking his paws as he observed Abillon playing with Polwin.

"Abillon stands out. He's clearly the most promising."

Aratus didn't seem to hear him, though he did.

"Aratus, you agree with me, don't you?" Balfort asked again.

"They're all promising. None stand out yet."

"None but Abillon," Balfort corrected him.

Aratus saw Maddocq become alert, then picked up the same transmission vibrating through his pads.

"What marvelous creatures these elk are!" Balfort exclaimed. "Why it's as if they hear my stomach and come to answer its call."

Cob-Ash stood and stretched. It was no mystery why he was the facet of the pack. "Facet" literally meant "the face of us." Others in the pack could stand behind him and proudly say, "Cob-Ash is the one we choose to represent us to the world, he is the best of us, *the face of us.* When other packs think of me, let them think of Cob-Ash, for he is our best." He was a stunning beast, with powerful, hulking shoulders and bold markings around his eyes and mouth which accentuated his intelligence and, more importantly, confidence. He rarely had to tell others what to do, they eagerly tried to please him, to be in his good favor. The power of eight wolves looking up to him fueled the furnace of his authority, which he abused no more than any other facet.

The excited pups tried following the hunting party out of camp, so Hesser, the pack's kickaround dog, acted like a panicky elk to distract the needle-toothed pups into chasing him instead.

Cob Ash kept the five hunters in sync, traveling briskly but conserving energy for the hunt. They ran up-slope and stopped to watch the elk come down from the mountain to forage on Cob Ash's prized aspen groves.

Maddocq and Balfort sauntered into the valley to agitate the elk, while Cob-Ash and Aratus stood together scanning the herd for slow, sick, or old. Cob-Ash found his prey and they stormed into the valley to kill it.

Upon realizing that it had been selected, the elk overcame its injury enough to stir up some anarchy, driving the herd out of the valley and to the east. Balfort and Maddocq raced ahead to keep the herd within their borders, but they were not fast enough and the elk thundered into neighboring Draguignon.

Cob Ash was so maddened that he violently lashed Aratus. Then, without saying anything he sprang across the creek, stepped over Draguignon scent posts, and entered hostile territory. The others looked at each other queasily, then took their positions running behind Cob Ash.

They were deep within Draguignon when they brought down the elk. Cob-Ash ate first, eating the heart, kidney and liver without contest from his brothers. Once these were finished, the others vied for turns. He aggressively asserted his status and did not let them eat, bitter as he was.

"Cob-Ash, our facet, who we can always count on for good judgment," began Balfort with his singsong voice, "given how we are quite far from home and might be joined any moment by our unfriendly, murderous cousins -- who, I must say, would be within their right to kill us..."

Aratus and Maddocq casually moaned in agreement.

Balfort's voice turned to a whimper, "Perhaps, my facet, you would let us take meat by your side? That way, if we are forced to defend ourselves, we are well-fed and have strength."

Cob-Ash growled, his mouth overflowing with meat. "If you're hungry, come and take it."

It was an invitation that none of them dared accept.

They smelled an approaching wolf and hunkered close to the ground. Surveying the open meadow they saw a lone black pup bouncing through the snow racing eagerly towards the elk carcass. Then the wolfmother appeared -- a big, majestic old ramblefoot, off her turf like them -- chasing after her errant son.

This gave Aratus an idea for how to steal meat from Cob-Ash. He shared the plan with Balfort, and Balfort lured the big female into challenging their facet wolf for the elk. The stratagem was a success, and they each managed to sneak off with a piece of the elk as we have already seen.

On the way home, Cob-Ash, madder than before, was soothed by Balfort, "My facet, you recognized our hunger, you invited us to eat and you kept your word. What a fair and decent facet you are!"

They felt the marching of wolves through their pads and smelled the scent of Draguignon wolves, whose province they'd just poached in, grow thicker. Then the marching suddenly stopped, creating a silence that seemed to defy time. The terrible silence was interrupted by a single howl. Another wolf added her voice, then another, and the droning howl grew more powerful and ominous as all those individual threads wove into a loud grim dirge that penetrated deeply into the trespassers' guts where it seeded fear.

"They have the numbers," Aratus whispered confidentially to Cob Ash. "And if we head directly home right now, we will find them holding the border."

To help him decide whether to fight or flee, Cob Ash looked up at the moon dimly glowing in the afternoon sky and felt empowered by the fact that the eye of the ancestors was nearly fully open. And just as Balfort and Maddocq had to wait in anxious agony for their facet to dictate their fate, the eager reader must be asked to have patience as we explain the importance of the eye of the ancestors.

While it can't be called a religion, the eye is a belief that every wolf has. He isn't born with an innate sense of it, nor does he learn it from other wolves -- he couldn't, no wolf dares talk about it because the eye looms over them constantly. This shared belief is self-learned.

The baby wolf, once he is old enough to see his mother's and father's eyes, quickly learns how those golden orbs can spoil him with attention when he is good or make him shrivel in humility when they judge him harshly for being bad. They can ignore him when he is needlessly craving attention, and they can shower him with pride when he shows good sense. They can laugh with him when he takes a risk and fails, or laugh mockingly at him when he talks big and then does nothing.

And once a young wolf understands the language of his parents' eyes, it is natural for him to make the same association with the radiant orb that watches over him in the sky, the moon.

Now, since there is no oral tradition (and certainly no written scripture), the mood of the eye is open to interpretation from wolf to wolf. A wolf may grow to think that the mood of the eye is a reflection of approval or scorn. Another wolf may see the mood of the eye as a predictor to the day's fortunes or misfortunes and act accordingly.

Since there are no conversations on the interpretation of the eye, there is no consensus, no disagreement or argument between wolves because, simply, there cannot be. However, if two wolves were to have that conversation that is impossible for wolves to have, and they were to talk about the meaning of the eye, they would most probably agree on a few things: First, they would both agree that it is the eye of a great wolf, greater than their facet, for it is the eye of an immortal beast who stands above them all in the sky. Like a parent, it is loving and patient and also critical and punishing. The eye can't force you into doing things the way a facet can with his teeth, but it watches and judges you, and the commanding stare of a righteous being is more powerful than the sharpest of fangs.

The second thing these two wolves would agree on is that this beast is the sum of all dead wolves. That means that when the eye is watching you, your dead aunts and uncles and perhaps even your dead children are watching you. That can mean shame to one wolf, and pride to another.

The third thing these two wolves would agree on is that when the eye is just a sliver of itself, when most of the eye is shadowed and only one sharp crescent remains, the eye is at rest It is a good time to steal your neighbor's retch, hump your facet's bitch, and cower from lesser wolves when the eye is resting.

When the eye is fully open, however, every wolf acts in top form. Wolves will show off for the eye when it is fully open, but this should not be mistaken for hubris. Wolves like to entertain the eye, to share their glories in the same way a pup enjoys impressing its parents with its achievements.

Our two wolves having this impossible conversation might even say, "If I am going to do something noble and valiant, I want the eye's full attention. For why should I take such risks and attempt such ambitious feats if the ancestors are not watching?"

And so Cob Ash, divining that the eye, attentive looking as it was, wanted to see him achieve victory and attain glory, looked away from the moon and turned so he was poised to face the arriving enemy.

"We fight Draguignon."

***

An All Around Bad Idea

"What?! Surely flee is what you mean," Balfort exclaimed.

Before Cob Ash could lash Balfort, Aratus stepped between them and offered the facet his counsel. "We will gladly take them on and kill as many as we can, for our facet is great and his judgment good. But it will cost us all our lives."

"So what do you suggest we do?"

"Retreat."

"You said retreat was impossible."

"I said direct retreat was impossible. There are provinces to the east, in the Valtige. We don't share a border with them, and we did not just poach their meat."

"Our meat," Cob Ash corrected him.

"It stopped being ours when it passed their scent posts."

"You want to circle mountains? That will take us days to return home. And you don't know for sure that a fight doesn't wait for us in the Valtige."

"That is true."

"A fight against the Valtige would be pointless, it would gain us nothing but safe passage. But fighting Draguignon -- tensions have been brewing, and one day it must happen."

"Perhaps on a day when your brothers are better fed."

"Mercy for you I don't have time now to kill you for that remark."

"I'm just assessing the situation as it is, my facet. You are bordering on meatdrunk, while we are bordering on starvation.

Our enemies are waiting for a response from us. Do you have a decision?'

"It is obvious to me," Cob Ash began, appraising his neighbor's land casually as he spoke, "Why they would desire to invade our province."

Aratus indulged Cob Ash's nonchalance while his other brothers fretted nervously behind him.

"Look at their land," he continued. "It is beautiful, yes, but they don't have the aspen groves of Cob Ash."

"No, they do not. They cannot boast, as you can, of the prime meats that are drawn to your aspens. They are stuck with our leftovers."

"Maddocq believes they had two bitches with healthy litters this year."

"Maddocq's nose is impeccable, so I do not doubt it."

"Draguignon will have the numbers when all those pups are grown."

"My facet, any time you would like to augment the size of your pack, I am at your service."

Balfort, eavesdropping behind them, snickered.

"We will leave now and save fighting for another day," Cob Ash said softly, and they ran east, towards the mountain range that loomed over the eastern border of Draguignon.

They were fifty lengths from the border when Balfort, unable to control the churning of his anxious gut, suddenly stopped, curved his back and unloaded his bowels.

The others looked at him and laughed one by one, and then Cob Ash shat as well, followed by Aratus and Maddocq. Of the wolf's many great joys in life, shitting inside an enemy's province ranks very high, and higher still if the experience is shared with friends. Our heroes now had something victorious to remember when they looked back on the awful day when Draguignon made them retreat.

Once they crossed the border into the Valtige, they traveled in morbid silence through the crescent-shaped province that curved around the mountain. Uneasiness plagued each of them

Cob Ash stopped and surveyed.

"We are deep into the Valtige. Where are they?" Cob Ash said while his nose searched the air for clues. "They should have made themselves known by now."

"Strange." Aratus agreed. "All the scent posts are dry, I barely smell them." He sniffed again. "And why have no other wolves moved in to claim this vacant province?"

They continued on, traveling a serpentine route that winded through the foothills. Anxiety had seized each of them, but none more so than Aratus who thought, *How can a province where there is not a wolf to be heard be more frightening than one where there are fifteen shrieking for my death?*

They looked for refuge, not because any of them imagined they could sleep in this eerie place, but because they were horribly worn down, dispirited, and starving.

They took refuge under a cantilevered rock ledge where they flopped restlessly, haunted by the uncanny absence of wolf howls and fresh scent posts in a territory that was once vibrant with them. Balfort cheered them up briefly, reminding them that they shat in Draguignon.

As they traveled again, Maddocq, who possessed the most sensitive nose in the group, picked up the bright and shocking flare of youthful wolf piss. Aratus saw Maddocq honing on the scent, whining as he did. He followed Maddocq until he smelled it too; shutting his eyes he fathomed the wayward black pup from the day before. He opened his eyes and charged into the timbers where he raced quickly, darting side to side until he arrived at the site where the black pup, separated from his mother, lay dead alone in the snow.

His heart felt heavy enough to fall out of his chest as he gazed into its open, lifeless eyes. It was so sad a spectacle it would have broken even the most cold-hearted wolf's spirits. Aratus, whose heart was obliged to take on all the grief of the world like the tiny ant carrying five times its body weight, began to moan and cry uncontrollably over the body of this young wolf. In his howl he fathomed the moment from yesterday, seeing the wolf bounding bravely into a dangerous pit of hungry wolves like he had some rightful place there. He saw the resolve on his snow-covered face every time he crested a hillock, and then his huge mother, cresting the hillock after him, unable to catch him.

What he saw was exactly what was missing in Cob Ash's latest brood. It was here, laying dead in the snow, and Aratus looked so devastated and sang with such melancholy that the others, who'd arrived shortly after him, worried that their brother would keel over and die from sadness in sympathy with the unfortunate pup.

And then the tiny animal's glowing eyes blinked.

Aratus's heart sprang back into his chest. He gently nudged the wolf with his nose and saw it spastically kick out its hind leg. Aratus licked and massaged his underside with his long warm tongue.

Aratus looked over and saw Maddocq and Balfort sniffing at the regurgitated snake in the snow. He imagined how the little pup had valiantly fought, killed, and ate its prey, not knowing the snake's poison would sicken it. He licked the wolf's face, feeling his shallow breaths on his whiskers.

Cob Ash arrived and took a cursory sniff of the black pup.

"The mother must have died. Let's go," Cob Ash said, impatient to get home. Only Maddocq followed him as he trotted out of the clearing.

Aratus stared at the pup with admiration; he had performed an amazing feat by traveling and hunting alone. His only mistake had been his choice of prey, and this, he predicted Balfort would comment on.

"Not such a good choice of food, eh Aratus? A wolf, even in youth, should hear the voice of his ancestors warning him not to eat a snake. Mercy."

"If he hadn't overcome his natural fear of snake he would have died."

"*Would* have died?! Aratus! He's two breaths away from death!"

Balfort's bombastic certainty on all subjects no matter how far out of his scope irritated Aratus when they were younger. Then, one day, Aratus realized that whenever he faced indecision, he could always reach a sound judgment by doing the opposite of whatever Balfort suggested. So Balfort's blustering only made Aratus even more sure of his inclination to save the pup.

"In any case, Cob Ash has commanded us to leave without any mention of rescuing half-dead babies."

"Ah," Aratus said with a glint in his eye, "But he has also *not* mentioned leaving him here to die."

"Ah! So your plan is to exploit the vagueness of his command, which will only add insult to insult -- disobeying a command, and abusing the non-specifics of it."

Aratus looked at the pup. A raven landed near him and trilled at Aratus. He lunged at the raven, spooking it away. Balfort was growing impatient and made his case again:

"If I were you -- and you never take my advice even though you always thank me for it -- I would leave now without the baby and not anger your facet any more than you already have."

And that was exactly what Aratus needed to hear.

"Thank you, brother! Your advice, as always, is as reliable as the sun rising in the morning and setting at night," Aratus said with sincere appreciation.

Balfort smiled proudly then ran to catch up with the others. Aratus smiled into the pup's eyes, unable to tell whether the paralyzed animal could see or hear him.

"You took a risk eating the snake. I will take a risk bringing you home."

Aratus gathered the pup in his mouth, hoisted him up, and caught up with the others. When Balfort saw the child in his jaws, he just shook his head, mystified eternally by his brother's logic.

***

Returning to Cob Ash

The following day, when the bedraggled hunting party returned to camp with no meat but another mouth to feed, the sick black pup was greeted with skepticism. But by nightfall, worrying about the fate of the new addition to their pack became the predominant activity around camp, casting a gloomy shade over everything they did.

Knowing that Cortess, Cob Ash's mate, would not allow a sick, strange pup in her den with her own litter, Aratus built a small, impromptu den that was just outside their camp and slept with his body curled around Raspail for heat. Every wolf except Cob Ash came to visit the pup and offer Aratus some relief.

As the pup went in and out of sleep for three days, his dreams and nightmares were filled with unfamiliar faces looking at him with worried eyes, poking him with their wet noses. He howled weepily to them, *"Maaaaam! Maaaaaam!"* And when the helpless innocent cried, the wolves could not eat, play or sleep, for it was so demoralizing a song it was as if it were a curse sent to them by some dead enemy.

On the fourth day, his howling suddenly stopped, and the wolves grew even more anxious waiting to see which direction the pup's life would go.

As a diversion from this somber vigil, Hesser, the lowest ranking wolf in the pack, engaged the pups in a game he initiated by picking up a long stick in his mouth and running around camp scratching the pups with it. The pups then chased him trying to wrestle the stick from his strong jaws. Cob Ash, eager for distraction himself, joined in the game and soon play broke out everywhere. Even Aratus, who desperately needed to shake off some of the gloom hanging over him, left the den to play.

"Maaam..."

Aratus, wrestling with Maddocq and Cob Ash, looked up to see Raspail standing outside the den, listing to one side, his eyes squinting in the searing sunlight. Aratus bolted back to the den.

Many strange characters visited Raspail in his dreams. One of these strangers -- a calm, reassuring wolf who smiled with his eyes and not his mouth -- visited his dreams more regularly than the others. So when this wolf greeted him in the flesh, it was as if he already knew him, that he was an old friend from his imagination who had become real.

"I'm Aratus. I found you and brought you here."

"Maam?"

Aratus fretted for a moment over how to respond, then pressed his muzzle next to the pup's and softly said, "I'm your new Maam."

Balfort, who was standing behind Aratus, howled uproariously, "Splendid! Aratus a maam! Now I've seen everything!"

The mood in the pack lightened as if a new brood of pups had just been born, and the dazed Raspail was swarmed with curious guests. They licked, they poked and pushed, they retched up food, and even Cob Ash, who had been bitter with Aratus for his insubordination, seemed to let his grudge pass as he was so overwhelmed with joy.

Aratus noticed the normally upbeat Polwin hanging back from the spectacle and acting aloof, so he trotted over and engaged the young wolf in play. Polwin soon shook off his jealousy and, when he could no longer suppress his curiosity, sprinted off to wiggle his way into the fray and look at his new brother. Aratus couldn't be more pleased.

Polwin swatted at Raspail playfully, knocking him over easily to the amusement of his aunts and uncles. Raspail got back on his feet, and the chance to swat him down a second time was irresistible to Polwin. This time Raspail fought back, biting his leg and wrestling him to the ground. The entire pack watched excitedly, yipping joyfully at the indomitable spirit of their newest member.

Over the next few days, Raspail grew strong enough to walk around and eat but too weak to really play. Polwin and Abillon kicked him around to show off for their sisters, and when Raspail fought back, which he always did, he was no match for the bullies, malnourished and out-numbered as he was.

When Aratus returned from the hunt with meat for Raspail, Polwin and Abillon would team up and steal it from the weak pup. Aratus watched him take on fights that he couldn't possibly win, fighting with the self-taught thrashing of an orphan who had never played with peers. It bordered on unwatchable.

He thought: *His mother was a massive thing. He'll have size too, he just needs to learn how to fight.*

Balfort was nearby grooming the fur on his feet with a euphoric fury. "I told you a wolf who doesn't know better than to eat a snake wouldn't thrive--"

"Two breaths from death, you said! I've lost count myself," said Aratus proudly. He got up and loped away before Balfort could respond.

He trotted along trying to rein in his many thoughts, when a hare crossing his path woke him from his introspection. He pursued the hare, not out of a desire to eat it, but to play. Casually chasing the hare he reminisced on the many skills he had honed play-fighting with Cob Ash, Maddocq, Balfort and Hesser when they were young. Raspail had no experience with brothers and sisters, and so he had never learned how to play or be social. He ended the game with the hare and returned with it to camp thinking: *It is time to stop being his mother and start being his brother.*

He was surprised to see Raspail waiting for him so far outside the camp. Raspail had figured out that it was possible to shake off his harassers by venturing beyond where Cortess allowed them to go. Raspail, who was by nature disliking of boundaries, was rewarded in his endeavor by the look of surprise and approval on Aratus' face. So he was confused when Aratus, who was normally fair and generous, sat down with the rabbit and guarded it like he intended not to share it.

Raspail stared quizzically, whining in protest. He hopped on his hind legs, and patted his front feet lightly on Aratus. When that didn't work, he rolled on his side and whined louder, but Aratus just ignored him and played with the rabbit, throwing it around and retrieving it as if to amuse himself. He rubbed his muzzle in its thick fur, inhaling its musk with exaggerated glee, cruelly stoking the flames of Raspail's desire, envy, and frustration.

"Mine!" the pup yipped earnestly. Aratus remained aloof, pretending to ignore him. "Mine!" the pup repeated, then he lunged at the rabbit. Aratus blocked with the hard crown of his skull. The pup bounced off, rolled over and got up, looking defiant and determined.

He dodged at the hare again. Aratus whipped the hare away as the young wolf corkscrewed at it and fell with a mouth full of air. Aratus blocked him with his hips as he came a second time, keeping the hare as far away from him as possible. Then he began to peel open the rodent, slowly, tauntingly. The pup paused for a moment to gaze at the delicacy that had just been cracked open.

"Yes, it's yours." Aratus slowly started eating the rabbit.

"Then why don't you give it to me?" he asked, frustrated.

"It's only yours once you've taken it. Until then, it is *mine.*"

The dejected pup took on a look of resignation and walked back to camp. When Raspail was out of his sight, Aratus felt regretful that he had gone too far teasing him. He got up from the hare to seek Raspail, and followed his trail twenty lengths to where the scent suddenly went cold. Raspail was nowhere in sight. He heard a light rustling behind him, spun his head around, and that is when he saw Raspail running away with the hare in his mouth.

"You cunning little thief," the wise wolf laughed in delight. Raspail growled at Aratus to keep his distance.

Aratus lay down, elegantly resting his head on his crossed forepaws, and watched Raspail devour the hare. *Perhaps I am not your mother or your brother, but your student,* he pondered.

Raspail took his food this way from then on, and every day Aratus thought of new lessons for his student. He taught him how to defend what was his in a game that involved a pine cone. Aratus showed him how to keep the pine cone clutched between his front paws and pivot from that point, using his hips to block, his back feet to kick and mouth to bite. Aratus worked him like this until both were panting from exhaustion.

Then he taught Raspail how to steal what wasn't his. He demonstrated by making feigning lunges at the pine cone. Aratus swiped the pine cone from Raspail several times then let him copy him. Raspail feigned very convincingly because, as with nearly everything, he committed his heart to it fully. They destroyed twenty-four pine cones and five sticks playing like this.

In the flurry of fighting over the last pine cone, Raspail suddenly found himself wrestling with himself over the coveted object, because his opponent had vanished. Aratus was nowhere. It was as if the wolf had disappeared into the granite boulders.

"Aratus!" He cried.

Then the student was suddenly standing under his teacher's shadow, and the wolf reappeared as if he'd walked out of the solid granite. Raspail was awed.

"I want to play *that* game!"

Aratus grinned, "I'm sure you do."

"Where did you go?"

"I was right here. I just didn't let you know I was here."

"I don't understand"

"Klooting is for later on."

"Later today?!"

"No."

"Tomorrow?!"

Seeing the eagerness in his young eyes, and remembering how fascinated he was watching the older wolves make themselves disappear before his eyes when he was a pup, he softened.

"Tomorrow, maybe. If you can do something."

Aratus looked around, his eyes landing on a young apple tree with a willowy trunk. "I want you to get me an apple from that tree."

The pup jumped at the tree's lowest hanging branch. Even if he were twice as long he would have been too short. It seemed he'd been assigned an impossible task.

After jumping from every possible angle, he faced Aratus and asked him, "Can I do it?"

"I will never ask you to do something that is impossible," the fair Aratus assured him. "I must go now. Bring me an apple and tomorrow I will show you how to kloot." Aratus trotted off, leaving him alone.

Raspail jumped a few more times at the apples till he fell and rolled into the tree's rubbery trunk. The tree's branches rustled, and some dead leaves drifted to the ground. This gave him an idea. He pounced on the tree, pushing the trunk. The branches shook as the tree swayed, but no fruit dropped. He charged at the tree, harder and harder until the tree was rocking back and forth under its own momentum, then jumped at the tree's branches as they craned low and tore an apple off its stem.

He crashed hard to the ground and his fangs punctured the prized apple in his mouth, the acidic juices burning the tender lining of his mouth. It was a taste he would never forget. Tomorrow he would learn how to disappear.

The next day, after Aratus and Raspail destroyed more pine cones and branches stealing from each other, Aratus led Raspail up a stack of boulders that had been locked in precarious, gravity-defying positions for millennia. Raspail was agile and had no trouble keeping up with Aratus, who barked back to him, "Don't let me out of your sight."

Halfway up, Aratus vanished as he did the day before, and again, Raspail was dumbfounded.

"I'm here," Aratus' soft voice echoed through the rocks. Raspail could not locate him.

"Come find me," his voice echoed again. Raspail circled the area, jumping from boulder to boulder, diving between the gaps. He ran like this until Aratus appeared running beside him. The startled pup, not watching where he was going, ran head first into a rock wall. He shook his head and gathered his wits.

"When you howl, you make your presence known. When you kloot, you do the opposite -- you vanish from nose to tail," Aratus said.

He took a deep breath and Raspail copied him. Aratus said, "Now breathe out slowly, and don't breathe again." Raspail exhaled through his open mouth, which Aratus closed tight with his own, clamping it shut. "For smell, your mouth must stay shut. For sound, your insides slow down. And for sight, choke the light out of your eyes so they are dark and invisible. Raspail watched with wonder as the seasoned wolf's eyes squinted and the yellow light seemed to extinguish.

"Always be aware of the landscape around you, find places to kloot even when you don't need them. Make it second nature."

"How do I know where to Kloot?"

"My fur is the color of granite, so I kloot among the boulders, by aspen trees and in long, dead grass. Your fur is black. You are suited to klooting in the shadows of things, against dark timber."

"Let me try!" the student yelped.

"Run and hide. Don't reveal yourself until I find you, no matter how long it takes," Aratus told him. Raspail ran off, leaping from rock to rock until he was out of Aratus' sight. He stepped into the dark shadow of a crevice, then he breathed out, squinted his eyes, and slowed his excited heart. He froze like this, waiting for Aratus to pass.

Aratus did not immediately chase after Raspail. He first hunted a hare, and without killing it, carried it writhing in his mouth back to the boulders.

About the time Raspail was getting restless wondering if Aratus was ever going to find him, he smelled the hare getting near and he froze. His heart was trying to beat fast, but he steadied himself. The hare passed the crevice without sensing him, and Raspail launched himself at it, catching it before it saw him. His heart beat wildly at his victory and he began to drool. But eager as he was to eat it, he was hungrier for something else. With the hare in his mouth and confidence in his heart, he raced back to show his brothers and sisters what he had accomplished.

***

The Fortitude of A Wolf Who Has Faced a Thousand Deaths

Raspail had no position of rank whatsoever among the pups and desperately wanted to impress them with his worth, which in his mind at this moment, was considerable. He returned with the rabbit in his mouth and paused at the edge of the camp.

He saw his sisters Kileo and Moorea fighting over a hawk feather. Kileo was a magnificently speckled creamy gray wolf. While the markings that highlighted her mother Cortess' eyes and mouth suggested confidence and consistency, Kileo's were erratic, exciting and unpredictable, like her nature. If there were any wolf he wanted to impress more than others, it was Kileo.

Raspail strutted over and began casually flinging the hare in the air and catching it, but Kileo denied him the attention he craved.

"I hunted it myself," he finally said.

Kileo ignored him, but Moorea sniffed the hare. "You liar. You can't hunt."

"Yes I can. I killed it like this." Raspail reenacted his heroic deed, freezing with squinted eyes, then darting dramatically at the dead hare.

Polwin blindsided him, ramming his shoulder into his chest and knocking him over. Abillon then scooped up Raspail's hare and took off with it.

Raspail chased after Abillon, but before he could reach him Polwin jumped on his back and brought him down. While the two tussled, Abillon started tearing open the hare. Raspail saw the thief's blood-stained muzzle and felt the cold rush of fury that innocents feel when fair play is not abided by.

Raspail heaved Polwin off his back and attacked Abillon, feigning like Aratus showed him, then biting at his face and neck while wrestling him down, punching him unrelentingly in the ear with his hard snout.

Abillon yelped in pain. Polwin came to his aid, jumping on Raspail's back again, but to his surprise he could not bring him down as he could in the past. Ten Polwins could not bring Raspail down, and it was not because of Aratus' rigorous training.

It was because Polwin had that which all innocent creatures in their youth deserve to enjoy. He had the safety and comfort of a dependable and caring family, with aunts and uncles watching over him, lavishing him with love and affection. He did not have to fight for his survival in his mother's body, the way Raspail had, or seek food after she died. Raspail was that much wiser, that much stronger, that much more defiant to any challenge that would come his way, for he had survived a dozen deaths already.

Polwin's sharp fangs dug into Raspail's shoulder as the two ran side by side. Raspail twisted his head and butted his skull into Polwin's right eye hard and painfully until Polwin released him and cowered back, giving Raspail the victory.

Abillon saw the hare laying unguarded and went for it a second time. But as he picked it up he felt Raspail's jaws close around his muzzle. They spun in the dirt, and the fight quickly ended with Raspail sitting on top of Abillon, eating his precious hare in a show of dominance that verged on comedic.

Raspail looked around and saw that this comedy was playing to every member of the pack but, of course, Kileo.

The hare incident was the first of many exploits in which Raspail demonstrated that he was not just strong and brave, but did things with humor, charm and brio. He turned mundane activities into extravagant misadventures, upending the ordinary as if to wring more out of it, always getting in way over his head and then achieving victory through cleverness and tenacity.

His amusing antics were a welcome diversion in the life of a wolf pack that spent long hours between hunts laying around. One afternoon the pack woke to the sound of Raspail storming into camp chased by a bear cub twice his size. He was not crying for help, as another wolf might have. In fact, he had brought the bear into the camp so that he could be emboldened by the approving laughter of his family while he fought the beast. But the bear, upon seeing a dozen wolves leap to their feet, turned around and retreated quickly. Raspail stormed back out of the camp as quickly as he'd entered, only now he was chasing the bear.

He was gone for three hours when Aratus began to worry. He looked to Cob Ash for silent approval then began a long howl, calling out for Raspail. He was joined in by his sisters and then Balfort, Maddocq and finally Cob Ash, whose broad, round voice weaved all of their voices together.

Raspail returned the following day, limping into camp with clumps of fur gouged off his bloody hide. The pack stared curiously at him, but Raspail was in a bad temper and growled at them, deterring them from inquiring about his night out. Later that day Maddocq found the remains of the dead bear during his daily rounds. Raspail, at five months old, had killed a bear cub twice his size.

***

An Encounter with Draguignon

As they prepared for the hot, enervating days of summer, Aratus, Balfort and Maddocq did perimeter scouts every day, during which they refreshed the scent posts along the borders. It was an opportunity to play in the fresh cool grass and vibrant streams and talk, free from the eyes and ears of their facet.

"It is finally clear to me why you rescued Raspail. You have a *plan.*" Balfort's eye twinkled.

"Really. Perhaps you'll share my plan with me so that I can benefit from it?"

"You are going to ramble once the pups are able to hunt."

Aratus remained coy. "And what has this to do with Raspail?"

"You're not very impressed by young Abillon or Polwin."

"Don't speak for me."

"Zut!" Balfort said in frustration.

Maddocq continued for him, "Brother, we all know your heart is too noble to depart Cob Ash and leave the hunting party in disarray."

Aratus looked stupefied. "The hunting party in disarray? Neither of you makes sense, and when I put your mad thoughts together I am doubly confused."

"You saved a half-dead baby without Cob Ash's blessing, then became an obsessive wolfmother dedicating untold time and effort to making him thrive." Balfort emphasized his point by jabbing his muzzle at Aratus. *"Admit* that was uncharacteristic for wise Aratus! *Admit* that you had a purpose, a plan, in which Raspail plays a role!"

"You are right, Balfort. I would not normally have bothered to save Raspail, certainly not if it risked the wrath of our great leader. But I met his mother. And though I never ran beside her in a hunt or howled with her, I could see she was a formidable beast worthy of respect. That respect I showed her by saving her child."

"But Cob Ash didn't wish to save him. Shouldn't you concern yourself more with *dis*respecting him?"

"Cob Ash *should* have saved him, not me," he said with casual impertinence.

"Artatus -- *shame!*"

" In any case, I don't know why he didn't. Perhaps he thought the pup was beyond saving."

"You say you respected the dead mother, I say you saw the son of a giant! One big enough to fill your vacant position on the day you leave Cob Ash... *and ramble!"* His voice warbled into whining.

"So that is your worry, Balfort!" Aratus laughed.

"My worry -- our worry -- is that you would ramble without us." Balfort said, "For we would like to go wherever you lead us."

Aratus affectionately swatted his muzzle against Balfort's and threw his arm over Maddocq's broad shoulders. "I brought Raspail into the pack to spark the litter, to give Abillon more competition. I am surprised myself at how remarkable he has turned out. But I promise, I have not thought beyond that. Any future plan I make will of course include both of you. You are my friends, my brothers."

Several birds burst from the bushes, and they all took notice.

"We are being stalked," Balfort said, poised for a fight, "Maddocq and I will --"

"Not necessary," said Aratus calmly. "Look in the shadow of the bush, you'll find your fiend there."

There, klooting invisibly in the shadow of the bushes, was Raspail. Seeing them staring at him, he bounded forward and lunged playfully at Aratus. He had grown so large in the last few weeks that he nearly knocked Aratus over.

"He followed us, the devil! And us none the wiser!" Balfort exclaimed. They played briefly, then Raspail quietly trailed behind them the remainder of the patrol.

As they reached the northeastern border of their territory, they saw birds circling overhead, which meant that meat was below. The meat in question was a moose, and feasting on it -- on *Cob Ash territory* -- were six members of the Draguignon pack. Aratus and the others spied on the situation, acid pumping through their veins.

"Three more than us," Maddocq said.

"No," whispered Aratus. "We are four."

His brothers looked dubiously at the gangly-legged Raspail. At this pre-yearling stage, all his body parts seemed to be growing on different schedules. And nowhere was this more evident than with his muzzle. This highly important piece of wolf anatomy had recently attained full size even though Raspail's body was still filling out.

"Oh you can't be serious! He's a baby! He'll be killed and so will we!"

"He's as big as their females and nearly as big as me. He doesn't need to fight. He just needs to fill out our numbers. "

"His legs look like weeds! He wouldn't fool a rock!"

"He'll stand by me. They're off territory. They'll flee without a fight."

"You can count on me," Raspail said, barely containing his enthusiasm, "to do whatever you ask."

"Stay in my shadow, walk tall," Aratus told him, "Mouth shut, breathe through your nose so they don't smell the youth on your breath."

"While we are on the subject of your mouth, be sure and let them see that snout in profile," Balfort added. "Hopefully they'll fathom the rest of you as big."

Raspail, having no idea that his nose appeared anything other than normal, became self-conscious at a moment when he needed confidence. He turned to Aratus to ask him if his nose was overly big, then gaped in amazement for his three uncles had already klooted into the fabric of the landscape and he alone stood there in the open.

Raspail slowed his breathing and dropped his heart rate, then camouflaged his dark body in the shadows of the trees downwind from the enemy. He moved invisibly through the folded creases of the terrain, crouching low and leaping from shadow to shadow if necessary, never once putting his body in contrast to something lighter than him. He went as far as he could go without revealing himself before the enemy. Just as he was starting to feel vulnerable, Aratus grazed his shoulder and signaled him to follow.

The four wolves of Cob Ash appeared before the intruding Draguignon pack by degrees. First, they saw Maddocq with a hideous display of fangs, jagged and broken from a habit of chewing on rocks. Next to him they heard Balfort, the honey-throated voice of the pack, humming with nonchalance as his tail swagged musically in the snow. Six lengths away appeared the gimlet-eyed Aratus, carefully keeping Raspail in his shadow.

Draguignon did not look too impressed. He was a large old wolf who possessed that distinctive and rare feature which all wolves are envious of. On the huge ruff that enveloped his neck was an exquisite filigreed crest. It was an arabesque of tawny hues, perfectly symmetrical, set against fur that had become silver with age. His broad chest inflated this marking, making it even more voluminous and multi-dimensional. It was the kind of feature that through his life other wolves would see it and think, *This wolf has the stamp of greatness upon him*, and he was treated accordingly. Great things were expected from Draguignon because of his exquisite and unique crest, and he did not disappoint. He was a bold and confident facet, but also tyrannical in the control he maintained over his family. He did not let his sons and daughters ramble from Draguignon, and as a result his pack was large, with nearly three generations of sons and daughters filling his ranks.

"If you want meat, wait your turn with the coyotes," the facet growled at Balfort. The other Draguignon wolves laughed approvingly.

Aratus counted an additional wolf among them that he hadn't seen earlier, a white bitch who was klooting against the snow. It was Sarrassin, Draguignon's favored daughter and his only offspring to inherit his crest, which was subtly emblazoned across her white breast in a golden-orange hue.

Balfort spoke up: "You must be lost, cousins. This side of the creek is Cob Ash."

"You were *lost,* I suppose, that day you poached an elk in Draguignon?"

"Elk is bountiful here, we needn't do our business in that foul smelling valley east of our creek. I would rather eat my own scat in Cob Ash then the fattest elk in Draguignon."

Raspail was in awe of Balfort's voice. Someday, he dreamed, he would have wit and panache like this uncle.

"And if you haven't the ability to protect your borders," Balfort continued insulting their facet to the outrage of his sons, "then at least be courteous enough not to take your business into our province. For we wolves of Cob Ash are quite able to protect our borders."

Draguignon casually tore off some meat and ate it, "There's two of us to kill every one of you."

"We don't bother to fight unless there's a good three wolves for each of us. And strong males at that. Why, all I see are bitches! Bitches here and bitches there -- why it's bitches everywhere!"

At this, Raspail uncontrollably laughed, unwittingly spitting particles of information at the enemy.

Draguignon was approached by Sarrassin, and as she spoke her red eyes directed her father's attention to Raspail.

Aratus breathed soft words in Balfort's ear, "The white female sees Raspail is young. They know they have the numbers."

"The big brown-gray one is wounded," Maddocq interjected, "I saw him favor his right side."

Aratus agreed with his observation and made a decision. "Leave with sullen faces and tails tucked." Without another word, the Cob Ash wolves sulked off to the derision of the Draguignon wolves.

As they smugly packed their stomachs with moose, Draguignon and his family grew more and more meatdrunk. And this is when the four Cob Ash wolves sprang out from behind them. Aratus and Raspail attacked the big brown-grey wolf while Maddocq took on Draguignon, and Balfort fought Sarrassin, the white bitch.

Sarrassin, seeing her beloved brother Denalfi under attack by two wolves, pushed Balfort off her and went to Denalfi's defense. A vicious, bloody brawl erupted. Sarassin, knowing that her brother suffered a kick to his ribs from the moose, lashed out at Raspail and forced him away. Raspail, desperate to not disappoint his uncles, fought valiantly against her, feigning expertly and drawing blood from his more experienced opponent.

Aratus, caught in a life or death battle with the bigger Denalfi, glanced quickly to check on his young ward Raspail. Denalfi took advantage of this distraction and lunged at him, catching him off guard and digging his teeth into Aratus' back bone. Aratus, a moment away from death, let out a squeal of pain that got Raspail's attention. In a half-breath, the young pup shoved off of Sarrassin and came to his aid. Seeing Aratus with the vice-like bite of Denalfi about to end his life, Raspail viciously launched himself on top of Denalfi, knocking him to the ground. Before he could rise to his feet Raspail rammed into his wounded ribcage, sending searing pain throughout his body.

Sarassin, seeing her brother wincing in pain with the young black wolf positioned over him, raced to his aid screaming "Brother, I'm coming!"

She was too late. Raspail darted at his neck and crushed it, piercing flesh with his sharp young fangs. He felt the warm blood trickle through his mouth while life drained from his enemy's jerking body. Aratus watched in disbelief.

Sarassin, seeing her brother dead, charged at his killer, her red eyes blazing with vindictive fury. Aratus came to Raspail's aid, and it took the two male wolves to suppress the white banshee.

Meanwhile, Draguignon found an equal in Maddocq, the fiercest fighter in Cob Ash. Maddocq, normally a self-possessed and quiet wolf, was abnormally territorial. He didn't even like his own brothers rubbing next to him unless he solicited it. So when foreign wolves crossed into Cob Ash, this territoriality transformed him into a manic, killing machine. And though his teeth had been blunted and broken, his jaws had adapted accordingly with massive muscles protruding luridly on either side giving the short-snouted wolf the visage of a bear.

Draguignon experienced the tenacious bite of Maddocq on his hind leg and wanted no more of it. With a shriek he disengaged himself and ran north to the creek. He was quickly followed by all the surviving members of his pack except Sarassin, who remained fighting Aratus and Raspail with demonic fervor. Draguignon called out to her and she disengaged from Aratus and Raspail even though the desire to finish off the young black wolf who killed her dear brother was strong. She retreated till she was standing over her slain brother's body. The four Cob Ash wolves snarled at her to keep retreating. Her eyes bore into Raspail's.

"You wear the blood of my brother on your muzzle."

"In a moment it will be yours on my muzzle," Aratus snarled back.

She glared defiantly as she slinked backwards away from them in retreat.

"Look! She walks with her ass for a head and a head for an ass!"

They all laughed with Balfort, who led them in a ripping howl that mocked their Draguignon neighbors:

I've told a lie
the culprit's us
who poached your elk that day
but even more fun
'fore rudely being forced to run
was giving it back when we were done.

The rest of Cob Ash would hear the howl and soon be there to share the bounty of their victory, so the hungry warriors wasted no time feasting on the moose carcass while the ravens tested their luck stealing bits of precious meat.

Aratus looked down at the dead Denalfi, then at Raspail. Aratus said incredulously, " You killed the biggest wolf in Draguignon."

"Well, he was going to kill you," Raspail responded sincerely. Aratus affectionately put his leg over Raspail's shoulder and pressed the side of his head against Raspail's so tightly the two lost their balance and fell down together, laughing.

The rest of the pack arrived and ate what remained of the moose while Balfort spun a ripping tale of the showdown. All four of the wolves took turns being immortalized in his description, but it was Raspail who emerged the star of the tale, dueling valiantly despite his youthful inexperience, killing the giant Denalfi.

Abillon and Polwin clung to Raspail, hoping that some of his newly acquired importance would rub off on them. But their acceptance of him no longer mattered to Raspail. He'd fought beside Aratus, Balfort and Maddocq and earned their comradeship by showing his heart to be noble and true. He'd discovered true fraternity with his uncles.

He looked at Kileo. This was his moment, and yet the mesmerizing beauty remained unimpressed, unreadable, unattainable. Raspail, undeterred by her impassiveness, strutted towards her, hopped up and put his legs over her back playfully. She withdrew with a growl and trotted away. He waited for her to look back at him with an inviting glance, a look of annoyance -- anything -- but he got nothing. He chased after her anyway, and when he mounted her the second time, she growled and bit his neck hard, the pain of which he savored and thought about endlessly.

**

Hesser

As the sweltering summer days overflowed into fall, the older wolves, enervated by the heat, relegated the boisterous half-yearlings to Hesser, the kick-around wolf. The pups adored Hesser. When Hesser hopped about on his hind legs and growled at the pups with the grumpy, ferocious scowl of a Grizzly, it was as if he'd actually transformed into one. When he limped like a wounded deer and made the little ones chase him, you could almost hear their bellies growl in anticipation of an imminent meal as they nipped at his rump, bringing him down. He was a master actor, and even the elders never tired of watching him run through these hackneyed routines.

But when hunting was poor, or when there was strife in the camp, Hesser was the first to get blamed, lashed, and spat on. Hesser's acting skills were so masterful that not a single wolf was aware of his suffering, or that his heart pumped cold malice through his veins for every wolf stationed above him in life, which was all of them.

Hesser's actual size was incalculable. His bony back arched upwards, shortening his length, and his shoulders swooped so low his elbows almost scraped the ground when he walked, lowering his height. He gave the impression of a walking bat. As a pup he was hapless and fretful. His muzzle was too tapered for his broad face with its smallish, closely set eyes. This, combined with the dark, downward highlights at the corners of his mouth, made him appear perpetually nervous.

The master actor didn't flop with the others. His private domain was a sliver of granite that protruded from a shallow cave several lengths above the ground. Stuck in perpetual shade, the floor was slippery with moss and difficult not to slide out once inside. So Hesser devised a way of sleeping propped half-upright against the wall with his extended leg supporting him, and once he'd gotten into this restrictive sleeping position he could not freely move.

Hesser's miserable abode was accessible only by climbing over and under prickly, blood-drawing bramble that was drenched in his urine. Only Hesser knew how to navigate the serpentine route and gain access to this morsel of granite. With no prospects of ever rising above his current station, Hesser had found a piece of the world that no wolf would ever desire enough to challenge him for, and indeed no one ever had.

This perch was where Hesser retreated to when he needed solitude from the pups, when their nipping and aggressive craving for play got to be too much. And no pup craved to play with him more than Raspail. Raspail adored Hesser. His innocent eyes were dazzled by the magic of his craft, and, greedily wanting more, he put up strong resistance when Hesser grew tired and wanted to be alone. Every day, when Hesser retreated to his private sanctuary, Raspail would follow and stand at its edge whining persistently for him to come down. And every day he studied how Hesser navigated the maze of bracken, memorizing where he stepped and how he shifted his weight, so that one day he could follow him and continue harassing the actor on his special ledge.

On this particular day, perhaps emboldened by his recent heroism, Raspail decided to make a go of it. He made his first step where Hesser did, on a thick stump bare of thorns. The sharp smell of Hesser's urine filled his flaring nose. He took another step on to the same springy branch Hesser did, then another, and then he froze balancing on the rickety bramble thinking that this was not perhaps his greatest idea.

"You are crazy," Kileo said, without any hint as to whether crazy meant good or bad to her.

Raspail nearly lost his balance on hearing her voice because she had never once spoken to him or responded when he spoke to her. And here she was, standing behind him near the edge of the bramble, watching him.

"You don't think I can do it?" Raspail asked.

"I can't think why you'd do it."

"To see Hesser!"

Apparently "crazy" was something worthy of her attention, because she sprawled out on the ground and waited for the show to start. This was just what Raspail needed in order to take the plunge. He stepped forward and climbed quickly up the springy bramble. About halfway up the treacherous ascent, he walked afoul of the safe route and was lashed by long nasty thorns across his legs and feet. Raspail suddenly could not recall the rest of the route and froze.

Kileo started to lose interest and sighed loudly. Raspail heard her sigh and, full of that carelessness for consequence that spurs young creatures to do impulsive things, plunged again into the bramble, this time shredding his body as he swam through the web of thorns. He didn't stop moving until, after losing a lot of fur and blood, he reached the granite ledge. His claws battled to get traction on the moss-covered rock and eventually climbed on to the perch where Hesser lay.

"Hesser, I made it!" Raspail greeted him.

Hesser couldn't have acknowledged him any less. He didn't bother to stand or growl. He looked away as if to say he couldn't be bothered with this foolish young wolf.

But a line, in every sense, had been crossed. Hesser, teetering at that emotional threshold where anger turns to sudden violence, mustered all his self-control and acting skills to appear ambivalent.

In his young heart Raspail deeply loved Hesser, and he wanted Hesser to acknowledge him, so he licked Hesser's neck. Raspail was bewildered by the vibrating tension in Hesser's muscles. The great actor's mask said one thing, but the anger inside him was fighting to surface, and the restraint the beast called upon to save his revenge for another day made him all but explode. Raspail stopped licking him and stepped back.

After making sure that Kileo was still watching him, Raspail dived back into the bramble and began the trip back. He didn't feel any pain this time, exhilarated as he was. Nor did he see Hesser's hateful eyes watching him, or hear the silent curses of a wolf who had just been violated beyond what even the lowest kickaround was expected to endure.

   ***

Raspail and Kileo

Raspail emerged from the bramble as Kileo was walking off. He followed her, and when he was close enough he gently bunted her shoulder.

"What is wrong with you?" she said, acting annoyed.

It seemed to Raspail that her easy gait welcomed his play despite what her words said, so he continued to follow her.

"I'm invisible to you," he said. "Why do you ignore me?"

She picked her feet up and ran off. Kileo was a fast sprinter, able to achieve her top speed in three breaths. Raspail was in awe of her speed as he was of everything about her. He inhaled the area where she just stood, then, entranced by her perfume, took off after her, weaving through trees and crashing through streams.

To Raspail, Kileo was his sister as much as she was Polwin's or Abillon's. As far back as Raspail (or any of the pups) could remember, he was the son of Cob Ash and Cortess. This meant that one day Raspail would instinctively know that Kileo was off limits to him, that they could never be mates. But that day was not today, and he flew up and down hillocks chasing her, unburdened by the natural politics that awaited him further down the line.

Kileo finally felt secure that she'd lost him. She looked around to make sure, then sighed, *Why am I disappointed that I lost my annoying brother?*

As she turned to head back to camp she saw the black wolf suddenly appear beside a tree, standing there casually as if he'd been there waiting for her. Just as she surprised herself to be disappointed when she lost him, she was now relieved to see him there -- maybe even impressed.

"Why are you following me?" he said to her.

Maddened by the insinuation that she liked him, she pounced on him and bit him sharply. She chased him now, fighting as they ran up a hill, and as they crested it, Raspail jumped on her back, clamping down hard with his forelegs and throwing his weight on her so she lost balance. They fell, tumbling down the other side of the grassy slope on top of each together. When they stopped rolling, Raspail didn't get up, he just lay there with a satisfied smile on his face. She jumped to her feet and stood over him, then stepped on his face with her muddy foot.

"You really are an ass, you know that?"

He gently bit her foot and gnawed on it. She made no effort to pull away.

"I'm going to eat you," he said.

She pulled her foot away and snarled in his face. "Maybe I'll eat you first."

They nipped at each other, snorting and smelling each other's breath. Then he became annoying and she pushed him away. He bit her foot again, this time licking the soft fur between her pads. She let him do this a moment, then growled and kicked his head away, and he laughed, happy for whatever he could get. She flopped next to Raspail, and they quietly lay together. Kileo noticed him staring at something, a raven, five lengths away on the ground, staring back at him.

"Why do you stare at her?"

His eyes stayed on the raven. "She lives in our camp. She follows me, watches me. From the tree. From the ground. From the sky."

Poitu hopped a length closer and kawed shrilly at Raspail.

"She's talking to you," Kileo marveled.

"She does that," Raspail said, remaining still as the raven hopped yet closer until she was so near he could strike her if he wanted. The bird didn't seem worried.

Poitu heard something and flew off. A moment later, Raspail and Kileo heard the pack trotting off to hunt.

***

Polwin's Deception

Over the past two weeks, the young wolves began joining the older wolves on hunts. They were given minor tasks that allowed them to observe how the group chased and killed prey without getting in the way of the experienced hunters.

Raspail and Kileo caught up with the pack and ran silently with them until they reached the elk. The hoofed beasts, some weighing five times as much as the biggest wolf, seemed relaxed about the arriving wolves; the healthy amongst them had little to fear; it was the sick and the old that the wolves were targeting.

The wolves casually broke up and spread out, individually weaving in and out of the small groupings of elk at an easy pace, looking for a fearful reaction, a limp, or an infant who could be separated from its mother. They took their time doing this, some running around, others sitting, communicating to each other with silent signals, while Cob Ash studied the movements and reactions of the elk.

One elk who earned his attention made unsuccessful attempts to hide among healthier cousins, but these elk eschewed the pariah's company knowing he had been chosen. Cob Ash signaled Cortess and she was off.

Cortess ran low and fast, her head and neck in a perfect line with her body. When the old elk saw her coming, he wedged his way into a group of six hoping to get lost. He glanced back to see if this had thrown off his pursuer and saw the wolf's deep yellow eyes locked on to him as she bobbed and weaved through the ranks of healthy elk towards him.

The prey bolted. Cortess was the fastest runner in the pack. She chased the elk a good long time before she ushered the beast towards Balfort. Balfort, being overly confident that he could kill the beast, diverted it away from Cob Ash so that when he brought the beast down the first bite of meat would be his. Cob Ash saw what his advantageous brother was doing and barked a reprimanding warning to him.

Balfort adeptly redirected the elk back towards Maddocq, who lunged at the elk from the side, digging his teeth into the beast's neck. The elk fell and Maddocq tumbled over it. Maddocq got back on his feet and resumed the chase. He was so close to his quarry that its hind legs whipped at the fur on his muscular cheeks. When the elk quickly darted left, its hoof connected hard with the side of his broad skull, the concussion knocking him out of the game.

It was Aratus' turn to hunt.

Raspail loved to watch Aratus hunt. Aratus had an uncanny ability to shadow prey. Now that the elk's stamina was dwindling, it tried to lose its pursuer by dodging left and right. But as it did, Aratus was always right behind it dodging in tandem, anticipating its moves as if he had tapped into the mind of the animal he was chasing. The other wolves were great hunters, but Aratus was in a league by himself.

Somehow in the carefully orchestrated anarchy of the hunt a small spotted calf was separated from its mother. Escaping the hunters, it haplessly caught the attention of Abillon and Polwin, who wasted no time chasing it. Kileo joined them and looked back at Raspail shouting, "Come on!" Raspail tore his eyes away from Aratus and joined the chase with his siblings.

The wolves followed the small elk's agile, springy steps, towards a steep, rocky ravine. Raspail splintered off from the group and took a path beside the ravine. He was surprised to see Kileo running just behind him.

"Why this way?"

"Aratus has taken me here. I know the terrain, just follow," he said confidently, and she did. They swiftly jumped across boulders to the base of the ravine. In the spring, the ravine filled with rain and became a stream that fed a waterfall, and the waterfall emptied into a tiny lake. Aratus had taken him here so he could see his reflection in the lake contrasted against rock and tree during one of the many lessons devoted to klooting.

They reached the lake, which was now just a murky pool of shallow mud.

"Wait," he said.

The calf, as Raspail had hoped, arrived and jumped off the rocky ledge and landed in the muddy basin. The little elk, opening its mud-covered eyelids, looked relieved that it had found safety from its pursuers. But then Raspail and Kileo appeared before it and the deer's look of hope vanished.

The two young wolves strutted around the perimeter of the mucky basin, penning the deer in.

Kileo laughed, "Did you see his face when he saw us? He was like -- *I live!* And then -- *I die!*"

"I'll kill it," Raspail said excitedly. "If it tries to get away, block it."

"Okay," she said, as excited as him.

Abillon, Polwin and Moorea reached the cliff's edge and looked down at them.

"Don't kill it!" Polwin shouted.

"Why not?"

"Wait there." Polwin shouted again, as Abillon, Moorea and he climbed down the ledge and formed a circle around the trapped deer.

"You can't kill big prey without Cob Ash's authority." Polwin said.

"He'll be proud we killed it." Raspail said. "Besides, he's not here to ask him."

"Raspail is right," Kileo agreed.

The calf made a weak attempt to run, but on seeing the wolves react, it crouched low and waited, its legs shaking. The young wolves looked at each other. It was the first real decision they would make as a group, one with consequences.

"We should wait, Raspail," Abillon said sincerely. "We don't have the authority to hunt and kill yet. Cob Ash will be upset."

Before Raspail could take either course of action the elders arrived. They had been unsuccessful in bringing down the old elk and were pleasantly surprised to see that the pups had trapped their own prey.

Raspail was excited to tell Aratus how he outsmarted his brothers and sisters and trapped the deer in the mud lake, and it was in his excitement that he missed the conspiracy brewing. Polwin stepped in front of Raspail, blocking him while Abillon, in a flashy leap that was intended to impress his father and uncles, boldly attacked the deer and killed the weak, terrified creature before their very eyes.

Raspail was devastated. He watched Cob Ash lavish praise on his bold son. Kileo looked at the dark expression on Raspail's face -- he was suddenly a different animal than the carefree one she had been frolicking with earlier. He had depth and anger that came from an intrinsic nobility. She liked this side of him.

Polwin brushed past Raspail with a smug look on his face and said, "See? Aren't you glad you waited now?" Raspail flew on to him, pitilessly biting him, pushing him into the mud where he continued to lash him It took Maddocq and Aratus to pry him off his whimpering brother.

"What's up your fur?" Aratus said.

"Nothing," Raspail said.

Cob Ash let Abillon take the second share of meat, proud as he was. Every wolf vied for food except Raspail, whose appetite was dulled by bitterness. Kileo sat out the meal in solidarity with Raspail and softly laid her head on his back. She heard him sigh and let her placid heart calm his.

"That should have been your kill," she said.

He licked her face with shut eyes. When he opened his eyes again he saw the mysterious raven who often visited. When more ravens arrived to strip the carcass, they heckled her until she flew off.

***

The Mocked Raven

Poitu knew the arriving ravens would mob her if she lingered, but she lingered anyway, trying to make sense of what had just happened to Raspail. When the viciousness of the mob became overwhelming, she flew off.

During the last winter, when Poitu shockingly chased the black wolf pup from the ravens waiting to eat him, it took those fifteen ravens less than four days to tell every raven in Warmpools that she was mad. The reputation stuck. It was unlikely, unless she flew very far way, that she would ever rebound from her scandalous deed and find acceptance again.

Being an outcast from the raven community was of no consequence to Poitu. She rediscovered her black wolf shortly after he'd been absorbed into the Cob Ash pack, and the uncanny connection to him that she'd felt the day she'd first encountered him was instantly rekindled. She moved into their camp and shared Raspail's triumphs and defeats from a branch in a cottonwood tree.

The bond she had with him was, so far, one-sided. In the few occasions where she got him to look in her eyes and acknowledge her, she could see that the wolf did not share the connection that she had with him, that whatever ancient memories she had of him were as of yet dormant in him. But Poitu did not lose hope; she had the immense patience of a raven.

***

The Cold Heat

The wolf owns autumn. Hunting is at its best, with elk coming down from the mountains and migrating from the south to forage on aspens. The climate is at its most comfortable, and family bonds tighten as the long cold nights bring wolves close together, pooling their collective heat.

Raspail looked almost full-grown with his heavy winter fur filling him out. It was his first real snow (since he could not remember the snow that fell the first two months of his life), and he and his siblings tumbled down snow-covered slopes and dived into snow banks with utter recklessness, knowing the soft snow would cushion their blows. And of course they ate mouthfuls of snow until their stomachs rumbled.

It was an equally festive occasion for the adults who saw themselves reflected in the pups the first time they saw snow. Every wolf, old and new, frolicked with the spirit of youth in them, and even though opportunities to hunt arose, Cob Ash often let them pass by so they could simply play.

If there was one benefit from the deception that Polwin and Abillon played on Raspail, it was that it strengthened Raspail's bond with Kileo, and they spent more and more of their day together. During hunts they worked and ate side by side. They slept curled next to each other in the snow, their tails brushing each others' noses.

With the pups old enough to travel, the pack left camp and became nomadic during these cold months, camping wherever the day's hunt took them. And as it got colder, the wolves spent more time sleeping between hunts to conserve energy and maintain their size.

The one exception to this was Cob Ash and Cortess. The facet and his mate would disappear for hours, then return in good spirits. They did this every day for a week, arousing Raspail's curiosity.

"Where do they go?" Raspail asked Kileo.

"I'm trying to sleep. Don't you ever sleep?"

"No. Let's follow them."

"No. Let's sleep."

"I won't leave you alone till you come."

His persistence was at once charming and bothersome to her. She reluctantly got up and joined Raspail, staying close as they followed their parents, which wasn't difficult because of the thick, musky odor that trailed behind Cortess.

They climbed a ledge that looked down on a frozen lake where they saw Cob Ash and Cortess playing like pups, with Cob Ash jumping on Cortess, Cortess biting him and growling but eventually submitting. Then all similarities to childish play ended. Cob Ash mounted Cortess from behind and curved his back as he thrust his hips at her. It was over in a moment, and the two wolves laid down near each other, Cob Ash curled around her back, moaning.

Raspail, immature in matters of mating, could not restrain his laughter. When Cob Ash saw his son and daughter spying on him he tried to get up but could not because he was locked together with his mate. Every time he tried to rise he dragged Cortess up with him and, pulled off balance, he would fall, dragging her back down with him. The regal Cob Ash appeared clownish as he struggled to pry himself from Cortess.

"He's stuck in her! How is he stuck in her?!" Raspail whispered urgently.

"I don't know! Let's go!"

The insatiably curious Raspail could not tear his eyes away from the fascinating spectacle and Kileo had to bite him hard on the tail and yank him. The two ran back to camp laughing.

When Cob Ash and Cortess returned an hour later, father said nothing to son and both happily pretended that nothing had happened.

Cob Ash wasn't the only wolf tantalized by the female scent during those weeks in winter. The alluring perfume tortured the lonely Hesser who, because of his low station, had no chance of ever taking a mate.

One afternoon, when the pack left the rendezvous camp to hunt, the same intriguing perfume that seized his every thought over the last three days became so thick it was obvious that the bitch was near. He impulsively followed the smell, getting as close to the Draguignon border as he'd ever dared go.

He was about to turn back when he saw her. The bold white wolf stood ten length away watching him with an innocent smile, then bolted away coyly. Hesser, not the most vigorous wolf, huffed as he chased after her.

"Come back!" he pleaded, "Please, slow down so that I might meet you."

She finally stopped, allowing Hesser to grind his muzzle in her fur, but as soon as his nose went to her hind quarters she jumped back and snarled at him. She did this many times until Hesser was deranged with lust and drooling uncontrollably.

If Hesser had kept his wits in that moment he would have realized that this white wolf with the cornet of gray speckles blooming up through her plump brisket was way out of his league and that something was not quite right. But Hesser's desire strong-armed away all suspicious thoughts and he awkwardly tried to mount her. On his first thrust she violently threw the love hungry beast off her and on to his back. The bitch attacked him, biting his throat just hard enough to scare him. To kill him would have defeated her purpose.

"I'm sorry, please don't--" he begged as he squirmed submissively and looked away from her eyes.

."You want to dominate me?" Her voice, haughty and confident, terrified Hesser. She sounded nothing like how he imagined she would.

"Yes, no -- I-*I don't know!*"

"You think I give myself to any wolf? Look at me!"

Hesser barely had the courage to stare into her red eyes. "You think I let just any wolf dominate me?"

Then, as if she could read Hesser's thoughts, her voice transformed to a soothing, vulnerable lull, to the voice he wanted to hear.

"Don't you want me to be yours?" she said. "I could be...yours."

"Yes. Please be mine"

"No. You don't desire me enough. I was wrong about you." She turned and sashayed off.

"No! You weren't wrong! I'll do anything for you!" He whined as she ran off, vanishing beyond the curtain of falling snowflakes. He was going to chase after her, then he heard her voice:

"Next estrus... *maybe.*"

With that seed rooting in his mind, Sarassin headed back to the Draguignon border.

***

Returning Home, Leaving Home

In February the pack returned to camp where they would again live until the next autumn. Cortess was greeted at the entrance of her den by another expectant mother; a coyote had moved into the sacred dwelling in her absence. Behind her stood her mate, trembling in terror. The wolf pack played with the unfortunate couple, and when they were finished they left their lifeless bodies for the birds to feast on. Balfort howled out a beautiful and comical sonnet.

> *Mother coyote, trying to save time.*
> *Squatted in our den singing, 'What was yours is now mine.'*
> *You should have known better, should have used your head.*
> *But you did not, so we used it instead!*

The other wolves sang along with him, howling with laughter at their great voice, Balfort. When outsiders heard Balfort and the hearty howl he provoked in his pack, they imagined a group with healthy bonds, ones that were forged by good humor, love and playfulness. And that meant their pack had solid leadership from a facet who was strong, fair, and consistent. There was harmony in their diverse voices, there was light in their song, and while it was impossible not to be enchanted by the howling wolves' celebration of unity and harmony, one dared not provoke a well-oiled wolf pack, as the dead coyote couple would testify if they could.

Cortess refurbished the den, scratching away the outer layer of dirt to reveal the fresh smell of damp earth, then gave birth several days later to six healthy pups. The pack, which had been waiting impatiently, rejoiced at the news, but none more than Aratus. He had been planning his ramblefoot for almost a year now, and with the increase in the pack's numbers, Cob Ash would surely give him his blessing to leave. Aratus felt immense relief as he let the good news soak in. The winter had been long with the sticky scent of bitch heat lingering in the air, and he was lusting, while hunting and marking, to ramble.

Watching Raspail become a sure-footed hunter and cunning fighter under his tutelage proved unexpectedly rewarding to Aratus, and it made him yearn to start his own pack and make his own decisions about their fate. Raising Raspail gave him confidence that he could be greater than he was, that he could be a facet, even if he wasn't as beautiful or physically strong as Cob Ash.

While Aratus waited for Cob Ash's invitation to see the new brood, he watched Raspail play with Kileo. Aratus knew that Raspail would be facet someday, of this pack or his own. Kileo would be his natural choice for mate -- they were madly attached to each other -- but because of their sibling relationship, they would never allow themselves to mate. Aratus knew that Raspail had every right to know that their sibling relationship did not extend to their blood and that he could some day mate with Kileo. But he didn't dare let Raspail know this now -- he worried that the young couple, at Kileo's first heat, would ramble off together, and this would leave Cob Ash depleted of its best hunters.

As Aratus considered how to solve this dilemma, Cob Ash approached him with a warm smile. "Cortess would like you to see the new wolves."

Aratus jumped eagerly to his feet and licked Cob Ash's face with gratitude. Balfort tried to join them but Cob Ash growled at him to stay back. Cob Ash had been the only wolf to see the pups so far, and the suspense that surrounds a new birth during that first day when the matriarch nurses the litter alone filled everyone with ecstatic jitters. The two brothers trotted to her den, and Cob Ash gestured for Aratus to enter. He crouched low and entered the tunnel, walking to the birthing chamber at the end.

Hope and calm filled Aratus' heart as he gazed at the future of the pack, blind, deaf and uncoordinated as they were, nursing on Cortess, who smiled at him in the darkness.

"Thank you for the honor, wolfmother" he said with a bow of his head.

He closed his eyes and breathed; the sweet smell of new life filled his head and lightened his heart, awakening memories of the time a year ago when he built a den for Raspail and lived there with the unconscious pup, nurturing him and watching him recover from near death. He looked at the pups, six healthy, beautiful wolves, but it was Raspail he thought of and Raspail who made him smile. He licked the babies and murmured, "I regret that I will not get to know each of you."

After leaving the den, Aratus walked with Cob Ash and they played, chasing each other and wrestling in the snow.

"You've created a big family," Aratus said. "I would like to do the same."

"Would you," Cob Ash said.

"I'm sure of it, yes. I have an itch to ramble."

Cob Ash was in good spirits and not in the mood to hear of Aratus' wanderlust. "You'll stay in Cob Ash. The itch will go away, Aratus. The risks are too great, to Ramble, a wolf alone."

"Yes, risks. You are very wise to bring up the risks of a wolf traveling alone."

"A wolf traveling alone, no matter if he's as good a fighter as you, is sure to die."

"Yes, again your wisdom and your care for my well-being humbles me. Perhaps, then, given your worry, you'd be more inclined to let me take this risky step if Balfort and Maddocq accompanied me."

Cob Ash, irritated that Aratus was persisting with his request, growled low in his chest. "You -- that's one thing -- but you ask to take my two best wolves--!?"

His anger surged and he snapped his jaws at Aratus' neck and forced him to the ground. He stood over him threateningly, and Aratus knew that his facet had every right to kill him.

With disgust in his voice Cob Ash asked, "Do they wish to go with you?"

"They have said they do, my facet, yes."

Cob Ash calmed himself but remained annoyed. "Get up." Aratus rose but kept his head bowed. After a long moment he asked, "When would you leave?"

"I will not go if it displeases you--"

"When will you leave," he asked again.

"Soon."

Cob Ash said nothing but looked resigned to his request. Aratus licked his brother's cheek in gratitude.

"You must do me a favor," Aratus said.

"I do you a favor by letting you live."

"Yes, it is true. This is more a favor for your son."

"Which son?"

"Raspail. This favor -- and it's more than a favor, it is an oath you must take -- " Aratus paused, seeing the look of bedevilment in Cob Ash's eyes. "You must promise me that someday you will tell Raspail that Kileo is not his sister."

"But she is his sister. Raspail is my son, Kileo my daughter."

"In one sense. But in the other sense -- their love for each other is beautiful and they should know that, if they wanted to, they could make a family."

"Hmm." Cob Ash pondered this, as if for the first time. Aratus wondered if his facet hadn't been astute enough to notice that Raspail and Kileo had a unique bond.

"Why don't you tell him yourself?" Cob Ash finally asked.

"I'm afraid if I do they will ramble at Kileo's first heat. There will be a time to tell him, later."

Aratus saw he'd convinced Cob Ash. While he waited for Cob Ash to compose his thoughts he looked around at the home he would be leaving.

"After the next healthy brood is born I will tell Raspail that Kileo is his *half*-sister." Cob Ash tried to hide the look of discomfort on his face. Then, with an intimidating growl that was intended to quiet Aratus, he said, "Any other favors... or oaths you would like me to make?"

"Only that you and Cortess live long, eat well, and bear many children, my good brother." Aratus' soothing words brought out Cob Ash's good humor again. The two wolves played in the snow till the sun went down, playing like they did when they were pups, before hierarchy mattered.

There was one more thing to do before he left, and that was tell Raspail, the very one who had made his ramble possible, that he was going. He explained to Raspail that he had earned the position of second in command to Cob Ash, the position that he was resigning from, and that he would eat third at the hunt after Cortess. It was difficult for Aratus to say goodbye with Raspail's brooding head downcast and his eye averting his gaze. Aratus waited for him to respond, but Raspail was too angry to talk. Deeply ingrained in Raspail's memories were wolves he'd lost, wolves somehow important to him, and he knew this because the hollow pain they left in their absence --that ancient wound in his heart -- suddenly became raw again.

He watched bitterly as Aratus, Balfort and Maddocq left the camp, and pretended to be indifferent. Kileo tried to soothe him, but he was inconsolable.

***

The Three Ramblefoots from Cob Ash

Aratus, Maddocq and Balfort, the three ramblefoots from Cob Ash, ventured southwest into the Neparaise valley searching for an unclaimed territory they could agree on calling home. Without Cob Ash as their facet, the threesome soon realized they had grown comfortably dependent on their leader's firm decision-making.

Through many open territories they passed, but there was no facet among them to say, *"This land is good. This is where we'll put down roots. I will stand by my choice!"* So the only decision the three brothers reached, after much arguing, was that all decisions needed to be made by a majority of two. If two out of three agreed on a territory, they would stake their claim. But

Maddocq, who refused to give his opinion on anything, automatically withdrew his vote. This left all decisions to be made by Aratus and Balfort being in agreement, and this, as has been said, rarely happened.

It was an anxious week of rambling. Maddocq tested the patience of his brothers by lingering for excruciatingly long stints smelling the local scat. Balfort, thinking he was lifting his comrades' spirits with song, instead irritated them with verses like:

> *Three idiots we be, three idiots lost and hungry.*
> *Come kill us, mercy be, for we left Cob Ash stupidly.*
> *But beware if you eat us, what might happen to thee*
> *You might get stupid like we three.*

He repeated the ditty for hours, driving them scatter mad. Aratus, nagged by self-doubt, could take no more of Balfort's song.

"ZUT! I'll be singing about TWO idiots if you don't shut up!" Aratus growled with flashed fang.

Balfort responded to the threat with a new song:

"Two idiots we, for the singer would not end his reverie--"

Aratus attacked him. They wrestled in the dirt and battered and bit each other as viciously as they would an enemy, if not worse.

Maddocq looked around him at the lay of the land and thought, *There is nothing wrong with this place.* He walked to a tree, humming Balfort's annoying song, and lay in its shade. While his brothers gnashed their teeth and ripped into each others' fur, he closed his eyes and tried to sleep. The two brothers broke from fighting and looked at Maddocq strangely.

"I am done rambling. This is where I am staying," he said.

Aratus looked around. He'd been so harangued by Balfort's singing that he overlooked the merits of the territory where he stood. It was small and manageable with their tiny numbers. As time passed they would find mates, make sons and daughters till they had the numbers to push their boundaries outward. Balfort and Aratus surveyed the area for a long time then looked at each other, their faces matted with each other's blood, in unanimous approval.

Aratus led them as they marked the old scent posts which, according to Maddocq's precise nose, had been last refreshed three years ago. Why such a lovely territory would lay vacant plagued Aratus.

"Say! Look here!" Barked Balfort. "Does our wolfmother approve?"

Aratus saw Balfort standing at the entrance of an old abandoned den, dug under a tree stump.

The brothers pissed the territory's perimeter and pissed it again, then on the third pass encountered a strange, bison-like animal that was ridiculously easy to kill. They ate until they were meatdrunk and sick with satisfaction.

***

Raspail and the Natural Law

Taking Aratus' place in the hunting order at so young an age was a huge honor which Raspail rose to effortlessly. Working in tandem with Kileo, with whom he shared an intuitive connection, they nearly measured up equally to the three wolves they were replacing.

Their closeness made Abillon jealous, and like all cold-hearted beings who relish telling others gloomy news, it was he who one day informed Raspail, "You know you can't take her as your mate."

"Not yet, I can't. But some day--"

"Not ever, Raspail. She is your sister."

Young Raspail looked at his brother confused.

"You don't feel it?" Abillon asked, as if he were an idiot. "You can't mate with your sister. It's wrong."

Raspail thought Abillon was playing a cruel joke on him.

"You have to find a mate outside the pack," Abillon said with authority.

"Why should I look outside the pack when what I want is right here?"

"You don't feel it's wrong?"

"No."

Abillon chortled and walked off, delighted by the tumult he'd started in Raspail's mind.

Raspail, not being a blood relation of Kileo, did not feel any instinctive repulsion to wanting her. There was no internal argument raging inside him, dissuading him against his deep affection -- his attraction to her felt normal and healthy. Yet somehow what Abillon told him seemed truthful, even if it was delivered with too much pleasure for his liking.

He cursed Aratus for not being there when he needed his wise counsel most. Then he spent a week thinking of a way to ask his mother Cortess about the subject so as not to give away the full agenda of his embarrassing curiosity. She was resting outside her den watching the pups, who were now four months old, play.

"Was Cob Ash your brother?" Raspail asked.

She laughed good-naturedly, then said, "No, Raspail, of course not. Brothers don't mate with their sisters."

So friendship, it turned out, was as far as their love was intended to go.

What tyrant makes this unfair law?! Raspail wondered angrily. *And who upholds it if it is violated?!*

Kileo saw him in this agitated state and came to his side. He ran away from her and she chased him, finally stopping him by wrestling him to the ground.

"You are so serious lately."

"I'm unhappy."

"You can't always be happy."

"That is true. But I refuse to forever be unhappy."

"Why would you be?"

He stood to leave, but she knocked him down again. Finally he talked:

"When you look at Polwin, or Abillon -- could you ever imagine being with them the way Cortess is with Cob Ash?"

Kileo laughed uproariously. "Of course not. Abillon is a fool, and Polwin is ugly."

"Besides their character and appearance -- do you feel in any way repelled by the notion of --"

She bit his muzzle shut, silencing him. "Just speaking of it fills me with disgust!"

"But you don't have that feeling of disgust for me?"

"No."

"As I don't feel anything other than attraction for you. But as it turns out, I am supposed to feel something in my heart that makes me repelled by the notion of being with my sister, as you admit to feeling towards Abillon and Polwin."

Now she too looked concerned.

"Moorea says that if brothers and sisters mate they give birth to coyotes."

"What do you think?"

"I think you think too much."

She ran off, but he didn't follow her. Instead he went alone to the small lake where Aratus took him, the one where Polwin had deceived him with the elk.

The crashing sound of the waterfall composed his whirling brain. He could not reason to himself why he could not have Kileo. He knew what it felt like to instinctively be repulsed by something -- like the notion of eating a fellow wolf. There were no internal boundaries warning him, like a scent post which says, "Don't cross here." There were only others telling him "No," and this was not a powerful enough incentive to deter him from adhering to his own principles and make him stray from his own will.

He looked at the moon, a faint glimmer in the clear, sunny sky, and howled determinedly, "Whatever fate has in store for me, I accept it! I will bask in the scorn of other wolves -- I will father coyotes if I must! -- but I will not veer from the course my heart navigates me on!"

He bounded back to camp with a lightened mood. He thought of Aratus affectionately, for even though he was not there to seek advice from, he had given him the tools to figure out on his own what was right to do.

"Aratus! I love you!" Raspail howled, hoping that his friend could hear him, wherever he was. He bounded faster and faster, weaving through standing timbers, diving under fallen ones, leaping off rocks.

The raven soared by his side the entire trip back, infected by his indomitable spirit.

***

Hesser's Revenge

While Raspail was making deals with fate at the lake, Hesser was busy being a grizzly bear for the benefit of his newest audience. It was torture for him, having to play with pups while obsessive thoughts of the tantalizing, white-furred goddess begged for his complete attention. He wished desperately that the jumping, snapping pups would tire themselves, but they, like Raspail and others before him, could never get enough of the actor. Hesser was on the verge of exploding.

Raspail galloped into the camp and the first wolf he saw was Hesser, towering over the pups like a cornered bear. Raspail, brimming with optimism and hope, decided to join the game.

"Mean old bear! I'll kill you!" he said as he exuberantly reared on his back feet and jumped on Hesser.

Hesser had festered with hatred for him since the arrogant youth trespassed on to his perch. And though he hadn't planned on exacting revenge on him, he'd reached a state where he could not take any further humiliation.

Hesser toppled under the power and weight of Raspail and hit the ground to the amusement of the laughing pups. Raspail laughed with the pups, then went to lick Hesser's face affectionately. As his tongue slapped against the fur of his cheek, Hesser sprang at Raspail's throat. Raspail, being trustful of Hesser, was so dumbfounded that he had no chance to parry or retreat, and now he was peering into the actor's true face for the first time, glaring terrifyingly at him with his jaws clamped tight on his throat and fangs digging deeper into his neck. Raspail tried to wend his throat free, and as he did something tore in the muscular fabric of his neck, in that mysterious part of the wolf anatomy where speech is generated. The pain washed over Raspail with such dizzying acceleration that he nearly passed out.

Hesser quickly disengaged and shuffled back nervously from his victim. Realizing the lashing he would receive for harming a high-ranking wolf, Hesser was worried not for Raspail, who struggled mightily before him in his attempts to breathe, but for his own hide. His mind raced, fathoming what lies to tell the others.

Raspail alternated between gasping for air and coughing blood. In a desperate effort to cancel the pain with more pain, he dragged his head violently along the rocky ground.

"Help! Raspail is hurt! Oh dear me, come quick!" Hesser cried to the others. Every wolf in the pack came running, but none faster than Kileo, who shoved them all away to reach Raspail first.

His eyes conveyed terror that she had only seen on elks moments before they died. She had never seen that pathetic wild-eyed look on a wolf.

"RASPAIL!" she shouted helplessly at him, for there was nothing else she or any of them to do but cry and whimper at the misery unfolding before them.

Hesser shrank back from Cob Ash, whining, "Raspail threatened to kill me! I-I was protecting the pups, I thought he was going to hurt them, I swear it, my facet!" He curled up on the ground, urinated on his tail and licked Cob Ash's massive foot as he squealed for mercy.

The anxious wolves mobbed Raspail, watching to see how the morbid spectacle of Raspail's untimely death would end. But the fire in his eyes wasn't flickering out, it was glowing hotter as if he was whipping every atom of his being into a frenzy to stay alive. The wolves watching were mesmerized by the fight Raspail was waging to continue living, thrashing about heroically like he were battling some invisible fiend. Poor Kileo almost died from grief watching.

The crowd was suffocating him. He needed air. He rammed his way through the claustrophobic group. With great racking pain he pitched his head back -- for this was the only way he could get air down his injured neck -- and blood and air filled his lungs, giving him relief, such as it was. He arched his head back further, to the point where the pain was so unendurable he wished it would kill him, when the blockage inside his throat painfully sprang loose and he could suddenly breath again.

His legs gave and he crumpled to the ground where he filled his lungs, over and over, waiting for his balance to return.

Kileo looked in his eyes, sensing his relief.

He opened his mouth to tell her he was okay, but no sound came out. He tried again, harder this time -- the look of worry on her face pained him as much as his throat -- but all that came out was silence. He became frantic and ran shaking his head to and fro like he had the scatters, hoping that when he stopped in a new location things would be normal.

Kileo chased him, barking at him, "Stop running! What's wrong with you?! Say something!"

She furtively followed him until he arrived at a place where he thought he'd found privacy. She watched him open his mouth and try to utter sounds, over and over again, the ground around him splattered with his blood.

He heard her crying and looked over.

"What is wrong with you?" she pleaded.

It was the same question she asked him when he was a charming nuisance, only now the coyness was gone and replaced with anxiety. He stared back with an unfamiliar look in his eyes that scared her.

"Just talk!" she shouted at him. She bunted his face and bit his shoulder angrily. He didn't bite back. He always bit her back.

She ran back to the camp alone, crying the whole way.

Standing alone, with the sounds of chirping birds, bugling elk and howling wolves swirling around him, he fathomed the cold reality of this new circumstance.

Hesser's attack had left him mute.

***

Raspail and Poitu

After several days, the pack, disconcerted by Raspail's dark, inward gaze, stopped trying to engage him in conversation.

He was no longer invited on the hunt. To hunt in the group you needed to communicate, and he could not howl, he could not growl, grumble, whimper, moan, yip, cry, sigh or laugh. So

Abillon took over the post vacated by Raspail, Polwin the position left by Abillon, and so on down the line, leaving room for one more wolf, and that wolf was Hesser.

In fairness to the wolves who loved Raspail, they did not comprehend his condition, and in their minds he had not just become mute, but deaf and dumb as well. He was a ghost now, lingering invisibly at the fringes of the camp. Only the pups acknowledged the ghost, but feeling like a pariah, Raspail withdrew from them when they tried to play with him.

While Raspail may not have been able to vocalize his thoughts, he maintained an inner dialogue that was drenched with anxiety and despair. He asked himself, countless times during the long, agonizing hours waiting at the camp while the others hunted, *What is wrong with me? How did Hesser steal my voice? When will my voice return?*

The answers were more silent than his questions.

Kileo brought back food for him from the hunt. He felt the crushing humiliation of being unfit to hunt for his own meat and couldn't look into her beautiful golden eyes. He stopped regarding her as the object of his passion -- it was far too painful -- so he submitted gratefully to her when she arrived with food for him. It was more than she could bear.

Two weeks passed, and Raspail not only suffered from his woes but from a fever, brought on by infection, that throbbed through his body. He watched the hunting party return, starving for the meat Kileo brought him. But on this day she brushed past Raspail and said, with every bit of love gone from her voice, "Get your own food."

She continued past him and laid down with Abillon, Polwin and Moorea.

It was the hardest thing Kileo had ever done -- it would have been so much easier to just bring him back meat. But she had to jolt him out of his passivity somehow, and it wouldn't be by feeding him like some wolfmother.

Raspail shuffled out of camp, gripped by the fever which made his dwindling stature feel huge and cumbersome.

He killed a rabbit, and while he ate t it he remembered the time when Polwin and Abillon stole the bounty of his first hunt and he alone fended off the two thieves, impressing his uncles and aunts.

A joyful memory from another wolf's life, he thought.

He was still hungry after finishing the rabbit, but rather than hunt some more, he succumbed to his feverish body and fell asleep. In his sleep he dreamed that his voice had miraculously returned, and that he was laughing about it with Aratus. In the dream a raven landed near him, the same raven who he often saw watching him.

Poitu had in fact landed near the prone wolf and was watching his legs and eyes twitch while he slept. She was so close she could feel his warm breath ruffle her feathers as she examined the wound on his neck.

Unable to lick the wound, and without a friend to lick it for him, Raspail had innocently tried to heal the wound by rubbing it against trees and rocks. She hopped closer and smelled the sickness inside the swollen lump. The scab's crystalline crust glistened in the sun, tempting the raven.

She pecked at his neck and ripped the scab off. Raspail shot to his feet and looked around for his attacker, but there was none he could see. *I have the scatters,* he thought.

Then he heard a guttural rattling sound and looked down. There was the raven, standing in front of him, and in her long bill she was holding the scab. As if he were still dreaming, he saw white puss drip from his neck on to his foot. He licked it off, then looked at Poitu curiously. She croaked at him, then flew off with the delicate scab held firmly in her beak.

***

Poitu's Cache

Just as terrestrial animals, using a little imagination, can connect points of light in the sky, grouping them together into memorable images so they can be catalogued for future navigation, so does the Warmpools raven using stands of spruce trees. Eight out of every ten trees in Warmpools were these tall, conical-shaped behemoths, and viewed from above, contrasted against the rich volcanic soil or pure white snow, they provided endless patterns for the raven who needs to refine its search on a finer map than the stars. Poitu, flying high, located the constellation of spruce trees which had been recorded in her head as resembling a wolf's head in profile with its mouth hanging open.

Poitu landed on the top of the tallest spruce in the stand and, under the calm sway of the massive timber, scanned the skies to insure no other birds had seen her.

Satisfied that she had no watchers, she began her cache ritual, climbing down the tree in small sections, patiently surveying for spies each step of the way, until she jumped off the lowest branch of the tree and was on the ground. She rotated so she was facing north, then strutted forward, counting her steps: *eight north, four east.* She opened her wings and flapped them explosively, the bursts of air sweeping the pine needles off the softly packed dirt. Kicking the dirt away with her talons, she excavated something glittering in the dark soil, and as always, her heart beat faster. Being overly cautious she flew up into the tree and waited for any opportunists. None came, so she flew down and brushed away the remaining dirt. There she found the prized possessions she'd collected through her life and hidden. This was Poitu's cache.

The impulse to collect shiny things occurred after she witnessed a fellow raven fly into a window of some man-made structure on the southern edge of Warmpools. The window shattered and the raven disappeared. On the ground, to Poitu's fascination, shards of glass were sprinkled everywhere. *Perhaps there is a connection between the raven's sudden death and the sparkling dust that fell from the sky around it,* she pondered. She gathered a chunk of the glass in her mouth, noting that it had neither taste nor odor, and carried it to a hiding spot under the stand of trees that resembled a wolf's head. She made over seven trips to recover the precious glass before she developed a clever idea. She found a discarded sardine tin and filled it with the pieces of glass. It took just two shuttles with the sardine tin to recover all the glass.

The next object to fascinate her was a shiny porcelain handle that had broken off a tea cup. Then some fishing hooks she stole off a frozen lake.

But once she encountered the black wolf pup, she only hoarded things from his life. There was a shiny black claw that was Parsay's (the fleshy pad was still attached, as was some of the gray fur), two of Raspail's milk teeth, and a clump of his black winter fur. She added the scab to the cache, then covered that layer with enough dirt to conceal what was below. Over that she sprinkled the glass. If another raven raided her cache, they would see the glass, take it and leave the wolf things safe in their second compartment. She would gladly sacrifice her stardust to protect these more cherished items.

She started to cover the glass layer with dirt and leaves when she felt eyes spying on her. Quickly she jumped up into the spruce and scanned the area and saw Raspail calmly watching her. She had no idea how long he'd been there.

She fanned her wings and croaked loudly at him. Undeterred, he walked to the cache and dug the dirt off the hole. She croaked madly again at him, but he was entranced by something emanating from her cache.

The odor was incredibly faint, but the source of it -- his mother -- was not; she was powerfully embedded in his memory as some ethereal, omniscient guardian. He stared into the mysteriously sparkling fragments, thinking the mesmerizing smell radiated from them.

Poitu flew over his back and pecked at his rump. He backed away from the cache and watched the strange bird obsessively cover the hole with dirt and pine needles.

When she was done, she flew off and, without Raspail seeing, alighted on a tree behind him where she waited to see if the wolf would raid her cache. If he did, she would need hours -- maybe days -- to find a new cache and re-hide her possessions.

But he didn't. He lay reverently on the ground with his heavy head sinking into the loose bed over the cache, inhaling whatever faint molecules of his mother he could. He slept peacefully for the first time in weeks while his body, drained of its toxins by the strange raven, recovered from the infection that the wolf, starving and heart-broken as he was, could not fight alone.

***

Returning to Poitu's Cache

Cortess approached Raspail the next day with her brood trailing behind her.

"I would very much like to hunt today. Will you watch your brothers and sisters?"

He gratefully licked his mother's ear and wouldn't stop until she lovingly nudged him away.

When she left, the pups attacked Raspail with such infectious vigor that for those four blissful hours that he was alone with them he was distracted from his many sorrows. When Kileo and the hunting party returned, so did his woes, so he left camp and searched for Poitu's cache where he would rest peacefully like he did the day before.

Poitu, flying over the southeastern corner of Cob Ash territory, discovered a dead deer being eaten by a ramblefoot who had sneaked into Cob Ash.

She landed by the carcass, and the skittish wolf darted at her half-heartedly. While waiting for an opportune moment to feed, a mob of ravens descended. The smart ramblefoot, predicting that the noisy mob would attract the guardians of this province, fled with as much meat as he could carry in his mouth.

The mob, recognizing the infamous Poitu, blocked her from getting meat. An aggressive young female stepped forward and challenged her, lunging at her wing. Poitu quickly parried and counter-riposted, stabbing the tender flesh between her left eye and beak. Her victim shrieked in pain, which started a hideous cacophony of raven hysteria.

Using the anarchy to her advantage, Poitu peeled off a stringy mass of meat and flew away in search of a quiet place to dine alone. She glided low over the trees that surrounded her cache, and there she saw Raspail sleeping with his head on its unmolested cover of pine needles.

She landed in front of him with the meat and saw his tail brush back and forth as his mood lightened. He craned his head forward and sniffed at the food, then darted at it, but Poitu hopped backwards too quickly for him. He tried again to snatch the food from her and this time she flew up to a branch. He sat under the branch waiting hopefully for bits to fall.

Poitu awkwardly ate the ungainly meat on the willowy branch, disconcerted by the drooling wolf below, then screeched in dismay as the meat accidentally sloughed off the branch. Poitu swooped down just as Raspail jumped up and caught the morsel in his jaws. She landed at his feet, and now she was the one scrounging the ground for scraps.

When the meal was devoured, Raspail curiously examined the raven as the raven hopped around examining him. She walked between his legs and looked up at his chest, noticing the poor condition of his hide. Poitu knew firsthand that one of the hardest things about life as an outcast was staying well-groomed without the help of others. Raspail's fur, the victim of neglect, had been taken over by lice and mange.

She pressed her head against his chest, seeing how his hide hung from his pronounced ribcage. He skittishly jumped back, and she hopped back over to him fearlessly.

Her mind drifted to the raven mob eating the carcass. *Should be his,* she thought, *his and mine.* She rushed into the sky, and in seconds she was within view of the carcass and the ravens that jeered her earlier. She reversed course to figure out a plan to lure Raspail to the carcass. But as it turned out, she didn't need a plan. She could see Raspail was already on his way, chasing the shadow she cast below on the ground.

***

A Raven Execution

Poitu's brazen return to the carcass was greeted by looks of disbelief. One raven chanted, "Kill her!" Then another joined her, and another, until all of them were screeching, vulgarly pumping their bodies up and down and flexing their closed wings. In a moment the mob transformed from a group of individuals into a single entity. And the entity determined that Poitu needed to be killed.

She had once witnessed a raven execution, and it was a morbid spectacle she had tried to forget. Now she was the one to be executed. She leaped off the ground and tried to take flight, but a gauntlet of hovering ravens blocked her escape. She hovered there, trapped, her wings flapping against the thrusting spears and scooping hooks of her prospective executioners.

To her immense relief, Raspail appeared cresting the hill. With a surge of adrenaline Poitu forged her way through the chaotic flapping of wings, tumbling through a barbed, black cloud of pecking bills and scraping claws, and soared clumsily to the wolf, landing solidly on the giant animal's bony back.

Her executioners stopped their death chant and stared, wondering, *Are this raven and wolf an alliance? Or is it a bluff and the wolf will kill the raven?*

Their eyes marveled at the sight of Poitu's claws clamping tightly into the wolf's sagging fur. The wolf did not shake off the raven and try catching it in his jaws. On the contrary; it was as if he understood that the pain was a signal meant to goad him forward, which he did, walking casually and confidently to the carcass, carrying the raven safely on his back.

Now, ravens are no strangers to exploiting elk and deer and other herbivorous animals for the sake of transportation. But never had any of them seen a raven being taxied on the back of a meat eater.

As Raspail got closer the spellbound mob dispersed into the air and recongregated about two lengths behind the carcass. Raspail swallowed rapacious mouthfuls of meat while Poitu ate next to him, and to the mob's further amazement the wolf indulged the raven's intimate company.

One of the ravens strutted forward. Raspail didn't waste a moment -- he leaped forward and pounced on the culprit. Five other ravens suddenly dived at Poitu from her right side, wedging her away from the wolf and the carcass so they could kill her. At that moment Raspail jumped over the carcass and helped fend off her foes.

The ravens chaotically fanned out into the sky then formed a neat roost in the nearest tree. They yammered noisily among themselves until a consensus was reached: They had all the proof they needed; this wolf and raven, mad or not, were clearly in alliance. This was way too much for them to comprehend, so rather than analyze it any further, they flew off to look for food somewhere else where things weren't so queer.

While Raspail and Poitu ate voraciously side by side, the wolf watched with fascination as the raven industriously removed a long rubbery string of flesh from the backbone by tugging with its beak and holding the slack down with her claw, working like this until she removed the long strand of flesh.

Raspail was meatdrunk and feeling stupid. He snapped at Poitu's hard-earned delicacy and tugged it back so roughly that Poitu, whose beak was clenched tightly on the cord, flipped over and landed on her back. What Raspail had longed for most in the last month was a partner to play with. Poitu eagerly accepted his invitation, having also missed the absurd games that ravens engage in.

She righted herself and flew at him, feigning, then soaring under him and between his legs, landing behind him and biting his tail and yanking it. Raspail whipped around and she flew back under him, grabbed the end of the stringy meat and flew up in the air with it. A powerful tug of war ensued with the raven pulling vertically on the meat while suspended in flight. As Raspail's neck arched back, he felt the stinging pain return in his throat and released his grip on the meat.

Poitu flew off with it and landed a safe distance away, proud that she'd outwitted the wolf. She coiled up her trophy so it was more portable and flew off with it, bobbing in the sky, weighed down not just by the heavy cord in her beak but by the meat filling her stomach. She sagged in the air and dropped the meat several times during the course of the trip. Raspail laughed silently as he watched, thinking, *Hesser has at least not stolen my laughter.*

***

Was the White Bitch Real?

While Raspail was forging an unusual alliance with a raven, Hesser was dreaming of forming one with a white wolf. He had, over the year, alternated between optimism and doubt. Now that winter was here, and her return to him overdue, he fretted that she was conjured up by his hungry imagination while gazing at suggestive shapes in the clouds. Then, one afternoon, during the course of a hunt, all doubts about the existence of the white goddess eroded as her unmistakable scent was delivered to him on a crisp wisp of wind.

Hesser quickly broke from the pack and followed her scent, acting like he was on the trail of prey. The scent got thicker -- she was near him, watching him, he could feel her eyes. He straightened his back and took on an important posture, looking confident even though his heart pounded like it was trying to escape from his chest. Just as his eyes registered the sudden movement to his right, she tackled him and laughed playfully.

He shriveled back in fear and at once corrected himself upon seeing the white bitch standing there, swinging her tail back and forth with an easy, friendly flourish. He jumped up and cautiously approached her.

"Is it you?" he said, "Or do my eyes play tricks on me? Be fair to me and don't wound a good wolf's heart."

She regarded him as if he were noble and said with passion, "It's as if you are reading my mind! For I too wonder if you are just a dream from my sleep and not flesh and bone!" She rubbed her flank against his, feeling the nervous tension in his muscles. "You *are* real!"

"Yes. I am," he said reassuringly, posturing as nobly as he could.

They leaned against each other for a long moment then chased each other playfully. "If we were to mate, you might lose your place as your pack's facet."

Hesser suddenly felt insecure; *had she mistaken him for the pack's leader? Would she still fancy him if he were not?*

"You flatter me, goddess, but I am not my pack's facet."

"Impossible! Surely a wolf like you, with your superior physique and flawless face -- you can't be serious! You are a superior wolf, a natural leader! You can tell me honestly that there is one better than you in your pack?"

"I did not say he was better. I say he took power and there were no challengers."

"Show me this wolf, for I cannot believe that you have an equal in your pack."

The bold request frightened Hesser, who hesitated and stammered, "You -- you wish to see my facet?"

"Yes."

Hesser whined, "I worry that is not a good idea."

She performed the most ribald gesture she could, turning so that her rosy vulva was planted squarely in his face. If she leaped off a cliff, he would have gladly followed her to his death at this moment.

"No wolf is superior to you. I will return again to look at him, my white body klooting in the snow so he doesn't see me, and I will judge this wolf who thinks he is better than my wolf," she said possessively.

Hesser heard Cob Ash and the rest of the hunting party howling in celebration in the distance. Sarrassin sidled next to him, her warm breath filled his ear. She slowly bit down on his ear, her fangs piercing it. He tried to withdraw, but could not without tearing the ear further.

She whispered in his bleeding ear, "Tell them you fought a Draguignon wolf and chased them off." She gently released his ear. He gaped at her, terrified by her beauty.

"I would never chase you away," the romantic wolf said reassuringly to her.

He almost passed out as she licked his blood off her muzzle. She turned and left, and as she sashayed back to Draguignon, he flared his nostrils at the departing bitch and sucked frantically at her essence till the rush of cold air made it impossible to smell anymore.

***

A Mysterious Discovery

Since the Cob Ash ramblefoots had settled their province, there had been no trespassing interlopers contesting their claim, and life had been relatively easy if not boring. On some nights they discerned the familiar howls of their old comrades ringing through the valley. But something had troubled Aratus in recent weeks, and that was the notable absence of Raspail's voice in the chorus.

When he mentioned this to Balfort, he responded, "I hear him. *There!* That's him!" But the voice he heard was not Raspail's. Aratus was sure.

While this was worrying Aratus, something else was nagging Maddocq. During the night he frequently woke from his sleep, smelling something unfamiliar in the air.

One day, after waking up to the smell, he woke the others and asked them, "Do you smell that?" The others sniffed the air.

"Smell what exactly?" asked Balfort

"That smell. I don't know what it is. I smell it all the time." He sniffed the air and said, "There it is again."

"Nobody has a beak as keen as yours, Maddocq. Tell me, is it a good smell?" Aratus asked.

"No. It's most definitely not good."

"It is close?" Aratus asked.

"It is not far."

They returned to sleep, only to be woken again by Maddocq, snorting at the air. Seeing them awake, he eagerly exclaimed, "You smell it now, don't you!"

Aratus kindly said, "Maddocq... we wake from you snorting loudly at the air, not from any smell." Maddocq was disappointed.

When they returned to sleep, Maddocq wandered off in search of the smell. With Maddocq gone, Aratus and Balfort slept righteously until being jolted to their feet by the far away howl of Maddocq. Without hesitation they followed their friend's howling until they rendezvoused with him at the southwestern perimeter of their territory under a cloud of hovering birds. He appeared to be okay.

Maddocq stood over another wolf, a big male with a white-tipped tail and a brown head, who was lying dead on the ground.

"Nicely done, brother!" Balfort said, "And not a scratch on you!"

"It wasn't me who killed him."

They saw the wolf's leg was locked inside something that looked like the stripped down jaws of a big beast. The jaws had teeth, but unlike the teeth of animals, these were uniform in shape and size. Aratus smelled the wolf and then the metal jaws. None of it made the slightest bit of sense to them.

Aratus looked up at Maddocq and asked "Is that the smell?"

"Yes. Only there's more. It's coming from the south."

"It's a bear jaw" Balfort concluded.

"It smells nothing like a bear," Maddocq said.

"Not like any bear we know from Cob Ash, but a bear nonetheless."

"There are no claw marks on the wolf. No sign of a fight." Aratus said

"The bear was dead. This unlucky fellow stepped on a dead bear, and like the elk which quivers and spasms after it has been killed, the lifeless bear's jaws snapped shut on his leg, killing him."

"And where is the rest of this bear?" Maddocq asked dubiously.

"Coyotes tore the bear apart and dragged it off, leaving only the jaw behind."

"We would have heard coyotes." Aratus said.

"We are sleep deprived," Balfort said pointedly to Maddocq, "and our wits not at their sharpest."

Aratus smelled the jaws again, this time closing his eyes. They had a scent, the scent of a strange animal, but it did not originate from within as the smell of marrow radiates from inside bone. These jaws had a lifeless lack of smell, like rock, which gets its scent from things that rub against it.

"The coyotes obviously ate the bear before we claimed the territory, leaving behind its jaws, stripped of meat by scavengers. On these jaws the hapless wolf stepped, triggering a muscle spasm that caused them to shut on the wolf's leg," Balfort said as if it were established fact.

"It's not from a bear," Aratus said conclusively.

They left the dead wolf and quietly walked back to where they slept. Now that Aratus had smelled the trap, he could smell in the air what Maddocq had been smelling all these days and, like Maddocq, found it hard to smell anything else.

***

Three Bitches for Three Brothers

Several days later, there was a new odor passing through their territory. Balfort got up and stretched, then said very casually, "I'm going to mark the perimeter."

"I'll join you," Maddocq said, eagerly getting up.

"No, no. I think you should stay, otherwise we would be leaving Aratus alone."

Aratus raised his brow and said, "Why don't we all go?"

"It's unnecessary. Besides, I like to walk on my own time to time." And before anyone could protest, he trotted off.

An hour later, with Balfort still gone, Maddocq got up and said, "I feel hungry."

"Why don't we hunt for something together? I'm bored and keen for activity," Aratus said.

"I know you are saying that for my benefit, but you needn't, kind brother. I feel like hunting alone," he said, and he walked off leaving Aratus bewildered and alone.

Aratus muttered to himself, "They are acting rather strange."

He tried to sleep some more, but Maddocq had put the idea of food in his head and it wouldn't let him drift back to the pleasant state of slumber he had been in. He got up irritably and went hunting for rabbit. A new scent, the smell of a young bitch in heat, overwhelmed his desire to eat, and took him on a different course entirely.

In the past, when his sisters or matriarch went into heat, he was able to ignore the smell. But now that he was free to mate, the smell cast a spell on him, drawing him closer to its source. This meant crossing the western border of their small province and stepping over the scent posts of a neighboring pack that, from what he could determine with his nose, outnumbered them by four.

It was crazy what he was doing, yet he couldn't control himself from indulging his desire to meet the owner of this perfume, for it seemed singularly created and released for Aratus' benefit alone.

He suddenly sensed he was being watched. He glimpsed a wolf klooting behind some trees without looking at it directly, then klooted himself so he could lose the wolf spying on him and sneak up from behind it. He successfully disappeared from the wolf's vision, then made a broad, creeping circle and leaped into the crevice where the other wolf's shadow was visible. He pounced on the beast, surprising it, then withdrew from his victim upon seeing that it was Balfort.

"Brother! Why did you attack me like that!" Balfort exclaimed.

"I didn't know it was you. Anyway, I thought you were marking the perimeter."

Balfort looked embarrassed. "Yes, I was doing that.... and as I finished my business a moose appeared before me."

"A moose appeared before you?"

"Yes, exactly. As close as you are to me now. Of course I chased the fat old thing. You'd think I'd never learned from that dreadful hunting trip where Cob led us into Draguignon. You remember, the day you found Raspail." Balfort amicably rubbed his neck against Aratus' as he remembered fondly the old days.

"Please, continue."

"Ah, yes. So I stupidly ventured across the border in pursuit of this meal. I am more than relieved to see you here, Aratus."

"Obviously."

Balfort saw that wise Aratus doubted his story. "And of course by now you've guessed that the elk got away."

"The *moose,*" Aratus corrected him

"Yes, that's right. Thank you, Aratus. It was in fact a moose." Balfort paused. "Now that you know how I ended up crossing our perimeter, what brings you here?"

"I couldn't sleep. I fathomed something dire happening to you so I followed your scent here."

"That must have been difficult. Scent is thick in the air today, eh?" Balfort said, arching his brow suggestively.

"Almost as thick as brothers," Aratus replied good naturedly. They both heard a rustling and klooted between the rocks. They watched the jagged top of a giant wolf in the distance move slowly behind the shallow cover of a snow bank and blend with the trees behind it.

"Maddocq!" Balfort called. Maddocq raised his head and looked surprised and embarrassed to see his two brothers. He plodded over the snow bank towards them.

"What are you two doing here?" he asked.

"Balfort chased after a moose that briefly became an elk," Aratus said, "I sensed he was in danger and came to his aid."

"Oh." said Maddocq, thinking quickly. "That explains why you weren't at camp when I returned. I was worried and went looking for you."

Balfort looked at Aratus dubiously.

The sound of wolves arriving from two directions saved the three brothers from admitting the true reasons for exploring the enemy's turf. The damp air fell silent for a moment. They looked at each other, knowing that one of them would have to step forward and make a facet-like decision. There was no time for voting, consensus, or petty arguing now.

Wolf howls ripped through the sky. Balfort and Maddocq felt suitably threatened. Aratus, who was less impressed, said with a smile, "Let's greet them."

"With our asses disappearing over the hillocks you surely mean!"

"There's no reason to retreat." He sniffed the air and was reassured. "There's not just one bitch. There's perhaps three."

"Ah, that is reassuring me, Aratus. Three bitches in heat, their sixteen uncles, and forty-two brothers. Yes, let's greet them, indeed." The storming footsteps grew louder. Aratus remained steadfast.

"Brother, trust me and summon your most affable voice," he said. "I have an idea."

"Share with me this idea first."

"No."

"Fine," Balfort responded. "But at least share it with these ravens, who seem to be betting on us losing this one."

Aratus looked up at the gathering ravens. He laid down in a relaxed posture and excitedly faced the incoming wave of wolves. He had one last word for them:

"Let us not forget, they don't have a facet."

Balfort and Maddocq, reassured mildly by the cryptic Aratus, struck a similar reclining pose as him.

The sight of these three prone wolves, looking without a worry in the world -- eager to meet them even -- was so unnerving to the advancing wolves that the instant their ranks charged out of the trees and caught sight of the bold strangers they became stupefied.

Aratus was acutely aware of their youth and disunity. He invited them to come closer, to smell him, paying special attention to the three fine bitches in their ranks.

Balfort said graciously, "Cousins, we apologize for trespassing on your province. The thick scent of your bitches colored the scent posts and thus we wandered blindly here where you find us with no malintent, I assure."

The big gray male, who could not have been older than Raspail, lunged at Balfort. Balfort dodged the wolf and sent him rolling on his side. Maddocq pounced on the big gray before he could get to his feet while Aratus snarled a warning to the gray's brothers and sisters, cautioning them to stay back.

"Lucien! Disengage!" The three sisters barked. Lucien, who was looking into Maddocq's abyss of a mouth, obliged.

Maddocq backed off from the gray and let him stand. Aratus addressed him, "You are the facet of your pack, then? *Lucien?*"

"Obviously," he responded. It was less obvious to his brother, who growled challengingly at his brother.

"Do you need a moment to determine who is your facet?" Aratus said kindly.

"No!" The big gray said confidently.

"Our facet disappeared two days ago," one of the females said.

"What about your matriarch?" Aratus asked.

The second bitch spoke up. "She went looking for him. She hasn't come back."

"None of this is your concern," Lucien said, flashing fang.

"Perhaps it is," Aratus said. "We found a wolf in our territory. A large, brown-headed male with a white-tipped tail, and high shoulders like my brother here."

The description resonated with them.

Lucien tried to incite the others, "They killed him!"

"Zut, Lucien!" The females growled back, quieting him.

Aratus continued. "He was killed, yes, though not by us."

"By who then?" one of the females inquired

"I don't know. I invite you to cross into our territory to verify if this wolf is your facet."

The neighboring wolves murmured to each other.

"We do not trick you. There are just us three. You will not be greeted by more of us."

Balfort's tongue hung luridly from his mouth as he gaped at the bitches, their perfume crazing his thoughts. He could barely see straight, but nonetheless had an idea and expressed it:

"We are willing to stay here, under guard of course, while you verify the identity of this wolf who might be your facet. If we have misled you, then pass your judgment on us."

The neighboring wolves huddled again.

Balfort continued with an ominous tone; "Take your strongest wolves, for though there is no threat of attack by more of us, whatever mysterious creature killed your facet *still lurks about.*"

The neighboring wolves fell for Balfort's subtle manipulation and agreed to leave their three sisters and one brother in charge of guarding the trespassers, which was exactly what Balfort desired. Lucien and his brother then embarked into their province in search of their slain facet.

Aratus, Balfort and Maddocq romped lustily with the young bitches the instant the search party was out of sight. Wasting no time, the wolves paired off, found some privacy, and played for the next hour.

Feeling useless, the young male guard ran off to catch up with his brothers.

The search party returned with low hung heads and grim faces that required no explanation.

"It seems you were right," Balfort muttered to Aratus.

The three of them strode back home with no resistance from the grief stricken young wolves.

During their journey back, Aratus meditated on their good fortune. The slain facet had presented an excellent opportunity to expand their numbers and territory by leaving behind an inexperienced, disorganized pack. Without leadership their hunting would suffer, and hunger would further divide their ranks right about the time that the bitches showed they were pregnant. When that time came, Aratus figured, they would return and merge with their ranks, raising their pups and organizing the hunters.

Reaching their camp, Aratus curled up on the piece of land he'd tried sleeping on before, and though his stomach was even more empty then before, his mind was so sated by the fortuitous events of the day that slumber came easily.

***

How a Raven gets a Wolf to Hunt

Raspail convened daily with Poitu. And while this unique bond strengthened, Raspail slipped further and further out of rhythm with the pack.

As weak as his connection to family life had become, it was still something he was unwilling to give up. Being optimistic by nature, he held on to hope that his voice would one day return for real as it did in his dreams. For that reason he did not consider rambling.

He stopped sleeping in camp and began flopping on his own, far away from the others. He found comfort in the large piles of leaves and pine needles that collected in the crevices between boulders, and hiding his body in the natural bedding he slept soundly without feeling vulnerable.

Poitu camped with him at his flop. She was there when he went to sleep, and there when he woke. She traveled with him to camp to watch the pups for Cortess when she hunted, she included herself in their games, and she left with him when the hunters returned.

Like all desperately lonely creatures, Raspail was grateful for any company he could get. He would have gladly accepted a cactus as a friend-- and to a wolf a raven was not regarded much higher than that prickly plant. But as he found out, the raven's complex personality was not so different from a wolf's. His obsessive mind, which grinded endlessly trying to make sense of his reversal of fortune, welcomed the challenge of understanding his strange new companion. The little bird was, after all, his only friend.

Raspail's inability to talk gave him an advantage understanding the raven, simply because he was forced to watch and listen without being tempted to interrupt. On any given day when no wolf talked to him, Poitu, lonely as she was, gladly kawed, cooed, trilled, clucked and snapped her bill to him for hours.

He quickly became attuned to how her vocalizations changed in intensity, duration and rate. Her accompanying postures and facial expressions allowed him to assign meaning to these calls, which he catalogued in his head, and over a short period of time he began to comprehend the building blocks of her speech. She could convey to him when she was hungry, when she was mad, when there was danger, when she wanted to play, when he played too rough, and when she was territorial -- and she was keenly aware when the wolf understood her and when he did not.

He became so familiar with her voice and flying style after those first few weeks that he could easily distinguish her from other ravens. Shortly after that he ceased thinking of her as a raven and him a wolf, for together they forged into something that was much greater than the sum of its parts.

Poitu, empowered by their bond and true to her resourceful raven ways, set her mind to exploiting her powerful new friend. From her aerial vantage point, she, like other ravens, could pick out elk and deer who were enfeebled by injury or age. She even devised a way to track them by dropping her scat on their wide flat backs, leaving a distinctive white splatter that she could easily identify from the air. But sometimes it took weeks for one of these animals to die or be killed, and the task of monitoring them and waiting was tedious.

Having invited herself on many Cob Ash hunts, Poitu correctly identified the primary reason wolves hunted in groups: The stamina-intensive task of finding and flushing out the weakest prey in the herd required a relay of runners, each performing at their peak then passing the task on to the next wolf. With her unique point of view she could direct Raspail to the ailing prey and eliminate all the running around. So she dedicated herself to devising a way to convey this complex notion to him.

While Raspail did his pack task on this day, Poitu went scouting for one of her marked quarries. After locating one, she caught up with Raspail leaving camp and raced with him through the timbers and into the valley. But instead of soaring into the sky at this point as she usually did, she stayed low and continued racing him, leading him to an aspen grove where elk were foraging.

The big animals regarded the lone wolf with vague interest, knowing that a solitary wolf would not waste his energy on the impossible feat of taking down an animal many times his size. They leisurely chewed on bark as if he weren't there.

I am invisible even to those who once feared me, he thought despondently, turning to leave. As he did, he saw Poitu fall from the sky and land on the back of an elk. She paused, then flapped her wings the way she did when she was being proprietary.

Raspail stared at her, trying to make sense of it.

She launched off the old elk and raked her wing across its face, making the startled animal rear on its hind legs. The animal's fractured hip could not support its weight and it buckled, toppling over on to its back, then struggled to get back on its feet.

Raspail gleaned in that one awkward slip instigated by the clever raven's ploy what it would have taken an entire pack an hour's worth of running around to figure out:

This one was prey.

Raspail stealthfully drove into the herd. He chased his prey to separate it from the others, then, running alongside it, jumped at its throat. He hung on by his fangs as the elk took off running, trying to shake off its attacker.

Poitu was overjoyed. She flew overhead and watched the wolf get flung around by the elk, laughing at her success.

Raspail, still malnourished and weak, lost his stamina and fell off the elk with a silent grunt. He sneezed to clear his head, then pursued the elk again. He leaped on top of the elk, but his legs, cramping from malnutrition, could not steady him as the wounded elk buckled under his weight. He slipped off its back and watched the elk disappear into the timbers.

At camp that night, Cob Ash was feeling the loss of his three brothers and called out to them with a mournful howl. The others joined in, "Aratus, Balfort, Maddocq!" they cried, "Have you settled? Are you alive?" They repeated the howl until a response came from their absent comrades.

"Cob Ash, good facet, we are alive and well and rooted like trees," Balfort's howl resounded over mountains and rivers.

By degrees, the inquiring howls of other forlorn wolves seeking news from their departed relatives and friends turned the airwaves into a communal web of calls and responses. So keen is the wolf's ear that he can pluck the sound of his friend out from this fusillade of chatter.

Raspail could no longer howl, but this did not keep him from trying. He arched his head back, suffering the pain that this triggered, opened his mouth and called out Kileo's name. His silent howl was the most mournful cry in all of Warmpools.

Later that night, Poitu crashed into the leafy bed where Raspail flopped. He tried to ignore her, but it was clear the strident raven had urgent business for him. He climbed out from under the leaves, stretched, and followed her to the creek. There he saw the prey that had evaded him earlier that day laying on the ground breathing heavily and looking dazed.

Upon seeing the wolf, the elk tried standing but failed. Raspail crept up to it cautiously then suddenly lunged at its neck. He watched its blood drain into the creek.

He tore open the large animal's chest and excavated its heart. This glistening treasure, so fresh and sparking with the life and energy of its former owner, lay before him. Remarkably, it was his and his alone, to eat uncontested. He watched mesmerized as the violet hues glowed with dazzling fluctuations of iridescence. He could hold off the temptation no longer and swallowed the heart, not tasting it so much as feeling it buzzing like a million microscopic bees as it slid down his long tongue into his stomach. The feeling was transcendent.

He cracked back more ribs and dug for the next treasure hidden inside the beast, tossing away the stomach and exposing the red-green phosphorescent halo of the liver. He licked it and enjoyed the buzzing on his tongue as he watched the liver's halo change color where he had touched it. He gently took the liver out of its harness of veins, careful not to puncture it with his fangs, and swallowed it whole like he did the heart.

These two jewels, safely stowed in his stomach, began their transfer of energy to the wolf. And with this sudden charge of power Raspail stared incredulously at Poitu, standing inside the cavernous ribcage of the animal eating, as if she'd suddenly sprouted antlers. Not only would he be able to hunt big prey again, he would only have this tiny bird, doing the work of five wolves, to share it with.

He ran up and down the creek, stomping in the water, rejoicing over his incredible good fortune.

Over the next month, wolf and raven perfected their unorthodox hunting technique and Raspail ate so well his size came back twofold. When he went to camp he carried himself with the pathetic posture of a kickaround dog -- spine arched and crouching -- in order to disguise his newly acquired bulk.

He was becoming massive.

***

Sarrassin's Stratagem

Hesser, in order to oblige the white goddess who possessed his every thought, invited Cob Ash to a site where Sarassin told him she would be watching. There, he engaged Cob Ash in some playful grappling.

"Ah, to play with my facet, what a delight. It has been too long since we played as brothers, alone, like pups."

Hesser, aware that the white goddess was observing, broadened his shoulders and deepened his growl to appear his brother's equal. Cob Ash suddenly sensed something, stopped playing and scanned the area.

Draguignon and five of his children emerged from where they were klooting in a circle around Cob Ash and Hesser.

Sarrassin growled at Hesser, "Step away!"

Hesser stepped back from Cob Ash. Cob Ash saw betrayal in the eyes of his brother and lunged at him.

"Traitor!" He bellowed as he sank his teeth into Hesser's croup. Before he could do any damage, the six Draguignon wolves descended on Cob Ash. Hesser groaned in horror as he watched him get ripped apart with violent glee until finally the great wolf was dead.

Four of the assassins, their muzzles covered in blood, dragged the limp body of Cob Ash across the border into Draguignon territory.

Sarassin, standing next to her father, took a new tone with Hesser. "I have slain your facet."

"I did not ask for that!" Hesser responded in a panic.

"Didn't you?" she asked. "I have freed you to become facet of your pack, which is what you want, what you deserve."

Hesser whimpered nervously, "But..."

"At an appropriate time I will return to you and an alliance will be forged between Cob Ash and Draguignon."

Draguignon glanced at him contemptuously, then led Sarrassin out on the route taken by the assassins.

Hesser began his terrified trek back to camp, trembling and fathoming lies.

Once in camp Hesser innocently asked Cortess, "Where is Cob Ash?"

Cortess looked confused. "Weren't you with him?"

"I was," he began. "But something was making him uncalm and he unexpectedly left my company."

As the day turned to night, Cortess' worry rubbed off on the others, but none appeared as concerned for Cob Ash's well being as Hesser, who paced back and forth from one end of camp to the other, making his anxiety appear like worry for his brother.

At dawn, Cortess, Kileo, Abillon, and Polwin went searching for Cob Ash with no success. Cortess howled a heartfelt plea for her mate's return. The mood at camp grew grimmer still, and Cortess went inconsolable with grief.

***

Exile

On the day Hesser was unwittingly drawing Cob Ash into
Sarrassin's deadly trap, Raspail and Poitu were enjoying the
bounty of another successful hunt. When he was meatdrunk like
this, Raspail felt all his misery slough away. Naturally, he
pursued this state as often as he could.

They flopped near the carcass, guarding it so they could
feed off it the next morning, which they did until his straining
belly pleaded for pity and the euphoria returned. Laying there
meatdrunk, he heard Cortess' distressed howling for Cob Ash. As
heavy as his body felt, the call was so powerful that he could not
stay idle any longer. He bounded to camp, his legs resenting him
for calling them to duty.

On route he picked up Cob Ash's scent and diverted
towards the bloody stain where he had been ambushed and
assassinated. Raspail sniffed dilligently at the blood and
recognized his father's scent. Sniffing at the ground he smelled
other wolves, and one of them was Hesser.

Oh, the agony of lacking a voice! he thought. *I must share
my discovery with the pack -- but how?*

He then had an idea. He rubbed his muzzle in the blood of
Cob Ash while Poitu watched.

*When the others smell and see the blood, they will follow
me back here and understand.*

He rushed home uplifted by the promising notion that, after
bringing the news to his family, Cob Ash would be found and he
would be regarded once again as a vital member of the pack,
even if he were mute. This morsel of hope put speed in his legs.

He entered camp, hunkering low to hide his girth. As he
headed towards Cortess with the information he carried, he was
intercepted by Hesser, who stood before him imperiously,
blocking him. He saw immediately the blood on Raspail's
muzzle, smelled that it was the blood of Cob Ash and thought,
Ah, so the mute wretch has seen things he shouldn't have.

Hesser recoiled back in a show of shock as he cried:

"The son carries the blood of our great father on his
murderous jowls!"

Polwin and Abillon rushed over to smell Raspail's muzzle, confirming what Hesser had just told them.

"It's true!" Abillon declared. "Cob Ash's blood is all over his face!"

"You! You murdered our facet!" Hesser paced, as if the thought of this betrayal filled him with untold horror. "Oh, treacherous wretch, oh wretched traitor -- what have you done!"

Oh why can't I speak, now of all times, he fretted. The other wolves surrounded him, suspiciously sniffing the blood on his face. With looks of shock and confusion they cried in agony. Even Kileo seemed convinced of his guilt. Raspail knew he was doomed.

Hesser stoked the fervor of his audience, howling melodramatically at the eye of the ancestors. "Oh, my facet! Good and decent Cob Ash, you are gone to the ancestors! Slain by your detestable son, the black devil!"

The six yearlings, seeing their beloved caretaker persecuted, ran from Cortess to his side, but they were quickly ushered away.

"You silent, gloomy black misfit! You *murderer!*" Hesser pounced on him, spitting, "Hesser will avenge you, Cob Ash! Though I cannot bring you back to life I can at least end the life of your murderer!"

And then he thought cynically to himself, *And surely my pack will make me facet then! Oh white goddess, I pray that you are watching, for this is the performance of my life.*

Raspail's heart beat faster as Hesser whipped the mob into a frenzy. *Death,* Raspail prayed, *Take me at your will. But not for a crime I did not commit, and not with the lying traitor who did it as your agent.*

Hesser opened his gaping jaws, revealing teeth as white and pretty as the day he weaned on his mother, for they had not been dulled or broken by hunting. And as he lunged at Raspail -- who up to this point had maintained a submissive posture -- Raspail dodged the strike and bit down hard on the base of Hesser's ear. Raspail used Hesser's force against him, flipping him over his back and throwing him to the ground. Hesser lay there, blood dripping from where his ear had been attached a mere moment ago.

Raspail slowly straightened his compressed spine and crooked legs and brought his huge head up, letting his body expand to its full and natural stature. He was as big a wolf as any of them had seen. Kileo barely recognized him.

Raspail spit Hesser's bloody ear out and stared darkly back at them. The pack retreated a length in fear.

It seemed like they were going to let him go free, when Polwin and Abillon suddenly darted at Raspail from opposite sides. Raspail reared up, towering over them like a black mountain. When the mountain came down it was an unstoppable avalanche sending the three wolves tumbling in a mortal broil.

Cortess, already grief stricken over the loss of her mate, watched in horror as her children tried to kill each other. Crying hysterically she stepped into the fray and pleaded, "Raspail! Stop!"

Raspail, his heart full of love and respect for her, obeyed her command without hesitation and retreated from his attackers, his fangs still drawn defensively.

"Leave Cob Ash! Now and forever! Never come back!" Dismal sadness filled her heart as she uttered these words, for she could not comprehend that Raspail would murder his father.

Polwin, Abillon and Moorea advanced at Raspail and forced him to the edge of the camp. Though Raspail resisted with the valiant heart of a wolf unjustly persecuted, he could not hold his ground.

Kileo begged her crying mother, "You know Raspail didn't kill Cob Ash! Help him!"

But her mother, her heart so tormented and her head so addled, could do nothing.

Polwin, Abillon and Moorea pushed Raspail step by hard won step to the border between Cob Ash and Draguignon. With gnashing teeth and vicious pummeling they finally forced the brave Raspail across the threshold into enemy territory. The three wolves then spread out, aggressively blocking Raspail's efforts to reenter.

"Our mother commanded me not to kill you. Mercy you," Polwin said.

Then he started to howl, exaggerating his melodic voice to torment his voiceless enemy. Abillon joined in, and there was no doubt that their goal was to lure the Draguignon wolves to Raspail which, of course, was no different from killing him.

Raspail felt the ground tremble as Draguignon wolves rose to their feet and coordinated their ranks. The tremble quickly became a rumble; the entire Draguignon wolf pack was marching towards him, and death was looming over him once again.

"Raspail!"

It was Kileo.

The Draguignon wolves were so close now, he could hear them inhaling and exhaling in tandem, sucking in his smell, locking on to him. If he stood where he was, they would kill him in twenty heartbeats. He tried once again to enter Cob Ash, but Polwin, Abillon and Mooria were tenacious in preventing him, biting him viciously. Blood rained off Raspail's wounded hide and he was losing strength. Polwin tackled him over the threshold back into Draguignon.

Again, Kileo cried out ruefully:

"Raspail!"

Polwin snarled at Raspail from across the border, confidently standing his ground. "Move on, ramblefoot."

Raspail now could see through a screen of timbers the white wolf Sarassin, fifty lengths off, leading the pack towards him.

He could stall no more.

He turned and bolted through the unfamiliar enemy terrain, his only chance at survival outrunning his pursuers long enough to make it past their scent posts.

He saw a stream ahead and, hoping it was their border, flew at it.

The surface was frozen. He clawed aggressively at the slippery ice to keep his momentum going, but as he reached the middle of the stream the ice shattered beneath his forelegs and he fell headfirst into the hard ice, his legs flailing in the water below. With each effort to get up, the broken floes supporting him bobbed and threw him off balance. His body was trapped between these dueling sheets of ice when his pursuers reached the shoreline.

"He killed Denalfi, I'm sure of it!" said Sarrassin.

"Stay back!" Draguignon commanded his children, who waited at the shore with flashing fangs. He stalked across the ice to finish off Raspail.

Raspail thrashed his body violently against the ice, forcing enough of it away that he could dive down into the freezing cold water. With the thick ice pressing down on his spine and his feet sinking in the sandy stream bed, Raspail held his breath as he traveled underwater with the unnerving sound of wolf claws skittering on the ice above him.

The ice thickened as he reached the shore. He forced his back up against it, but his feet just pushed deeper into the sandy bed. He could not hold his breath a moment longer. He bowed his head down, then pitched it up as forcefully as he could against the ice.

Draguignon watched in amazement as the black wolf smashed through the ice trapping him, then launched out of the stream as if nothing in nature could hold him down.

Raspail did not waste a moment looking back. He ran like the hunted animal he was, sure that even if he evaded this enemy he would deliver himself into the jaws of another.

A dark angel flashed by his right side. He surrendered his fate to the raven and followed.

She navigated him up steep, crooked stairs of jagged rocks that brought him above the timberline of the mountain. He did not slow down or look behind him until he reached the mountain's barren peak. There, he passed out from exhaustion, protected only by the stiff winds that swept his scent into the clouds.

Poitu watched over him as he trembled violently in his sleep, not from nightmares, but from his wet hide's exposure to the harsh winter wind. She spent hours kicking dirt on top of his curled body, but the gusty winds took away what little protection she could give him.

Throbbing pain woke Raspail at morning's first light. He stood dizzily and looked down from the mountain's peak. It staggered his mind to see how high he had climbed, beat up as he was.

He lay down again and licked his wounds -- terrible glistening gouges that ached to the very core of his body -- then nodded off to sleep again. At around that hour when the winter sun shines its brightest, he woke with a jolt as if suddenly under siege by the Draguignon wolves. What woke him, in fact, was a nightmarish recall of the name that Polwin called him during the mad fighting of the day before.

He was a *ramblefoot.*

Book II:

RAMBLEFOOT

The Law of Nature

If you are by nature strong, take as much as you can fight for.

If you are by nature big, take as much as you can defend.

If you are by nature cunning, take as much as you can steal and hide.

If you are by nature noble, take only as much as is fair.

But if you are by nature all these things -- strong, big, cunning and noble -- then you don't need to take at all, for *it will be given to you.*

Coming Down

Getting his fragile, wounded body down from the steep mountaintop proved harder than the impossible feat of climbing it. With no enemies in pursuit, Raspail had the leisure to tally the painful toll of the previous day's fight and chase. There wasn't a muscle that he hadn't torn, not a vein that hadn't spilled blood, not a limb that hadn't been bitten, and not a bitter emotion he hadn't considered and reconsidered. Hunger plagued his stomach so badly he threatened to feed it never again, dying if he had to, for that would silence the hateful beast inside him forever.

As he made this slow and painful descent, Poitu occasionally left his side to survey the area for food. He watched her in the air, never straying too far for too long. *Poitu,* Raspail thought, *my one and only friend.*

The mountain leveled out into a grassy bluff that overlooked a vast series of plains below. Raspail drank from one of six narrow streams that radiated outward and divided the plains into a chain of wolf provinces as old as the plains themselves. Viewed from the bluff's edge where Raspail stood, the territories wrapped around the angular western shore of a massive lake like the crooked arm of a wolf, and so the six provinces were known as the Coude Fou, or "the crazy elbow." But as in the Valtige, wolf life had vanished from this once bustling territory.

Poitu returned from her survey and flew low for Raspail to follow. His slow, cautious pace was wearing on her, so she impatiently darted ahead, disappearing then reappearing behind him, landing on his back and motivating him by digging in her talons.

She led him to a small group of grazing deer, one of which was wearing the raven's distinctive white mark on its back. Raspail, who no longer needed Poitu to land on the prey once he could identify her signature white stain, slid into the herd of deer and harassed his fake target. His raw muscles ached intensely as he ran, and his head pounded as he concentrated on not getting kicked. He was into his last reserve of energy and needed to bring down his real target. Pivoting on his forelegs, he changed course in a start, charging at his real mark.

His battered body responded slowly to the rapid change in direction. He could see, by the deer's quick response that he had attacked too soon; the mark hadn't let its guard down yet. The deer took off. He didn't even bother chasing it; he was done.

An hour later an unlucky rabbit crossed his path and Poitu shared the meal with him. After eating, Poitu played with the bloody pelt, taunting Raspail with it, urging him to join her and make it a game.

She croaked while tossing the pelt in between him and her. He had no interest in play, he only wanted to sleep. She retrieved it, whipped it around fanning his nose with it. Again she threw the pelt between them, teasing him to get it.

Just as Poitu was ready to give up, Raspail lunged at the fur. Poitu quickly stabbed her bill deep into it, anchoring it with her body weight. Raspail jerked his head and tossed the pelt -- the raven attached to it -- into the air.

Poitu twisted with it and crashed to the ground, shrouded in the fur. She shook it off and looked for Raspail. The dejected wolf was back on his feet, limping slowly into the valley.

***

Smelling Like a Bear

Raspail needed a food source that didn't require strength or stamina. Bears thrived in Coude Fou, feeding in the trout rich streams in the spring. With Poitu watching from above and guiding him safely between bear territories, Raspail caught seven large fish on his first day. They flopped near the stream for several days, Raspail getting his strength back with the nutrient rich fish, sometimes catching twenty in a day.

On the fifth day he became self-conscious that he had taken on the smell of a bear. Bear smell was universally detested by the pack, and often one wolf would start a fight by suggesting that the other smelled like bear. Even though there were no other wolves in his company to mock him, such vanities still mattered. It was time to hunt again and smell like a wolf.

At midday he happened upon a conflict unfolding by the stream. A bear was forced to defend a deer carcass from two wolves challenging him for it. The two sides were so evenly matched that the stand-off went on indefinitely, with the wolves unable to gain an advantage and the bear unable to eat without being harassed.

Raspail circled through the trees and klooted behind the bear. He was six lengths away when the wind direction shifted, blowing his scent towards the conflict. The wolves smelled Raspail first and, thinking he was a bear, they stepped back from the carcass and scanned the trees. The bear, thinking they were finally giving up, hunched over the carcass and immersed himself in his meal. A half-moment later, he had a massive black wolf on his back, digging its long fangs into his neck.

The bear stood and emitted an intimidating roar, but Raspail's jaws stayed locked on him as he hung from the tall bear's hide, feeling the roar vibrate through his sternum. From the corner of his eye he saw the two wolves join him, biting at the back of the bear's thighs. Raspail dropped from the bear's back, and before he could get up to continue harassing his victim, it was galloping off into the woods.

The two wolves raced to the carcass. Raspail charged at the bigger of the two, jumping on him as he had on the bear, then flipped him into the air. The terrified animal landed on his back and whimpered away while his friend took a huge mouthful of meat and ran off.

Raspail and Poitu ate uncontested until they could eat no more. Raspail flopped in the darkest shadow he could find, but sure enough, the rest of the impromptu hunting party joined him once they had finished his leftovers. The smaller one sniffed Raspail till he grew annoyed and flashed fang.

They stepped back and waited until Raspail's lip drooped back over his long fang. The smaller one spoke with an agreeable voice and said, "Respect."

They lay down near him. Raspail pretended to ignore them.

"Which way you traveling if you don't mind my asking?"

Even if I could speak, Raspail thought, *I would not tell you.*

The wolf made several more attempts at conversation, and then the larger one spoke. "His ears are dead."

Raspail jerked his head and looked directly in his eyes. The gesture, as it was intended to, proved the wolf's ears were quite alive.

The smaller one spoke. "We don't care where you're rambling. Just where you been."

Raspail gestured with his muzzle at the mountains to the north.

"We're traveling that way. What's the attitude towards Ramblefoots up there?"

Raspail shrugged.

"You aren't headed south, are you?"

"Stop asking him questions you idiot, his tongue's dead."

"Fack off, I'll ask him what I want."

Raspail gestured with his muzzle towards the lake.

"Don't go, cousin. Do you smell good things down there?"

Indeed, Raspail smelled what Maddocq had smelled, and what every wolf smelled as they got closer to the lake, and that was the smell of vanishing scent posts, disappearing from neglect.

Raspail flopped the night then parted ways with his two companions the next morning. A cold miserable rain started to pour down on bird and wolf as they continued south.

***

Hagi Shan

The heavy rain battered Raspail so mercilessly that it no longer sloughed off his thick fur, but soaked into his hide, chilling him to his bones. If he were with a pack, he would have huddled with two or more other wolves to pool their body heat, and so the chills were a bitter reminder of how alone he was. Even Poitu had stopped to get shelter in a tree.

The sky was still light but the moon was starting to emerge, and Raspail needed shelter. As he searched for an abandoned den he saw a wolf staying dry under the ledge of a boulder. The wolf saw him and shouted out:

"Hoy!"

Raspail looked at the wolf. Through the screen of rain he could only make out one feature of the wolf besides his reddish brown coloring, and that was his missing rear foot.

"Hoy!" the three-footed wolf shouted out again. His voice was old but robust.

Raspail kept walking. Along the stream he saw a hole that had been dug into the soft sandy wall of the stream's bank. He cautiously stepped through the rushing stream, climbed the bank and entered the den, crawling five lengths through the dirt tunnel until he reached a birthing area spacious enough for Raspail to shake the rain off his fur. Shivering, he circled, softening the floor with his claws. He curled up and went to sleep listening to the rain pound the stream.

In his dream he heard Kileo's voice, calling out to him, and he was able to respond with a sonorous howl that flowed easily from his throat. His voice sounded different, beautiful, not his, making him wonder -- *Have I forgotten what my own voice sounds like?*

When he awoke, it was still night. He thought about Kileo and felt shame that she might believe Hesser's lie, that he had killed Cob Ash. He thought about Hesser, who he had loved, who had stolen his voice, killed his father, and accused him of the crime. He thought about Polwin and Abillon, who didn't hesitate to believe Hesser, so happy were they to be rid of him.

He fell asleep again, this time dreaming that the three-footed wolf he'd passed that day was entering the den and calling to him.

"Hoy!" the wolf said. Raspail woke. There was no intruder, like in his dream, but a wolf was indeed calling to him, muffled as it was by the driving rain.

Raspail crawled to the opening of the den and saw that the stream was now a fast moving river which had risen to the mouth of the den. Lightning illuminated broken trees and brush speeding past him. The prospect of leaping into the river terrified him, but if he waited much longer the rising river would flood the tunnel and drown him. Raspail's heart raced as he realized he was imprisoned in the den with time running out.

He heard the voice again coming from above, "Hoy!" Raspail craned his neck and looked up at the three-footed wolf he had seen under the ledge, now standing above him on top of the river bank peering down at him with a look of concern. He barked loudly over the sound of the rain.

"Go back in and dig! As soon as I hear where you're digging, I'll dig too," the old wolf said.

He would have to dig a tunnel two wolves high to get out, and in that time the water would be high enough to drown him in the cave.

There was no other way. He crawled quickly back to the birthing chamber and, in the cramped space, dug frantically at the ceiling. He clawed at the moist soil, whipping dirt clods and rocks to his feet. The small space filled quickly with dirt, and Raspail stood on the growing mound to dig higher. As he pitched his head back to dig, his throat felt like it was being crushed by a huge beast. The muscles in his throat, which had healed and scarred in a way that stifled his voice, were being stretched to their limit.

He heard something and paused. The old wolf was indeed digging right above him as he had promised. His terror abated with that bit of hope, but the moment was brief, for the river had reached the lip of the den's mouth and water began to splash into the den and pool at his feet.

Raspail dug and dug, his eyes blinded by falling soot. Water flooded in and quickly filling the birthing chamber. His lungs choked on the thickening air. In an instant the chamber filled with water to its ceiling and was rising up the escape tunnel he dug. It reached his neck and he fought the panic rising in him. He could hear the old wolf barking to him, but in his panic he could not make sense of him.

Suddenly the ceiling collapsed on his head as the two tunnels the wolves were digging connected. Fresh air poured in and rushed into his lungs. With a mighty heave he scrambled up through the part of the tunnel that the other wolf had dug. Losing his foothold he slipped back down into the drink, but the old wolf bit into his thick withers and dragged him up and out of the hole.

Raspail collapsed and caught his breath as the rain washed the mud off his fur. He glanced at the old wolf who saved his life, licking the calloused end of his amputated leg, which bled from being used as a foot. He paused to let out some of the air he'd swallowed licking his leg, then said with good humor in his voice:

"Lucky for you old Hagi-Shan was lookin' out for you."

"Gratitude," said Raspail, surprised at the hoarse wisp of a voice that came from his mouth.

***

Newhouse No. 4 1/2

Hagi and Raspail sat under the rock ledge, sheltered from the rain.

"I can take you to a place where the gloom of the past and the uncertainty of the future lift like the morning mountain mist."

Hagi knew his audience well; he had tempted many ramblefoots in his life.

"Paradise meat -- the cloudbeasts, the slow-footed bison -- you'll do well there, a big wolf like you."

When Raspail did not respond, he continued.

"They say the ramblefoot travels alone. Well that's a lie; he has the company of his many woes, eh?"

Hagi stared dreamily through the sheet of rain pouring off the rock ledge they stood under.

"Well whatever your woes, they won't haunt you in Ramblefoot. There's no borders. No facets. You answer to one master, your stomach, and he, I promise you, will be a happy master indeed."

Raspail was intrigued by the old charlatan and enjoyed hearing him speak even if he doubted such a place as he described existed.

"You're a real talkative fellow, eh?" Hagi Shan said with a laugh. "It's alright with me. I'll do enough talking for two of us." He laughed and saw that Raspail was in good humor as well.

"Friend, when this rain stops falling I'll take you to a place called Ramblefoot. You'll need a guide, for there's more ways to die there than to live. In return for this knowledge I only ask for a small share of your meat."

He saw Raspail's brow change and look away.

"You'll be eating more meat in a day then your facet ate in all his days."

They both heard a strange sound outside their shelter. Raspail was about to step out when Hagi Shan blocked him protectively.

The sound got louder, and to Raspail's ear it sounded like one animal dragging another. Then he saw it, coming towards their shelter. It was a gray wolf, walking unnaturally slow, struggling with each step because it was dragging something, a dark round object attached to both back legs. Both his legs were bleeding terribly.

On the wolf's face was a look of pure, unadulterated fear. Raspail, who had just barely escaped death himself moments ago, was transfixed by the look of dread on this wolf, struggling as he was against the massive weight of whatever he was dragging.

"Should have listened to Hagi Shan. You won't make the same mistake."

Hagi loped outside the shelter, followed by Raspail, and they approached the traumatized wolf. The wolf immediately crouched submissively and lowered his trembling head, his torpid eyes avoiding contact.

"Get them off me, mercy!" he begged them in a terrorized voice. "Get them off!"

"You're young with strong jaws, my sad friend. Only one way out of them." And Hagi gave a little gesture with his leg, the one without the foot.

"I tried--" he started to say, then shuddered to a stop.

Raspail investigated the devices that had come caught on the wolf's hind legs. He nudged one of the black boulders with his nose. It was heavier then rock and tasted bright on the tongue. Hagi was next to him, examining the wolf's leg. It was chewed into. Hagi looked into the wolf's eye.

"Finish the job. You're halfway in."

"I can't!"

Hagi could finally see what the wolf's problem was. His teeth were ground down and broken.

"Cause you tried chewing through the trap first you fool! Didn't work, did it?" Hagi shook his head sadly and faced Raspail.

"Want to save a wolf? I've done my good deed for the day."

Raspail was unsure what Hagi was suggesting.

"You chew through his legs, just above the shackles. I'll hold him down."

Hagi threw his arm over the wolf's back. The wolf was twitchy and agitated, and Hagi had to use more force.

"You got to do it now."

Raspail sniffed at the leg.

"Come on!" Hagi shouted at him.

Raspail carefully positioned his jaw around the wolf's bloody leg, the metal trap stinging his lip where it touched, and quickly crushed the bone with his back teeth and masticated it further. The startled wolf shrieked and jerked, but Hagi pinned him down, cursing the beast to stay still. Howling flared from the south in response to the suffering wolf's cry; they howled in sympathy, for many of them recognized what that horrific squeal meant all to well.

Raspail then sawed at the skin with his front teeth until the leg ripped in two, freeing one of the legs. Blood spewed from the amputated leg. Raspail quickly repeated what he had done on the other leg and the squirming, frantic wolf passed out. Hagi and Raspail dragged the unconscious animal back to their shelter and licked his severed legs till they stopped bleeding.

There was silence, even from the loose-tongued Hagi, as they waited to see what direction the sleeping wolf's life would take.

The rain began to taper off halfway through the night. Raspail slept poorly. Hagi woke him, nudging him with his muzzle. His voice was soft and grim.

"Time to move." Raspail looked over at the other wolf and saw immediately that he was dead; he didn't survive the double amputation.

"He's not waking up. And I don't sleep with the dead."

Hagi Shan walked out into the rain where he could smell the sky and look at the moon, and he determined the rain was going to stop. His good cheer returned.

Raspail's frozen stare was stuck on the wolf whose legs he had cut off the night before, dead where they'd dragged him and set him down. Raspail didn't know the wolf -- he was neither an enemy nor ally -- yet seeing him dead after his own recent escapades made him feel humbled, stupefied, lucky, and strangely immortal. Remembering the fear projected from the eyes of the wolf that night, he tried fathoming the pain of being snared and dragged down by the weight of two giant boulders, trapped and helpless, unable to run, the only way to freedom being chewing your leg off.

He finally registered that Hagi had left the shelter and now stood outside under the moon. He joined his side, and Hagi said, with his now familiar good cheer, "Well, I think it's going to stop raining."

They passed the two wolf traps as they started their journey towards Ramblefoot. Already a hawk had claimed the wolf's severed limbs. Raspail scared the bird off as he crouched forward to analyze the traps, keeping his distance as if the object might hear him and suddenly wake up and snap at him. On either side of the toothy iron jaws were two massive leafsprings, and these looked similar enough to muscles he'd torn from the jawbones of elk and moose that he concluded they were analogous.

He cautiously poked his foot and nose around the round pan at the center of the iron jaws -- a Newhouse No. 4 1/2, as it was known to some -- with the word "WOLF" embossed right where the eponymous animal had stepped to release the compressed leaf springs on either side.

Don't ever step on one of these you, he told himself, *or you'll be dragging rocks up a hill to your death as well.*

"There's three ways of learning about traps. You get bit by one, like me, and you live to know never do that again!" He laughed at his own bad fate. "You get bit by one and die like our poor friend, mercy. Or you're lucky and you witness what you just saw and keep all your feet -- and your life, eh?"

Growing restless with Raspail's thorough investigation, Hagi nudged him and said, "Come on. You'll see plenty more of those, hopefully not with wolves in them."

***

Hagi and Ravens

In that rare moment when all living creatures are captivated by the same thing at once, the sun burned through the dense clouds and lifted the humidity off the ground in thick, opaque layers of steam that hovered above the valleys and in the canyons and ravines between mountains. In that steam cloud was the swirling essence of all living things, and as it levitated from the ground, every animal ate the thick perfume with its nose. And though no specific information could be deciphered within it, the same sentiment was shared from mouse to moose, and that was, *That is all of us together.* And for that brief moment, all creatures feasted on perfumed vapor and the good feeling it induced instead of on each other.

Poitu had been looking for Raspail since before the sun came out, not knowing that he was hidden under the rock ledge. When the low heavy clouds rose and obscured her view of the ground, she landed in a tree and waited impatiently, looking for something to occupy herself with.

Below her she saw anthills rippling with industry as the tiny residents worked busily to rebuild their homes after the rain. She dropped to the ground, hopped on to an anthill, scooped up a bill-full of ants and gently crushed them. She then spread the slurry on her wings and under her feathers, using the liquefied insects as a protective balm against other bugs, a habit she'd learned from watching an older raven when she was little. She made herself comfortable on the anthill as she got more involved in the activity.

In a moment word spread through the ant colony that there was trouble. Poitu saw to her distress that ants were climbing up her quicker then she could kill them. She leaped into the air and began flying as fast and erratically as she could to rid herself of the unwanted guests but the ants stayed on her, biting viciously and leaving a fiery sting. She panicked and flew into a tree branch. Stunned, she dropped to the ground. The ants continued to nip her with increased fervor. She rubbed her body along the rough earth, continuing to do so even after she had angrily ground every last ant to death.

When they were all dead, her angry mood turned itself on her missing wolf. If circumstances had been more conventional -- that is, if she had a mate or was part of a roost -- another raven might have warned her about the type of ant she had chosen or at least helped her get them off. Alas, Raspail could do none of those things, and even if he could he was nowhere to be found at the moment she needed him. "Dumb useless wolf," she screeched.

Moments later, she went flying low looking for him and recognized the black wolf's brooding gait in the distance, heading to a stream. Her heart raced with excitement and love for him, her resentment gone.

Raspail and Hagi stopped at the stream to fill their hollow stomachs with water. Hagi felt a duty to keep his companion in high spirits by talking about food.

"I knew a wolf..." he began, the glint in his eye promising a captivating story. "This wolf died from eating too much."

Raspail's mouth hung open. It was like hearing that a wolf died from being too happy or sleeping too much, because to a wolf, any pursuit that feels good generally is good, and not something that induces death. Hagi was pleased with the look on his face, and continued.

"Hard to believe, I know, but it's true -- I was there, I saw it. There were three of us. We had a challenge to see who could eat the most. The winner of the challenge, he ate enough to make three wolves meatdrunk. It was so much facking meat he killed his stomach, and when his stomach died, he died too." Hagi shook his head, amazed at the words of his own story. "Died face first in a pile of meat. Just like this."

And Hagi imitated the dead wolf, shutting his eyes and letting his tongue dangle from the side of his mouth with a look of euphoric bliss. Raspail laughed.

At that moment Poitu swooped down and landed between Raspail and Hagi, trilling at her partner and cawing at the stranger. Hagi nervously recoiled from the raven with a startled "Hoy!" Poitu hopped closer to Raspail's companion, examining him. Hagi bellowed at the raven, and she took off into the sky with a fright. Raspail laughed uproariously.

"I don't like ravens in particular. Some wolves don't mind them, I know." Hagi dramatically prepared to launch into another story as captivating as the one about the wolf who ate himself to death. He spoke in a hushed tone full of awe.

"I've heard tales of a wolf who travels with a raven. Hunts with it. Eats with it. Even sleeps with it." Raspail wanted to laugh, but he kept a serious face. Hagi mistook the look as one of shared disbelief and said, "I know, incredible."

Poitu bombed out of the sky as if she had been waiting for the moment of maximum shock value, then landed with boisterously flapping wings on Raspail's back, digging her claws deep into his thick fur.

Hagi recoiled back again. The raven preened against Raspail's ruff, trilling as she did. Raspail didn't flinch; he just stared at Hagi waiting for his reaction.

His reaction was worthy of the moment; his ears perked upwards and his head cocked sideways as he realized that the black wolf before him was in fact the very wolf he just painted in such illustrious tones. Hagi, the wolf who had seen everything in his long life, was dumbfounded.

Poitu kawed at Raspail then flew off his back. Raspail raced her through the trees like they always did to warm up for the hunt, and he felt his healing muscles performing like they should.

Hagi joined Raspail at the carcass late, having missed the bizarre spectacle of wolf and raven hunting together. Raspail was a generous host, letting his companion take what meat he wanted, since he'd already devoured the heart and liver.

When they were all good and meatdrunk, Raspail played a lazy game of tug of war with Poitu using a long piece of sinewy viscera. When Raspail tired of the game, she hopped over to Hagi, who was sleeping, and inspected the calloused stump below his hock. A scab was hardening where he'd injured it digging. Poitu pecked at the scab, as she had at Raspail's, and ripped it off in a shot.

Hagi sprang from the ground in a fright, looking at the shiny black culprit in horror. "Devil be gone!"

Poitu tried to engage him in a game of tug of war, but the distrustful wolf looked sick at the idea.

"You wretched black demon!" Hagi said. "I'll feed off the milky tit of a bear before I play with a facking raven!"

***

The New Cob Ash

Since Raspail was exiled, many unfortunate changes had taken place in Cob Ash. Hesser, who had come out of the conflict looking authoritative, decisive and confident, took over for their slain leader as provisionary facet. Neither Polwin nor Abillon (who could have easily challenged him) protested his ascent.

What Hesser lacked in natural leadership he made up with acting. As has been said, his ability to mimic other animals was uncanny, and so he applied his art of imitation to Cob Ash. It was not difficult, with every wolf confused and anxious, to reinvent himself as a strong and clear-headed leader.

Kileo was forced to take over as caretaker of the yearlings because Cortess, her mind scattered with grief over her mate's death, could no longer watch them reliably. Kileo took the yearlings on hunts and always brought back meat for Cortess until the day Hesser stole the food from her and growled, "No more meat for Cortess." She saw that Polwin, who had risen in status by becoming Hesser's main enforcer, fixed his stare on her, ready to carry out his facet's law.

Returning to camp with no meat in her mouth and sadness in her heart, she saw that Cortess had left to go searching for her lost mate who she still could not fathom was dead. All that kept Kileo rooted to the camp now was the welfare of the yearlings.

"The others have been fed the lie that Raspail killed his father," she secretly told Carel, Navarin and the other yearlings. "Only I know it is not so, for Raspail revered and loved Cob Ash. Yet this lie festers in their guts and sickens their minds and makes them strange and unpredictable."

Cortess never returned to camp.

About the time that Raspail was trapped in the flooding den, a loud moan, loud enough to rise above the pounding rain, was heard in their territory. Hesser immediately recognized the voice and led Polwin, Abillon and Moorea to where Sarassin lay in the grass giving birth and groaning in pain as the first pup emerged.

"Mercy, I don't mean to trespass, but as you can see I was forced by nature to stop my ramble within your borders and -- aaaaahhhhh!--" She moaned again as she birthed another.

All eyes turned to Hesser to see whether he commanded them to kill the mother and her offspring or give them sanctuary.

"Why are you rambling, white bitch from Draguignon?" he said imperiously.

"Why, you confuse me, sir. You should know the answer to that question. You put me in the condition that has made me an outcast."

The rest of the pack stared at Hesser, waiting for him to verify her bold accusation. He stood proud, as Cob Ash would have, and commanded his pack:

"Show this wolfmother hospitality and bring these pups to our den."

The pack worked together to bring the newborns, every one of them white like their mother, to Cortess's old den. Sarassin took up residency there, allowing only Hesser entry.

***

Kileo Learns Too Much

The addition of new pups was a much needed boost to the pack's morale. Even Moorea, who was Kileo's last ally among her siblings, seemed impressed that Hesser was bold enough to take such an impressive mate as Sarassin. Things were changing quickly, Kileo thought, quicker than she could make sense of them.

Sarassin rarely left the den, where Hesser frequently joined her. The yearlings were immensely curious about the arrival of new young wolves, and it was difficult keeping them away from the den. Carel, the bravest of the yearlings, succeeded in making it into the entry tunnel to the den to get a glimpse of her new siblings before the white tempest lacerated her nose with a vicious bite that went beyond the normal protectiveness even of a wolfmother.

Carel scurried back to Kileo, bleeding. While Kileo licked her wounds, Sarassin appeared behind her.

"You."

"Yes?"

"You're in charge of the yearlings?" She said with annoyance.

"Yes, I am."

"Do not let them near my den."

"Your den?" Kileo said aghast. "I was born in that den. As was Carel, who was justifiably curious about your children."

"Next time I will kill."

"Let me remind you; Cob Ash is their home. You, white wolf, are a stranger and a guest here."

Sarassin smiled as if she knew better, then sashayed back to the den with her tail high in the air.

That night, Hesser joined Sarassin in the den. He lavished her with licks and she let him taste her milk.

"You are a brilliant, natural leader of wolves." And she bowed her head to him as she felt his ego grow. "Nothing stands to change your status, which has improved with my arrival. I worry of only one thing."

"What is this thing, mother of my children?"

"There might come a day when the yearlings seek vengeance for their father's death. I know this feeling, and it does not fade in time, it ferments like fruit on a tree that ripens too long."

"What does my wise bitch, who troubles herself with my fate, think I should do?"

"The pretty one who cares for the yearlings. She seems unhappy with my settling here. Her young wards heed her. They will be influenced by her. Make me not just mother of your children, but mother of all Cob Ash's children -- of the yearlings, of Abillon and Polwin. Announce me as your mate."

"Is it not too soon? I fear it will make them suspicious."

"Fear? A facet has no fear. Others fear him."

"I will announce you as my mate when the eye is full. That's in nine days."

"I prefer earlier. However I will defer to your judgment."

Outside the den, Kileo floated like steam from a secret tunnel that connected with the birthing chamber. Carel, when she was just three months old, had dug a tunnel that gave her access in and out of the den. Cortess marveled at this extravagant feat, so they left it out of respect. Only Kileo, Cortess and Carel knew of this secret passage.

"Good old Carel," Kileo thought to herself as she shook the dirt off her back and rolled in the leaves to cover the sweet scent of the den that stuck to her. She made her way back to Moorea, Abillon and Polwin.

Polwin and Abillon slept with their backs together. Kileo curled up so she was intertwined with Moorea and fathomed a memory of Raspail that cheered her so that Moorea would not hear her beating heart and suspect her anxiety.

Moorea saw Kileo grin. "If you have reason to laugh, don't be selfish. You know two wolves make one joke funnier."

"I remembered when Raspail fell into that disgusting thorny bramble around Hesser's cave."

Moorea and Kileo laughed together. Kileo turned serious. She spoke quietly.

"How did that wretched Hesser become our facet?"

"You loved him when we were little," Moorea said surprised.

"He's a clown. Children love clowns."

"He's changed. He's different since father's death. Sometimes he reminds me of father."

Kileo felt it was unwise to speak from her heart anymore. Moorea was agreeable with the group on all matters. She was a follower. There was no doubt, Kileo's only allies were the yearlings.

She had to ramble. Wherever she went, she would take Carel, Navarin, and the others. She would die before leaving them at the mercy of a clown and that white bitch in the fractured remains of the once great Cob Ash. Getting them all across the border of Cob Ash before the pack woke and noticed they were gone would be difficult and dangerous.

She had nine days to plan their escape.

***

Two Eager Parties Merge

As the day approached for Aratus, Balfort, and Maddocq to reacquaint themselves with the three bitches from over the border, mood around camp was tense, and each wolf was at his personal worst. Aratus was solemn and self-absorbed as he strategized. Maddocq, tortured with worry by his hypersensitivity to smell and sound, paced and snorted. And Balfort, seeking to remedy the boredom of his brothers' company, dredged up inane subjects for discussion thinking this would invigorate the solemn crew.

"I believe the bear is more clever than the moose. Care to know why, Aratus?" When Aratus did not answer, Balfort turned to Maddocq, who was smelling something at the bottom of a tree.

"Maddocq, can I interest you in this comparison? Or is the smell of that owl turd so mesmerizing you must keep your nose in it another day?"

Aratus farted. Maddocq lurked pathetically over to Aratus and began sniffing at his ass. Aratus angrily watched him, then flared his lip in warning. Maddocq was so intoxicated by the smell that he didn't care. Aratus finally flashed fang and snapped at him. Maddocq backed off, but not without inhaling as much as he could as he retreated.

So as it was, they'd become so sick of each other that the idea of fresh company was more than just appealing; it was necessary to them not killing each other.

At the border they were surprised to see the three young males excitedly waiting for them with sweeping tails. The young brothers, who were brooding in their last encounter, were now bright with hope, eagerly welcoming their new uncles.

As for their new attitude towards the Cob Ash wolves, it must be said that the three pregnant bitches had set the mood around camp for the last month. The poor young males had no elders to explain to them that their sisters, who they loved, did not have the scatters but were exhibiting the many strange moods that pregnancy brings. They were grateful to add more males to the pack.

The Cob Ash wolves followed their hosts, admiring the land that would be merged with theirs. They reached the outskirts of their camp, where one massive den had been tunneled under the vast root mass of what had been a huge tree. There the Cob Ash brothers saw their three future mates weaning the pups that they'd sired.

Aratus rubbed shoulders with his brothers. Whatever love was lost between them in the last days was regained in a heartbeat.

"We have our numbers now, eh?" Balfort said.

Aratus licked him in agreement, then ran over to meet his new family.

***

Kileo Shares her Plan

With three days till full moon, Kileo thought of nothing but escape. In preparation she looked for a safe route along the western border. The western border to Cob Ash encompassed a low, flat-topped mountain chain. Cob Ash wolves rarely explored these mountains, and Kileo figured she could flee with the yearlings and hide there until the yearlings were mature enough to hunt, fight and ramble.

While Navarin and the male yearlings went with Polwin and Abillon to mark the scent posts, Kileo took Carel up-mountain with her to explore. Kileo found the area hospitable, with enough hunting to provide for the six of them.

Carel was climbing rocks. From her perch she barked down to Kileo, "I'm higher than you!"

Kileo climbed up the rocks and joined her.

"You like it up here?" Kileo asked.

"You knew I would," Carel responded.

"We are going to live here for a while."

"All of us?"

"No. Just you, Navarin, and the rest of your siblings."

Kileo saw the confusion in Carel's eyes.

"We are leaving Cob Ash. First, we'll come here to this mountain, where we'll hide. When we're ready, we'll move on and find a new home somewhere else."

Kileo let Carel consider this. Carel curled her lip and squinted her left eye. Kileo adored this expression which she often made.

"You don't like the pretty white bitch, do you?"

"No, I do not. She wants to be your mother."

"I have a mother."

"Hesser is making her our matriarch at full moon. That is why we must leave in such a hurry."

"Is that why you brought me up here?"

Kileo nodded. Carel felt proud and could not hide her excitement that Kileo had chosen her as her confidant.

"I have no wolf but my yearlings. And of that precious brood, you are my most precious, Carel."

Carel licked her face. Kileo stopped her and continued.

"This will be dangerous. Your uncles and aunts don't want us to leave. That is why it is important that you repeat nothing we have discussed."

Carel scratched at the ground with her foot absent-mindedly while she looked troubled.

"What is it?"

"Navarin loves his uncles. He knows they are favoring him over Aboukir. He loves their attention."

"If Navarin were to stay, would the others stay too?"

"No. They will trust you and me over him."

Carel saw the worry that Kileo was carrying by the dryness of her nose and licked it. Kileo gently gnawed the hard top of her muzzle, then they flopped side by side and slept.

***

Talk of Fires Coming

A "no facet" policy may have worked for Aratus, Balfort and Maddocq, but with a large pack emerging around them a single leader needed to step forward. Balfort, who felt entitled to the position, made an impassioned and long-winded case to his brothers on why he deserved to be facet.

When he was finally finished, the young males looked at each other confused, then whined to Aratus with disappointment.

"We assumed *you* were our facet."

"Aratus?! Based on what!" Balfort demanded to know.

"Based on everything we've seen."

Balfort, too prideful to contest majority rule, removed himself from the ballot.

"Well, Aratus, if you want to lead a group of wolves with rocks for eyes, be their facet," And he gestured graciously.

Aratus made the fairest kind of facet in that he had no ambition to make law and exert power over others. His only ambition, being an intelligent, noble creature, was to be free from the whim of another wolf and not subject to his power and laws.

He lost no time turning the new pack into a hunting party as good as Cob Ash in their prime, and the pack ate well even though their combined province had half the elk-attracting aspen groves of Cob Ash. The huge litter of pups thrived (with only two dying), and all wolves seemed to get along well. The first real challenge the wise Aratus would face arrived on his sixth day as facet.

Aratus was playing with his mate Othenia and their pups when he heard the howling of a small wolf pack to the south. All ears at the camp locked on to the high-pitched chanting.

"Kill us not, stay we not, ramblefoots we not, hunt we not, kill us not..."

They repeated this over and over as they moved closer.

Othenia and her brothers ushered the squealing pups into the tunnels of the den that went deep under the tree.

"Balfort, Maddocq, Othenia and I will greet them," Aratus commanded them. "The rest of you stay here unless Balfort calls."

Aratus led Othenia and his brothers to the keening call of the intruders. Aratus was ready to protect their domain, and as his blood heated, he lusted for combat. When finally he laid eyes on the four travelers walking lethargically up the stream, his blood cooled.

The remnant pack was wretched looking; some were missing limbs, all had permanent looks of terror. They continued their gloomy chanting as they marched, blindly passing Aratus and company.

"Kill us not, stay we not, ramblefoots we not, hunt we not, kill us not..."

Balfort could not endure any more of their bleak howling and said, "We'll only kill you if you keep chanting that horrible song."

They continued to sing as they waded up the stream. Aratus moved closer to sniff them. The youngest in the group, a yearling female, looked at him and said chillingly, "The fires are coming."

"I don't smell fire," Balfort said dubiously.

Without another word she rejoined her mysterious companions as they wandered northward out of their province.

"Fires, honestly," said Balfort. "Fires make clouds, clouds that smell, and we have noses do we not? If I were facet, I would have killed them for fouling our moods."

Aratus needed no other proof than Balfort's quick disregard of the situation to start worrying. He thought, *They don't mean fires like we do. Somehow I fear I will learn what their fires are.*

***

To Ramblefoot

Hagi Shan was an excellent traveling companion, regaling his young friend with stories -- one after the other, and each more fantastic than the last -- about meat. Meat that he had enjoyed, meat that got away, meat that awaited them, and meat that, no matter how much it tempted him, he refused to eat. He even repeated the story about the wolf who had eaten so much he died, and Raspail enjoyed it even more the second time.

When Hagi ran out of stories about meat, he talked about exceptional wolves he had met in his rambles. Like the wolf Repetto, who though fully mature had never grown bigger than a half-yearling, and who by all accounts looked like a harmless infant. The only thing that gave the dwarf's age away was the yellow tint of his milk teeth, which had stayed rooted in their gums even though his adult teeth had moved in behind them. This gave him four rows of teeth which served him well for he had twice the temper of a normal wolf at half the size.

Another character earned the name Siksak by merit of the exaggerated size of his scrotum. As Hagi put it, "He frequents the same low haunts I'm bringing you to, so if you pass a grey and brown wolf whose sack hangs like two ripe pomegranates straining their branch, stay clear. He's not one to mess with."

Hagi's banter kept Raspail's mind off the persistent thought of Kileo. Day and night he heard her howl, calling for him like she did the day he was forced out, and he could no longer discern whether he was hearing her actual voice or if it were conjured by his beleaguered mind.

Hagi was halfway through a story about an infant moose carcass that he'd torn open to find that it had two hearts when Poitu alighted on Raspail's back and kawed in his ear. In a split-second they were gone, and Hagi struggled to follow Raspail, cursing the raven for disrupting his story.

Hagi reached them and watched Raspail weaving through a small herd of elk, harassing his fake target. Hagi laughed dubiously as any wolf would, knowing that one wolf, no matter how accomplished a hunter, cannot pick out his prey and take it down without the help of several other wolves.

Raspail suddenly pivoted, changed direction and struck his real target. He drove his fangs into the thigh of the deer and forced the beast into another deer running fast beside it. The deer collided and tumbled on to its side, and before it could get back on its feet, Raspail lunged at its throat. It stood once more, but Raspail dragged it down and held it there till it died.

Hagi watched in disbelief. The storyteller had just acquired another story.

Raspail dug inside the animal and took its exquisite treasures, the heart and liver. Hagi, knowing a wolf can quickly change its temperament at the side of a meal, cautiously sidled next to Raspail and helped pull apart the carcass.

"I like you," Hagi said. "The raven, not so much."

Raspail laughed. *"Pwah-too,"* he corrected him, sounding like he were blowing a feather out of his mouth. Poitu landed next to Raspail and ate.

"It has a name, does it?" Hagi marveled as he ripped off a mouthful of meat. Poitu flashed his wings in Hagi's face. Hagi dropped the meat as he recoiled, then watched Poitu steal it and fly off.

"Cursed devil," Hagi said. "That's my name for you."

By night they reached a high sheer cliff overlooking a deep canyon, at the bottom of which was a broad, fast-moving river. On the other side of the canyon, beyond the cresting mountains, was Ramblefoot, the province named after its illustrious denizens.

Raspail was restless and eager to continue their journey, but the older Hagi desired sleep and, being his guide, set their pace. They flopped at the edge of the ravine, but Raspail could not sleep so he watched Poitu tease him by gliding across the huge chasm, back and forth, making him wish he were a bird.

At dawn they descended into the ravine along passages that Hagi knew and carefully crossed the river. When they had succeeded in ascending the other side of the canyon, Hagi led Raspail through secret corridors and up precarious trails carved into the mountain. They reached an overlook where Raspail could see what was obscured the night before. The mountains flattened out into one endless plain, which unlike the plains of his old home, continued on indefinitely. The scope of the world he knew had just doubled in size.

Like Hagi said, their were no boundaries in Ramblefoot. Raspail tried to catalogue the new smells, but the wolf piss zig-zagged eccentrically, offering no boundary information. As he tried to make sense of the new land, he picked up another smell that gave him caution. Hagi saw the look of concern.

"You smell the fires, eh?"

In fact Raspail could see the narrow plumes of smoke rising in the distance.

"Stay away from smoke."

Raspail stayed close behind Hagi as he navigated carefully marked routes through the thick timbers.

"Hag-iiiiii!" a wolf howled out.

Raspail looked around, then heard more wolves cry out:

"Hagi Shan the old scoundrel is back!"

A chorus of howls broke out. They were not unified like a pack's, but disparate and unorganized with no central voice. And they all had a distinctively lazy, slurred patois that came from being meatdrunk more often than not.

A savage looking grey wolf appeared to their left, happy to see Hagi. Hagi let the wolf merrily sniff him from nose to tail. The wolf cared little about Raspail, which allowed Raspail time to take note of him. He was well-fed and missing two toes on his front right foot. Raspail glanced at his ball sack, as he would with every wolf he encountered after hearing Hagi's warning about Siksak.

"Boonbrekker," Hagi said, "How is hunting?"

"The hunting, if you can even call it that, is so fine that if it were any finer I would swear I were dead and eating with the ancestors."

Hagi laughed, "You won't eat this well when you're dead, that I can tell you."

Boonbrekker led them at a gallop out of the woods and into the flat plains. Fear mixed with excitement as Raspail ran exposed under full moonlight through an unknown quarter with confusing scent posts. He saw Poitu's shadow, then looked up and saw her fly ahead, perching on a tree. If there were danger, he knew Poitu would fly back and warn him.

Boonbrekker escorted them to an isolated grove of trees where they paused. Raspail looked around, smelling such a wealth of meat his mouth watered. The smell, as it turned out, was wafting from the breath of four wolves with distended bellies and blood splattered on their jowls klooting out of the shadows. Wolves of ramblefoot weren't a pack, as Hagi had told him along their journey; they were more akin to a raven roost, where the birds rendezvous in large groups to socialize and exchange information. Violent fighting was uncommon here because, as Hagi said, "Wolves with full stomachs are too content to fight."

And these ramblefoots shared a common look of satedness that came with being well-fed all the time.

"Hagi!" they all yipped as they leaped on the old wolf, knocking him down with affection. In doing so, they had each abandoned a slab of meat big enough to feed a pack.

Raspail looked at these unguarded treasures with wide-eyed amazement and thought, *They leave their meat unattended here, that is how abundant it is.* His stomach was crying for food and he was tempted to steal some of the unguarded meat.

Hagi saw the temptation in Raspail's eyes and said loudly, "Let us show our new friend the riches of Ramblefoot."

     ***

The Riches of Ramblefoot

The world that Raspail knew, the world he had been banished from, seemed distant and irrelevant -- even Kileo seemed inconsequential -- because he was so meatdrunk he could barely see straight.

"The gloom of the past and uncertainty of the future will disappear," Hagi had promised him. He hadn't lied.

The sun was coming up and Hagi, who had dined with him and Poitu for hours, stood with a cautious look in his eye.

"You gotta move when the sun comes up," Hagi said.

Raspail looked at the sheep carcass, not ready to part ways with it quite yet. Hagi hobbled off without another warning.

As Raspail struggled to stuff another mouthful of meat into his stomach, a loud crack pierced the air and echoed around him. He looked around and saw two other wolves dart in different directions. He stood up, balancing his engorged torso on willowy legs. He had no idea what direction to run in, and there was nowhere for him to kloot in the open meadow.

Poitu flew down as urgently as he'd ever seen her and navigated Raspail safely away from the mysterious danger. There was another crack and a wolf running beside Raspail yelped and tumbled to the ground. Raspail looked amazed and terrified at the bleeding animal, thinking, *What can do that?*

He stayed on course with Poitu until they were safely hidden in the timbers of the mountain foothills.

There he rendezvoused with Hagi and the others who were watching something below. The wounded wolf was back on his feet and limping through the open plains struggling to reach the cover of the wooded foothills.

There was another crack in the air and the wolf fell again, only this time he did not get up. The ramblefoots dispersed in different directions, disappearing into the mountain along well-traveled escape routes that were marked with scent posts. Raspail knew he'd have to learn these escape routes if he was to spend time here.

Raspail followed Hagi to a secret precipice where they could watch the slain wolf in the open field. Two horses rode out into the field with men on their backs. Raspail watched, mystified and scared as the horses stopped and the men got off. One held up a long stick which he pointed into the trees. Pressed to his lips was a glowing ember. Smoke billowed from his mouth.

This creature is so bold he eats fire, Raspail thought, terrified.

The other man lifted the limp wolf and placed it on top of his horse. The two men rode their horses through the field and stopped to look down at the sheep carcass that Raspail had left behind.

Fear paralyzed Raspail, his body tightened and he retched up some meat. Hagi laughed.

"I told you, there's more ways to die in Ramblefoot than to live. But those who live -- and you will -- live well."

Hagi walked off. Raspail quickly licked up his retch and chased after him.

***

The Meat Orgy

The three days that led up to the full moon were like a haze to Raspail, and it seemed to him that he'd eaten more in those days than he had in his whole lifetime.

At one point, while they were resting from the tiring activity of overindulgence, Hagi pondered, "When I first arrived in Ramblefoot, what troubled me was I could never remember my last meal. And then one day it all became clear: Ramblefoot is one long never-ending meal."

When Raspail was young he wished he could eat snow *because snow was everywhere.* Ramblefoot was that old dream come alive. Meat was everywhere.

Over the next days wolves would disappear in small, impromptu sub-packs and return dragging slabs of paradise meats into the orgy. The gathering of wolves, which at times reached the size of three packs, ate from the communal cornucopia without flashing fang or raising hackles. They ate side by side with an almost unwolf-like civility, and watching them eat gave Hagi all the pleasure of a wolfmother watching her young suckle.

Raspail assisted in these hunts, working alongside wolves he did not know, laughing drunkenly with them as they sloppily brought down the easy prey, hauling the bloody slabs of meat in tandem, tripping, tumbling and rolling on top of each other.

Games and challenges were invented to occupy them during the non-hunting hours of daylight when the wolves retreated into the mountain timbers. One such game involved the tiny wolf Repetto whom Hagi had talked about.

Challengers would stand with their meatdrunk legs splayed apart while Repetto would dive under the wolf and weave through his legs. The goal was to try and drop on Repetto, trapping the tiny wolf under their torsos. So nimble and fleet-footed was Repetto that his challengers almost never succeeded.

Raspail watched amused as several wolves failed at the challenge, then Repetto invited him into the arena. Raspail reluctantly accepted the challenge to the cheers of the other ramblefoots. He had no better luck than the others, and when he lost, Repetto mocked him by running up over his back and springing off the crown of his head.

The convivial atmosphere was disrupted by the arrival of a large handsome wolf who entered the gathering with his tail lifted ostentatiously high so that his puckering, scented asshole was exposed, like a facet flaunting his authority. This allowed

Raspail to see his dominant feature, the gargantuan balls that hung, as Hagi had testified, like pomegranates.

Raspail was struck by Siksak's flagrantly imperious body language. Most wolves do not become aggressive until they have to. But Siksak roved menacingly from slab of meat to slab of meat, pissing near the food, snarling at any wolf he caught looking at his sack. When he ate, he ate alone, for nobody was brave enough to eat beside him, so infamous was his territoriality.

Hagi whispered to Raspail, "We talked about this one, right? Look how he shows us his asshole, eh? I'm not sure I can smell it. Har, what an asshole."

Siksak heard Hagi talking and swiveled his head to land his angry gaze on Raspail. Raspail looked away.

"Hey Black. Look at me."

Raspail, who was awash with a sense of belonging for the first time in a long time, wished the antagonistic wolf with the freakish balls would realize he was unwelcome and go away. But Siksak thrived on the fear and discomfort his presence caused, mistaking it for envy and respect, so he lingered, trying to provoke fights, like he was with Raspail at the moment.

"Why not look at me when I talk to you? Do you fear me?" His eyelids drew back and his eyeballs jutted forward as he growled, "Look at me."

To look into his eyes would be to accept an invitation -- not to fight but to engage in the dance that occurs just before the fight, when both wolves get the chance to gamble on their life or pull out, depending on what they see in the eyes of their opponent.

Since all wolves turned down the invitation to connect with Siksak's awful gaze, no wolf had ever stared into his eyes, and no wolf knew what fatal, omnipotent force emanated from them.

Raspail, who was not shy about exploring the unknown, raised his head and peered into Siksak's eyes. Those watching stepped back as if flaming snakes might suddenly explode from Raspail's head. But Raspail saw that the eyes of Siksak were not in fact horribly massive orbs of destruction as the orbs between his legs suggested, but were small and undaunting.

It was now Siksak's turn to respond. Though he was skilled in intimidation, the well-hung wolf knew very little about actually fighting. Through his life he had been so successful at intimidating wolves that he'd acquired little fight experience. He saw in the large calm eyes of Raspail a creature he was loathe to acquire that experience from, so he craftily diverted his rage to Hagi.

"Do you know why that old liar brought you here, Black? To hunt for him." He chortled contemptuously. "Because he's weak and the weak cannot hunt for themselves. He survives on mercy. And thems who give mercy are as pathetic as them seeking it."

Siksak moved on, but Hagi remained agitated. He ate more and more meat to flush the distressing Siksak from his mind. A wave of nausea passed over him and he suddenly had to retch. He stood up while his gut spasmed, uttering an uncontrollable *Gwa! Gwa! Gwa!* that was a clarion call to the other wolves.

Every wolf in the camp, no matter what they were doing, diverted their attention to Hagi, for they knew he was about to retch and wolves are endlessly curious about another wolf retching. Hagi roamed looking for a private place to throw up, but the mob followed him wherever he went. Finally Hagi, unable to find privacy, heaved out a slew of liquefied meat, and every wolf stared and sniffed at it with fascination.

Hagi caught his breath. The noisy crowd cheered at him to eat his retch. As he prepared to consume it, Siksak swaggered over, unrolled his massive tongue and slurped up Hagi's vomit. Silence and shock seized the spectators, because in the hierarchy of affronts to a wolf, stealing his retch sits alone at the pinnacle.

Siksak turned his asshole to Hagi, swinging his balls in his face. He was giving Hagi the opportunity to defend his honor, knowing that the old three-footed wolf would never take it.

"Welcome back, Hagi," he said as he licked the foamy retch off his lips and swaggered off, leaving the gathering.

***

The Favor

Siksak's transgression came and went in the haze of celebration for every wolf but the one who was being celebrated. Raspail was half-asleep when Hagi whispered in his ear:

"Come walk with me."

Hagi took Raspail far away from the group. Only Poitu followed them, watching them talk from a tree.

"You like it here?"

"What is there not to like?" Raspail answered in his hushed voice.

"Oh, I can think of one thing." Hagi laughed, then turned serious "No wolf should steal another wolf's vomit. Not here where food is in abundance. If I were younger -- if I were not short a foot -- you can be sure I would have killed him."

Raspail felt bad for Hagi, and made sure his friend knew that he thought no less of him for not defending his honor.

"I can't fight Siksak. He knows that -- everyone does." Hagi's eyes narrowed with intensity. "But you could, my friend. *You* could kill him! I would be forever indebted. All here would. No wolf will miss him."

Raspail was surprised at the request. He was new here and didn't want to make his first impression as the wolf who settled grievances and arbitrated disputes. This reeked of being a facet, and it was obvious to him that no wolf needed or wanted such authority in Ramblefoot. Here, all disputes were settled by the parties involved.

Hagi saw the look of consternation on Raspail's face and thought better of his request.

"It's too much to ask of another wolf, I know. Forget I asked you."

They walked back to the gathering. When Hagi saw that Siksak had returned, the distress upset his stomach and he was tormented by the need to vomit again, which he suppressed for fear of a second humiliation. Unable to control himself any longer, he regurgitated another wad of juicy retch from the depths of his gut.

Again, the crowd formed, and again Siksak swaggered over. He bent his head low to eat the vomit. The silence was so intensely quiet that Raspail's murmur of a voice could be heard by all twenty-three wolves.

"Meat is plentiful. There's no need to take another's."

Siksak looked up from the retch and saw that it was Raspail challenging him. Raspail looked relaxed, lying on the ground, front feet crossed, his hackles down and his fangs concealed.

"And if I don't heed your advice -- weakly uttered like the fart of a butterfly -- will you *punish* me?" Siksak said.

"No, I will not punish you. I don't have a grievance with you. The wolf you insulted, however, will."

Siksak looked at the old, three-footed Hagi and snickered. Hagi looked shocked as well that Raspail would volunteer him to avenge himself.

Siksak, empowered by the large crowd and the near-full moon, licked up Hagi's retch.

With the instantaneous acceleration from standstill one sees in a hummingbird as it darts from one flower to the next collecting nectar, Raspail lunged at Siksak's back right leg, which was, not coincidentally, the same leg where Hagi was missing a foot. Using the same force he used with mercy to crush the poor wolf's leg in order to free him from the trap, he crushed Siksak's hock with his back teeth. He twisted the broken ankle in his mouth, tearing the muscles inside like blades of grass.

Siksak shrieked in pain. His eyes, which moments ago had projected a fearless, impassive aggression, now were trembling pools of vulnerability and paranoia as he looked back at his foot dangling uselessly from his leg.

Raspail returned to where he had been lying previously next to Hagi, looking as relaxed as he had before.

Hagi slowly realized the incredible favor his friend had done for him. Raspail had equalized the battleground for Hagi so that he could avenge the crime against him himself. He was giving him the opportunity to win back his honor in a fair fight. He looked into Raspail's eyes long enough to communicate his sincere gratitude.

Hagi rushed at Siksak and mounted his back, biting him from every angle with unbridled hatred. Siksak finally stopped the lashing by locking his jaws on to Hagi's. They grappled like this until Siksak disengaged, ripping off part of Hagi's lip as he did. Hagi, looking demented with his face streaming with blood, bit on to Siksak's bad leg and twisted him on to his back exposing his prized anatomical feature.

Hagi threw himself at the massive ballsack, snapped his jaws and bit it off like he were plucking an apple off a tree. Hagi let the trophy dangle from his mouth for the mob of ramblefoots to see, and they howled hysterically in approval.

Nobody had ever seen Hagi fight. Hagi was considered a sweet-mannered wolf who survived by his wits, not his strength, so expectations were low for a great fight. When he showed such sadistic passion in his vengeance, the spectators soared adoringly to Hagi's side, loving him for putting on such a ripping show. That he did it under a near-full moon invested the fight with even more ceremony, and all who watched felt they were witness to one of Hagi's great yarns come alive.

The pain of having his balls ripped off caused Siksak such a traumatic shock that he was unable to defend himself against Hagi's offense, which grew more merciless as his advantage increased.

To Siksak's good fortune Hagi's brutal slaying was interrupted by a third urge to vomit. Siksak seized on the moment and escaped limping into the mountains. Hagi, egged on by the mob to finish the fight proper, overcame his nausea and pursued the slow moving Siksak. The mob chased Hagi, reaching a precipice where he confronted Siksak for the last time.

Hagi feigned at Siksak's wounded leg and the wolf skittered back. Hagi then charged, digging his fangs into his loin, sending the two warriors tumbling over the ledge. The crowd rushed over and watched the two wolves cascade down the cliff to a basin clouded by the steam of warmpools.

Through the bluish haze the spectators could see the frenzy of two wolves fighting to the death, but could not discern which wolf was winning. One of the fighters, retreating on to the brittle crust of the warmpool's perimeter, suddenly disappeared as he sank into the boiling cauldron shrieking in agony.

The watching crowd fell silent with anticipation, waiting to see who the victor was.

Hagi emerged from the steamy netherworld and looked up at the cliff where the ramblefoots stood watching.

They erupted in a howl of excitement, *"Hagi Shan lives!"* *"Hagi Shan is the victor!"*

Hagi, covered in blood, slowly limped back up the mountain where the cheering mob enveloped him. He scanned the mob for Raspail but did not find him.

Raspail retreated from the crowd when the fight ended, walked off and looked for a flop. He found a pile of leaves and pine needles trapped between two giant boulders and burrowed deep inside the decomposing foliage as was his custom. He needed to think. He needed to rest. He needed to stop eating.

He couldn't slow his mind down. He restlessly shuffled under the blanket of leaves, burrowing deeper. Sleep was not coming and he could not understand why.

Poitu quietly landed on the boulder and stared down at him in the leaves. It was one of her games, staring into his eyes until one of them grew bored and looked away. She always won, and when she did she trilled happily.

He knew that if there were trouble, Poitu would wake him. Feeling safe under her watchful gaze in this strange new place, his eyes drifted shut, Poitu trilled at her victory, and sleep came easy.

***

Kileo's Escape

On the day that Kileo was planning to escape with the yearlings, the early sunlight made the dew that covered Cob Ash twinkle more alluringly than she could remember ever seeing it. Entranced by the beauty of her home on the day she was planning to leave it, Kileo quietly left the sleeping pack to run off some of her anxious energy.

She was near the southeastern boundary when she heard a strange chorus of wolves chanting:

"Kill us not, stay we not, ramblefoots we not, hunt we not, kill us not..."

She cautiously got closer to the disaffected troop that Aratus and company had encountered, then froze upon seeing the strange melancholy band of wolves trespassing through Cob Ash.

She howled a warning to the rest of the pack. They responded, and in a moment the sound of marching grew louder, not just from the west where the pack was arriving from, but from out of Draguignon as well.

Polwin, Abillon and Moorea arrived first, followed by Hesser and the yearlings. They surrounded the chanting trespassers, who didn't seem to notice or care that their lives were in peril.

Of equal urgency was the arriving Draguignon pack. The neighboring packs sized each other up for the first time since Cob Ash had lost five of its great wolves. Draguignon, with a disingenuous air of diplomacy, addressed Hesser.

"Cousins to the west, let us put our differences behind us for the moment and address this new problem which arrives first at our border and now at yours."

Hesser fathomed Cob Ash for the sake of imitation and said, in a convincingly distinguished tone, "We have no problems that cannot be handled by us alone."

"Are you now the facet of Cob Ash?"

"He is!" Polwin barked.

"He is!" the others repeated, even Kileo.

"Respect to you, cousin." And Draguignon gestured for his pack to lower their heads, just enough to convey respect and not submission.

"Your ability to handle these four ramblefoots will have an impact on Draguignon. They are part of a larger wave of remnant packs moving north. We have killed many of them already trying to cross through Draguignon. Now they stand at your threshold. What will you do, facet?"

Everyone waited for Hesser to declare his intentions.

"I will do... what I do... in the interest of my pack, and my pack alone."

The pack approved of their new facet. Even Kileo was impressed.

"May I point out the bloodline of Draguignon now runs through Cob Ash," Draguignon said as he stalked Hesser. He spoke menacingly, for he was losing patience with the imbecile he had helped elevate to power.

"My daughter has taken refuge here as your mate. Though she is not under my care and protection any longer, I haven't stopped caring for her. I will protect her from the dangers I have already spoken of."

The chanting wolves were getting agitated and tested the wolves penning them in. Polwin and Abillon aggressively kept them in place.

"The same is true for her sons and daughters, for they are half Draguignon," he continued. "They will be protected by Draguignon wolves, for I am unimpressed by your numbers, facet. Very unimpressed."

Draguignon was now two lengths away and appearing very formidable.

Hesser spoke in a pompous voice to compensate for his insecurity.

"If your patronage towards Cob Ash comes truly from your desire to share in the protection of our children against this *threat* -- these ramblefoots who are a burden on our resources and a plague on our borders..." and he threw a disgusted look towards them, subtly shifting the focus towards a mutual enemy, "Then we will not regard this trespass as hostile."

There was a long silence, during which Draguignon remained stoic and unreadable. Then he lifted his foot and stomped his foreleg on the ground. Four shrieking Draguignon bitches flew out of the woods and on to the chanters. The chanters didn't defend themselves, they just took the lashings. Kileo saw in their pathetic eyes that they were accepting death without resistance.

Polwin and Abillon looked to Hesser for leadership -- trespassers were brazenly spilling blood on their territory, right under their noses.

"Assist our neighbors ! Eradicate these wretched ramblefoots!" Hesser commanded.

Abillon and Polwin entered the frenzied slaughter, but young Navarin was unable to summon the hatred needed to kill another wolf he had no dispute with. He looked towards Kileo for guidance. Kileo shook her head no, and Navarin stepped back from the bloodbath.

"Spread their guts along the Southern border," Draguignon commanded his sons and daughters.

They were an efficient team, some wolves tasked with ripping and gutting, others with carrying and running.

Kileo watched bitterly as the Draguignon wolves roamed freely within central Draguignon doing their business. As soon as she was able to see beyond the immediate shock of the invasion, she was at once seized by the realization that the window of opportunity to escape had closed, and that now her problems were significantly more complicated than they had been. She cursed herself for not leaving earlier.

***

Repetto the Tiny Wolf

Poitu grew bored waiting for Raspail to wake. Standing on the rock ledge above the bed of leaves and pine needles that he'd disappeared into, she hopped into the air and let herself drop on to the soft bed of leaves, cushioning her fall. The unexpected thrill of this activity motivated her to do it again and again, each time using less and less wing to slow her fall until she was dropping like a pine cone. She knew she was irritating Raspail.

Finally Raspail's head emerged from the bed, followed by the rest of his body. He shook the leafy debris off himself and stretched, yawning contentedly, his tongue rolling out.

The day, he decided, would be spent familiarizing himself with the escape routes that undulated through the mountains. Poitu joined him, either flying above him or perched on his shoulders, and they voyaged leisurely along the scent-marked paths, enjoying the day.

One of the objects of this trip was to find a dwelling where he could have privacy. He stopped at the first den he saw and sniffed at its entrance. In a moment he heard the tempest of a woken wolfmother barking viciously as she charged at him;

"Stay away from them pups! Stay away from them pups or I'll kill you!"

Raspail retreated from the deranged mother. He was ready to move on when he heard the son bark at his mother from inside the cave, "Nin! Enough from you! Shut up, crazy bitch!"

The pup was no pup at all but Repetto, the diminutive wolf who, when standing at full height, could walk under Raspail's body with his hackles barely grazing the lowest point of the bigger animal's chest.

Dwarf wolves rarely are allowed to live past infancy by their mothers, so Raspail, like every other wolf in Ramblefoot, had never seen an example of his kind and could not help but gape at the miniature wolf. His upper arms bowed in giving him a jaunty gait that appeared jolly even when his mood was anything but. His gravelly voice gave away his maturity.

"Back in the den, bitch, and don't you come out!" he commanded the wolfmother. Her tail curled under as she disappeared inside the den, but Raspail could see her watching protectively from the shadows.

"Don't mind Nin. She takes care of me, like I'm her pup. Brings me food. Fights for me. She's a good old mam."

"You're not her son?" Raspail asked.

"Nah, them all got killed. I keep her from getting the scatters." He laughed.

Repetto joined Raspail on the trail, and Raspail welcomed the tiny wolf's company. He had an instantly likable nature to Raspail as there was with Hagi, and so starting a friendship with him -- the real kind, where wolves can take the piss out of each other without flashing fang -- was easy.

"You think you made that an even fight, breaking Siksak's leg." Repetto shook his head. "Nah, not hardly. I'll tell you why: The wolf with the new wound, he fights with a disadvantage against the one with the wound that's healed."

"Yes, you're right. But I didn't tell the two wolves *when* to settle their differences."

Repetto looked at him, not knowing if he were being earnest or facetious, and not knowing how to respond, said nothing.

"I suppose I could have given Hagi bigger balls, too, so they were equal to Siksak's. But only a father can do that for his son."

Repetto burst into laughter.

"Say, that as loud as you get?" the dwarf wolf asked curiously

"That as big as you get?" Raspail said.

Repetto laughed so hard that he fell, somersaulted and flopped on his back, sneezing uncontrollably. He recovered from this sneezing by rubbing his snout along the ground. He gave one final sneeze to blow out the dirt and they continued walking. Repetto didn't ask where Raspail was going, and Raspail didn't ask why he was joining him. They had both traveled like this together before, it seemed to both of them, though neither said a thing about it.

"We ate good last night."

Raspail acknowledged the comment with a grunt.

"I heard of some wolf..." Repetto started, pausing dramatically like Hagi, "This wolf ate so much, he died. He ate, ate some more, then he ate a lot more. Then he just died. From eating too much meat."

Raspail's lackluster reaction to the greatest story he knew bothered him.

"I heard of a wolf, he ate so little, he died." Raspail said. "Ate nothing but air, and when the air ran out, he just died."

"That dumb wolf didn't live in Ramblefoot," Repetto said and they both laughed so hard Repetto broke out into a sneezing fit again.

"I heard of this wolf, he sneezed so much he died. He sneezed and sneezed until one day he sneezed his life out." This just made Repetto sneeze more.

The route they were on took them to the cliff that Hagi and Siksak rolled off of. They peered over the edge and saw Hagi below, pacing around the steaming warmpools where Siksak had died. Raspail and Repetto snaked their way down the mountainside to meet up with him.

Hagi was troubled, but seeing Repetto and Raspail sweetened his mood. He stared lingeringly at them, happy that of all the wolves in Ramblefoot, Raspail had gravitated to Repetto.

He finally broke his stare and threw his fore leg over Raspail's shoulder and poked his muzzle affectionately into the thick ruff of his neck.

"You're some kind of wolf, you know that?"

Raspail shrugged off the compliment. Hagi talked softly. "Doing what you did last night for me -- that speaks of your honor, sure. But more so, *something* else." He didn't give any clue as to what that 'something else' was, but Raspail liked hearing that he had it anyway.

"I never met my sons or daughters, but I could only hope they were like you."

Raspail was moved by his praise. Repetto was happy for his new friend, who had earned the flattery, but nonetheless wished there were a scrap of praise for him.

"What about me? Don't you wish those sons were like me, Hagi?" Repetto asked in jest, for around friends he had good humor about his physical shortcomings.

"Repetto, if I'd sired a runt like you I'd have surely asked my bitch to kill you or leave you in the timbers for the hawks and eagles." They all laughed.

"But knowing you as I do now," Hagi continued, "I would have been mistaken to do so, for you have turned your size into an advantage, and your demeanor shows no bitterness for what you lack, only joy for what you have. And that makes you the biggest wolf I have ever known."

Repetto almost fell over from the old wolf's praise.

Raspail looked down and saw footprints in the sandy edge of the pool. They didn't look like a normal wolf foot; the toes had somehow melded together into one. He couldn't smell anything in the acrid sulfurous vapor. He wondered, had Siksak emerged alive from the warmpool -- alive but changed?

Impossible, he told himself, *No wolf could survive having its leg broken, its balls ripped off, and then being boiled.*

When he looked back up Hagi was staring at him with a look of worry. He himself had seen the odd footprints and pondered the same improbable thought as Raspail.

Neither spoke a word about it.

***

A Memorable Smell

The wolves galloped back into the timbers. When night fell, the three wolves cruised for food in the flats, and Hagi wanted to show Raspail one of the "fightless bison." Along the way they encountered a slab of meat gleaming in the moonlight. To Raspail's surprise, the meat did not tempt his two companions.

He was about to claim the meat when he heard Hagi calmly say, "No."

No sooner had Hagi uttered these words when two wolves, a male and female, darted out of the timbers and claimed the meat. To Raspail's eye, the female wolf's aquiline muzzle, upturned mouth and speckled tawny coat suggested that she was part coyote, something he had never seen before. Hagi stepped up to her.

'Strangers, I'll give you the same advice I give my friends: Don't eat that meat."

"There's no territories here," the young female wolf growled while her mate ate, "We can eat what we find."

"Yes you can. But if you eat that you'll be dead before that cloud passes the moon."

Raspail looked up and saw that a cloud was indeed about to pass the moon.

The male gulped the meat down with a very defensive posture. He flashed fang at them while he greedily tore off a second bite. "If you want to fight me for this meat, fight me! I'll kill you!"

"You're not getting it, are you boy," Hagi said.

The wolf swallowed the second bite. Raspail looked up at the sky and watched as the cloud slowly reached the moon. He heard a gagging sound and looked back down at the wolf, whose muscles were convulsing as he stumbled around the meat still trying to protect it.

His legs tightened and he fell to the ground, dying from asphyxiation just as the clouds passed the moon, restoring full moonlight to the area. Raspail was astonished.

The female barked at Hagi, "What did you do to him!?"

Hagi ignored her and gestured with his muzzle to the meat, saying to Raspail, "Go -- smell it."

Raspail circumspectly approached the meat as if it could at any moment leap up and strangle him. He sniffed it. It smelled like meat and he began to drool.

"Keep smelling it."

After a few moments, as soon as his nose's excitement settled down, he could smell the bitter scent of strychnine that radiated from inside the meat.

"Remember the smell. And when you smell it, think of your poor cousin here laying dead, not two mouthfuls in his hungry stomach."

"This is 'the meat you never eat?" Raspail asked.

"The very one."

Hagi walked off with Repetto. Raspail drew a few more breaths of the strychnine laced meat, cataloguing it with the smell of the trap.

He ran to catch up with Hagi, and as he did was joined by the dead wolf's partner, running alongside him.

If she were any smaller he would have sworn she were a coyote.

***

Navarin's Bravery

Under the full eye of the ancestors, on the night when Kileo was to have taken refuge in the low mountain to the west with the yearlings, Kileo instead sat uneasily listening to Hesser reassure the pack that the merge with Draguignon would be "beneficial" to Cob Ash as the brash howling of Draguignon wolves swirled around them. Already, only two days since the invasion, the once comforting smell of their scent posts was being overwhelmed by the unnerving smell of foreign wolves.

It sickened Kileo so much that it rekindled her loyalty to what remained of the pack.

The next morning she woke and saw that Navarin was missing. The other yearlings knew nothing of his departure.

Kileo took Carel and the others and went searching for him immediately.

They found him roving the north-western border alone, marking the scent posts. Kileo ran towards him, and when she reached him she pushed him down with authority. He resisted and stood, trying to look more formidable then he was.

"What are you doing?" Kileo asked.

"What my uncles and aunts should be doing."

"There's a reason they're not marking the periphery. You'll be killed."

"I'll die defending Cob Ash before living under their law."

She heard marching to her right and saw three Draguignon wolves approach in the distance. Running was an option, but in the time it would take to convince the stubborn young Navarin to go they would lose their lead.

The Draguignon wolves walked to the border and smelled where Navarin had pissed. The wolf named Asper talked to his sisters Selon and Jacier.

"That's not how it should smell. This is how it should smell."

He lifted his leg and pissed on top of Navarin's piss, then stared intimidatingly at Navarin, trying to provoke him. Navarin avoided his stare.

Asper, insuring his dominance not just be known but felt, walked over to Navarin and lifted his leg, sprinkling urine on the young male's tail.

Navarin showed incredible restraint, unlike his sister Carel who lunged at Asper and rolled him on to his side Navarin was as quick to her aide as she was to his, driving his sharp young fangs deep inside Asper's neck, locking on as the bigger wolf thrashed wildly.

The world around them slowed to a halt as the life and death play unfolded at what seemed to be a hundred times longer than the fleeting moment in which it actually occurred. Carel defended herself against Jacier, Kileo found herself sparring with the vicious jaws of Selon, while Navarin was using all his wits and strength to drain the life out of Asper.

Now, it must be noted that while the three Draguignon wolves were very experienced in the slaying of wolves -- the females were half of the quartet which exterminated the chanting trespassers -- none of the young Cob Ash wolves had ever killed another wolf.

Kileo gained the advantage over Selon by ripping her thigh open, but in doing so slipped and lost her balance and the wounded Selon bolted off.

Kileo chased after her, knowing that Selon was looking for a high point from which to howl for help. Kileo knew the terrain of her home and, anticipating where Selon would go, took the quicker route there.

Selon reached the precipice that fed the mud basin and pitched her head back to howl for help. Kileo charged at her from where she klooted in the conifers. As she rammed into her enemy she closed her jaws on her throat and went flying with her off the slippery ledge and into the mud basin below.

The two wolves splashed into the mud, Selon's throat still clutched tightly in Kileo's jaws. Kileo pushed Selon's thrashing head under the mud, and held it there.

Kileo finally saw the bubbles of Selon's dying breaths stop rising to the surface of the mud and released her.

Dire thoughts of her beloved yearlings being slain filled her head. She ran back, whipping herself to speeds she had never run at.

When she reached the border, things were not calamitous as she'd imagined. Carel was licking Navarin's wounds, wounds he'd received after killing Asper and helping Carel fight off Jacier, who had managed to escape. The wolves took a moment to huddle and rub their muzzles together, bonding over their unlikely victory.

Howling erupted around them. It was a warning from Jacier, alerting Draguignon about the attack. The Draguignon wolves responded quickly with their droning howl.

"We have to leave. Now."

Navarin looked at Kileo defiantly. "We just killed two of their wolves. We can kill more. Cob Ash is ours, not theirs. I won't run from them."

"Navarin, your courage brings me joy and sorrow, for it's that courage I think of when I remember what Cob Ash was, and it is that courage that I thought had disappeared forever from our home. But in a moment there will be three times as many of them as us here, and no amount of courage will keep us from being slaughtered."

"I will not die," Navarin said boldly.

"Shut up, Navarin!" Carel barked at him fiercely, "So what if you killed one of theirs. You couldn't have done it without my help, which means you are half as strong as you think."

Navarin could not make eye contact with her, knowing she was right.

"We are going where Kileo leads us," she said flashing fang, "And if you don't come I am killing you myself!"

"Where will you take us?" Navarin sheepishly asked Kileo.

"Just follow," Kileo said confidently.

Kileo led Carel and the others into the ravine and along the stream that winded up into the low mountain where she had taken Carel days earlier. Carel immediately went to her perch and surveyed Cob Ash.

In a hushed voice she said, "Come!"

Kileo and Navarin sprinted to the perch where they could see a patrol of five hyper-vigilant Draguignon wolves arrive at the border where the fight had taken place. They were sniffing the ground and talking.

Navarin felt ashamed by his brashness; Kileo was right; they would all be dead now if they'd stayed to fight.

"The others will be punished for what we did," Navarin said regretfully.

Kileo knew he was right. Cob Ash blood would be spilled in response to the two murdered Draguignon wolves. But there was nothing they could do.

While Carel and the others quietly explored their provisionary mountain home, Kileo's mind drifted to the mud basin, back to when Raspail and she ambushed the fawn.

Raspail might be dead, she thought with a shudder.

It hadn't occurred to her before. Ramblefoots lived hard, short lives, and he was at even more risk having no voice. The prospect of never seeing him again made her heart stop. She could remember the time, before she was smitten by Raspail, when she ignored him, when he was, as he'd put it, invisible to her. Now, with him so gone from her life and possibly dead, she hated herself for all those times she rebuffed him and caused him anguish.

What has become of you? she asked. *Are you fighting for survival, moment by moment, running and hiding in the shadows of enemies?*

No matter how bad things looked from up here, she knew that Raspail had it much worse.

***

Looking For a New Flop

Unable to find any place better to sleep, Raspail wandered back to his original flop. He stumbled and tripped the entire trip there, and he was so meatdrunk it was a miracle he made it there at all.

He flopped on to the soft pile of rotting leaves and needles. As the spell of sleep cast deeply on the tired wolf, flies burrowed their way through his fur to his hide and feasted on him as freely as he had on elk. When he woke, his groin and ears itched and stung and he swore to himself that if he did nothing else that day he would find a better place to flop.

Laying beside the pile of leaves waiting for him was Ipsy, the mate of the wolf who did not take Hagi's advice. He ignored her and walked immediately to a tree to relieve himself and rub his rankling skin against a rock.

Ipsy came to his aid and began to lick and gnaw at the insect bites under his fur. Raspail growled at her to stop, but she was persistent, and Raspail, having missed the sensation of another wolf grooming him, gave in and let her work on him. She was tireless and eager to please. Raspail sensed her desperation for male companionship. Desperate or not, it felt good -- she had a pointy, delicate mouth with fine long teeth which was quite like a coyote's because half of her was.

It is not uncommon for wolves and coyotes to mate, especially during the strange, changing times they were living in. What was different was that Ipsy's mother was the wolf, and not vice-versa. In her heat, she had accepted two wolf suitors in one day. While resting from these amorous pleasures, a coyote smelled her perfume and, unable to control his desire, rushed at her and became her third lover of the day. Ipsy's mother slayed the Lothario mounting her, but not before he had finished his business.

Ipsy was weaned and raised like any other wolf, but as she matured and her exotic coyote features, like her wing-shaped ears, became more prominent, it became obvious to her mother that she was the daughter of the coyote and, as she wanted no reminder of the indiscretion, banished Ipsy at a year old.

Ipsy survived by her wits and her exotic beauty. Her heart was badly damaged by the cruelty of her mother and she sought acceptance wherever she could find it, choosing friends and mates poorly.

Raspail smelled her strange scent while she ground her teeth on his skin. Her allure was not lost on him, but the immediacy with which she pursued him after her mate's death cautioned him.

Poitu dived down and wedged her beak between the two animals, startling Ipsy. The raven then landed on Raspail and dug her claws into his back possessively, made a territorial gesture with her wings, and began vigorously grooming the filthy black wolf.

Raspail shook Poitu off his back and went on his way with Ipsy following him. Not wanting her company, he snarled at her and flashed fang. She stopped and watched the wolf gallop off with the raven flying above him.

Raspail found Repetto drinking from the stream near his den. Nin stood guard there, watching him protectively. As soon as Raspail got close she smacked her feet at the ground and quivered her lip, barking viciously at him:

"You son of a bitch! Don't come here no more -- leave my son alone!"

Raspail was sufficiently frightened of the wolfmother and backed away. Repetto said that he had kept her from getting the scatters. To Raspail's eye she already had them.

"Oh, enough goddammit! I won't take your stupid barking at my mates no more!" the little wolf barked back at her. "I bite your tongue off you don't stop! Or maybe I just leave you, eh? Find another wolfmother take care me!"

She drooped her head forlornly, whining submissively.

Their bizarre dependency was comical to Raspail, and he knew that one day he would either win the wolfmother's trust or be ripped to bloody shreds by her.

Raspail, true to his morning resolution, went searching for a better flop. With Repetto at his side, running two paces for every one Raspail took, they scoured every abandoned den from the old beaver lodges in the streams to tree trunks that had been hollowed by lightning. At each entry a wolf appeared giving him the once over and telling him, "Keep moving."

Repetto split from Raspail whenever they found a den, posting himself so that if a hostile wolf charged from one of these holes he was behind the attacker and ready to defend Raspail. He didn't ask Repetto to do this, he just did, and Raspail was somehow not surprised by his inherent loyalty and cautiousness.

The day progressed with no luck. Occasionally a wolf would squeeze out from the tunnel of his or her den and, recognizing Raspail as the wolf who evened the fight for Hagi, would tell him, "Sorry mate, hole's taken. But down the way there's a hole so-and-so used to sleep in but he's since gone and..."

By afternoon they'd seen every den there was to be seen and flopped under the shade of a pine tree, enjoying the silence around them.

Both wolves leaped back as something crashed to the ground in front of them. It was a squirrel, stunned into unconsciousness. Raspail heard Poitu above them and looked up to see her diving at a second squirrel running the length of the branch to the trunk. She kicked it hard with her claws, and it dropped to the ground in the same condition as its friend.

Raspail and Repetto ate the squirrels, grateful for the snack that would silence their stomachs until dark when they would go out to feast in the plains.

Poitu played with Raspail using the long tail of the squirrel, and Repetto was amazed at how gently the giant wolf interacted with the fragile bird.

When they were finished playing, the two new friends continued their journey, Raspail lowering his standards and looking for something that could perhaps be converted into a den. But wolves had lived in these mountains for thousands of generations, and anything that could be made into a den had been.

As darkness fell Raspail sighed resignedly and returned to his old flop so he could rest before dinner. Repetto joined him, copying how Raspail burrowed into the debris for cover.

"Don't you worry. Wolves die all the time. There be an open hole for you soon enough. Besides, this not too bad, eh? This kinda good."

Raspail started to drift off to sleep when Repetto woke him. "Hey, if you don't find something, you know, you can flop with me."

Raspail looked at him. "Thank you. If I was looking for a place to be mauled to death, I'd accept your offer."

Repetto yipped with laughter. Raspail, excited to fill his stomach like the night before, did not sleep. Once the howling began, he jumped to his feet and ran with Repetto down the mountain.

***

Walking Meat

Raspail beheld the fightless bison, grazing alone under the moonlight, with an expression that was probably no less full of awe than the first bear to watch as a salmon leaped from the stream into his hands.

Repetto, Boonbrekker and Hagi were by his side, watching his reaction with pleasure.

"There is no way that animal is real." Raspail said, and Repetto instantly began sneezing with hilarity. Hagi silenced him by biting his mouth shut, but the cow heard the wolves and started to ambulate backwards.

"Look at it. Why it's as if someone went through the trouble of stripping the beast of his armor to save us the effort of tearing it off," Raspail said. "How do you hunt it?"

"But you've seen the hunting style of Ramblefoot!" Hagi laughed, surprised by his intelligent friend's question.

"I was drunk. Everyone was drunk."

"That is the Ramblefoot way to hunt."

"Drunk?"

"As drunk as you can trick yourself into being with an empty stomach. Once everyone starts acting drunk, you'll be as drunk as you'd feel with a stuffed stomach, only it won't have a drop more food in it than it does now."

"I'm very sure of two things." Raspail said

"Two things only?"

"For now."

"Go on."

"One is, I doubt I can make myself *feel* drunk, stumbling and clunking about like an idiot, with my stomach torturing me."

"That will change. What's your other thing?"

"I'm pretty sure that beast weighs as much as a bison. While he's obviously not that formidable a creature..." and he was interrupted by their childish laughter, for this was an understatement. "Just the same I don't want it falling on me. Therefore, charging at it like some scatter-headed maniac with no particular plan -- it seems a bad plan, frankly."

"It is the plan that works. And as I said, it *is* the hunting style of Ramblefoot." Hagi surveyed the pasture where the cow stood as he talked. "Raspail, since you're the newest hunter here, you get the privilege of playing the stupid meatdrunk wolf who happens upon a cow all alone in a meadow. Remember -- you're so full you couldn't possible be interested in that dumb cow. Then, you jump around drunkishly. You'll get her agitated, but you'll also get her confidence up cause she thinks you're alone. Then we three come out, drunkishly, and we beleaguer the thing."

"Then?"

Hagi shrugged. "Anything goes, just drag it down."

"Chaos."

"Exactly. They're big animals with small heads--" Repetto's infantile laughing interrupted them again. "You stun them with chaos then drag them down."

It began to make sense to Raspail. He fathomed a drunken state and stumbled out goofily in front of the cow. The cow didn't seem very concerned. Raspail polished his acting skills up a notch, and wobbled on rubbery limbs before the cow, moaning contentedly like his stomach was full.

Up close, the creature was even more astounding. He laughed hard as he assessed it thinking, " It's walking meat. All I have to do is stop it from walking, then it will just be meat!" He couldn't help feeling amused, which helped him conjure himself being drunk. His movements grew looser and sillier.

In the distance his friends laughed at him making an ass of himself in the moonlight. He took the joke well because he knew it was made with good humor, and laughed at himself, all the while forgetting about the "walking meat" that was suddenly charging at him.

"Run!" Repetto shouted.

No animal, no matter how brave, wants to be in the path of a moving animal that is ten times its size, so Raspail turned and sprang off the dirt.

In his haste he lost his footing and tripped every bit like a meatdrunk wolf, and as he tumbled over he saw the underside of the cow traveling over him.

The cow, still thinking it had only one foe, stopped, turned and chased Raspail. Finally his comrades ran out and joined him, howling and flaunting their mirth -- not drunkishly but *full on drunk,* for they were so intoxicated by the hilariousness of their prank.

The mood was contagious as Hagi promised. Boonbrekker bit the cow's throat and hung from the animal's huge neck trying to drag it down. Repetto ran circles around it and weaved between its legs, nipping at its joints. Boonbrekker fell from the cow with a chunk of flesh in his mouth and swallowed the meat as its angry owner nearly trampled him under its massive body. The cow put up with these shenanigans for about another five minutes, then fell, unable to defend itself any longer. Impatiently filling their stomachs with meat, they seamlessly transitioned from being pretend drunk to meatdrunk.

Everyone urged Raspail to take the heart and liver since he was the victim of the prank and they were grateful for his good humor. Raspail divided the shimmering treasures with Hagi.

Poitu dived in front of him and tore half of the heart out of Raspail's mouth and flew with it to the safety of a tree.

"That's what you get for friending a Raven!" Hagi laughed with the others.

When Repetto stopped laughing he began a drunken howl that, though it lacked the sophistication of one of Balfort's poetic sonnets, brought just as much happiness to his heart.

When the four wolves were satisfied with what they'd eaten, they rested by the carcass waiting for their hunger to return. Two new wolves, themselves already meatdrunk, wandered over, greeted Hagi playfully, and joined them around the carcass. Neither party acted threatened or threatening.

Hagi bragged about the meat they'd just eaten, and he demanded that the guests at least try a bite of their kill so they could see how superior their meat was. The guests ate from the carcass, agreeing that it was a fleshier cow then the one they'd just eaten.

Watching their guests eat made them all hungry again, so the four hosts joined their guests, eating side by side as peacefully as wolves are able to.

Raspail saw Poitu drop in front of him and fan her wings, croaking with urgency. He stood up, backing away from the carcass.

"They're here," he said.

The others stopped eating and listened and smelled. Nothing was in the air.

Boonbrekker resumed eating. "The moon's still high. We have hours till the sun comes out."

Hagi watched Raspail follow Poitu back to the mountains. He rose up with great difficulty.

"Raspail's right." Hagi said. "We gotta move."

Repetto and Boonbrekker reluctantly stepped back from the meal. Hagi was getting impatient with them, so he flashed fang and they quickened their step.

To the two wolves who were their guests Hagi smiled and said, "Eat to your heart's content, but if you're smart you'll leave."

The two guests stayed.

Raspail waited in the shadow of the timbers, comforted by the dark recesses and shadows he could kloot in. In a moment, he was joined by Hagi, Repetto and Boonbrekker, none of whom looked happy about abandoning their meal.

"I don't get it." Boonbrekker said. "Why we leave them wolves all our meat?"

Gunshots rang out, cutting him off. They could see their guests, now running to the timbers, suddenly fall yelping to the ground. A moment later, men on horses came to collect them.

Boonbrekker moved close to Raspail, looked him over then said, "You come hunting with us anytime you like. You say leave, we sure leave." And Boonbrekker rubbed his head against Raspail's.

***

The Notoriety Of Raspail

Raspail gained notoriety in Ramblefoot very quickly. Four factors contributed to this, the first being his clever disposal of the hated and feared Siksak, which almost every wolf in Ramblefoot was witness to.

The second was his uncanny ability to know when to leave a meal. When there were fewer ramblefoots, the men came only in daylight to hunt the wolves. Now, with so many wolves raiding their meat, the men were less predictable.

Nobody but Hagi knew that Raspail's intimate bond with the raven allowed him to detect danger early, so Boonbrekker and other wolves attributed this to some special sense that he had. Several times (since the time just described) he proved his accuracy, and in each instance those who followed him lived and those who didn't were killed. Word spread quickly, and his popularity as a hunting companion grew.

The third factor was something he'd learned from watching Poitu roll her body on dead ants and coating her feathers with their juices. He decided to try it out of sheer curiosity, to see why she did this seemingly counter-intuitive activity.

She laughed clangorously as she watched him imitate her, toppling the anthill as he rolled his giant body on it. There was no immediate benefit to this -- it certainly wasn't that enjoyable or pleasant -- so he didn't give it another thought. That night he enjoyed the best sleep so far in his bug-ridden flop. Three days later, when the pesticide had rubbed off and the bugs attacked him in his sleep again, he realized why Poitu (and all ravens) smear dead ants on themselves.

Anting allowed him to sleep comfortably in the leaves and pine needles and so he stopped looking for a hole. Wolves who hunted with Raspail began copying this bizarre ritual. For the dozen or so wolves who had not found dens, anting allowed them to flop in any of the many leafy piles abundant in the timbers. Again, Raspail could not take credit for knowing how to ant, only for obtaining the knowledge through observing Poitu's behavior. Credit was heaped on him anyway. Ramblefoots quickly took up the fashion of flopping in these soft crannies (now that it was comfortable to do so with the ant balm), and some even vacated their coveted dens to do so and not appear out of rhythm with the others.

So Raspail had demonstrated bravery and honor in the justice he had administered to Siksak. He showed good judgment during the dangerous activity of eating in the flatlands and a preternatural ability to know when hunters were coming. And he had panache; others liked his style and sought to imitate him.

The fourth factor wasn't something that Raspail did, but rather something he did not do.

Hagi was approached by eight ramblefoots led by Repetto. They asked the old wolf if he would get a feel for whether Raspail would want to be their facet.

Hagi was shocked. The main lure of Ramblefoot, besides its easy paradise meat, was the freedom from having to follow another wolf's law. Hagi was the closest thing to a leader they had or wanted, so they deferred to his judgment on how to proceed.

Hagi went to talk to Raspail in private (though the assembly of eight wolves followed him not so discreetly). He found him playing with Poitu outside his flop and waited for them to finish.

"Things will really have hit bottom around here the day every one of these wolves gets themselves a damn raven just because you have one."

"She's not a raven. She's a little wolf who flies." Raspail's voice sounded stronger every day, though it would never sound like it had before.

'And to her you're a big raven who hunts."

"Perhaps I am," Raspail said. After a moment he said, "Tell me a story, Hagi. I don't care if it's one you've told me a dozen times."

Hagi laughed. "Have I a story for you my friend."

"Waiting on a good one?"

"Oh yeah," Hagi laughed

"So it is not one I've heard before?"

"I'm pretty sure not."

"Then why hesitate? Speak, Hagi. You know our journey here was an experience all the more memorable because of your stories. Now enough with the suspense."

Hagi lay down next to him

"Some ramblefoots came to me inquiring about you."

"What about me?" Raspail looked anxiously into Hagi's eyes.

Hagi hesitated. Raspail had to nudge him to continue. "Now I'm against this, because things is what they is without much need for changing it, and I have never been approached by such a large number of Ramblefoots in order to carry out a request--"

"Not only is this the worst story you've ever told, Hagi, but I'm about to fall over dead worrying how it ends!"

"They want you to be facet."

"A facet? Here? *Me?*"

"Apparently."

Raspail rolled on his back and laughed uproariously. Hagi didn't find it so funny.

"Who asked you to do this?"

"You can see for yourself." He gestured with his muzzle, and Raspail saw the others hiding about, watching and waiting.

"Huh." Raspail pondered it for a moment. "Tell my friends that we are doing quite well without a facet."

Hagi nodded and turned away to walk off, happy with Raspail's decision. Then Raspail sighed and said "But also tell them... if a situation should arise where we need a facet, I would honor their request."

This natural nobility was the fourth factor that contributed to Raspail's notoriety.

***

The Secret Cave (and a Brief Lesson on its Origin)

The ruckus had brewed at the foot of Raspail's flop since dawn, but he was indifferent to it, for he was enjoying the blackest of sleeps as the sun's rays toasted the womb of nature's detritus enveloping him.

The fighting grew louder and meaner, Poitu croaked more irritatingly, and finally two wolves tumbled into Raspail's flop on top of him, gnashing teeth and wrestling each other, leaves flying everywhere.

This woke Raspail. He heaved the two wolves off him and emerged from his flop irritated. Immediately he gave reprimanding bites to the two wolves who woke him, and to his surprise they rolled on their backs and lolled their tongues in submission to him. Behind them were several more wolves.

"Can't a wolf sleep around here?!" He said to all of them in his hushed voice. "What's the meaning of this?"

They all spoke at once, but through the confusing din he discerned the fact that they were each waiting for his counsel on some problem they were having with a neighbor, friend, enemy, or lover. Poitu croaked at them to quiet, but it just made the fusillade of complaints all the more unbearable. Raspail was horrified.

"Go home, all of you! I have no opinion and furthermore I don't care! I'm not your facet! Fack off!"

Repetto stepped forward. "But you told Hagi--"

"I told Hagi that if a problem arose which--" and his low voice was drowned out by their arguing.

Repetto wanted him to settle a dispute he was having with Nin; another wolf who Raspail had never met wanted him to punish some other wolf who had pissed too close to his flop, and so on and so on.

Accidentally, and to his dismay, he had given these Ramblefoots the impression that he had the solutions to all the many problems that had been festering in the absence of a facet. In a most un-facet-like display, he ran as fast as he could from them. They barked their woes at him as they chased after him, but because of their discord he quickly lost them.

Along the way he felt the need to shit, so he curled his body and strained until his legs were shaking wildly, but all that came out were three hard pebble-sized turds that would have embarrassed a rabbit. He was constipated and hadn't had a decent movement in four days.

Poitu landed near the meager turds and pecked and sniffed at them. She was aware of his irritable mood, brought on by this inability to ditch the sensation of a full bowel.

Raspail ate some grass, hoping this would alleviate his woes, and finally met up with Hagi who was grooming himself by the stream.

"I need a place to sleep and think without every wolf and his cousin and his cousin's cousin coming to me with his problems."

The two wolves ventured westward looking for a cave that Hagi remembered exploring before he had developed his fear of entering dens and other such underground holes.

They walked through a rocky field pocked with small craters. Unlike the warmpools, these craters did not vent steam. They reached a large, cone-shaped mound and Raspail followed Hagi up to its rocky lip and peered in.

The hole was about eight lengths wide and shallow. On the flat basin at the center of the crater there was a pool of water that seemed to glow as if lit from below. He looked at Hagi. It did not look remotely habitable.

"Not as you remembered it?" he asked Hagi.

"Exactly as I remembered it. There's more to it, you have to go in."

"You'll come with me?"

"Ha! No, I don't go underground."

"Why not?"

"I'll tell you another time."

Raspail carefully circled the perimeter, perplexed by the water's glow. He leaped on to the basin, splashing in the water, which went up to his hocks. Peering low in front of him he saw that the basin he stood on continued under the rock mound. He looked up at Hagi, watching him.

"You wanted privacy. You'll find it there."

Raspail crouched and ventured forward into the tight low crevice between the basin and the rock ceiling. The space eventually broadened as the basin angled downwards, revealing a vast cave, lit by sun beaming down through holes above and reflecting up off the shimmering pools of water below. He took small steps down the slippery inclined basin, but it was a futile precaution; he slid down the rock and splashed in the water below. The ceiling above, dripping with stalactites, vaulted high above his head. The floor of the cave was like a lake dotted with inter-connected rock islands. Tunnels and caves radiated in all directions, up and down.

"How does one exit from here?" he shouted up to Hagi, who he could no longer see.

"You'll figure it out."

Raspail jumped from island to island. There was an ample selection of dry sleeping places. Still water, steeped with minerals leeched from the basalt, gave the cavern a foul smell, but it was no worse than the dead leaves he'd been sleeping in. He tested out one of these islands, sprawling on its smooth convex surface, and decided the place would serve him perfectly.

The unique space Raspail found himself in had been formed millions of years ago when the massive volcano at Warmpools' core erupted and spewed its hot magma so rapidly that the rock mountain it erected collapsed under its own weight, leveling the area above into a huge plateau that sealed off the powerful cauldron that had created it. To relieve this massive pressure, hundreds of small warmpools perforated the plateau allowing steam to escape from this sleeping volcano and keep things in relative peace.

Raspail's cave was a warmpool that had, like the volcano, collapsed on itself, sealing it off from the hot mantle below and diverting the high pressure steam somewhere more porous. Left behind was this smooth basalt chamber, unchanged from how it looked the day it was created.

Skrish...Skrish...

The strange sound echoed around him making it hard to locate. If he'd had a strong voice, he would have warned it to go away. But he didn't, so he cocked his ears and waited for the noise to come again.

Skrish... Skrish... Ping

He saw a huge shadow dart across the end of the tunnel to his right.

Skrish... Skrish... Ping

He quietly entered the narrow tunnel and floated like a phantom towards the faintly lit void where he'd seen the amorphous black shape.

FWAAAAAAAH!

The shadow passed again. He froze and choked the light out of his eyes. He waited, but nothing happened.

"RAAAAAAAAAAAAAAAAAA!!!!!!!!"

It came straight at his face, shrieking as it attacked. His heart hammered against his ribs with fear and he fell back against the rock wall, his jaws agape and ready to snap.

The phantom shrank back into the light of the void and Raspail saw it was Poitu.

Poitu cackled as she disappeared up through the vent hole above.

He suddenly had the uncontrollable urge to shit, such was his fright. There was a nearly vertical pile of rocks that led out of the hole. He ran up it and emerged at the basin of another crater into the daylight.

Hagi was waiting for him, smiling, but Raspail raced past him until he could not control his urge anymore, curved his back and pushed out the turd that had been plaguing him for days. Poitu flew down behind him and looked at it, laughing, for she had scared the shit out of him.

A New Worry for Kileo

Seclusion in the low mountain was idyllic for Kileo in some ways. The hot months were more tolerable here than in the valley, they were all eating well enough, and they had so far evaded notice from Draguignon. Soon Navarin, Carel and the others would be mature enough to ramble and they could start a new life.

But it was difficult to relax knowing that at any moment a Draguignon wolf might find its way into their secret realm and expose them. All she needed to do was visit Carel's perch and look out to be reminded of the insidious dangers that lurked all around her, and she did this obsessively, never letting her guard waver.

The yearlings remained carefree and played with each other constantly, and though she was happy that this would give them preparedness for fighting when they rambled, seeing them play sadly reminded her of times with Raspail when they were young and innocent.

She slept poorly. She missed being free to howl and bark at will, and her appetite suffered. The cold months were coming, which meant that soon her body would change and attract a mate whether she wanted to or not.

Navarin and Carel were playing too noisily for Kileo's comfort. She turned and went to scold them as she often had to, but when she saw them they were with a third wolf whose company they were enraptured to have.

It was her brother Abillon.

He ran to Kileo and played with her. Though she was wary of his presence, she was undeniably excited to see another grown wolf and eager to hear about the politics of pack life since she had left.

"They went looking for you at first," Abillon told them. "Hesser ordered us to find you because Draguignon was putting pressure on him, but after a few days everyone assumed you'd rambled so they stopped looking." This was relieving news to her. "Draguignon is more concerned about the ramblefoots migrating north, trespassing on his land. Polwin leads the patrol that protects the border."

"I've seen them. They're very busy."

"Polwin's had an easier time joining the Draguignon wolves than me."

He looked around him at the inviting mountain-vista. "This is paradise."

"One would think. But it's not, brother. I am full of fear constantly."

"I can imagine. Why, if Hesser knew that I'd found you... Well, let's say I'd gain favor because Hesser would impress Draguignon with your capture."

A chill went up her hackles.

"You should see the pups. They are fierce and serious for their age. They are more Cob Ash than Draguignon."

She doubted it. It was hard to tell where Abillon's allegiance was. Though she had been happy to see him, having him know where they were hiding was distressing. Abillon was weak of character, and she was sure he would use his knowledge of their whereabouts for currency in the new hierarchy if he had to. She needed to be careful.

"Brother, you must never tell anyone we are here. If we are captured, Navarin and Carel will be killed."

Abillon laughed, "Why would I give your secret away?"

"You wouldn't. Of course you wouldn't."

Abillon played with them for a while, and then Carel asked the question that Kileo was wondering but was too afraid to ask.

"How did you find us?"

"Yesterday there was a wounded calf that I watched flee from this mountain. I could see that wolves had wounded it, and so I came up to see who these wolves were."

Indeed, Kileo had worried that the elk he described would give away their secret. She had reason to worry, as it turned out.

"Well I'm lucky it was you who found the elk and cleverly deduced we were up here rather than some other wolf," Kileo said.

"Of course you are! If they found you you'd be dead!" He laughed, and she pretended to laugh with him.

"I meant I'm glad that you found us, because I've missed you, brother."

He was flattered as she hoped he would be. He looked at her a long while, investing her comment with even more meaning.

"I can come and visit you. I can come every day."

"Oh brother, how I wish. But you could be caught and then you would be implicated along with us."

"That's true," he said. "Still, you haven't seen the last of me."

"Be careful when you leave so they do not see you. And soak your body in the stream so they do not smell us on you."

He left thinking about Kileo in a way that he shouldn't have. He thought about her trapped and lonely on top of the mountain. He imagined her dreaming of him returning, the way she used to dream about Raspail returning to Cob Ash. Abillon had always been jealous of Raspail's relationship with her. And now, with the cool months approaching, he imagined visiting his sister again, only this time satisfying himself the way Raspail never had a chance to.

***

Blood, Smoke and Horses

"Kill us not, stay we not, ramblefoots we not, hunt we not, kill us not..."

"Shut up, Balfort," Maddocq said.

Aratus was busily weaving through the elk herd with his mate Othenia when he smelled smoke -- too small to be a threat, but too much, nevertheless, to be ignored.

"Honestly, Maddocq. What happened to the love of a good song? Why I remember the days when you used to beg me to sing."

"Sing. Just don't sing that."

Aratus locked on to his quarry. Othenia approved his judgment, and the hunt began. But it was not more than a moment into the hunt that they heard a series of loud cracking sounds.

The gunshots whipped the grazing elk into a stampede, and Aratus and Othenia suddenly found themselves fighting for their lives as the panicky animals moved over them like an avalanche. Aratus ran against the herd, diving under the legs of fleeing elk, and was knocked over and kicked in the groin. Othenia made the wiser choice of running with the flow of the herd and splintered away, escaping the throng of frenzied elk with no injury.

Aratus got back on his feet and led them quickly to camp. As they approached, they smelled blood, smoke, and horses.

The smell got thicker as they neared the den. Othenia barked to her sisters but there was no response. Maddocq entered the den first. At the end of the tunnel he could see eight of the pups. None of them moved or breathed, dead as they were. In his fury he did not see the traps set on the ground.

Aratus heard Maddocq shrieking and ran into the den where he saw him biting frantically at the metal jaws that had closed on his front ankle. Aratus saw the other traps just as Balfort charged in.

"Stay out!" Aratus cried at him.

Maddocq threw his weight against the heavy chain that held the trap in the dirt. He heaved against it again and again, ignoring the immeasurable pain, and yanked the iron spike that rooted it to the ground free. He bolted past Aratus and out of the den.

Maddocq collapsed outside the den and attacked the trap with his blunted teeth, trying to free himself from the lifeless jaws, desperate and determined to not let his fate end like that of the dead facet he'd discovered.

Balfort and the younger males howled mournfully, adding to the atmosphere of hysteria. As a last resort, Maddocq wrapped his massive jaws around his foreleg and experienced pain that was usually reserved for enemies. In a moment the worst of it was over and he was free from the trap, passed out on the ground

Aratus followed the smell of smoke to a glowing red ember in the dirt. Its flame was dying, but smoke -- the smoke he had smelled earlier -- still emanated from it. He moved away from it and raised his nose, shutting his eyes and tucking his ears in. He sniffed at the air and smelled the smoke in the distance. It would not be difficult to follow.

He barked at the young brothers, "Stay here and tend his wound -- don't let him move!"

Aratus, Othenia and Balfort followed the trail of the smoke, traveling to the southeastern border of their territory and beyond. They were finally close enough to hear and smell horses. They climbed to an overlook where they could see them.

There were four horses with riders. Behind one of the riders Othenia's lifeless sisters were stacked on top of each other. Another rider traveled with a cage that contained some of their pups, still alive, inside. Aratus could not see their faces, but recognized their squeals as those of his children. The overwhelming agony of being impotent to protect them afflicted Aratus with a pain in his heart as great as the jolt Maddocq endured amputating his own foot. The only relief he could fathom would be saving them, and so he leaped forward and raced towards his children, which, if he weren't blinded by pain and sadness, he would have known was suicide. Fortunately Balfort and Othenia caught up with him and tackled him to the ground. He fought with them to release him, biting his mate and kicking Balfort in the face, until Othenia said fiercely to him through tears of her own:

"Get your children back, but not stupidly and with anger in your head."

***

Where The Scent took Aratus and Othenia

What Aratus and Othenia beheld as they followed the path of the men on horses was so incomprehensible, so alien and disturbing, they could barely fix their stares on it.

Death was everywhere, hanging from fences, walls, and carriages. The sheer multitude of wolves on display would have been a marvel on its own, for Aratus could not have imagined that this many wolves existed in all the provinces. And here they were dead, strung from their heads next to each other, organized neatly in rows upon rows, and where there was no room left to hang them, they were stacked on top of another, their black eyes looking back emptily at Aratus wherever he went. He could not look back at their horrific stares and kept his eyes on the ground before him.

The sight of dead wolves was nothing Aratus hadn't witnessed before. He had seen wolves in many of death's grotesque poses, but death never posed them in such a fashion as this, one after another, preserved from the onslaught of scavengers. This defied nature and his understanding of it, and crippled him with anxiety. He looked at Othenia and saw she was trembling pitifully.

And so the couple's concern for their brood was overshadowed by this huger terror, this hell they'd followed the men into. As brave and clever as Aratus was, he knew he was no match for *This*. There was nothing he could do to penetrate this terrifying scourge and rescue his sons and daughters. Here before him was the entire population of wolves staring at him from the other side of life, warning him, *Get out of here while you can.*

Aratus, with his tail curled between his legs, his back hunched in shame, and his strong rear legs trembling in fear like a child's, turned and led Othenia back along the route they'd come on, secreting through the timbers along the plain.

They traveled with heavy hearts, barely feeling their hunger until Othenia caught the scent of meat and ran to it. Aratus, not far behind her, heard the sharp sound of the trap shutting followed by her shriek of pain. When he reached her, he saw the trap on her leg. She struggled to extricate herself from the vicious jaws, but the more she moved the more the jaws dug in. She eventually stopped moving and looked into Aratus' eyes as she whined in pain, begging him for help.

There was nothing Aratus could do but share the deep wrenching pain that his mate was feeling, as if this would somehow lessen it for her. She said nothing for hours, just moaned helplessly.

The wolf has but one instrument for healing injury and pain, and that is its tongue. So Aratus licked her legs and face with unbridled commitment, but her eyes were focused beyond him, on their way to becoming the black, empty stare of the wolves he'd just seen.

When night ended and the sun rose, birds were gathering above them in anticipation of her death.

Aratus smelled the man coming.

He inched back from Othenia, but was so gravitated to her dying body he was unable to leave her side. He lay down next to her and waited with foreboding. He heard the horse, then saw its rider guide it to the timbers where the man got off and walked towards them.

He could not face the creature as it approached, so great was his fear of it. It spoke directly to him as it walked closer, as if expecting him to understand it. Aratus, paralyzed by grief mixed with fear, did not flee. Something dropped on his head, and as he flinched back the loop of rope tightened around his neck. Aratus, compelled to run at this sensation, choked as he reached the end of the tether, with the man holding the other end. He gasped for air as he watched the man open the trap with his feet and pull out Othenia. He dragged her body by the tail to his horse, where he hoisted her up and draped her across the animal's broad back. The man then mounted the horse and with one hand holding the long rope tied around Aratus' neck, rode quickly, forcing the wolf to run at his pace or be dragged and choked to death.

***

The Brave Rescue

It was the middle of the hot season, when the sun won back dominance of the sky and pulled back the cloak of darkness under which ramblefoots plundered the riches of man. This factor, along with the increasing haste in which Ramblefoots had to leave the side of a good meal to avoid getting killed, meant getting meatdrunk was harder than in the winter and spring.

This irked Raspail. Through his kinship with Poitu he had adopted the thinking process of a raven, which is to say when he faced a challenge he focused all his cunning on cracking that challenge.

So after much trial and error he figured out he could drive the cows towards the mountains where he could feast in the safety of the timbers. No longer did he have to eat the cow where it died -- which usually meant in the open plateau with nowhere to kloot. Now he could make it die and fall where he wanted to eat it.

This approach to hunting was quickly adopted by others, and the number of mortalities in the area diminished. Where ramblefoots were dying as quickly as they were arriving, now their numbers were growing.

Raspail, who had turned down their invitation to be facet, could do nothing about the fact that whenever some problem or conflict came up, he was the default wolf they went to for a solution. Such was the case on the day that three wolves ran up to Raspail and Hagi barking a confusing litany of hysterical claims that made no sense. Raspail and Hagi followed them a ways to an empty den that was located so close to the plateau that no wolf claimed it. Huddled around the entrance of the den were ten other wolves, including Repetto, Ipsy and Boonbrekker. They were howling a wretched, heartbreaking cry.

Raspail snarled at the mob to hush them, and in the silence he heard the squeals of infant starvation coming from within the den.

Repetto came to his side, his voice warbling from the morbid sadness in him. "There's six of them! One is dead and the others will be soon! Hear how they starve, I can't take it!"

Raspail circumspectly entered the den with Repetto behind him. He saw the pups, just a few months old, curled together and clamoring for food at the end of the tunnel. Between the pups and him there were six traps, but one of the metal jaws had already closed on the body of one little wolf who had ventured from the birthing chamber.

Repetto began whining, and Raspail snapped at him to be quiet. Hearing Repetto cry made the pups crawl towards them thinking the grown wolves were arriving with food. Raspail's eyes widened in horror as they neared the deadly jaws.

Traps put the fear of all fears in Raspail. They were the most dangerous part of the animal, the jaws and teeth, isolated in terrifying coldness from any sort of body, with no eyes to read or ears to reason with. They were neither dead nor alive, there was no understanding them, they were just pure terror to Raspail, clear and simple.

Crouching low in the tight tunnel, he stepped awkwardly between the unpredictable monsters, thinking that at any moment they might jolt awake and start some feeding frenzy. On his fifth step his bent hock triggered one of the traps and it slammed shut. Raspail quickly raised his leg, but not before the jaws clipped off a hunk of fur from his rear foot.

He stood there frozen on three legs above the traps, blood dripping from his back foot, unsure of what to do next, his confidence dwindling. The pups cried as they walked closer to the traps.

"Go over my back!" he barked at Repetto.

"You gotta crouch lower!"

Raspail crouched as low as he could go without touching the traps. Repetto jumped on his rump and bounded across his broad back. Raspail felt his body cave as the wolf sprang over his spine and land safely on the other side. He grabbed the first pup in his mouth, jumped on Raspail's bowed head and bounded over his back with it, continuing out of the tunnel.

When the desolate onlookers saw Repetto run out with the first pup, they gasped in disbelief. They mobbed Repetto wanting details, but Repetto just dropped the pup and said, "There's more!" and ran back in the den.

He repeated the rescue until only one pup remained. That last pup, anxious from being separated from the others and fearing he was being left alone, aggressively made attempts to cross the traps. Each time he did Raspail flashed fang at him and nudged him back with his nose. Raspail finally cried out:

"REPETTOOOOOOOOOOOO!"

Repetto's claws dug into his croup and he was suddenly climbing up his back and springing over his head into the chamber where he arrived in time to knock the pup over before crawling on to the trap.

Outside, the crowd's suspense was at its zenith as Repetto's mounting achievement approached its grand finale. These normally rowdy, boisterous wolves grew so silent with anticipation that they could hear the heart of that last baby wolf beating. Their hearts all began drumming in sympathy with his little heart, and they imagined with horror the moment that heart stopped beating if fate delivered him into one of those jaws.

When Repetto emerged from the tunnel with that last pup in his mouth, the crowd erupted in rapturous howling. He saw Nin at the front of the crowd of wolves laying on her side nursing the pups.

The last pup dropped from Repetto's mouth and waddled over to this brothers and sisters and wedged his way into the feeding frenzy. Hagi urged the mob to leave the lowlands and return to the safety of the timbers.

Nin herded the rescued pups back to her den where the onlookers reconvened. Repetto basked in his glory, rightfully so, for he had performed a selfless deed in a heroic fashion.

Raspail, however, remained exactly where we last saw him, crouching frozen above the traps with his wounded foot trembling in the air. He could not exit the den backwards for fear of stepping blindly on the traps behind him. The only way out was to continue forward, turn around in the birth chamber, and head out. But he couldn't move, so terrified was he by the prospect of getting caught in the traps.

Maybe a better solution will come as I wait here, he consoled himself. It didn't.

His leg cramped and he accidentally stepped on the trap that he had already triggered. He braced for it to snap at his foot again, but it didn't bite a second time. While he thought about this, he felt his other leg cramping. He had to move. He thought back to the day he tried to reach Hesser's perch and got snagged in the bramble. He fathomed the rush of excitement he'd felt when he leaped into the thorny bushes, empowered by the knowledge that Kileo was watching him. He pretended Kileo was watching him now.

He bolted forward, stepping off traps that had already snapped shut, turned in the chamber, and ran outside the den, greeting the outside air with immense relief.

Once outside, he heard the festive howls garnishing Repetto with praise for his heroic deed. Where any lesser wolf would have said, "But half that glory belongs to me!" Raspail thought, *It looks like I will finally get a decent sleep for once.*

He headed back to his old flop (even though his grander, more accommodating cave awaited him), wanting to fall asleep with the sound of merry howling in his ears.

***

How Raspail and Repetto's Amusement Turned to Disaster

After some time, the party in Repetto's honor came to an end and he returned to his den where the hero was greeted by Nin in the same fashion she greeted his friends, which is to say, very inhospitably. Sobbing, he wandered to Raspail's old leaf pile to flop. There he found Raspail, who refused to wake, but who he told his story to regardless.

Later that night when Raspail woke, Repetto told him the story in earnest. Raspail got a big laugh, after which he immediately invited Repetto to come live in his cave as Repetto had invited him early in their friendship. Repetto jumped around in excitement at the notion of flopping with Raspail, then inexplicably burst into tears. He finally explained, "She let me drink from her teat. Now she will only feed those pups. And I will not get any more of her sweet milk!"

Life in Ramblefoot could not have been more pleasant for Raspail over the next months. The pups were thriving under Nin's obsessive care, and their arrival was seen as a blessing. The area outside Nin's den was rife with well-wishers, and even Nin's demeanor changed, letting the ramblefoots admire her precious pups without a rancorous display of fangs and threats.

Repetto flopped in Raspail's cave every morning when they were done eating. As they waited for sleep to take them, they engaged in ridiculous amusements.

They of course played the game that Repetto excelled at, of weaving between Raspail's legs until he trapped him. They also invented some new games. They barked gibberish that echoed off the curved basalt walls. They took turns, making the calls more and more bizarre and complicated, while the other would try and imitate them until he got tongue-tied. The ensuing laughter, echoing forever, sounded like a hundred happy wolves.

They played tug of war with a long piece of animal viscera they found, and when Poitu perched herself on the taut cord the wolves worked together to shake off the raven. Poitu would hang on until she was flung into the air where she would hover for a moment then come down for more.

Repetto convinced Raspail to play a version of the weaving game in which the bigger wolf had to weave under Repetto. Of course there was no point to this game since Repetto's low torso did not have much room under it, and their first challenge ended with the little wolf sitting on Raspail's head laughing hysterically.

Outside the cave, Hagi eavesdropped on the wolves amusing each other. Their merriment tempted him every day to join them, but because of his fear of caves and dens, he was unable to participate. He often sat at the rim of the crater enjoying their playful sounds, but it was as torturous as smelling meat and being unable to eat it. The mirth was so contagious that Hagi needed either to leave or overcome his fear and enter the underground cave where he could then participate in his friends' antics.

Hagi ultimately could not resist joining them. When he entered the cave, Raspail and Repetto were playing a game in which Raspail stood on a slippery rock partially submerged under water while Repetto would charge at him from the far end of the cave trying to knock the bigger wolf off his perch. They stopped to greet Hagi and applaud him for overcoming his fear of going underground.

Hagi discovered to his surprise that the cave wasn't as oppressive as he had imagined, and his fear and caution quickly subsided. He watched Raspail and Repetto play their weaving game (which was as much fun to be a spectator of as it was to be a participant in), and with the addition of a spectator, the gamesmanship went up twofold.

In Raspail's ardor to trap Repetto he dropped his meat gorged body on the cave floor so hard the ground quaked, but still the little wolf evaded him. Hagi's muscles tightened upon hearing the noise, and he tried to follow the hollow sound as it reverberated eerily around him.

Raspail, his frustration mounting as the game progressed, dropped his body with such force that it cracked the already weakening basalt floor which, unbeknownst to them, was barely thicker than the ice surface of a frozen lake. The thin, brittle floor suddenly shattered and fell away, dropping our heroes through a hole and into another chamber not far below.

When the dust cleared, they could see the new chamber they were in. The remaining ridge of the old floor above was just out of jumping reach. Raspail made several efforts to leap out of the low chamber, but only his forelegs made it over, and as he scrambled to pull himself up, his huge claws scratched furiously to get a foothold, he degraded the crumbling rock even more and fell back to where Hagi and Repetto were.

Hagi was in a panic. "Even if you get out, it don't do us any good! Repetto's too small and I have only three feet!"

Raspail ignored him and jumped again. It was his most successful effort so far, but when he fell back down the force broke the thin floor of that chamber as it had the one above. Again they dropped into another chamber below that one, landing on a heap of rubble.

Hagi was in a frenzy.

"You jump one more facking time I'll --!!" and he bit Raspail hard on the face, making him yelp.

Dim light illuminated their prison. Tunnels and chambers riddled the underground area, with occasional pinpoints of light suggesting ways out if one dared enter the confusing maze.

Raspail began exploring. Behind him Repetto whimpered like a pup and Hagi cursed himself.

"We'll never get out of here! I should never have come down here! I deserve to die!"

As the sun began to set, the thin slivers of light that illuminated the caves subsided and darkness filled the void. Before darkness completely enveloped them, Raspail noticed a series of footprints in some sand that looked familiar. Hagi and Repetto saw him looking at the ground and came over.

In silence they looked at the large prints. They were as big as Raspail's with a stride equal to his, but the toes were melded together like the footprints he remembered seeing near the warmpool that Hagi threw Siksak in. Their terror, which was already quite high, escalated to another level.

"You seen everything, Hagi! What has four feet that don't match?" Repetto asked, his voice quivering.

Hagi didn't answer and Repetto grew more agitated. "Hagi knows everything! And if he don't know what animal that is, it's some kind of monster that's gonna kill us!"

As it grew darker, the dangers of walking became apparent. There were long chutes that dropped from the floor, so if one were to blindly step into one they might drop even deeper into the warren of chambers. With that in mind, they used their last bits of light to find a place to wait out the night. Finding a recess in the wall big enough for the three of them, they huddled with their shivering bodies pressed close together.

None of them had ever experienced darkness as complete as that which they found in the cave. Only the dim light shining from their eyes gave definition to each other's blurry movement but nothing beyond. Hours passed in silence. Finally, a feeling of unease hit each of them simultaneously as they sensed another living creature in their midst watching them. Hagi was the first to acknowledge it.

"You feel it watching us?"

"Shhh. It's on my side, about twenty lengths off." Raspail said.

"No, it's on my side," Repetto said, his voice cracking.

"Repetto -- growl your most fearsome warning, show it we are formidable," Raspail said.

Repetto hesitated, straining to fathom bravery while such terror plagued him.

"What about Hagi? Let him talk to it. Everyone likes Hagi."

"We aren't trying to make friends with it! Do as Raspail says!"

Repetto made a hostile growl that sounded like it came from an animal ten times larger because of the amplification of the cave. They waited for a response, and it came.

"Haaaaaaaaaaaaaagii."

Hagi's blood chilled and his whithers stood so erect they nearly blew out of his back.

"Who are you?!" Hagi barked at it.

"Siiiiiiiiiksaaaaaaaaaaaak," the voice said.

"Siksak is dead!" he shouted in all directions, not knowing where the creature was. "The dead don't speak!"

Raspail could hear Hagi's heart thumping.

"Do you not see me?" it asked.

They saw nothing. In the total darkness of the cave, without any illumination from the sky, their eyes were dazzled by blackness.

"What do you want!" Hagi yelled at it.

"I want to *eat* you!" he proclaimed with frightening honesty. "Meat is all you are to me. I've been living on spiders and lizards. I want meat!"

"Even you wouldn't eat another wolf!" cried Repetto with terror.

"I don't want *your* meat. I want the meat inside your bellies!"

"Kill me already! I can't take it!" sobbed the suffering Hagi, "I can't take any more of this!"

Raspail bit his ear to shut him up.

"Do you see me now?" Siksak hissed.

They couldn't, though his voice was getting closer.

"Now? *Now* do you see me?"

He was very close. They could smell his breath.

Hagi finally cried out uncontrollably with woe in his voice, "Oh, to die in a hole, without the moon over my head, to have my stomach ripped open by my worst enemy and all the delicious meat stolen from it -- it's too much! Hoy, kill me already you sackless bastard!"

"No! When you fall asleep tonight I will come to kill you. All of you."

"We won't sleep then!" Shouted Repetto, thinking he was clever.

"You'll give in to sleep eventually. You're wolves, after all."

***

Hagi Calms Himself by Telling a Story That Reveals a Key to Raspail's Past

Raspail was terrified by Siksak's threatening presence, but compared to Hagi, who was pleading with his enemy to show mercy and kill him, and Repetto, who was crying and whimpering like the pup his tiny stature suggested, he kept the coolest head of the three.

"He was surprised that we couldn't see him," Raspail said to them in a calm whisper, "He can see us, but that is his only advantage. We are three blind wolves, he is one with sight, but that will change as our eyes adjust to the light."

"I'm still blind! It's impossible for a wolf to see down here."

"Siksak is a wolf. He sees because he has been down here longer than us."

"He's a ghost!" said Hagi.

Repetto squirmed between Raspail's forelegs and whimpered, "Ghost? What do you mean he's a ghost?!"

Raspail nipped at both of them. "Keep your heads or we will die! Hagi -- distract us, tell us a story."

Hagi whimpered and cried senselessly, unable to speak anymore. Raspail sighed, then rubbed his skull affectionately against the old wolf's shoulder.

"I should never have let you go in the cave. I know how you hate caves and dens."

Hagi rubbed his head against Raspail. "Will you do me one favor?"

"Of course."

"Would you kill me? Right now? Please?"

"Try and tell us a story. It will distract you, it will calm poor Repetto here, and we need to stay awake till our eyes adjust. It's going to be a long night."

Hagi reluctantly began a story, a good story that he told absolutely terribly. His second story was slightly better. His third story was absorbing and the three wolves started taking their minds off of their dire and terrifying situation. Their eyes had begun adjusting to the severe darkness, and that further helped erode their gloom. Repetto even interrupted the story to point out, "I am starting to see again. I can see you, Hagi, but not Raspail, because his fur is so black."

Raspail began asking Hagi questions, for he needed to be prodded to talk.

Raspail finally asked him, "So Hagi, tell me -- why are you so afraid of going in dens and caves?"

"That reason should be obvious right now."

"And it is. But I am interested in the original incident that put fear in you."

Hagi chuckled to himself. "Now that *is* a good story. Would you like to hear a good one, one I never told before?"

"More than anything in the world besides freedom from this despicable place."

Hagi had never told the story before, so he took a moment to compose the remembrances in his head with a bemused smile on his face.

"I was some bit younger. I'd just lost my foot. I was scared, I don't even know where I was going, I was going nowhere. I found this old den, went inside it looking for shelter. It was empty, or so I thought. Then suddenly these two little yellow eyes open and scared me half to death."

Hagi imitated the eyes opening. Raspail and Repetto were rapt.

"He was a little thing, two months old at most. I gave him some food. I should've know his mother would be back. Anyway, back she comes, drags me out of her den by my tail. I'm outside the den, and I can see her now -- she's this massive gray wolfmother, as big as Raspail."

At this point, Raspail had a strange sensation that he'd heard the story before.

"Hagi, surely this isn't the first time you've told me the story."

"I said I've never told it before. To any wolf."

Repetto, captivated by the story, angrily nudged Raspail, "Let him tell the story!"

"She tells me she's gonna kill me, she's going wolfmother crazy on me like that damn Nin, I got away, but she almost killed me. After that, I never went inside a dark hole, den or cave ever again. Except today, mercy."

Repetto was particularly amused because of the personal reference to Nin. But the story resonated within Raspail more profoundly.

"You're sure this wolfmother was gray?" Raspail asked. Hagi was confused by his question, for it had little to do with the actual story.

"I don't forget anything. She was gray, with a big long muzzle. Rambled down from the north, most likely. Wolves are bigger up north"

"What color was the pup?" Raspail asked.

"I don't know -- who cares?"

"I care. Try and remember!"

"Why, it was as dark inside that den as it is in here. I couldn't see him until his eyes opened--'

"If he was gray, or tan, you would have been able to see him -- just like Repetto could see you and not me in this darkness. The pup must have been black."

"So he was black! Why does it matter?"

"Where is this den? If you had to find it again, could you?"

"Oh, I could, I suppose. But why I would go revisit that damn place I don't know. Especially since we're for sure going to die down here." Then he started another story to prevent Raspail from continuing his inane questioning.

Raspail was beset by a strong emotion that was neither good nor bad. He had on many occasions dreamed of the time before he was adopted into Cob Ash, and one of those dreams Hagi had just described with exacting detail, including the giving of food to the pup. Was it possible that his dream had really happened? Had he met Hagi when he was a pup? And if this were true, what did it mean that the wolfmother he was in the den with was not Cortess -- for the wolf he described was definitely not her, and he knew that Hagi's memory was uncanny.

I asked for a distraction and I got one, he thought to himself with a sigh.

   ***

Deceiving Siksak

Time passed in the blackness with dreary, unreal slowness. Raspail, who felt even more vulnerable in the situation without Poitu to watch over him, remained hyper-vigilant.

He guessed it was halfway through the night, and already he was able to see six lengths ahead of him, though with very little detail. It was exhausting, mindbending tedium trying to pick Siksak out of the grainy darkness, and Raspail could finally empathize with Hagi's wish to be put out of his misery. So when he finally saw the misshapen silhouette of Siksak enter the large chamber as quiet as a breeze, he was more relieved than frightened.

"He is approaching from my right but don't look directly. Let us pretend we are still blind," Raspail said in a voice so faint it was only a sliver above a thought. They obeyed and resisted the temptation to turn their heads or whimper in fear.

"Oh misery -- If only we could see!" Repetto clamored with acting skills that Raspail thought rivaled Hesser, mainly because he managed to cry it without revealing his chattering teeth. "I can barely see the top of my nose! How will we know when he is come to kill us!?"

"Maybe he has left, mercy." Hagi said with respectable enough believability to keep their ruse going. "Yes, maybe he's changed his mind and won't kill us after all!"

"I'll bet you anything he just wanted to terrorize us. Wolves like Siksak are cowards, they just flash fang, they don't use them. No, an ass like Siksak is probably hiding from us in fear right now!"

Siksak was maybe four lengths close now and completely fooled by their ruse. Their vision allowed them to see the new form which Siksak had taken since his "death."

Before we describe what a wolf who falls into a pit of boiling water looks like if he survives, let us try and imagine the inexorable pain Siksak suffered. It was a pain so intense that to Siksak it seemed like a lifetime of hurt was being heaped on him in one blow. This surge of pain lasted but an instant before the nerves in his skin were melted, and after that he was rewarded with a body that would never feel pain again other than the discomfort of hunger.

The scalding water, in addition to melting his nerves, bonded his fur and skin together into a molten, impermeable mass. It was this outer shell which miraculously protected him from death. When he emerged from the hellish pit, he rolled his tortured body in sand and rocks, unwittingly and permanently embedding the detritus from the earth's floor into the new fabric that surrounded his body.

What Hagi and Repetto could see of him from the corner of their eyes with their limited vision was terrifying.

Hagi was so full of anxiety he was unable to keep the ruse going a second longer. He lunged at Siksak. The deformed wolf, thinking they were still bind, was caught by surprise.

Raspail and Repetto jumped on Siksak and helped Hagi wrestle him to the ground. Repetto drove his sharp fangs into his neck, but sharp as they were, they could not fully penetrate the thick, reconstituted hide. Siksak whined in submission, not from the pain, which he did not feel, but from fear of death.

This was a far cry from the old Siksak, the intimidating browbeater. He cried so pathetically that, as inclined as they were to kill him, the sympathy they felt overwhelmed their better judgment and they let him plead his case.

"Mercy! Haven't you done enough to me already! Look at me! Look what has become of me!" He hardly needed to invite them to stare, transfixed as they were by his hideous appearance.

Hagi said, "Why should we let you live! You wanted to kill us and eat the meat in our stomachs! Eh?!"

"I know the underground routes. I can show you a way out of here. If you kill me, you'll die too."

Raspail considered this.

"I say kill him!" Repetto said.

Raspail pressed down hard on Siksak's neck with his foot "Show us a way out of here and *maybe* we will spare your life."

Siksak looked grateful at the acceptance of his offer.

"But if for any moment I think you are tricking us--"

Siksak looked suitably intimidated. "Mercy, no. I will show you a way out. But we must wait till sunrise. Sun needs to shine through the holes to navigate."

They waited in silence while making sure that Siksak, who they depended on for survival, did not escape. As soon as the first weak shafts of light began stabbing the darkness, Raspail kicked Siksak to get him moving.

"A little meat, mercy? There's three of you. Surely one of you can cough up a little meat?"

Raspail flashed fang at him and he rose quickly to his feet. As he led them through the maze of narrow basalt tunnels, Raspail could smell where Siksak had marked routes with his piss.

Siksak sidled next to Repetto and inhaled his exhaled breath.

"I bet you pack it in, little wolf. I smell that tasty meat inside your tiny belly."

Repetto snarled at him and he backed away.

Whenever they passed a spider web, Siksak delicately extracted the insect and whatever victims were stuck in the web. Hagi tried keeping track of the number of spiders and lizards he ate along the way but it went beyond the highest number he could count to, which was 26.

Unlike the night, which seemed to go on endlessly, the day moved exceedingly quickly with the sun setting before they'd found the cave's exit. They stopped and chose a place to flop. When they settled in, Raspail assured the others he would stay awake all night and keep watch over the prisoner, and the exhausted wolves who had not slept in two days gladly accepted his offer.

Repetto curled on his side and tried to sleep. He immediately sensed something alarming and opened his eyes. Siksak was staring lustfully at his belly with drool dangling from his glossy lips.

"He's staring at my stomach!" Repetto cried.

"Sleep, Repetto. He won't bother you."

Repetto turned, curling his body protectively around his stomach. He still felt the monster staring at him.

It was torture for Raspail to stay awake. The other wolves, including Siksak, were sleeping soundly and their snoring, echoing through the caves, lulled him into a relaxed state that eventually led to sleep.

"Aaaaaaaaaagh, son of a bitch!!" Repetto screeched.

Raspail woke and jumped to his feet. Siksak stood over Repetto, pinning him down. He spit out a mouthful of Repetto's belly fur, then prepared to lunge at his gut.

Raspail knocked the beast off him just in time, sending him hard against the wall.

"He tried taking my meat!" Repetto sobbed like a traumatized child, over and over.

Siksak licked Repetto's blood off his lips with gusto.

"Like the taste of blood, do you?" Raspail asked. Before Siksak could answer he lashed him, his strong jaws puncturing the monster's armor-like hide above his neck. Once he hit a vein, he pumped it and splattered his blood on the ground

"There. Eat your own blood."

To Raspail's shock, Siksak did just that.

The night was interminable and Raspail, who promised he would not fall asleep again, again failed at keeping his promise. Sunlight finally filtered in through cracks and holes, and Raspail saw immediately that the angled basalt wall they were sleeping against offered escape from the cave. He sighed in relief and looked back at the others.

Siksak was gone.

"Bastard got away before we could finish him off," Hagi said regretfully.

Raspail nodded in agreement with him, but in truth he did not care whether Siksak was executed or not. Their imprisonment had come to an end, and freedom awaited him.

***

Raspail's Request

The three wolves burst from the hole and into the light of day as if being born a second time. Raspail ran in circles like an idiot, and Repetto chased him.

Hagi, who in his youth had spent days in a metal trap unable to move until he bit his own foot off, knew that freedom was best appreciated by those who had lost it and then rediscovered it. He let his friends run in celebration while he looked up at the sky and saw the last remnants of the moon in the morning sky and moaned gratefully to the ancestors, who were watching with a half-closed eye.

Poitu, who was waiting perched on the ridge of Raspail's cave, flew over and joined them, diving around them biting their tails. When they were finished, the three wolves parted ways and Raspail returned with Poitu to his old flop, so exhausted he felt like he could sleep for a week.

He felt another wolf in the pile and kicked it. It was Boonbrekker, with Ipsy flopping near him.

Boonbrekker asked him where he and Hagi had been. Raspail grumpily told him to ask Hagi later. He added that it might be the greatest Hagi story yet, and that if he were to tell it now, tired as he was, he would not do it justice.

Boonbrekker whimpered anxiously to hear this incredible story no matter how poorly it was to be told.

Raspail warned him that if he or anybody else pestered him or woke him, he would kill them. Boonbrekker was pretty sure it wasn't just an idle threat, so he prodded Raspail no further and left the flop accompanied by Ipsy.

Raspail lay in the soft, crunchy bedding and stretched out, inviting each and every fly, ant and spider to come have a bite of him.

By the time darkness fell, Boonbrekker had spread the word that a great story -- maybe even the *greatest* --was about to be told by Hagi. Hagi was woken by fourteen anxious wolves begging to hear the story. He said he would oblige them after stretching and taking his morning drink and piss.

They hung on every expression and imitation Hagi made as he told the story. Their cackling and gasps of amazement attracted even more wolves until there were twenty-one rapt wolves hovering around him attentively. When Hagi reached the end of the story, he was asked to repeat the first half by those who arrived late and missed it.

Raspail joined the group at this point and was greeted as a hero, for Hagi made sure that his audience knew that of the three captives only Raspail kept his cool during the nightmare, while Repetto and he were scatter-headed with fear, whimpering for death to swiftly take them. It was Raspail who outwitted the terrifying, deformed Siksak and freed them.

Once again, his notoriety grew.

The trio's successful escape from the hole was of course more than enough cause for celebration. The night was an orgy of meats that lasted till sunrise without any of them getting killed. Hagi was drunkenly performing an imitation of Siksak eating spiders for three laughing wolves when he saw Raspail watching him with a serious facade, waiting for a word. He excused himself and walked over.

"You and I are going to ramble," he told the old wolf. "You're taking me to the den that wolfmother dragged you out of."

"I am, am I? And for what benefit would that be?"

"Do you remember where it is?"

"If I lie and tell you I've lost all memory of its whereabouts, would you believe me?"

"No, your memory is perfect. Hagi, you must do this for me."

Hagi looked as confused as he felt.

"I would do anything for you, Raspail. Just say when you want to leave and I will lead the way."

"We leave now."

"Now?!" Hagi cackled. "I may have entered your cave old of body and young at heart, but I came out three years older which means I am practically dead." He waited until Raspail stopped laughing, then said, "You can laugh all you like -- I'm not the only one changed by the fright of that adventure. Look at your ruff."

Raspail looked down at his ruff. Indeed, the massive collar of fur had received a shock of silver that formed a simple cottonwood leaf-shaped crest below his neck. Though not as ornate as Draguignon's or as exciting as Kileo's, it was a mark of distinction on his otherwise monotone coat. He was fascinated by it, even proud.

"It will take at least four days of slow, careful travel if we are to arrive there alive," Hagi said. "If you rush me along the way, I'll only drag my three feet and make us take six days."

"We go at your pace. You have my word, Hagi."

At that, they walked away from the last remaining revelers. Raspail followed Hagi, who, true to his word, kept a tedious pace that seemed twice as slow because of his nagging anticipation.

Repetto heard about them rambling north and, feeling bonded to them by their last adventure, caught up with them even if it meant leaving the "walking meat", as they now all called it. He was easy company, eager to help them and keep their spirits up, and they were both glad he'd joined them.

The three wolves talked little along the way, each of them enjoying the silence. Raspail let Hagi concentrate on the route without begging for stories.

Hagi reached a crossroads where his sense of direction failed him. He cursed his aging mind for losing its ability to recollect, as well as his noisy stomach for drowning out what few thoughts he was able to recollect. He asked Raspail and Repetto to let him be alone.

Repetto wanted to sleep. Raspail wandered off and hunted an elk brought to his attention by Poitu. Repetto, who could not sleep, went looking for Raspail and found him bringing down the elk. He ran immediately back to Hagi to tell him excitedly what he'd just witnessed:

"Hagi, he hunted and killed an elk on his own! Hagi, you have to see! It happened like *that!* Hagi--!"

Hagi, who was trying to concentrate, showed his irritation at being interrupted.

"He hunts with that damn raven. You didn't know that you idiot?"

The poor little wolf was hoping to hear Hagi say, "Impossible! I must see! Thank you for telling me!" Instead, he received a verbal lashing and was called an idiot. Repetto, whose mood was already fouled by hunger, resented Hagi at that moment and refused to believe his preposterous explanation.

"He doesn't hunt with no raven! Fack off!"

"Why else would he travel with a raven?!"

Repetto's hackles sprang up, his eyes widened and his lip quivered.

"I'm not no idiot!" Repetto barked at him. "You think you're smart, and I'm some idiot?!"

Repetto angrily sprung at Hagi. The two rolled around in the dirt until Repetto, suddenly feeling at fault for starting a pointless fight, rolled on his back and cried for the elder to forgive him.

Hagi's blood was up and he needed to take out his temper on him. So rather than accept his submission as an apology and let the matter drop, he goaded the hot-tempered runt on so that he could lash him to his full satisfaction.

With mean spirit he said, *'I'm the little baby, don't hurt the baby."*

Hagi was harkening to something in Repetto's past, before he'd gotten over his fear of hunting big prey. In those early days he socialized with ramblefoots and challenged them to the game that we have seen. If they failed, they shared a bit of their meat with him. If they trapped him -- which rarely happened -- they quickly released him and enjoyed the praise of their friends.

One day, a big wolf accepted Repetto's challenge and adroitly pinned Repetto under his massive weight and wouldn't release him. Repetto gasped and strained to move while the big wolf howled for more wolves to come over so he could show off his prowess.

On the verge of dying, Repetto cried pathetically, "I'm just a little baby, don't hurt the baby."

He broke four ribs squirming free from under his sprawling oppressor. He crawled into the timbers and was amazed when he woke that night to see that he wasn't dead. He waited three days for his body to heal.

On the fourth day, the big wolf was eating a calf with two other ramblefoots when Repetto appeared beneath him, scrambling between his legs, playing his game again, laughing with good cheer. The big, meatdrunk wolf took the challenge and, not knowing that revenge had been brewing in his small opponent, underestimated him. He plummeted his torso to the ground, then looked down expecting to see Repetto there. Not only was he not on top of the runt, but the runt was on top of him, slashing his neck. Repetto did not have the jaw strength to mortally crush his opponent's throat, but he could bleed him to death, and that is what he did. After lacerating his throat in front of the two other wolves, he waited for the big wolf to expire, then took his position at the carcass, eating the meat that had been his victim's.

So when Repetto heard those pathetic words that he said on that humiliating day, his anger turned black.

"I never said that! That's a lie! It ain't true! Take it back or I'll kill you!"

"I'm a little baby, don't hurt the baby!"

Repetto launched himself at Hagi and resumed the fight. While the two hungry wolves went at it the smell of fresh meat hovered past them. With no real grievance to settle or stakes to be won, the two fighters quickly made peace and ran to join Raspail by the elk carcass.

Repetto filled his stomach with meat while staring at Poitu with new respect.

"If ever this big dumb black slob be mean to you, you come right to Repetto, I take care of you."

Poitu kawed back at him and they all had a laugh. Full stomachs of meat not only restored their good spirits but revived Hagi's memory as well, allowing him to regain his bearings.

After they rested, Hagi charted an indirect route that took them through provinces where he was known and would be welcomed. But this terrain, like so many others, had vanishing scent posts. Worse still was the absence of wolf howls. Coyotes howled a discomforting greeting to them:

> *Welcome wolves*
> *Come on through*
> *They won't catch us*
> *But they will catch you.*

For the three heroes who survived the fright of the cave, courage was not in short supply. Nevertheless, they traveled anxiously and without pausing, eager to be back in the realm of wolves and not ghosts.

Having traveled all night without hearing a single wolf howl, they became sullen and Hagi made them rest by a stream noisy enough to fill the void left by missing wolves.

The trip, which Hagi had warned would take four days, took just two and a half.

***

The Old Den and the Faded Memory

The den was exactly as Hagi had last seen it. Raspail stared into the dirt tunnel.

"Worth the trip, I'm sure," Hagi said sarcastically, because there was nothing exceptional about this hole in the ground, even to Raspail, who had been so eager to gaze upon it.

"We shall see," he said.

He entered the tunnel, crouching low as his statuesque mother had long ago, and walked three lengths till he reached the birthing chamber at the end. He sniffed at the bed of leaves hoping to recognize something, but it bore the smell of dozens of animals who had taken refuge in the den since that day years ago.

He lowered his hulking body and curled up on the leaves. With closed eyes he tried to conjure the faded dream that he often had when he was young, that of being alone in a den and being confronted by a wolf with a missing foot who seemed both scary stranger and benevolent kin. He drifted off to sleep in the dark birthing chamber, hoping to revisit the dream. Instead he dreamed of Kileo, a vivid, violent dream that he could not wake himself from.

Outside the den, Repetto was tormented by the nightmarish sounds of Raspail whinnying in his sleep.

"You gotta wake him from that," he told Hagi.

"I ain't never going in another hole long as I live. You go."

"This is between you and him. Don't you hear how sick his sleep is?"

Hagi knew he was right. He timidly entered the tunnel, quiet on his feet so as not to startle the sleeping wolf.

Hagi's vaporous entry into the cave registered in Raspail's sleeping head, and his violent nightmare mutated into the visit he was paid as a pup by the strange three-footed wolf.

His eyes burst open and he saw Hagi in the dark tunnel staring at him with worry. In that instant, the oddly familiar sensation he felt upon seeing Hagi in the den confirmed his suspicion; what he thought was a dream was in fact something real that had happened to him. Flush with excitement, he charged at Hagi. Hagi awkwardly retreated backwards out of the tunnel sure that the possessed wolf was going to kill him.

"Damn holes!" Hagi cried.

Raspail tackled Hagi outside the and affectionately licked his face the way a pup licks his father, then said in a voice that was loud in emotion if not in volume:

"It was me!"

Hagi was confused.

"The pup in the den -- the one you found here -- it was me, Hagi! That pup in your story was me!"

"Impossible."

"The wolfmother who attacked you must have been my mother. That means Cortess, who weaned me as her own, and who forever I will love with every beat of my heart, was not my flesh and blood. Which means..." and the thought of it excited him so much he had to take a deep breath before continuing with exuberance:

"Kileo is not my sister*! She isn't my sister, Hagi!"*

He ran like he had the scatters, bouncing and jumping in the air. His mood was contagious, and Repetto and Poitu joined him without understanding his reason for celebration. Hagi slowly tried to make sense of it all, but it wasn't until the moon came out that Raspail could stop running and jumping and settled down to tell them the significance of this amazing revelation.

He told them about his sister Kileo, who he loved in the way that a brother is not supposed to love his sister, about his despair over realizing that he could never mate with her, and about how he was muted by Hesser and forgotten by his pack members. Only through his unbreakable bond with Poitu, who kept him fed and played with him during this miserable isolation, did he manage to survive and keep his sanity.

Finally, he told them about the murder of Cob Ash, his facet and father, which was blamed on him. Forced to ramble, he met Hagi, and the rest they knew.

"Hoy," said Hagi, impressed with the story.

"Hoy is right."

Raspail looked at Hagi, indebted.

"So you see your story, which was meant to distract us in a time of stress and despair, has shined a beam of light as bright as the sun's on my life." Raspail respectfully lowered his eyes from Hagi's gaze. "You once said you hoped your sons, if you'd known them, would have been like me. I share that sentiment with you. I would like to imagine that the father I did not know was a wolf with as true a heart as you."

They all cried together, howling a melancholy ode to their friendship. When they were done, Raspail spoke again.

"I have no choice but to find Kileo now." Raspail said to them. "I must go back to Cob Ash and get her."

"They gonna kill you! To them you're some traitor!" Repetto barked. "Oh, that Hesser, he gonna kill you real good now you can talk!"

"Repetto is right. You can't ever go back."

"To not go back -- to continue living without her and with the knowledge I now possess would be punishment worse than being trapped in that black cave with Siksak." Hagi tried to interrupt him, but Raspail kindly stopped him. "No words that either of you can say will change my mind; so, mercy, let us say our farewells now, for if I have to wait another second I think I will go scattermad."

Neither of them said another word or whine.

Raspail turned and started on his way to Cob Ash, Poitu taking her position in the sky above him.

Repetto bounded underneath him and emerged before him, blocking his passage.

"You don't go without another wolf looking out for you, no way, that's just facking stupid."

Raspail nudged him appreciatively. "You need to keep Hagi company on the way back to Ramblefoot."

"Ah, what's to do there anyways but get drunk all night and sleep all day."

Raspail sighed knowing that they would not let him take the journey without them. Poitu dropped out of the sky and landed on his shoulders.

"I have my little black angel looking over me. You don't need to come."

"Ah, that's where you're wrong. You can't feed a story-teller the first half of the greatest story he's ever heard and then starve him of its ending."

***

Book III:

FACET

The Law of the Facet

The wolf who needs to feel important seeks to be facet so that others will respect him.

The wolf who has trouble getting what he wants seeks to be facet so that he has power.

The wolf who suffers under a lesser wolf's law seeks to be facet so that he has freedom.

But the wolf who does not yearn for respect, who has no trouble taking what he wants and deserves, and who knows true freedom -- that rare wolf is sure to earn respect, get all that he wants, and enjoy unbridled freedom through his life without seeking to be anything other than *what he already is.*

✳✳✳

How a Raven Pushes Two Mountains Together

The three wolves meandered along the south-western edge of the mountain looking for a vantage point to peer down at Cob Ash from. Falling snow limited their visibility in the high mountain.

"I guess you, me, and Hagi -- we like some little pack, huh?" Repetto said.

Raspail did not hear him, preoccupied as he was with a horrible, anxious thought that had begun, pleasurably enough, in the membranes of his huge, flaring nose.

It was an itch -- a pleasant itch -- that he savored without scratching. The itch traveled from his nose down to his groin, making his head whirl with arousing thoughts of Kileo. They were in the middle of the cold months, and the air was thick with the perfume of bitches attracting mates.

Repetto began laughing next to him, "You should see it growing down there!"

Raspail looked down and saw his lurid thoughts had unsheathed his "fifth leg".

The perfume had its effect on Repetto too, and when Raspail saw his little friend's fifth leg unsheathing, the pleasantry of the moment dissipated and he was seized by anxiety: *Every wolf in Warmpools will smell my bitch's irresistible perfume and desire her for themselves. If I do not act quickly, another wolf will take Kileo before me.*

This thought, combined with Repetto's innocent laughter, chafed the already impatient Raspail. He looked at the little wolf with the swinging fifth leg and saw not his loyal friend but a lecherous competitor for Kileo. With flashing fangs he lunged at him and lashed him with jealous fury.

Repetto was terrified and confused by Raspail's attack. Hagi separated them and looked at Raspail for an explanation. But Raspail was himself confused by his violent and unwarranted reprisal and said nothing, embarrassed as he was. Hagi led Repetto away, seeing that Raspail needed to be alone

When the clouds became transparent enough to afford Raspail a view of the land below, he stood and gazed down upon the two valleys between the mountains that were Cob Ash and

Draguignon, respectively. He had so many emotions for Cob Ash they cancelled each other out, all except one, and that was the feeling that he abandoned Kileo in this place.

Howls rippled like a wave from western Cob Ash to eastern Draguignon. Raspail felt uneasy. They were communicating with each other, these ancient enemies, as if they were one united territory. He recognized the voices of Polwin and Moorea blending harmoniously with the detestable sounds of their eastern neighbors. It did not make sense. And there was something else disconcerting; he could not hear Kileo's voice with the others.

Poitu heard noise and leaped into the sky, saw it was Hagi and Repetto, then croaked to herald their return. Raspail read on their eager faces that they brought new information.

"You picked a fine place to return to." Hagi said.

"There's joking in your voice." Raspail said.

"Yes, but it is no joke what we saw."

Repetto continued for him, describing small packs of large, menacing wolves patrolling the southern border. They witnessed a remnant pack of wolves trying to trespass. The howling that Raspail heard was the call to arms that brought three of these patrols together, eight wolves in all, to slaughter the three intruders and sling their guts along the border as a warning to others.

The uncontrollable optimism that surged through Raspail as he stormed from the cave with the knowledge that Kileo wasn't his sister was hard to maintain. Upon seeing Cob Ash, hostile and impenetrable, the old anxiety and fear returned, and it weighed heavily on him. He wanted to sleep and wake up feeling exalted again, and so he lied down in the snow and slept with Hagi and Repetto curled up pressed against him.

While he slept, Poitu occupied herself with two intruding ravens, chasing them away from her wolves. After they fled, she continued to circle in the sky above Cob Ash. As she hovered close to the low mountain she recognized Navarin, Carel and the other young wolves whom she and Raspail played with when they lived in Cob Ash. During that time, Raspail made them respect the raven, allowing her to play with the infants, and Poitu developed a bond with them.

When she landed amongst them, they stopped playing and stared at her. Carel darted at her, and she leaped in the air and landed on her back, trilling in her ear. In a moment, the five wolves were playing with the raven like she were an old friend. Kileo, who had been watching the massacre of the intruders from Carel's perch, came down to see what all the noise was about.

When she saw the raven playing with them, her heart beat quickly. She approached the black bird.

Poitu hopped into the air, landing on a boulder where she could safely look down at the gray wolf. Kileo looked up into the raven's black eyes, astonished.

"You're the raven who watches Raspail, aren't you?"

Whatever Kileo was expecting as a response, all she received was a silent stare. She eventually gave up on the ludicrous notion and turned her back on the raven. She took two steps then felt the raven peck her in the loin. She swiveled around and saw the raven hop back from her, a clump of her creamy gray fur held firmly in her black bill.

The raven then hopped into the sky and flew away. Kileo ran to Carel's perch and locked on to the raven as she flew above Cob Ash, past Draguignon, and descended into the tall mountains.

Raspail woke abruptly to Poitu frantically flapping her wings in his face. This was as serious as her alarms got and Raspail reacted accordingly, jumping to his feet, klooting in the shadows and scanning the area for trouble. When he detected nothing warranting such vigilance, he looked back at Poitu and saw that she had something clutched in her bill. She pressed the fur into the snow in front of him. He dropped his nose into the fur and immediately recognized it. The exaltation he hoped would return had come.

"Where did you get this?!"

Poitu hopped close to his face as if to whisper to him, then pecked at the long hairs that gathered inside the hollow of his ear and plucked them out. Clutching them tightly in her bill as she had Kileo's fur, she launched into the sky. Raspail watched her soar over Cob Ash and descend into the timbers of the low mountain. His eyes scanned the mountainside, hoping to discern something at the furthest limits of his vision. Like Kileo, he kept his eyes fixed on where Poitu landed.

Kileo, who was watching the mountainside, saw the raven returning. Navarin and Carel were fighting behind her and she snapped at them to be quiet. Her heart felt like it was going to explode out of her chest as the raven glided closer. She wondered, *What game is this raven playing with me?*

Poitu landed in front of Kileo and she saw that the bird still had the fur in its mouth. Before the disappointment had time to smother the spark of hope in her heart, she saw that the fur was too dark to be hers. It was, in fact, black. Poitu pressed the fur into the snow and hopped back as she had done for Raspail. Kileo dived forward and sniffed furiously at the long hairs before the wind took them away. She licked the last hairs -- hairs she had licked hundreds of times -- and was absolutely certain they were Raspail's.

Raspail stood as close to the edge of the mountain as he could. So determinedly did he search for Kileo on the mountain that his weary eyes formed shapes and patterns out of shadows.

Then he saw the tiniest movement. He stopped breathing to steady his head -- there appeared to be an animal pacing on a ledge. Now, if he did not have all the other supporting evidence provided by Poitu he would have never invested himself in making so much out of such an undefined blur, such a smidgen of motion. But knowing what he did, and knowing how Poitu, who loved mischief, would never make mischief with his heart, he continued boring into that faint dot and felt it boring into him with equal if not greater intensity.

It seemed impossible that he could be staring into the eyes of Kileo again. He looked away just to refresh his eyes and give the animal on the other mountain an opportunity to move on (if it were not in fact Kileo). He then looked back at the other mountain and saw that she was still there staring at him.

For her part, Kileo, who had better vision than Raspail, recognized those things which make a fellow animal recognizable in the absence of fine detail, and those things are gleaned from its unique posture and gait. Raspail stood and walked like no other wolf. So embossed were these traits in Kileo's memory that it took very little motion on Raspail's part to convey to her from across the huge plain that it was he.

The two wolves stared at each other silently for a period that transcended measurement. Time had stopped, essentially, and the moment belonged to them alone as they communicated, each hoping that the other could hear their thoughts and deep feelings of love and sorrow and hope. Then Raspail felt a peculiar impulse to stay where he was and wait for her, even if it took days or weeks, and that under no circumstance should he try and go to her. This impulse to wait for her ran counter to every instinct he had. And so even though he could not hear her voice, he felt she had spoken to him and told him to be cautious and wait.

Two mountains, spanning the distance of two wolf territories, had been moved together in this sublime moment, and if their moist noses were rubbing they would not have been any closer than they were right now.

***

The Facet of Ramblefoot

Repetto and Hagi heard wolves coming quickly and quietly approached Raspail, who they saw was transfixed by something. He did not heed them, even as the marching got closer, so Repetto and Hagi, unable to wait any longer, ran off leaving the immovable Raspail at mountain's edge in the state we have just described.

In short time a patrol of wolves passed behind where Raspail was rooted to the ground like the trees on either side of him. He heard the wolves stop and turn with the precision of a unified hunting party, and he felt them lock their gazes on him.

The patrol, which consisted of Polwin and two female Draguignon wolves, cautiously approached the big black wolf who kept his tail to them, ignoring them like they were insignificant.

What arrogance, Polwin thought, *That a wolf would appear so aloof in such a vulnerable situation, showing me his tail, when he is in such obvious danger.*

"You! Turn around and look at me if you can!" He said.

It anguished Raspail to break the connection with Kileo. He turned slowly and faced Polwin, staring directly into his eyes.

While Polwin scrutinized the arrogant beast, Raspail did the same of his opponent. Polwin had been eating well, and his size had increased. He had tasted the blood of many wolves in his role as master of the patrol, and he was full of swagger.

The two bitches flanking Polwin flashed fang and kept their muscles tightly sprung.

"You remind me of a brother I had. A mute brother."

"What happened to this mute brother of yours?" Raspail said with composure.

Polwin reacted with surprise to the low, hushed voice, for it not only proved that this wolf could speak, but it sounded nothing like the voice of Raspail before he'd lost it.

"I warned him that if he returned to Cob Ash, I would kill him."

"Well, since I am not your brother," Raspail said, speaking with authenticity knowing that he was born of a different mother, "And since I am not in Cob Ash, you are unburdened by the terrible task of having to kill a fellow wolf."

Polwin fought back his mounting confusion. As we have said, Raspail's muteness gave his pack the impression that he had lost all his senses, including intelligence. This wolf, who resembled Raspail, had voice and spoke with cunning. He even spoke in the patois of Ramblefoot.

"Who says it is a terrible task killing another wolf? Especially when we are talking about a wolf who murdered his facet."

"I have never killed my facet nor anyone else's. Again, I am quite sure you are mistaking me for another wolf."

Polwin gave a warning lash to the bitches creeping up behind him lusting for fight. Raspail stretched, enjoying his mastery of the situation, and spoke through his yawn.

"Surely if you recognize me, I should recognize you as well. But I do not. Now, I have given to you all the proof I can: I am not your brother, I am not mute, I never killed my facet, and I do not recognize you."

"You look too much like this wolf to not be him."

"You'd be a fool to let the color of my coat lead you to false assumptions, as there are nearly as many black wolves as there are gray and brown. But so as there is no confusion, let me ask you one more question: Does this wolf you mistake me for wear the silver crest you see on my ruff?"

Polwin looked at the leaf shaped crest on Raspail's massive winter ruff, the one that fright gave him during his imprisonment in the cave. Polwin, obviously, could not have possibly remembered a feature he had never seen.

"I am not sure."

"You had better be sure, because if you continue to harangue me, I will shed my good humor... and then..."

His voice trailed off, letting it linger in the air to torment Polwin.

"And then *what?*" Polwin said, unable to hide his anticipation.

"And then I will shed your blood."

And with this he flashed fang ever so slightly, for Raspail was not one for overstatement.

"You threaten me, do you?"

"Don't mistake a warning for a threat."

"You threaten three wolves when you are just one?" And with this he chortled, for the facts were plain to see, and no matter how well this wolf spoke, he could not deny the advantage that Polwin had.

"Again you assume, cousin. I am not one, I am many. All you need do is look behind you to see that you are mistaken."

Polwin cautiously looked over his shoulder and saw Hagi and Repetto standing above them on the earthy ledge that looked down on them. They were poised to leap to Raspail's aid, though Hagi prayed that he would not have to fight.

Polwin looked back at Raspail.

"I too have friends," Polwin said, then howled for backup.

Raspail lunged at him, feigning to his left leg, then driving his jaws bluntly at his face. Hagi and Repetto jumped down and engaged the two bitches. Repetto, with his unpredictable dexterity and sharp rows of teeth, got the better of his opponent, while Hagi, because of his age and disadvantage, merely kept his opponent busy without putting much skin in the game.

Polwin found himself underneath Raspail, who was making strike after strike to his wide neck. Polwin parried the powerful blows with his muzzle, so Raspail feigned for his neck then lashed at his face, goring the flesh around his eyes. Momentarily blinded by his own blood he thrashed frantically at Raspail. He would have surely been killed in the next few moments if Raspail had not been distracted by the sound of more wolves arriving -- droves of them. Polwin disengaged, retreating while shaking the blood off his face so he could see.

Raspail signaled Repetto and Hagi, and they converged on the route they'd come in on and ran pursued by Polwin and the two bitches. They lost their pursuers, but continued running till they found safety in the thick timbers on the other side of the mountain. There, they rested while licking their wounds, waiting for Raspail to announce his intentions.

When he finally spoke, he said that his plan was to wait for Kileo, even if it took days or weeks, and that he wished them to leave so that the foolish risk he was taking would not be shared by two friends whom he wished to live. They, of course, repeated their commitment to stay with him under any and all conditions, and Raspail was forced to acquiesce.

***

Abillon's Confession

Abillon played in the snow with Hesser's white pups under the protective eye of Sarassin. The young wolves were almost yearlings, and he was the only wolf that she let play with them, He regarded this privilege as a high honor, though Sarassin did not intend it as such. She recognized Abillon as a childlike fool, and she was gifting her children with their future kickaround dog.

The white wolves were a tight-knit unit, a pack within a pack, Abillon thought. His friendship with Polwin had become strained since the Draguignon takeover, and so he had tried to foster new alliances with these impressionable wolves. For that reason he took their abuse, which went beyond what a grown wolf would normally suffer before punishing the children. None of the white pups had any respect for Abillon, and Abillon, being a fool, had no sense of this.

Polwin approached, the flesh around his eyes still bleeding, and shoved Abillon away from the pups.

"He's come back."

"Who?"

"Raspail."

"No! He must be dead by now."

Polwin lashed at him, making him curl on his back.

"I said, he's come back. That means he is not dead."

"Mercy, brother, I didn't mean to upset you."

Polwin looked down at his pathetic brother with disgust and embarrassment. "Get up."

Abillon rose, but his tail still curled under his groin.

"I spoke with him."

"But Raspail cannot speak."

"I know that. Yet it was him, I'm sure."

"Why would he return?"

While Polwin pondered Abillon's question -- for it was a valid one -- Abillon answered it himself.

"Perhaps he has suffered as a ramblefoot. Perhaps he is returning thinking that enough time has passed that we would forgive him and grant him refuge?"

"This wolf has not suffered. This wolf eats better than me. And this wolf..." He hesitated.

"What about him?"

"This wolf isn't hoping for mercy. He made it clear that it is *he* who shows the mercy. It is this arrogance that makes me sure it is him."

"Why do you concern yourself so much with this, brother?" Abillon laughed, "You have two packs at your command."

Polwin could not say what worried him, because to say it would be to admit fear of another wolf, one superior to him, one able to vanquish him.

"Maybe he is here looking for Kileo? You know how close they were," Abillon said before he had the sense not to say it.

"Kileo rambled months ago."

Abillon's stance became more submissive, unable as he was to hide what he knew, and knowing that it would get him a lashing. He looked away from Polwin's eyes. Polwin edged closer.

"Why are you squirming?"

"I fear that if I say what I know you will punish--"

Polwin growled in his face and stared in his eye. "Say it or I will punish you *double!"*

"She is here -- in Cob Ash! She is hiding in the low mountain with Navarin and the others!"

Polwin lashed him hard.

"You didn't tell me this?! You *idiot!"*

Polwin felt someone watching and looked around to see Sarassin playing with her brood, but with an ear on their conversation. He ushered Abillon away from the den where they continued to speak privately.

"Do they still live in Cob Ash, in the low mountains?"

"Yes. I have visited them. I feared the Draguignon wolves would seek revenge, and knowing how you share ranks with them as you do--"

Again, Polwin lashed him. When he was done, he had a thought.

"He's here for her," Polwin said. "And he has come to take her before she goes into heat."

***

Carel's Impatience

In the low mountain, Kileo stood on Carel's perch where she had the best vantage point over Cob Ash, and strategized their escape.

There was one patrol of three wolves that monitored the border that enclosed the low mountain. Every day when the moon came up, this patrol was relieved by another patrol. Since the patrol being relieved was generally bored and starved for company, they would leave their post early to socialize with their relief crew, running inland and providing a window of opportunity for Kileo and the others to escape across the border. They would leave at dusk.

She had not told the young siblings about her correspondence with Raspail, and dared say nothing until she was satisfied with her plan of escape.

Carel walked up to her perch alone, and saw Kileo there, as she often was, gazing below. Carel sighed to show her displeasure.

"Why do I even bother maintaining my flop if you are always here?"

Kileo saw the pent up dissatisfaction in her face. In the last days she had been growing impatient and critical of Kileo's over-cautiousness, and expressed that they all wished to ramble soon. When Kileo told them they needed to wait until they were old enough to fight, Carel almost took it as an invitation to prove she could fight better than Kileo, and tension between the two had not yet been resolved.

"I am here because your perch has the best view of Cob Ash. From here I watch over the wolves who would kill you and me without hesitation. I obsess over routes that we might escape safely on one day--"

"That day will never come because you have too much fear to leave. We do not."

"That's because you are young."

"We will always be young to you, even when we are old."

"That is not true. I will respect you when you do not act rash like you are acting now."

"We're tired of being prisoners here. You don't dominate me. This is my perch, and you come here too much."

"You think I'm intruding on your territory to show dominance over you?"

"The others think so too."

Kileo gasped, for she was experiencing that unpleasant feeling which the mother of Raspail felt upon realizing that her family had been conspiring against her.

Kileo, however, was unburdened by age and a starving baby. She lunged at Carel and knocked her down. Carel was so shocked that she lay frozen where she fell, pinioned by the gravity in Kileo's eyes.

Kileo looked so formidable and dominant that Navarin and the others kept their distance and remained neutral.

"Fight me! Fight and kill me -- then you're free to do anything you want!" Kileo saw that Carel was not accepting the invitation.

Carel nervously rose to her feet and turned her back to Kileo, joining the others and leading them away. Kileo watched them walk off.

"We leave now," Carel muttered to them. "She can stay if she wants."

Carel broke into a trot, and the others followed her. Kileo raced after them to stop them, but when they saw her coming, they accelerated, widening the gap between them.

Kileo was flying down the slope when she nearly slammed into the five of them standing frozen in place, glumly staring down at the base of the mountain. Wolves were marching single file through the timbers. They broke up into four patrols, each with three wolves, and spread out around the foot of the mountain where they stationed themselves.

Carel, brimming with fear, looked back at the older Kileo, who stood there sage and brave, and trembled with shame for ever having doubted her. Kileo led them back to the top of the mountain where they all watched the terrifying patrols from Carel's perch. There was some relief that the wolves were not coming directly up to kill them, but it wasn't much.

Carel threw herself at Kileo's feet whimpering.

"Oh, sister, I am so horrible for doubting you and being so foolishly bold. Forgive me if you can."

Kileo licked her face in forgiveness. Navarin came over and licked her too.

"Please give us some hope," Navarin asked

"I will not lie to you, there is not much to draw on. There is something, though; something I did not tell you. Raspail has returned."

She waited till the excited wolves got quiet before continuing. "I saw him, on that mountain, earlier today."

Navarin wanted to believe her but felt dubious. "How could you see him that far away?"

"There's no way to explain it. You just... must believe me."

"But--" Navarin started, and Carel growled in his face. "Just believe her!"

Navarin shut up. "I told him to wait for us. I didn't want him to risk travel. I know he doesn't want to wait, but that is what he is doing. My hope is that he realizes something is wrong and comes for us..."

"But even then... he is one wolf," Navarin said.

"He is at least one more than us six. And with seven wolves, we might live a moment longer than without."

***

What Currency can Raspail Offer the Ramblefoot who has Everything?

Raspail had waited just one day and already the task of being inactive was tormenting him. Hoping to see Kileo again or make himself seen by her, he journeyed to an overlook and saw what Kileo had just seen, which was the heavy distribution of wolves patrolling the foot of the low mountain, effectively making Kileo a prisoner there. If Raspail had known that Kileo had Navarin and the others with her, he might have considered a raid on the mountain that would coalesce their forces. But he didn't, so the dire situation presented no immediate solution.

Hagi and Repetto, who had followed him to the overlook, saw what he saw and felt his gloom.

"Hoy. A dwarf and a ragged three-footed wolf won't get you through that I'm sorry to say."

"They're going to wait there till I come for her, aren't they?"

"It would seem that is their plan."

Raspail focused on the mountain and tried to divine her voice, but nothing came; the magic was not to be repeated.

"I know some fat wolves who would fight by your side," Repetto said.

"And for what in exchange? What is lacking in their satisfied lives that I can offer them?"

Repetto looked at Hagi. Hagi scratched at his ear as he thought. "You never asked me what I was doing that rain-drenched day you met me, why I was there so far from Ramblefoot."

"That is your business."

"But you were curious, eh? Once you got to Ramblefoot, you must have asked yourself why I would turn my back on all that easy meat."

"I admit; it had crossed my mind."

"I was leaving Ramblefoot. Because I am always trying to leave it, and always failing because it always tempts me back. It isn't a home. It's a place -- a very good one -- but it isn't our place. Its dangers are not ones that we can cope with, they are beyond our fathom and getting more mysterious, and they terrify me, as they should terrify every wolf to the very core."

"You're eluding me, Hagi: Tell me what currency I have to offer these ramblefoots who would wage their good lives for my own self-interest."

"If you had ambition, you would see it. But you don't. Your heart desires one simple thing, the prisoner on that mountain, but to get her you will need wolves, more wolves than your enemy has, yes?"

"Yes, ones I have nothing to offer, because they have everything a wolf can want."

"Everything but safety. Don't be fooled, they are all quietly afraid of what lurks out there, they are just too meatdrunk to recognize it. You could compel them to leave Ramblefoot and lead them to a new home far from the strange new neighbor who hates them."

"Ba! That sounds too much like I am their facet."

Hagi leaned his head in to Raspail and lowered his voice for emphasis:

"Raspail, I hate to inform you of this, but you already are the *Facet of Ramblefoot.*"

Raspail looked dubious.

"Whether you like it or not, there are twenty-some-odd wolves waiting for your command, ready to die for you."

"Hagi's right about that for sure," Repetto said.

"Safe land is in short supply these days. Where is this fantastic home I promise them, where they will be so well-fed that they do not rebel against me and rightfully kill me for uprooting them from Ramblefoot?"

Hagi casually looked out at the valley below, then said, "I see a lovely spread of land, rich with elk-attracting aspen groves, that encompasses two wolf provinces safely hidden in between mountains where our enemies don't venture."

Raspail, because he lacked ambition, had overlooked the fact that a battle to rescue Kileo would leave him in control of Cob Ash and perhaps Draguignon. He felt a surge of excitement go through him, as if the riches of the world were already his to give out as he wished. He could pay his mercenaries with the spoils of the conflict. It was so obvious now that Hagi had pointed it out, and Raspail reflected that it was wise to have clever friends, for often good ideas that we are blind to are in plain sight to them.

"He's right. That land gonna be yours soon as we kill all them wolves." Repetto said.

"So in return for a brawl I give those fighters who survive the provinces of Cob Ash and Draguignon."

"You can stay on as their facet, if it pleases you, or not. I see no other solution."

When Hagi, Raspail and Repetto returned to Ramblefoot at dawn, it was just as when they arrived the first time, with wolves appearing from shadows announcing Hagi's return, only this time they howled Raspail's name too. Wolves howled from every crevice of the mountain and within moments our heroes were surrounded by a throng of wolves overjoyed at their return. Hagi told them that they were all worn out from their travels and wished to rest, but that when the moon rose he would address every ramblefoot who wished to partake in an "epic adventure", as he called it.

Anticipation was so high that when the eye of the ancestors revealed itself, nearly full-open, there were twenty three boisterous wolves fighting to get close to Hagi, who was sitting, and Raspail, who was laying behind him with his fore legs crossed in a stately manner. Even Nin was there with her new litter (whose numbers we have not included in that count). Hagi spoke:

"Hoy now! Our cousin Raspail, our friend who you have expressed interest in being your facet in the past, is leaving Ramblefoot on an endeavor of serious consequence!"

At this his voice was drowned out by the worried whimpers and inquisitive murmuring of his audience. He waited for them to stop, then continued.

"If we have good sense, if we wish to live good and long lives, we will depart with him and join in this endeavor, leaving the bountiful easy meats of Ramblefoot behind forever."

As much as they respected Raspail, the crowd became restless with dissent, and each time Hagi tried to continue, his voice was drowned out.

Raspail finally stood and stepped next to Hagi, and the crowd grew silent again, knowing that Raspail's voice was unusually low and no wolf wanted to miss a single nuance.

"My home, or rather the land which was my home, is three long days' travel from here. In that land I left behind a wolf I loved deeply. I came to Ramblefoot, tempted by Hagi with promises that the easy meats would drown out my woes. He was truthful, and I have spent more days meatdrunk than not, as you've all been witness to."

The crowd, looking for a moment of gaiety to soothe themselves, laughed.

"I have been in a state of bliss since the glorious day that I set foot here. But in those moments when the drunk lifted, my woes returned and reminded me that my heart, like my stomach, will never cease being hungry until it is fed what it desires."

A feeling of unity fell upon the huge and diverse band of wolves. That is because Raspail, guileless in his plea to them, had articulated a feeling all of them knew. They had all, in some way or another, taken the same journey as Raspail to Ramblefoot. Every one of them had some unfinished business, some forbidden love they ran from, some friend whose company they yearned for, some pup they wished they could have seen grow to adulthood. And each of them knew that no matter how much they ate, the only way the food would permanently quell their heart's pain forever was if, like the hero in Hagi's story, they ate so much it killed them.

"It will take every wolf whose loyalty I can count on to reunite me with the bitch I left behind. My goal is my own, and I would not ask another wolf to shed his blood with me unless there were something for him to gain as well. It is not easy fathoming something that such well-fed wolves lack in. But Hagi, who has spent more time in Ramblefoot than all of us, warns us that things are changing too fast for a wolf to survive here anymore, and that this paradise will kill us all if we do not think beyond our next meal. To that I say, take the spoils of my endeavor-- all of it -- two meat-rich territories safely nestled in the valley between the mountains to the north. I offer you my home, Cob Ash, and the home of my damnable neighbor, Draguignon, for when we are done slaying every wolf who stands in our way, there will be a vacancy in one of the prettiest territories you will ever lay eyes on."

Repetto unable to control himself anymore, climbed up a large boulder and barked at the crowd, "It is true! Every word -- true!"

Clamoring and howling broke out.

His goal was suddenly their goal. And though not one of them had dared consider leaving the grand folly that was Ramblefoot to win back what they'd left behind, Raspail did, and this elevated him. He was each of them, but in their noblest incarnation, their best face -- he was truly their facet. To return with him to his homeland was for all of them to return to theirs.

All night long the celebration lasted, for they knew that they would be leaving it all behind soon.

Raspail was greeted throughout the night by his new pack as if they were meeting him for the first time, sniffing and licking him, rubbing against him and nibbling his fur respectfully. He had changed the moment he accepted their offer to be facet, and they all wanted to know what that change smelled and felt like, to literally have a little of him "rub off" on them.

An hour before sunset, a wolf was snared in a trap and his keening howl attracted men on horses with guns. They all watched from the safety of the timbers as the men shot him. The party, its purpose ironically validated by the unfortunate wolf's demise, came to an end.

Raspail wobbled back through the timbers, then spent his last sleep in Ramblefoot in the same flop of leaves he'd spent his first.

***

The Irony of Being Master

He was woken by Repetto diving into his flop off the rock above it. When Raspail gave him a harsh look, he became comically humble, saying, "Oh, my facet, mercy, I had no idea you were in there, mercy don't lash me--" and then his words lapsed into nonsense and sneezing because he was laughing so hard. The two wolves played in the snow until finally Raspail became serious.

"It's time to go." Raspail said. "You and Boonbrekker spread the word."

Repetto looked confused.

"What is it? "Raspail asked

"You know," Repetto said sheepishly.

"I don't know."

"No wolf thinks they are leaving today."

"Why not? Wasn't I clear to them?"

Again, Repetto looked sheepish, then glanced up at the eye of the ancestors, hoping that the eye had missed Raspail's indiscretion. Raspail suddenly realized what the matter was and groaned. He looked up to observe the moon, then said:

"It will take six days for the eye to fully open!"

"I understand that."

"This cannot wait six days."

Hagi ambled over. "It will have to. They believe this event to be so extraordinary that it demands waiting until the eye is fully open. They assume that you think the same way too."

Raspail looked at Repetto. "And are you one of these wolves who believes we must wait till the moon is full?"

Repetto did not answer, which meant the answer was yes.

And so Raspail, though he was one of those rare wolves whose noble heart navigated him on a valiant and courageous bearing through life regardless of the eye's capricious mood, was asked to indulge the pack's one caveat and wait six days so they could do battle under the full open eye.

Raspail's first challenge as facet was fighting the intense urge to abandon his pack in order to not be constrained by their whim. With all this supposed power he now had, he could not make them do the one thing he wanted them to do when he wanted them to it.

"I have been elected master, an honor indeed..." he muttered to himself, pacing, "And traded a free life with no master for a life bound by twenty!"

He found Hagi and expressed his urge to run, to go north on his own and get Kileo somehow. Hagi silently fathomed what Raspail's primary worry was, and went about soothing it.

"She's safe where she is. They won't make trouble for her cause they know it's in your nature to come back for her. They know it's so cause they saw you come back once, right?" Hagi waited until Raspail agreed. "No, they won't kill your bitch until they kill you. She's safe unless you go for her on your own. Then she's at risk."

"Six days. There are six days to wait till the eye of the ancestor is fully open."

Hagi laughed. "On the day you face your death you will wish there were six of those days, with legs to run and jaws to hunt and air to breath. Don't waste them watching the sun go from one end of the sky to the other."

Good advice was never wasted on Raspail, and so Hagi saved his best wisdom for his best student. But something else irked Raspail.

"I smell the fragrance of bitches in heat all around me, from Ipsy and Nin and the others. This delicious perfume is a scourge on me, because it means Kileo is approaching her heat and I am not there to take her. Another wolf will. She will attract suitors. I must get there first."

"You will, my friend. She will save herself for you. You know her heart is true."

Raspail licked his face with gratitude, then ran off and found Poitu. The two raced through the timbers like when they were outcasts living on the fringe of Cob Ash, running for its own rapturous sake, with no goal or destination other than to distract himself from his own impatience.

As he ran, he wondered what it would feel like to lead such numbers. They were a strong and well-fed lot, and with them marching beside him he could defeat any obstacle. He had never bothered fathoming true power, for the only power that could be relied on in his life came from within himself. But now, as he flew through the timbers, he imagined what it would feel like to radiate his will through an army of obedient subjects, to be the heartbeat of a powerful pack like that. His legs pumped as if involuntarily.

Yes, he told himself as he ran, *On the day that life drips away from me I will recall these six days that Hagi has given me, these days when I flew with Poitu knowing that Kileo would soon be my mate.*

And as this feeling washed over him, time sped up, and without his constant vigil over the sun's delicate movement, he was surprised by how it leaped across the sky. And then it all came to an abrupt and shocking end, this state of blissful fluidity, as the ground beneath his huge feet slipped silently away.

He almost made it over the pit. His head smashed into the dirt wall of the hole and he lost consciousness as he slid two wolf lengths to its bottom.

     ***

Waking Up in a Hole

Raspail emerged from the black sleep clueless as to where he was and how he'd gotten there. He could see the night sky, but he was walled in by thick dirt that seemed as if it had miraculously risen up around him. He tried climbing and jumping, but the hole was exactly too deep for any escape. In every way, the scenario resembled a nightmare come to fruition.

In his attempt to make sense of his predicament he wondered if he were dead, but then Poitu flew out of the sky and descended into the pit where she stared at him. Upon seeing her he remembered, vaguely, running with her through the timbers. But that was all he remembered.

After Raspail had fallen unconscious into the pit, Poitu flew to Hagi, Repetto, and several other wolves attempting to tell each of them that they should follow her. Lacking the bond she had with Raspail, she failed to communicate with these wolves and so she flew back to Raspail and was pleased to see that he was at least awake.

She spent the rest of the night in the pit with him trying to devise a way to get him out while Raspail, still rebounding from the blow his head took, phased between blacking out and waking up disoriented.

He woke to the sounds of barking, but not the barking of wolves or coyotes. He looked around for Poitu, but she was gone.

Four large dogs ran to the rim of the pit and barked down at Raspail. Two men then appeared beside the dogs and stared down at the wolf. One of them raised his rifle and aimed it at Raspail, but was stopped by his partner. A discussion ensued, an agreement was reached, and the men walked out of sight. Raspail's confusion was abetted by his head injury, and mercifully so, for his lack of mental prowess at the moment kept him calmer than he should have been.

The men returned to the pit's edge again, this time carrying a coiled rope which they threw down on Raspail. After the third effort, they snared his head in the loop, tightened it into a collar around his throat and heaved him out of the hole. He resisted, gagging for air as they yanked the rope. The only way to relieve the pain was to cooperate and climb up the vertical wall of dirt towards them as they hoisted him.

The moment he emerged from the hole the dogs were on him. Raspail kicked his legs out and ran until the rope tightened around his throat again, stopping him short. The dogs mobbed him with such frenzy that the men could not enter the fray. One of them raised a heavy stick, and the dogs cowered and whimpered in fear as if the man had put a spell over them with this wand. Raspail tried again to run, and again the rope went tight around his throat and he stumbled. The man came over and raised the same wand that he threatened to punish the dogs with. Before he could lower it, something black and huge erupted in his face from above.

Poitu drove her claws into the man's face and shrieked at her highest pitch. The startled man dropped the baton, giving Raspail the opportunity to run. The man's hands burned and bled as the rough rope was pulled through his tight grip by the terrified wolf. With the help of his partner they brought Raspail down again. Poitu made a second attack, but retreated when one of the men aimed his rifle at her and shot, missing her.

Seeing that they had a wolf determined to defy them, they tied a second rope around Raspail's neck. The two men, each holding a rope tied around the black wolf's neck, mounted their horses and rode home with their bounty whose exploits and elusive nature had earned him the nickname "Devil's Shadow". And whereas the head of any old wolf was worth fifteen dollars, the head of Devil's Shadow was worth four hundred and fifty dollars.

**

A Fellow Prisoner Resembles an Old Friend

Raspail's initiation into the world of man was rendered even more hazy and bizarre by merit of his head injury. He was promenaded past the walls of death, the images of tortured wolf faces with dark empty eyes burning into his throbbing head, and led to an outdoor pen. He was forced inside with lashings from the stick and beaten until the dark sleep fell on him as before.

When he woke he tried to open his mouth, but to his horror he couldn't; his face was encased in a mask of sharp interlocking metal bands that he could barely see from. A chain connected his rear legs together. He could stand and walk, but only with short, frustrating movements.

At the edge of the pen stood a number of people staring at him. He dared not make eye contact with them. They were interested in something at the far corner of the pen as well, and when Raspail looked he saw two other masked wolves, one who was so desolate and withdrawn he barely radiated life from his eyes, and another who seemed dead or near dead.

Raspail approached the live wolf, but as he got nearer to the animal, it turned its head away and tucked its muzzle under its forepaws. He was scarred and wounded and emaciated as any wolf Raspail had ever seen, especially in contrast to the well-fed wolves of Ramblefoot.

"Where are we?" Raspail whined to the desolate wolf. But the wolf either did not understand or ignored him.

The two men who captured Raspail entered the pen and approached the desolate wolf. One of them pinned him down with their foot on his neck and unlocked his muzzle. When the muzzle was removed, Raspail could clearly see his face. He shuddered at what he saw.

The spiritless, broken wolf resembled Aratus.

With disbelief he strained for a better view over the iron contraption that blocked his vision.

The men removed the muzzle on Raspail the same way, then left the pen. While the other wolf licked his wounds, Raspail crouched low and faced him directly, half a wolf length between them. The wolf's eyes, which were dim and fathomless, suddenly ignited -- not in recognition, but with rage as he attacked Raspail, forcing him back. Raspail looked deep into these fierce eyes, aflame with life again, and confirmed with certainty that it was Aratus.

"Aratus!"

Aratus' expression, frozen in a snarl, looked confused at this wolf who called him the name only a friend would know.

"It's me! Raspail!"

Aratus stepped back, unsure and unwilling to trust his judgment. It did not help that the voice sounded so different from his memory of Raspail's. His head shook dubiously and he looked down.

"Look at me, Aratus! Look in my eyes! You know my name -- it was you who gave it to me!"

Aratus suddenly stood, and at that moment he resembled the old familiar Aratus, proud and mighty. Raspail then heard what had caused him to rise. Barking dogs, five of them it seemed, were getting closer.

In a moment he could see them. The dog pack was led in by a different man than the one who captured Raspail. When the dogs reached the pen, they erupted in a manic, violent frenzy. The smallest was just bigger than Repetto, the largest the size of Aratus. The pen was opened and the dogs rushed in.

***

The Two Gladiators from Cob Ash

The moment the dogs rushed in, Aratus, whose scars and battle wounds bore witness to his experience in the ring, coiled his body like a spring and fought off the attacking dogs without using his shackled legs. The master fighter defended himself from two dogs at once, killing the small one while the bigger one freely took stabs at his neck. As soon as the little dog was defeated, Aratus bit into his bigger attacker's throat and flipped him, then positioned his shackled legs over his victim's flank, immobilizing his lower torso with the taut chain while he bled him from the throat.

Raspail, lacking Aratus' experience, clumsily relied on his bound legs to maneuver, but robbed of his agility he lost the advantage against the smaller dogs which attacked him as he stumbled on the ground, encumbered as he was by the heavy chain. His heavy winter coat and dense musculature deadened most of the impact of the wounds delivered by the smaller fangs of the dogs, but there were three of them tearing at him and his head, still pounding from the stick's blows, was ready to give up. Raspail abandoned all technique and skill and thrashed wildly.

In a flash, Aratus knocked one of the attackers off Raspail and pinioned him with his chain and killed him in the same fashion as the other. Raspail, with only two dogs to battle now, stood on his back legs and threw the one attacker off his back, pivoted on his chained legs, and struck with his jaws fully open. The dog might have just as likely died from fright upon seeing such a massive black beast descending on him as from the crushing force that closed on his neck.

The crowd of people, disappointed at the outcome of the fight, stoned the wolves. Only one dog had survived, a large female shepherd, and she cowered near the gate to the pen whining for mercy from the wolves. It was her human master, however, who raised his rifle and ended the dog's life.

Aratus quickly stripped open the biggest dog and ate its meat voraciously. Raspail was naturally repelled by this, since a wolf does not eat another wolf even under dire circumstances, and a dog was close enough to a wolf for the same law to apply here.

Aratus saw him watching judgmentally and said in a voice, familiar yet foreign, "Eat the dog. Quick, or you'll die."

Raspail, who was nurtured by this sage wolf from infancy, did not hesitate taking this advice which went against all his instincts, and he tore open one of the dead dogs and ate as much of its flesh as he could without retching in the brief moment he had before the men came in the pen and attached the iron masks back on their faces. The slain dogs, including the ones they were eating, were dragged out of the pen by the man who had brought them.

The human spectators dispersed and Raspail and Aratus were left alone. Aratus, his spirit broken by captivity, remained aloof to Raspail.

Poor Aratus had endured all the stages of misery that free animals go through when they are imprisoned. First, after his unsuccessful attempts at escape were punished, all wells of hope dried up. Then, memories of good times, which his soul relied on for sustenance, had gone stale. Death was all that was left to hope for, if in fact this wasn't death (as Raspail had also wondered). But Aratus' nature, noble as it was, deprived him of seeking this final consolation. He was not worthy of death, he felt from somewhere deep within him, and so he clung to life in order to continue suffering.

"Ignore me if you must," said Raspail, "but at least acknowledge that you know me. I will pester and beleaguer you until you do so!"

Aratus, broken as he was, recognized not just Raspail, but his steadfast persistence. And confronted by this, he quivered with the faint memory of what joy felt like, but it was fleeting for he knew that Raspail's indomitable character would be crushed as quickly as his had. And for that reason, he could not look in his eyes, for they were his own eyes when this nightmare began long ago, his eyes before they were drained of light.

Raspail prodded Aratus with his muzzle and declared, "Hear me, friend! I will bedevil and harass you with the last bits of my strength until you look in my eyes and confess that you know me!"

Aratus lifted his leaden head up and stared into Raspail's eyes.

"Raspail," he said through the mask. "I know you."

Raspail's heart flooded with great joy and sorrow at the same time.

"Oh, Aratus," Raspail cried as he pushed the crown of his head against Aratus' ear and held it there for a long and profound moment.

"I have yearned for and dreamed of our reunion, though not in this wretched way."

Raspail was wishing for a conversation, but his partner did not oblige beyond the simple acknowledgement that Raspail asked for. Still, it was enough to give Raspail hope. When night came, he circled the inner perimeter of the pen looking for soft ground, testing it by digging with his foot. Seeing that all the frozen ground was equally hard, he broke ground at the farthest point from the area where the men came in, and dug without stopping. He was fueled by the scent of the dead bitch dog which lingered in the air, for it reminded him of Kileo and her impending heat, on the other side of the fence, beyond this world of men. As the night grew darker, he heard howling from the mountains. He recognized voices of friends, some calling for him, but he dared not respond for fear of the man and his club. He kept digging, his feet torn up by the rocks that studded the hard-packed dirt.

"If you plan on surviving here, stop digging."

Raspail looked over and saw Aratus standing behind him.

"I don't plan on surviving here. I plan on escaping."

"You won't dig out by tomorrow; the ground is too hard. In the morning they will see the start of your hole and they will lash us both and close the hole," Aratus said "Conserve your energy, you will need it tomorrow."

"Is there no way out?"

"None."

"If ever there was a wolf to escape from the confines of a trap it is you. If you failed, it is only because of how they have bound you." And with enthusiasm in his voice he said, *"But there is now you and me here!"*

His rousing words did not impress Aratus, who sullenly walked back to his spot near the fence, curling into a ball, conserving his energy as he had recommended to Raspail. Raspail abandoned the hole and joined Aratus, laying down with a sigh and saying nothing. Raspail's silence provoked Aratus to speak.

"You've grown quite a bit."

"I have eaten well. But that seems like another life now."

Aratus smiled weakly. "You always found a way to eat. On the day I found you, you were alone and laying in the snow, poisoned by a snake you hunted and ate. That, at three months old."

Raspail smiled. "I've not heard that story before."

"I wasn't free to tell you it before."

"Why not?"

Aratus looked confused. "Did Cob Ash never tell you?"

"What exactly?"

"Our facet promised me he would tell you your story when the time came."

"I have made some discoveries on my own by chance. I know that Cob Ash and Cortess did not birth me, if that is what you mean. But I know nothing else." Raspail waited with intense attention for Aratus to talk.

"We were hunting, and we had misjudged the stamina of our quarry and ventured too deep into Draguignon. Your mother was rambling south with you. You left her side, drawn by the smell of the elk that Cob Ash had just split open. Then we met your mother, who had come to get you."

"Tell me of her."

"She was the biggest female I have ever seen. And cunning, too. Quite old, which is why I assume she was rambling, but very strong, strong enough to fight our facet."

Raspail savored every word, and as he put images to Aratus' memories the misery of captivity seemed to slough away.

"Then she and you went on your way. On our long march home I chanced upon you again, as I've said, near death."

"She was dead?"

"I presume she was, though I did not see her again." Aratus paused and looked confused again. "I wonder why our facet neglected to tell you all this. He made an oath to me."

"Alas, there was no neglect on his part, so do not hold any grudge towards Cob Ash. He was murdered before he had the chance to tell me."

It was now Aratus' turn to be attentive.

"How was he murdered?"

"I'm quite sure it was Hesser, but he didn't act alone. I was first witness at the site of his death. He'd been dragged off, but there was smell of Draguignon everywhere mixed with the smell of Hesser. When I returned to camp I was blamed for the murder by Hesser and then banished."

Aratus looked astounded. "Surely your word against a fool like Hesser's--"

"Ha! My word!" Raspail's laughter turned dark, "My word had been stifled long before. By Hesser. He crushed my voice in what was perhaps an accident, perhaps not. It is only recently that I have regained use of my voice."

Up till this point, reminiscing with Raspail and hearing news of Cob Ash had revived some of Aratus' spirit, but upon hearing of his great brother's death and Raspail's reversal of fortune, his heart grew heavy again and he cried at the eye of the ancestors:

"I have disappointed so many, even more than I fathomed. I have been untrue to every wolf who ever trusted me. Had I not selfishly rambled from Cob Ash, had I only stayed, so many would have been better off."

"Tell me, my friend: What has been so wretched in your life other than what is obvious at this moment? Share it with me so that I can carry half that burden with you, since it seems too heavy for you to carry alone."

Aratus told him of their ramble south, of the raid on their camp, of Maddocq's episode in the trap and of the tragedy of Othenia and their pups. At mention of the pups, Raspail stopped him.

"Tell me about your children."

"What does it matter. They are dead."

"Please - Describe them to me so that I may imagine them. This is important if I am to help carry your grief."

"I do not deserve your pity."

"Regardless, you have it as I would have yours under the same circumstances. So please, tell me of their color, their size, what they smelled like, what their fur tasted like."

With great pain Aratus then described the pups, leaving no detail out. As he reached the last description, that of his son Minou, his throat dried up and he stopped, unable to continue.

"You are right. You do not deserve my pity," Raspail said. "You do not even deserve to die. And I am sure you have made every attempt to escape this hellish prison, so I will not try and persuade you to do so again, even if you stand a better chance of escape now with my assistance."

Aratus' brow wrinkled as he sensed the words were loaded with some secondary purpose. He had taught this wolf the art of being cunning, and he was on the receiving end of it now as sure as the night was black. He let Raspail continue:

"That is... if what you are saying is true."

Aratus stood defiantly, the chain between his hind legs pulled taut as if he were prepared to use the weapon on Raspail. "Are you questioning my honesty? I have taken bad steps. I have made regrettable choices. *But I do not lie!*"

His eyes ignited again, but this time Raspail did not retreat.

"You said your sons and daughters were all dead."

"They are!"

"You presume they are, as you presumed my mother was dead without having seen her as such."

"And how do you know that I didn't see them with my eyes -- *dead!*"

"Did you?"

Aratus looked aside as he fathomed deeply into the recesses of his ravaged mind. His whole body quaked as he tried to resurrect the last visual memory of his children, and he saw them in the cage held by the men, alive.

"*Did you,* Aratus?"

"No," he answered weakly.

"That is because they are alive." Raspail stood dramatically and stared into Aratus' eyes with authority. "I have seen them! I have played with them, licked their fur--!"

"Don't trick me with lies!" Aratus snarled back.

"*Could* I lie to you? You who taught me all I know--*Aratus,* who does not lie?"

Aratus cooled down, but his body still trembled uncontrollably.

"The living, breathing bodies of your children were being used as bait, to lure wolves into a den where traps were set. I was one of two wolves who saved them. They are in the safe care of a wolfmother who lost her own brood."

And at these words, Aratus, still standing defiantly, let out a deep moan and collapsed in a heap on top of Raspail, realizing that the worst part of his nightmare was in fact just that, a nightmare, summoned by fear, and gone at dawn.

***

Coustat, the Challenger

When Raspail did not show up for meat, word spread quickly of his absence and every ramblefoot came to Hagi with concern, asking where their new facet was. Hagi assured them that he was okay, and told them that they should go on with their day as they did before they had a facet. But when the wolves left him alone, Hagi worried that the impetuous Raspail, unable to calm his nerves and wait the six days, had in fact fled North.

Poitu, herself vexed by Raspail's disappearance after returning to the pit and finding him missing, found Hagi and landed at his feet. Hagi sensed her agitation as she screeched at him.

"It's not enough I have to console all these wolves, heh?" He said to her.

She continued to chatter, and the attempts he made to run from her were futile.

"I suppose you're gonna plague me until he comes back."

She cackled as if she understood, then stayed with him throughout the day until Repetto visited Hagi, asking him the same questions as every other wolf.

Repetto had a more tolerant attitude towards the winged sidekick, and seeing that she was as lonely as he was, he picked up a long twisted branch in his teeth and charged at the raven, inviting her to play. Poitu acted disinterested and flew off only to suddenly drop from the sky and land on the branch, grappling it in her talons. She stayed perched to the branch like this, riding on it while Repetto ran in circles. The wolf, looking to shake up things, cocked his head left so the end of the branch where Poitu was perched dipped and dragged in the snow. Poitu jumped over his head, flapping her wings just enough to keep momentum with the wolf, and landed on the other end of the branch. Repetto then cocked his head the other way, and Poitu flipped sides. No matter how quickly Repetto switched the branch, no matter how many times he feigned and double-dipped, he could not trick the raven. Finally Repetto gave up, impressed at Poitu's quick reflexes.

After resting he said to her, "You and me, we'll look for Raspail. My nose and your eyes, we'll find him, sure thing."

Repetto wandered for hours with Poitu until he finally picked up Raspail's scent and followed the trail to where it ended abruptly at the pit. Repetto gazed in the hole while Poitu hopped around croaking frantically. Since he did not recognize the hole as a trap, he fathomed that perhaps Raspail's journey started here and ended somewhere else.

So he followed Raspail's trail, that erratic, joyful flight across the snow that he took with Poitu, and it led him back to Hagi's flop. Repetto excitedly searched everywhere for Raspail barking his name, not knowing that Raspail had in fact started at this point when he confessed his impatience to Hagi.

Poitu trilled with amusement watching Repetto zig-zag idiotically around the flop looking everywhere for his friend.

Repetto misinterpreted the trills as affirmation and navigation clues, hearing, "Yes! You're a genius! You're getting closer!" when in fact the raven was merely laughing.

That night, the second of Raspail's disappearance, a wolf who was keeping a cooler head than his neighbors stepped forward to address them. He was called Coustat, and unlike Raspail he had dreamed many times what it would feel like to have the power of a pack at his whim, though he had never imagined a way in which to acquire such power. Raspail's absence gave him such a way.

"We can still succeed at this, with or without Raspail as our facet," he told the worried wolves. "Our power, after all, lies in our numbers. Let me take you to this place up north, and I will serve you even better than Raspail!"

Repetto listened with outrage as he continued.

"Raspail did not even want to be our facet when we asked him. I, on the other hand, have always desired to be your facet!"

"Raspail will come back! He will!" Repetto barked at the crowd. The crowd shared his optimism.

"And if he does not? Should we wait here, getting meatdrunk until all of us..." and he gestured to Nin and the pups, "All of us, including these precious young ones, are killed?"

Repetto, whose own bravery had saved the infants, saw that the advantageous Coustat was playing off their anxiety. He rushed the bigger wolf and attacked him from every angle until two of Coustat's allies jumped him and tried to tackle him to the ground, which we know was near impossible to. Hagi stepped into the fray and commanded them all to stop.

When tempers calmed, Hagi said, "Raspail will return and we will have our facet. If he does not return--"

"Then *I* will be your facet! Yes -- I, Coustat, will be your facet!" Coustat roared at them.

And some of the wolves roared back in approval.

***

Romeo and Devil's Shadow

The captive wolves slept intertwined with each other where Aratus had collapsed on Raspail. The pleasant early winter morning sunlight warmed Raspail's head, but the moment of enjoyment was short for the two men returned to the pen and entered. They saw the beginnings of the escape route Raspail dug that night. The new captive had to be the culprit, for Aratus had already had his will pummeled out of him and given up digging after his third day of captivity.

Raspail received his lashing, but rather than wait for the black sleep to come, he let his body go limp and shut his eyes, falling listlessly to the ground even though he was still awake. The men stopped their lashing upon seeing him drop, and Raspail, behind closed lids, thought to himself, "There is mercy in these beasts, and so they can be tricked like a wolf."

Mercy was part of the equation. The other factor was the men needed to break him without hurting him too badly, for they saw in him a gladiator as worthy as Aratus, and with the two they imagined a very profitable enterprise.

Just as Raspail had been given the name Devil's Shadow by men, Aratus was known as "Romeo." Romeo did not have a bounty on his head beyond what any other wolf brought, but the story of how he waited by his dying mate's side was made legend in a pamphlet that portrayed him as a brave, loyal, amorous, and defeated outlaw. Visitors came at twenty-five cents a piece to see this wolf in the flesh even if he was curled in an amorphous ball at the back of the pen. In his first week as an attraction, his owners earned twice the fifteen dollar bounty on his head. When interest in viewing Romeo waned, the men made money inviting ranchers to challenge the wolf with their best dogs, and even though Aratus was handicapped by the chain on his legs, he proved he was just as much a fighter as he was a lover.

The man grumbled as he filled the hole. When he was done he kicked Raspail in the ribs three times, then left the pen, spending a moment latching the gate shut. Raspail, reeling from the pain in his ribs, studied through squinting eyes how the man fussed with the gate latch. As soon as he was out of sight, Raspail hobbled to the gate and pushed it with his foot against the latch. It rocked slightly back and forth on its hinge, and when he held his weight against it he created a gap big enough to stick his foot through. He looked up at the latch, having no idea what it did but aware that the man's manipulation of it allowed him to enter and leave as he pleased. He observed that when the man was inside the pen, the gate could be passed through, and when he left, the gate was secure and impenetrable.

There were men talking in the distance. Raspail backed away from the gate and lay down near Aratus. Aratus' vigor had returned, and Raspail was encouraged that he was possessed with something other than conserving his energy.

Aratus spoke:

"There are two of us, as you say. So tell me; what does this mean besides twice the failure and twice the punishment when we are caught?"

"We will think together and then we will work together. Right now, a plan does not present itself. But I have found myself in trouble more dire than this and lived to tell about it. An opportunity will arise, and when it does we must be ready to seize it."

"You say I taught you everything. That is flattering but not true, for these encouraging words could never have come from my lips." Aratus smiled at him admiringly.

"Show me how you fought those dogs." Raspail said. "I noticed you don't advance, you pivot on your hind feet. How do you control your legs to stay still under such circumstances?"

"When you hear the dogs, stand and part your hind legs as far as you can, till you feel the shackles digging into your hocks."

Raspail stood and did this, pulling the chain tight.

"Do you feel them digging into your flesh?"

"Yes."

"Let the pain remind you of how useless your legs are when it comes to movement. You can't chase or kick with them, you can only pivot, squat and thrust."

Raspail stood on his hind feet.

"Rotate side to side, but always keep the chain tight."

He hopped in order to turn, balancing himself on two legs. Aratus suddenly charged at him, easily knocking him down.

"If they try and knock you down, you must crouch on your rear legs to keep your balance. Fight them one at a time. If you try and fight three at once you will be killed. Make sure one is dead before you engage in the next fight, even if it means letting two of them tear your back open."

Aratus and Raspail practiced this fighting technique until Aratus stopped and said, "Good. Now rest a moment, save your energy, there isn't much food here."

They rested a moment, the subject of food hanging in the air.

"Do we only eat what we can get from the dogs?" Raspail asked, hoping greatly the answer was no.

"No. We are fed once a day. The meat is decent but never enough."

Raspail smiled wryly.

"What is amusing about that?"

"I know this story of a wolf. He ate so much it killed him."

Aratus laughed for the first time.

"Impossible."

"No, it is true, my good friend Hagi was witness to it. This wolf stuffed his stomach with three times what could fit inside it. He fell face first into the carcass he was eating, dying with his tongue hanging from the side like this."

And Raspail imitated the dead wolf exactly as Hagi had in the hundred times he had heard the master tell the story.

Aratus laughed. "While I believe that a wolf could kill himself that way, I don't believe there is a place where a wolf can eat that much."

"Ah, that is where you are wrong, Aratus!"

Raspail's eyes glowed as he told him of Ramblefoot and of the meat orgies. Seeing that his friend was starved for companionship as he had been after leaving Cob Ash, he regaled the despondent Aratus with every story he could remember, doing for him what Hagi had done for him on their way to Ramblefoot. Aratus delighted in these stories, for not only was he entertained, but he was proud of Raspail for prospering as he had, never failing to turn misfortune into fortune.

Raspail exhausted himself like this (and gained a new appreciation for Hagi's craft), but Aratus begged him to tell him one more story, specifying that he retell the one about the wolf who ate himself to death, just as every wolf is not content hearing it once.

***

The Escape

Food and water came as Aratus had promised. Their masks were removed and they ate and slurped at water voraciously while the men waited. Aratus was overly protective of his meat and even stole some of Raspail's, feeling justified to do so after hearing his stories of Ramblefoot. Raspail let him take his food and watched him greedily eat it, his ribs protruding pathetically as he devoured the meat. Though his body was diminished by starvation, his shoulders remained round and muscular, bulging atop his spindly, skeletal legs.

It snowed throughout the day, pausing for a short period during which the two trappers came into the pen to have their photographs taken with their live quarries. When the photographer's red-haired daughter set off the flash powder, Raspail lurched back in terror from the blinding explosion, knocking over the man holding the rope around his neck. For this Raspail received three blows from the stick. He sat still for the next two photographs, suffering the terror of the flashing light with pounding head pain.

There were no dogs to contend with that day, just visitors who paid admission to see the sullen outlaws. Children threw snowballs at the sleeping wolves to make them move, but even under this mild harassment they remained still.

The night was bitterly cold. Raspail woke to the foreign sting of alcohol in his nose. Peering out without raising his head he saw the white haired trapper approaching the pen accompanied by the photographer's daughter. The man carried a rifle in one hand and a bottle of whiskey in the other. He was walking funny, teetering and stumbling, and if not for the girl to lean on he surely would have fallen.

"Aratus," Raspail whispered. Aratus awoke and saw.

The man and girl watched the wolves from outside the pen, the man hoping that the romantic story of Aratus' loyalty to his mate would perhaps lead to some romance with the girl. Upon finishing the story he groped clumsily at her, trying to kiss her. The girl laughed as she pushed him away, and the man drank from his bottle again. They spoke for a while, then the man unlocked the gate and let the girl and himself in.

Inside the pen, Raspail felt the girl's fear. The man handed her his rifle and gave her a quick lesson on how to use it, then walked to Aratus and unfastened the mask and slipped it off. He did the same for Raspail, then yanked both dogs up by their rope collars. The smell of whiskey on the man's breath was intense, and Raspail observed that his reflexes were compromised. He looked up at the girl and saw that her fear of them had changed to pity.

The man released Raspail's collar but kept his hand tightly clenched on Aratus'. He shouted commands at Aratus while trying to drag him over to the girl. Aratus resisted, which caused the man to raise his stick.

Raspail saw Aratus shrink back in terror from the club hovering over his head. It was unbearable to watch, but to then hear the brave Aratus whine for mercy, drooling and pissing uncontrollably, enraged him beyond all self-control.

Raspail thrust upwards on his shackled legs and seized the man's wrist in his jaws. The man screamed, first upon seeing that the black wolf when standing was as tall as him. The scream then crescendoed into a shriek when he felt the full strength of the wolf's jaws, twisting and grinding, crushing his wrist bones. The man was no stranger to dog bites, but the wolf's bite, designed to tear through four inches of hair and hide, break elk legs and latch on to the backs of bears, has three times the strength of the strongest dog's.

Still, the man, with his fortitude augmented by the alcohol, did not pass out or give up the fight.

As man and wolf stood upright pushing and pulling on each other, the girl, who had shortly embraced a feeling of sympathy for the wolf, became terrified and, with eyes squinted shut, drunkenly pulled the trigger of the rifle, letting fate decide where the bullet should land.

The two fighters fell on each other, but it was the man who caught the bullet. And though he was shot and mauled, still he fought the wolf, not like a man but like an animal, thrashing on his back in the dirt, spitting and frothing and bleeding.

Raspail, who had imbued this mysterious creature with powers beyond his comprehension, was unimpressed.

The girl dropped the gun and ran screaming out of the pen. And though she slammed the gate shut behind her to keep the wolves in, it bounced back off the latch.

Raspail glanced up to see the gate was open. He leaped off the man and hobbled to the gate. With his muzzle he nudged the gate open more, and now freedom lay before him. He looked back at Aratus.

Aratus was at the back of the pen where he had huddled shivering in fear the moment that Raspail attacked the man. Raspail saw the man was dragging his body towards the rifle. He barked imperiously at the trembling Aratus, not like a friend, but like a facet:

"Stand! Stand and run or you will watch me be killed before you yourself are!"

Aratus stood and moved to the gate where Raspail was waiting. They ran as quickly as their shackled legs would go into the confusing man-made landscape that both had seen in those first dizzying moments when they were introduced to the prison. Raspail, whose memory was fresher, led them to the corridor of dead wolves, and the full splendor of its horror was not lost on him now. Beyond the corridor were the snow-covered plains where he'd hunted, and beyond that the mountains. They heard dogs barking.

Raspail knew he could make it out of the corridor, but Aratus was weak in body and spirit, and he lagged behind as the iron rings dug into the sores on his ankles each time they went taut. Raspail looked around, his nose stopping on a wagon overflowing with wolf and coyote hides. Its scent, surging with wolf, would cover theirs. Raspail awkwardly climbed into the wagon and burrowed between the dead animals. He felt Aratus climbing in behind him, and in a moment they were sidled together stacked among the dead.

The dogs arrived and by degrees each realized that the scent trail stopped and the two wolves had disappeared. Raspail and Aratus kept their eyes shut, knowing these glowing lamps would stand out in the sea of dead gazes and destroy their camouflage. Not one of the dogs thought of searching the wagon, and upon hearing a whistle they returned to their human masters.

The two wolves emerged from their hiding spot and ran the remainder of the corridor. They passed under the last of the man-made structures, an enormous arch of interlocked antlers and wolf skulls, and stepped over the threshold to freedom. Aratus attacked the long journey ahead with renewed vigor, for as Hagi could have told him, freedom is best appreciated by those who have lost it and just reclaimed it. Behind them, the confusion caused by their escape faded in their ears as they moved farther away from the prison.

***

How A Wolf Who Thinks Like a Raven Breaks Steel Chains Using What Resources Nature Offers

They paused in the plains so that Aratus could tend to the wounds on his ankles. While he licked his sores, Raspail went searching for nourishment. With each clumsy step the chain rattled and alerted his prey he was coming, and for the first time he realized that even though they were free from their captors, they were still imprisoned by the chains that bound them. He embarrassedly returned to Aratus with no food.

"We must do something about these," he told Aratus.

Aratus nodded. They continued without stopping until they reached a stream at the foot of the mountains where they lapped up water.

The journey up the mountain was slow and difficult. The steep slope was pitted with craters dug by bears looking for roots to eat before hibernation. It was impossible to avoid these deep pits, and every misstep from a back leg tightened the chain against the other. Aratus' leg was bleeding badly and he needed to rest, and Raspail, eager as he was to continue moving, obliged. While Aratus cared for his wounds, Raspail searched for a bird's nest to raid.

What he found was a rock crevice that narrowed into a large cave from which emanated a smell that was unmistakably bear. He stopped and listened till he heard the bear's slow, soft breathing -- the chain hadn't woken it, and he was safe to enter. Now as to why Raspail would want to enter this dark abyss in which a dangerous marauder was sleeping can be explained by an experience he had in his youth.

When he was young, Raspail entered a duel with a bear about his age. The duel, which lasted hours, ended with Raspail killing the bear cub and returning to camp beat to shreds the next day, as we remember. No wolf dared ask the grumbling Raspail what had happened, but if they had they would have been impressed by his boldness.

Before tangling with the bear on that day long ago, young Raspail let himself be lured into a vacant cave by the smell of meat. Because that year's exceedingly frigid winter lingered with snow falling deep into spring, some bears remained dormant in their dens in no hurry to wake. Such was the case with the den Raspail entered. There he found a sleeping adult bear, and by its side was the half-eaten leg of an elk. He gnawed at the frozen meat while the bear slept, and when he finished eating it, he went searching for more bear dens to raid. He explored two more dens, but without the good fortune of his first one. The fourth den he ventured into was occupied by a sleeping bear sow and her awake cub, the same cub that chased Raspail and which Raspail eventually killed.

So powerful was the memory of finding treasure in the bear den, that even though he never repeated the success of his first raid, he always imagined bear dens as secret caches of meat. Such was the case now, with Raspail desperate for food.

Raspail saw the bear in the darkness. It was laying on its stomach with its massive head resting on its arm. It was a full grown male grizzly bear, weighing five times as much as him. Raspail spread his legs while he walked to quiet the chain's metallic clamor, and as he got closer he saw the leftover carcass he had hoped would be there. He licked the meat to make sure it wasn't sick then tore off a mouthful and devoured it.

He looked at the carcass while he ate, impressed at how the jaws of the grizzly had broken through the thick thigh bone of the elk. He knew this bone intimately and shuddered to think of how strong the grizzly's jaws must be to snap such a bone. As he swallowed more food, he gazed at the prone bear whose meat he was stealing. An idea formed in his head, an idea that was as clever as it was crazy, for if it failed, this would be the last meal he ever ate. He tore off a large section of meat and exited the cave with it.

He brought the meat to Aratus, who practically ripped it out of his mouth. After he ate it, Raspail spoke.

"Are you afraid of bears?"

"Compared to the terror I have just escaped, the bear does not scare me, no. Why?"

"There is one thing in nature that can break these binds on our legs, and it is the jaws of a bear. I have found us one who will be willing to do the work for us. All we need to do is wake him."

"And how will you guide this freshly woken bear so that he does not crush everything but the chains?" Aratus asked.

"Ah! Good question. We will wake him by tearing his eyes out. In his blind rage we will feed him what we want him to eat, which in this case is the chain and nothing more."

"Is it the big bear or the smaller one?" asked Aratus with trepidation.

"Only the bigger bear would be appropriate for the task in mind, so for that we are lucky."

"Lucky!" Aratus laughed. "And we wake him by attacking his eyes?"

"Yes. I've woken bears before. They are slow to rise, and they remain confused. They are bears, after all."

Aratus could not comprehend how such an idea would have come to a wolf. It seemed to him, upon meeting up with Raspail further down the road of life, that he thought with Aratus' brain, expressed himself with Balfort's elegant voice, and bore all of their facet's courage and confidence. What he did not know was that Raspail, though he acted like a wolf in the ways his fathers raised him, cogitated with the ingenious logic of a raven.

Aratus looked at the sore flesh where the shackles rubbed, gave them one last lick and got to his feet.

"If I die, tell my story to my children."

Raspail laughed at his proud friend. "Either we both leave that cave alive, or we die together inside it."

They entered the crevice and walked as silently as they could into the dark cave towards the sleeping bear. Since Raspail had left, the bear had moved and now his massive paw rested on his brow, blocking his eyes. Raspail studied the situation with Aratus by his side. Aratus saw what the problem was and they communicated silently. Raspail lifted his forepaw and extended it slowly till the tip of his claw delicately parted the bear's fur, hoping that the bear would brush away the fly bothering him, thus moving his hand from his eyes. When the bear did not react, Raspail pressed his claw deeper into the fur.

The bear awoke in a fury, alert as if he had been merely lightly resting, and roared deafeningly.

Raspail lunged at the bear's right eye, while Aratus took bites at the other. The bear, whose eyes were obscured by blood, swatted blindly at his attackers as they continued their onslaught. He finally shoved them both off him. The wolves landed on their backs and stared up at the bear. Blood streamed from his eyes, and it was evident after a moment that the bear was blind. He swung his gaping jaws side to side, showing off the fat, blunt yellow fangs that studded the muscular gums. But he could not locate his oppressors, who lay as still as the mountain itself.

Then Raspail raised his hind legs. In the half-second it took Raspail to pull the chain taut, the bear's ears locked on to the sound and his jaws chomped down on the chain, mashing on it. The bear yanked the chain in its closed mouth, dragging a terrified Raspail on his back until finally the chain snapped.

The bear spit the shards of chain out and sniffed the air for his attackers. Aratus' stomach, bubbling noisily from sudden indigestion, gave his location away. As the bear charged at him, Aratus raised his hind legs so that the bear's jaws would fall on the chain. The bear smacked his teeth shut on the chain, snapping it off the shackles. As the bear bore down a second time, Aratus felt Raspail grab him by the fur of his neck and drag him back from danger. The bear made a clumsy attack at the empty ground where Aratus had just lay.

Together, Aratus and Raspail ran out the cave not just alive, but with freedom restored to their limbs. Only the bands on their ankles remained, and these would stay forever clamped on the legs of the two former prisoners through their life (and long past their death) as if they had become part of their bodies.

Raspail, not wanting to waste another moment, was heading for Ramblefoot the moment he stepped outside the cave. Noticing that the moon was two days from full, he realized that this was the night he was to have begun the journey to Cob Ash had he not been captured. He heard Aratus growling behind him. He immediately turned back towards the cave. There he saw Aratus jeering their angry victim, who was standing at his full, terrifying height in the crevice outside the cave. Aratus was trying to lure it out where he could kill it. He saw Raspail watching him curiously.

"You show me a better meal right now!"

The bear stumbled forward and Aratus lunged at its leg, tripping the blind beast. The mountain shook as the bear's body hit the ground. Aratus then jumped on its back and dug his fangs into its neck. The bear stood and tried to shake Aratus off, but Aratus tasted blood and would not relent. Raspail ran towards them, his legs pumping gratefully with no restricting binds, and jumped at the bear's neck. The bear lost balance and fell again, and then it was all over for the bear, blind and unable to defend itself from the lightning fast attacks of the two starving wolves.

There was a ridiculous amount of food to share and the two old friends got plenty meatdrunk. Raspail retired to the bear's cave first, but Aratus joined him soon after. He was so engorged with food, he stumbled through the cave as blindly as the bear had. After finding a suitable spot to sleep, he circled (as if he had the clarity at that moment to do respectable diligence), and then flopped on to his side. He let out a satisfied moan then said:

"My friend, I think tonight we will find out if, in fact, a wolf can die from eating too much."

They woke some hours later, filled their stomachs again, then journeyed on to Ramblefoot. It was unusually quiet, and thinking that perhaps the wolves had not woken yet, he visited every flop and den he knew of. There were no wolves in Ramblefoot.

The last place he visited was his old flop. There, perched on one of the boulders that cradled the bed of leaves, was Poitu. She flew at Raspail and landed on his back, rubbing her head on his neck affectionately. Raspail twisted his head back and darted his tongue at her. She pecked lightly at his tongue, a game that they often played.

Raspail saw Aratus' bemusement, but before he could say anything, Aratus spoke.

"There was a raven who followed you when you were young."

"This is her. Poitu, my angel."

She croaked four times, very loudly, and the bed of leaves, which was covered in a blanket of fresh snow, exploded away as Repetto woke and jumped out. He leaped at Raspail, licking him and sniffing him from nose to tail and withers to pads.

Over the next hour they shared stories, Raspail introducing Aratus and telling of the twist of fate that reunited the two old friends, leaving out the horrific details that Raspail wished he could erase from his thoughts. Repetto then had the unfortunate duty of telling how Coustat had assumed the role of facet in Raspail's absence, and that he had led them out yesterday to conquer Cob Ash. Repetto refused to accept anyone else as his facet, so he stayed behind with Poitu, having faith that Raspail would eventually return. Aratus asked about the welfare of the pups, and Repetto told him some stories that elevated his mood.

When the conversation was finished, they departed from Ramblefoot and followed the scent of the pack Northwest. They traveled quickly and only stopped when they heard the familiar sound of ramblefoots howling.

Aratus looked concerned. "How loyal is this pack which so quickly sought another facet in your absence?"

"They will be loyal to me," Raspail said confidently.

"How can you be sure?"

"Because you cannot be loyal to a wolf whose head has been separated from his body."

***

Coustat Gets a Chance to Prove his Merit

Coustat enjoyed being facet. He had not yet faced any real challenges, nor had he needed to draw on exceptional judgment or courage -- all he'd needed do was fill the void left by Raspail. In those few days since he seized his power, he mated with three bitches, lashed several wolves for no reason, and gave proprietary names to the pups which we now know to be the brood of Aratus and Othenia.

So when Raspail trotted calmly into their camp with Repetto, Aratus and Poitu, a miserable mood befell him because it meant that he would need to do something exceptional in order to upstage the big black wolf. Adding to his misery was the fact that upon seeing Raspail, the pack ran to greet him with such exuberance that Coustat felt disrespected. He lashed one wolf who was running around excitedly spreading the word of Raspail's return within a hair of his life.

Raspail greeted his pack warmly, and when they saw the shackles on his legs, it explained his absence without him having to do so. He inquired about Hagi and Boonbrekker explained that he had disappeared as abruptly as Raspail had.

Aratus darted amongst the wolves, unable to wait another moment to see his pups. Raspail badly wished to join Aratus and see the look on his face as he was reunited with his children, but at that moment Coustat waded through the mob and confronted Raspail, broadening his chest and shoulders to exaggerate his stature. The pack gathered around Raspail and Coustat, for this was a duel that was not to be missed.

Poitu, who had just gotten an unpleasant taste of life without Raspail while he was stuck underground, was not eager to see her wolf get killed by the imposing Coustat. She landed inconspicuously on a tree, then got closer by degrees until she was on the earth between the two wolves, ready to fly at Raspail's opponent if the situation called for it.

Coustat, like some of the ramblefoots, knew of Raspail's unusual alliance with the raven. But while others accepted it as further proof of Raspail's singular character, Coustat believed that without the raven Raspail would be as unremarkable as any other wolf -- vincible, even.

The opportunity to prove this came as the bird hopped closer to him and scanned his body for sores, injuries, and other vulnerabilities to exploit. When she got within an arm's length of him he lunged and trapped her delicate body under his huge foot.

Raspail shuddered knowing that the mere shift of Coustat's weight would be enough to end Poitu's life. His reaction of horror unfortunately lost him the advantage to Coustat. The wolf grinned, seeing the surprise he elicited from Raspail, and rolled the bird sadistically as she screeched frantically.

"You seem nervous," Coustat said. "You aren't worried that I'll kill this raven, are you?"

Raspail could not fathom losing her. He said nothing, just stared into Coustat's eyes as he continued.

"You've convinced these wolves that you are something great and powerful. But I have figured out that without this raven... *you are nothing.*"

Wolves in the crowd argued over the controversial claim.

"It is true," Raspail said calmly, silencing them. "That raven befriended me when no wolf would. She hunted with me -- *groomed* me when no wolf would even look at me. So in a way -- a strange way, I admit -- you are right: I am nothing without my little black angel."

Coustat, construing this admission as an advantage gained by him, felt emboldened and spat out, with utter contempt:

"I challenge you to the death, imposter!"

"I accept your challenge. But first release Poitu. She will not interfere in our fight."

"I can guarantee she won't!"

He was cheered on by the howling of several wolves. Raspail was as tense as he had been in the cave.

"If you kill her in such an unfair manner -- crushing her under your foot and with no means by which to defend herself, you will show yourself to be a coward. And this cowardly act will feed my need for vengeance; as I have stated, that raven is my loyal friend, and I would die either protecting her or avenging her death." Raspail's eyes intensified as he continued. "So, if you choose to kill Poitu, do so knowing that my anger towards you, which is only mild right now, will increase ten-fold and put you at an extreme disadvantage, I assure you."

Now, the truth was Raspail could not have grown any more angry or vengeful than he was at this moment.

"However," Raspail continued, "If you kill this raven fairly, vengeance will not be an issue. And then you will be free to defeat me without giving me the advantage."

"Ridiculous -- giving a scavenger the honor of a fight," Coustat responded.

"Yes, it would be embarrassing to lose against an unworthy little opponent like a bird, I know. You see how fragile she is and how strong you are."

The yammering started again. The idea of watching a duel between a wolf and a raven was so novel, so intriguing to the spectators, that once it was seeded in their imaginations by Raspail, no other course could be pursued by Coustat. Even Aratus, who was headed towards his long lost children, stalled and turned to watch how this strange confrontation would end.

Coustat looked down at the raven and thought, *It was easy enough to catch you the first time, I can catch you again.* He took his foot off of Poitu and she immediately leapt in the air and disappeared

Raspail exhaled a sigh of relief.

Coustat searched the sky for his opponent, but she was nowhere to be seen. He chortled.

"Your partner likes to flee when the pressure is on. Just like you."

At that Poitu dropped from the sky like a meteorite on to Coustat's shoulders, her talons grasping his fur firmly.

Coustat opened his jaws and swung his head left to bite at the bird, but she had positioned herself perfectly out of reach. Next, he swung to the right, with the same luck. Laughter erupted from the crowd, fueling his frustration. Poitu emitted shrill cackles behind his ear, putting his nerves on end.

Raspail's mood lightened significantly. He casually lay down to take in the show with the others.

As soon as Coustat realized that the raven could not be attacked while it was rooted on his shoulders, he tried shaking it off his back like he would water. This also failed, for Poitu was adept at anchoring herself to her host. He tried dropping on to his side to disable her, throwing his body against a tree, and several other strategies that all failed in everything other than making himself miserable and his audience howl with laughter. Repetto was entertained into such a fit of sneezing that he missed half the spectacle.

But because Coustat's reputation and power were at stake, he persevered against the antagonizing raven, jumping at it as it hovered just above his arcing jaws. Then, in a moment of clarity, a voice in his head asked: *Why waste your energy on this annoying creature when the one you really need to dispose of -- the one who has tricked you into making an ass of yourself -- is laying down and vulnerable to attack?*

Giving up on the raven, Coustat charged at Raspail. And though Raspail was caught off guard, he was not, like his opponent, in a state of agitation. Raspail killed Coustat with such preternatural speed and effortlessness that the gathering wolves who thought that the show with the raven was some warm-up for a great duel between two fierce wolves were startled to see that the fight ended before it even began.

"Dump him in the plains." Raspail's voice was soft but resolute. "I want no wolf to utter his name or think of him again; he has no name, he is nothing."

The wolves howled, thrilled at his spectacular return.

Raspail saw Aratus bounding towards Nin and the pups, and immediately went to join him.

***

Hagi and Aratus

Hagi had separated from the pack when he had the unsettling feeling of being stalked and hunted by an old and powerful enemy that he knew he had to deal with before it dealt with him.

The unique signature of Siksak -- four different disfigured footprints embossed in the snow -- was shadowing him. He first saw them in the camp at Ramblefoot the night Raspail announced his desire to be facet, and he saw them all along their journey north. This enemy, no matter how hard Hagi looked, evaded him. When he was sure that he sensed him in the tall grass that sprouted through the snow, he waited for wind to blow so that he could detect the contrasting motion between ruffled fur and bending grass. But when the wind blew, it did not help, for the fur of Siksak was not fur any longer, it was a mat of molten skin and hair, frozen in place like lava which, once flowing and free, has solidified in place never to move again.

Scanning the horizon he saw three bumbling ramblefoots dragging Coustat's body into the plains as Raspail ordered. Once they dropped the slain wolf's body they took turns shitting near his corpse, laughing deleriously as they did so.

"Hoy!" Hagi barked from the timbers.

"Hagi-Shaaaaan!" they howled as they ran to greet him with sweeping tails.

"Who is the dead wolf you're dropping turds by?" Hagi inquired.

"Coustat!" The wolves said in unison excitedly.

Hagi looked pleased. "Who killed him?"

"Who else!"

Hagi smiled and followed the three wolves back, cursing his missing foot for slowing him down.

Raspail cautioned Aratus about Nin as they neared the rendezvous site where Nin guarded the pups. It was apparent that Aratus was apprehensive, still holding on to doubts that the pups were his. Nin appeared and snarled at them.

"Let them sleep! Go Away!"

"We have a special visitor today, Nin. This is Aratus."

One of the pups ran towards Aratus.

"Minou!" Aratus exclaimed in disbelief.

Minou, who was the last pup that Repetto saved from the trap-laden den, barreled towards his father, yelping joyfully. Aratus let him nip at his ears and face. In a moment his other children -- children he'd imagined peering down at him from the sky when the moon was full, shaming him for his failure to protect them -- were on top of him mercilessly showing affection. Raspail's heart grew heavy with love, remembering how as a child he longed for Aratus to return from the hunt and attacking him when he arrived.

Nin was left out of this happy reunion and looked in every way threatened. Her lip quivered and she showed fang.

Raspail stood over her and spoke commandingly, "Show my brother courtesy, wolfmother, for he is the rightful father of these pups. His mate -- their mother -- is dead, so have no fear, you are their new mother."

Upon hearing the facet tell her that her role was not threatened, she relaxed her lip and watched the pups play, reprimanding them occasionally when they played too rough with their father.

Aratus looked at Raspail. "I have six children. Where is Raya?"

"Alas, we were too late to save them all, for one had already been taken by the traps."

Aratus, overwhelmed by the joy of seeing his children alive, did not let his woes over losing Raya overwhelm his appreciation for what he had not lost.

Hagi arrived and threw his arms around Raspail's shoulders. "Do you enjoy making me worry?"

The two friends played for a moment, then Hagi looked at his shackles inquisitively, smelling and licking them.

"There is a story that will scare the fur off your hide. But do not count on me telling it, because I do not have the fortitude to relive that misery again, the words to describe the horrors that I saw, nor the time to do the story justice. Full moon is approaching. We will be at the throats of our enemies soon."

Aratus turned his attention from his children to this new ally of Raspail's. Immediately he sensed he recognized him from an old memory, and though he strained to fathom how, he felt it was not a good association.

"Hagi, this is Aratus, who saved me from death as an infant and raised me like a son. And Aratus, this is Hagi, the greatest storyteller you will ever meet. If you smell his foot pads you will know the extent of his travels, which are vast."

Raspail saw Aratus' hackles go up.

"Aratus! Hagi is among the few creatures who I trust completely. As you are in that small group, I hope you will become fast friends with him on my word alone."

Aratus cooled himself and gestured agreeably, but his mind fathomed the deep recesses of his memory for a clue as to why this old wolf struck such a distrustful chord with him.

Shortly thereafter, Raspail gathered together Repetto, Boonbrekker, Hagi and Aratus to confer on the siege of Cob Ash. The strategy was simple: each of them (except Repetto) would lead individual sub-packs of five to six wolves in an assault on the southern border. These subpacks, spread out from the low mountain of the west to the Draguignon border to the east, would then fight their way into Cob Ash, pushing the enemy toward the center of the province where they would surround and hold them until they were defeated.

"We engage the enemy with the same mad drunken style we use to hunt in Ramblefoot," Raspail said.

Raspail knew that such a massive and bloody siege would draw the much needed wolf numbers away from the low mountain where Kileo was being guarded, and he and Repetto could then penetrate the mountain to rescue her. Repetto was flush with pride, being the wolf chosen to guard his facet.

The plan was agreed on by all with no further discussion.

They began their march towards Cob Ash, and spirits were high under the nearly full eye of the ancestor, though Aratus remained plagued by misgivings about Hagi.

***

Steeling for Battle

In Cob Ash at about that same moment, Hesser was experiencing a similar feeling of unease to what Hagi felt knowing that he was under the invisible gaze of a stalker who left no trace of his presence.

Siksak, like Raspail, was a quick adapter. Stealth was the upside of being boiled alive, and so he refined this ability to sneak up on prey and quickly disable them. And though his disfigured jaws inhibited him from chewing tough meat and breaking bone, he could easily tear through the thin hide covering a victim's protruding belly, puncture the stomach and slurp up its liquefied contents.

But Siksak stalked Hesser, not to eat from his stomach, but to feed his fear and manipulate him for his advantage.

"You are Hesser?" The voice drifted by like a breeze.

Hesser flinched and saw the disfigured Siksak peering at him through the frozen tangles of his facial fur.

"Who are you?" said Hesser backing away, afraid to look too closely at him.

"I am... *your friend.*"

"I have no friends who look like you."

"No, tis true, but two wolves who share the same enemy are allies."

"Who is my enemy?" Hesser challenged him "Answer this correctly or you will be killed."

"The black wolf called Raspail."

Hesser gasped in shock.

"This wolf will attack your province when the eye of the ancestor is open."

"But that is tonight!" said Hesser, unable to disguise his terror with his fine acting skills.

"Ramblefoots, enough to fill four packs, have been enlisted into his service. He will kill all who stand in his way."

Siksak knew this, for he had spied on the conversation we have just described.

"Why do you tell me this? What do you have to gain?"

"Do you see the wretched form my body has taken? I have the black wolf to blame for that. I cannot kill him on my own, and until he is dead I will be plagued by thoughts of revenge."

Polwin ran over ready to attack Siksak when Hesser stopped him and explained his presence. Polwin thought for a moment then spoke.

"We will need greater numbers. I will go to our border," Polwin said. "I'll find the fiercest and enlist them in exchange for residency in our province. Then we will have our numbers."

Hesser liked the plan and Polwin, joined by his patrol, scoured the border looking for recruits. Among the fittest were a remnant pack that had traveled north returning to their old home, the home they regretted ever leaving. When Polwin spotted Maddocq and Balfort with three strong young males in their ranks, he welcomed them back graciously into Cob Ash, though if they hadn't had need for numbers, he thought, he would have gladly killed them as if they were any other wolves trying to sneak across their border.

These returning brothers and their three wards entered Cob Ash. Balfort sniffed at the familiar sights and scents and said to Maddocq:

"Why did we ever leave this paradise to pursue such tragedy? This is where we belong. This is our home. Aratus is not wise in all matters, Maddocq. I hope you finally realize that now."

Maddocq, with his keener sense of smell and more pessimistic nature, registered the strange changes in the air as they walked and his brow showed his reservations.

"Really -- did we think we would find a place better than Cob Ash?" He waited for Maddocq's response. "Speak, Maddocq. Sometimes I swear it's as if I am traveling with a rock."

"It isn't Cob Ash anymore," Maddocq finally said. Cob Ash is gone, I don't smell him. I smell Draguignon on every boulder and tree."

They were brought to Hesser, who was relaxing with Sarassin and their brood of white wolves. The white wolves went to greet the visitors with vicious displays of territoriality, while Polwin addressed Hesser with respect.

"My facet, I have recruited the best wolves I could find at our border. There are seventeen in all. I think you'll find these five the best of the bunch."

"Facet?" Balfort muttered to Maddocq, who was staring down the young wolves. "Hesser is facet? Am I in some delirious state where everything is backwards?"

Hesser came over and greeted his two brothers hospitably. He looked well-fed, confident, and walked with the formidable stature of his brother Cob Ash.

"Welcome home, brothers. As facet of Cob Ash," Hesser gloated, "I grant you all the privileges you gave up when you rambled."

"Gratitude. Now tell me brother, what has become of our former facet, the great Cob Ash?"

"Let us just say that a certain member of our pack, embittered by unfortunate injuries from an accident, took out his anger on Cob Ash and heinously slew his father."

"What son are you referring to?"

"Why Raspail, of course."

The disturbing news stunned Maddocq and Balfort. Maddocq glanced at Sarassin, recognizing her.

"And Cortess? Where is our great sister?"

"No longer great, I tell you with sadness, because the tragedy so overwhelmed her she developed the scatters and went looking for her mate believing he was still alive. I was made facet by the pack and, seeing that it was impossible to defend our border from Draguignon with such diminished numbers, brokered an agreement that allows us to live in peace with our neighbors to the east."

Sarassin smiled at Balfort while she licked her paws. Balfort's suspicion was now on par with Maddocq's, but being the cunning wolf he was, did not reveal any of his misgivings.

"Hesser, I give you my full respect as our new facet, as does Maddocq," Balfort said bowing his head slightly and signaling Maddocq to do the same. "Merely say what it is you need from us and it will be yours as it would have been for Cob Ash."

"Tonight our home will be under siege by a massive pack of wolves. I ask you, my brothers, to be this facet's private guards. Guard me with your lives, for the good of Cob Ash and the future of its children is in my hands!"

Balfort gazed down at the white wolves who, at just eight months old, lacked the playful innocence of youth. Each was vicious -- unnaturally so -- like a creature mistreated from birth and learned to mistrust all. They formed in a crescent around Balfort and the others, and snarled with flashed fangs.

"For the good of its children!" Said Balfort with fake cheer as he smiled into the eyes of one of these half-yearlings. Eye contact caused the lithe white monster to lunge at Balfort. Balfort adroitly side-stepped his attacker, but the rest of them tightened their arc into a circle.

"Children," said Sarassin, "It is not play time."

"Play time indeed," muttered Balfort to Maddocq.

Balfort and Maddocq excused themselves so they could roam their old haunts. Wherever they went there was the smell of Draguignon and the feeling that some wolf was following them with their eyes.

"This intrigue we have found ourselves in is corrupt in every way," he whispered to Maddocq, "And never have I missed so much the sage counsel of our brother Aratus, for I have no clue what to do."

Balfort whined, and Maddocq moaned in sympathy.

The southern border of Cob Ash was fortified in preparation for the attack. This meant that wolves could no longer be spared on the far western border, at the low mountain where Kileo was being held captive. Polwin decided that only two wolves were needed to guard the mountain since there was only one way in and out via the steep ravine.

Abillon was posted here with an old Draguignon female. It was their job to howl an alarm if Kileo attempted to escape. Wolves billeted at the border would need just three minutes to reach the low mountain and thwart the escape, so the feckless Abillon's job was not a very important one in the eyes of Polwin who assigned him it.

It was a boring task and Abillon passed the time looking at the sky. Night was still hours away but it was dark as dusk because of the heavy clouds that blocked the sun. Abillon was transfixed by the long intervals between the sun hiding and exposing itself, and though his eyes were open, his mind was a void.

Then the smell came. It was an amorous invitation sent out by a bitch who was definitely not his partner in the patrol; she was too old. He lifted his muzzle and stirred the air; it was coming from the mountain, from Kileo.

The perfume got thicker and took control of his will, which was weak to begin with. His haunches and lower back jerked spasmodically, uncontrollably unsheathing his fifth leg and thrusting at the air under his chest.

The clouds, he figured, would obscure the moon during the night just as they covered the sun. With the eye blinded, he was free to follow the scent to Kileo, and the ancestors would not know what they could not see.

**

The Fickle Eye

The wolf pack, rolling like a wave of wolves, undulating over the hillocks and hummocks that peppered the meadows south of Cob Ash, looked every bit like a flock of birds to Poitu as she flew over them.

Raspail ran at the head of the pack, amazed at how silently this rowdy company moved when they needed to. When he stopped, they stopped in an orderly fashion behind him and awaited his command. Raspail told Aratus to watch the pack while he and Repetto scouted Cob Ash's border.

The ranks were eager to rest before battle, so Aratus had little to do but play with his children. While he played he spied Hagi walk among the troops, offering good cheer. It was uncanny to Aratus how familiar this old wolf seemed. He closed his eyes and listened to Hagi's voice, trying to fathom where he knew him from.

"You seemed to recognize me."

Aratus opened his eyes. Hagi was standing in front of him.

Hagi continued. "Well, you are familiar to me too."

Aratus was uncomfortable with Hagi's stare and looked away.

"I've spent my life traveling these provinces and you would be hard pressed to find a wolf who has met more wolves than me. Perhaps we've met before, no?"

Aratus looked back into his eyes. "I have no doubt I've met you. I just can't remember the circumstances."

Hagi laughed cryptically, inviting Aratus to stare into his gaze and jog his memory. Frustrated, Aratus looked away

"Hoy. We'll figure it out yet, my friend."

Raspail and Repetto were close to the border when they heard wolves. They stopped and crouched in the snow, listening. There were many wolves, more than Raspail had imagined there would be, waiting at the border, anticipating the siege.

How did they know to prepare this defense? Raspail wondered.

He looked at Repetto and saw that he was worried -- not because of the number of enemy wolves, but because the moon was half-obscured by thick snow clouds. This enormous cloud was moving so slowly it seemed to have dragged to a halt. They both stared at the eye, trying to speculate if it was going to open or close.

Raspail was driven to near madness as the clouds completed their obliteration of the moon at a sadistically slow pace. The arriving sky gave little hope to the eye making a comeback, at least for the next several hours. Raspail looked despondently at Repetto.

"Find out if they'll fight."

Repetto ran off silently back to the pack.

While Raspail waited, he looked at the low mountain. He was much closer than before, but in the poor visibility he could see less. His eyes bored through the fog for some sign of life but discerned nothing.

Repetto appeared back at his side, panting. He held his head low, hesitant to tell his friend the bad news.

"You needn't say a thing it if you are going to look like that."

Raspail looked up. The last remnant of moonlight was choked by the dreary, leaden clouds.

"The moment the eye opens, they are ready."

"Good for them," said Raspail as he began trotting towards the mountain. "But I am ready now."

Repetto whimpered, so torn was he between loyalty to his facet and fear of the eye.

Not far from where Raspail and Repetto were positioned at the border, Abillon stared at the sleeping Draguignon bitch, twitching from some dream where she was being chased. Even this battered, aged bitch, with her eye markings bleached off from the sun, looked inviting to him with Kileo's perfume drenching the air.

He looked up at the moon and saw that it was finally obscured by the clouds. He was free to unleash himself on his sister with no penance from the watchful eye.

"What it can't see it can't ever know!" thought the despicable wolf.

He followed the scent up the ravine to the top of the low mountain. As the elevation increased, Abillon slowed to a walking pace for he could see no further than a single length. It wasn't difficult to find her; when Kileo heard the wolf coming, she stalked it as it stalked her, klooting in the brush until she saw that it was Abillon.

"Abillon!"

Kileo walked to him, wondering what was wrong. Then she saw the lurid red shaft protruding from his sheath.

He hopped up and threw his arm across her back and mounted her. She tried to shake him off balance, but his forearms clutched her ribs with suffocating intensity. She felt his groin thrust at her.

"No!" she said as she twisted out of his grip and faced him. "Abillon -- we are brother and sister!"

"You are making me do this!" He mounted her again, only this time she flipped on to her back and kicked him off with her feet. He reeled back then pounced on her, not to mount her, but to show his dominance through bites and punches so she would end her resistance. Kileo fought valiantly, but Abillon was a big wolf. The horror of being raped by him seemed inevitable as her strength waned.

Then something powerful flew at them, knocking Abillon off of her and disappearing without a trace. Abillon lay confused on the ground. In the moonless night, with fog draped over every tree and boulder, he could not locate his attacker.

"Shame, Abillon, shame," came the hushed voice in the trees. Kileo did not recognize the voice, nor did Abillon, who looked around in a panic.

Two bright golden eyes ignited in the darkness as Raspail slowly stepped forward towards Abillon, his massive body taking form as it got nearer.

Kileo's eyes bored into this wolf. He was at once the Raspail she knew and a stranger, a wolf who had lived a thousand lives and deaths since she'd last seen him.

"Do you not remember me?" he asked Abillon "You once chased me out of Cob Ash, threatening me with death if I ever returned. You have the opportunity now. Why don't you kill me?"

"I will not kill my brother." Abillon said sanctimoniously, even though he was terrified. "I didn't then and I will not now."

"I too will not kill my brother." He saw Abillon look relieved. "You, however, are not my brother, Abillon -- at least not by blood." He continued, for Kileo's benefit, saying, "Cortess did not birth me as she did you. I came from another mother, I have learned."

Kileo heard what he said, but it did not quite register. Her life had been so beset by disappointment that her faculty for hope was diminished. This had to be a dream that she was weaving in her head; soon the ghost of Raspail would disappear and she would be under Abillon's mount again.

"Did we not share our childhood?" Abillon pleaded. "Did we not play and hunt together? Can you not think of a single happy moment we enjoyed together?"

Raspail cocked his head as if to fondly recollect. "I suppose we did share one happy moment."

"What happy moment that we shared together do you refer to, Raspail? I can think of many, not just one!" Abillon said hopefully, thinking it might dredge up Raspail's mercy.

"It was that happy moment... when I killed you." Raspail said.

And as Abillon arched his neck to howl (as he was instructed to do if there were trouble at the low mountain), Raspail lunged at his throat and pinched it shut before the vibrations fomenting in his chest could escape. Raspail sealed his windpipe shut and held it that way, pinioning Abillon to the ground until he suffocated to death. Raspail released the dead wolf from his bloody jaws and looked up at Kileo.

Kileo stepped back with raised hackles, flashing fang at Raspail.

"Who are you!" She snarled.

"Who am I?" Raspail laughed, confused by her cold greeting.

"You say you are Raspail. Yes -- that would be good, and even better if what you've said is true, that Raspail and I are not brother and sister. But nothing good has happened to me as long as I can remember, making me doubt what I see is real. My hopes and wishes, like the mute Raspail's voice, go unheard. You, black wolf who speaks and in a strange voice, are either an apparition trying to trick me, or I have the scatters."

"I am no apparition. I do not play tricks," he said as he walked closer, "And you do not have the scatters."

She flashed fang again, halting him.

"What are you then!" she snarled, her thigh muscles compressed and ready to release their power at him.

"Was I more real staring at you across that huge divide -- *a speck on a mountain!* -- than I am now, in the flesh, close enough to breathe your warm exhale?"

She had no answer. She looked weak, exhausted.

He walked closer to her. Though she was tense, she did not snarl or flash fang this time, but firmly stood her ground. When he was standing a half length from her, he bowed his head to her and stood stoically, inviting her to examine him. She circumspectly stepped closer and started at his tail, smelling his croup, burying her nose deep in his fur. She took her time, working her way towards his head, snorting at the fur under his loin. He remained as still as a rock while she diligently chipped away at her disbelief, one hair at a time it seemed, as he nearly exploded from the pleasure of her touch.

She sniffed at the pads of his rear feet, which she licked as well, then moved up to his ankle and paused at the shackle.

"What are those?" she asked like it were an interrogation.

"Freedom."

"Don't be clever with me."

Raspail remained stoic, with his neck craned down. He wasn't being clever. He had accepted the metal bands as part of his body since they could never be removed. As malevolent as the shackles were when they were connected by a chain, untethered they were benign and served as a reminder that freedom was his.

She lifted her right foot and pushed against his body as if expecting her foot to pass through something intangible like the fog. His body swayed slightly under the pressure, then rebounded like a branch bent by a gust of wind.

She slowly brought her muzzle to the side of his face and looked at his eyes, which were fixed on the ground. She sniffed at his ear, sniffed his cheek, and grazed her nose against the corner of his lip. He listened to her puff at him as she traced the crooked line of his lip to the matted fur under his chin. She lingered there. Then, with a tinge of surprise, outrage, and thrill, she felt Raspail's long tongue suddenly swab her nose.

She leaped back to a defensive position, snarling and flashing fang. "Would you like me to bite that tongue off?! *Would you?!*"

Raspail could see her tail from the corner of his eye. It was starting to sweep back and forth, but with a measured slowness on par with the dark clouds that concealed the moon. He was making some progress, but he concealed his satisfaction.

"No, my good bitch. I would not dare upset you."

Again she smelled at his face while he stared at the ground, and as she put her nose in range of his tongue again, he could not stop himself from imagining licking her nose again. Trying to remain stoic with this thought in his head made him lose all composure and he burst out laughing.

Kileo tackled him to the ground and stood angrily above him. She spoke fiercely:

"Only Raspail knows how to antagonize me and irritate like that."

"So you *do* accept me as Raspail then?"

"Even if I do, it doesn't mean I like you any better than I did a moment ago."

And she sprang off him and ran, vanishing into the fog. He leaped to his feet and chased her through the dark, misty routes between the trees and boulders, routes that she could easily run with eyes closed, routes that he did not know at all. He was navigated through bush and rock only by the invisible ribbon of her perfume.

Kileo thought he was doing an admiral job of chasing her, and slowed her pace to let him catch up. But then she heard a loud crash followed by Raspail's yelping. She turned around and ran back towards him.

Raspail had run headfirst into a tree, fallen, then slid on snow and rocks into another tree. The hit to his thick skull was hard enough to make him lose his balance, but he had suffered harder blows from the man with the stick. As disoriented and cross-eyed as he was, he got back up and continued chasing Kileo. He staggered and stumbled through the fog until he crashed into Kileo, who was running back to him. They tumbled in the air and Raspail landed on top of her, leering at her like a meatdrunk idiot. Then he fell over on to his side and tried his best not to pass out.

Kileo laughed until she saw blood glistening from the wound on the crown of his head, which had been gashed opened by the tree. She licked the bark out of his wound with her strong rough tongue as he lay there, dizzy in ecstasy. She saw other inflamed bumps on his head, and tried to imagine how he'd received them.

"Other trees you've run into?"

"Some ran into me."

His eyes were closed but he was not sleeping. "Why must you torture me so?" he said in a hushed voice.

"That is my role," she replied.

"Torturer?"

"Yes. If you are disappointed, go back where you came from, *ramblefoot.*"

He laughed privately at this, thinking that this provincial girl, who had probably never even met a ramblefoot but used the word for slander, was now laying with him, *facet* of Ramblefoot. His eyes radiated pleasure.

"I am anything but disappointed."

And he began to physically take charge of her in a way that was not unpleasant to her, though it was comically awkward for both of them. Cautious thoughts took control of Kileo's judgment.

"This must wait!" She said.

"All I've done is wait. We are finally on the same mountain, and we are alive. Everything else must wait."

"Let us escape this mountain first."

"I have faced enough trials today."

She rubbed her face against his and spoke softly.

"I am also eager to make children, but I would like to live to raise them."

"The storm conceals the moon and all is still below. We are free from danger at this moment."

She looked at him, startled. "I think you have gone from a mute wolf to one who is deaf, dumb and blind! Danger is all around us!"

"It always is and always will be." He laughed with genuine carefreeness. "Close your eyes. Fathom that moment that comes during big storms, that moment when the rain stops and the sun burns through the sky and we burst from our shelters to frolic in the warmth of the sun..."

She reluctantly shut her eyes, leaning her body against his.

"And we know that it will be a fleeting moment, we know that the storm clouds are due any moment, but we frolic up till the very last moment. We frolic hard, time stretches, it seems like the sun will never go away -- *that is this moment.*"

"I do not feel the warmth of the sun as you seem to," she said, her eyes still shut.

"Oh, the unfortunate irony that this moment comes during stormy skies," he moaned.

"Say something that will reassure me," her voice trembled, "because I would also like to feel as though the sun were on my back."

"For as long as the moon is obscured, no wolf will kill me. They will wait till the sky is clear so the eye, fully open, is witness to their grand deed."

She opened her eyes and looked at him again. In the dim night glow, with Abillon's blood splattered on his muzzle and his own blood dripping where he'd hit his head against the tree chasing her, he looked like he'd died and come back from the dead to get her.

At that moment, she felt the warmth of sun on her back as Raspail described, and the calmness she begged him to restore in her heart.

***

The Two-Headed Monster

For the male wolf who only gets one opportunity a year to mate (and that if he is lucky), there is such anticipation and sexual fervor stoked by the piquant scent of bitches during the cold months of December and January, that sexual climax happens rather quickly.

But that is not all there is to mating if you are a wolf. Once the male has climaxed, the genitalia of the two wolves swell and interlock to form an unbreakable seal that insures that not one drop of the precious juice, vital for the reproduction of more wolves, is lost. Thus, Raspail and Kileo lay cupped together embossed in the snow, stuck together in this blissful state.

All peacefulness was blown asunder as Repetto stormed through the brush yelping something incomprehensible at Raspail. Raspail looked up and saw that the moon had begun to appear from behind the clouds and was on its way to being fully open.

He heard three or four wolves coming. Raspail hoisted both their bodies up, but locked together as they were he could not use his arms to run, only his legs. He tried to withdraw from her but it was impossible without injuring both of them.

"We must run together," he told her.

Their first clumsy steps sent them stumbling to the ground again. They quickly got up and shuffled along until a gait that suited them both was found. They were moving too slowly to evade the attackers, who had just broken through the brush and were locked on to them.

"I feel them snorting at me!"

"Be calm," Raspail urged her, "Shadow my breathing, not theirs."

She tried to slow her breathing and heartbeat to synchronize with Raspail's. As she did, they started to move faster and with a semblance of grace, Raspail's torso rising and sinking with her back, his legs pumping in parallel precision with hers. And though they could not match the velocity of the wolves in pursuit, they gained the edge in another way. Their two bodies melded into one creature, one that shared two brains and two bodies. So when the three Draguignon wolves finally caught up with them, they faced not a bumbling, incapacitated coupling of wolves, but an agile two-headed beast.

Raspail had learned how to fight with shackled legs from Aratus, and fighting while anchored into the ass of his mate was not so different. Intuitively she pivoted when he needed her to pivot and advanced when he saw an opportunity to attack.

Kileo felt something graze her belly and saw it launch out from under her towards their opponents. It was Repetto. He slashed and shredded at legs, arms, and scrotum as he darted around the three Draguignon wolves like a deranged child. The three combatants quickly gave victory to their enemy and limped off yelping down the mountain.

Raspail was released from Kileo's clutch and fell to the ground panting. Kileo stared harshly at the little wolf, who was laughing hysterically at Raspail.

"Are you this boy's father?" Kileo asked Raspail angrily.

"Na, he just my facet." Repetto said.

In reaction to his voice, which was low like a full grown wolf's, she stepped back and looked to Raspail for an explanation.

Raspail had moved to the mountain's edge and was concentrating on the moon. The clouds had moved on, and the eye was not just open, it was crisply detailed. The mist on the ground had also lifted somewhat, and looking down he could see to the border from where he stood. All was quiet so far.

"This strange wolf thinks you are his facet," Kileo said to him.

"I am," Raspail responded, his stare fixed on the border.

"Really. You travel with a pack?"

"Yes."

"Are they all tiny?"

"No," Raspail said. "Some are quite enormous."

"I thought you were a lone wolf. A ramblefoot."

"I am *facet of Ramblefoot.* And that..." he gestured with his nose, "is my pack."

She looked at where he was staring and saw an avalanche of snow on the horizon. As her eyes adjusted she saw that the avalanche was in fact the snowy wake of a huge pack of wolves storming towards Cob Ash. The look of awe on her face as she watched this colossal wave of force drive towards Cob Ash thrilled him, and he thought, *So power has a drunk all its own.*

With their attention fixed on the coming tide of Ramblefoots, it was easy to not see the border recruits klooting invisibly within Cob Ash. These recruits, who offered their loyalty in exchange for a small parcel of Cob Ash, guarded their position as if it already were their home.

***

The Opening Skirmish

Hesser, giving the appearance of fortitude and leadership, surrounded himself with five brave wolves who he thought would fight and die for him so he would not have to, and these recruits included Balfort, Maddocq and their three young wards. They remained a safe distance behind the first bastion of border recruits and watched as the ramblefoots -- all well-fed and badly mangled -- spilled across the Cob Ash border and clashed with the defending wolves using their hunting style, which we remember was chaotic, drunken, and unpredictable.

Aratus, who coordinated the attacking ramblefoot sub-packs, was startled at first by the ramblefoot's disorderly style, but soon got caught up in the melee. They did not engage their enemies by clashing one-on-one. They rolled over the unfortunate enemy like a stampede, biting and gnashing without stopping, then moving on, letting the fresh wolves behind them heap more injury on the stunned victims as they passed.

In his first order on the battlefield, Hesser commanded his guards to retreat.

It was a swarm of bloody anarchy, and by dawn the defending wolves who survived the siege fled across the creek border and into Draguignon where they rested and licked their gory wounds.

In Cob Ash it was a different story. The ramblefoot pack, which suffered only two mortalities, was hungry to continue their assault into Draguignon and finish off the enemy. Hagi, who knew this was unwise, was unable to raise his voice above the clamor of the bloodthirsty celebrants to stop them. To his immense relief, Raspail appeared with Repetto and Kileo.

Upon seeing their new matriarch, the curious wolves climbed over each other to greet her, particularly Ipsy, Nin, and the other female ramblefoots. The pack howled in appreciation for their facet's good judgment, they howled at his successful rescue of Kileo, and they howled at their enemies for retreating without much of a fight. By the time they were done singing, their blood had cooled and their stomachs were demanding food.

Raspail commanded Aratus to take the pack hunting. During Draguignon's occupation of Cob Ash there was a parallel transformation in the elk herds that proved fortuitous to Aratus. When Draguignon absorbed Cob Ash's numbers, the elk merged their ranks as well, traveling in giant herds that surrounded their young. The disorderly ramblefoots thrived on this oversized herd (though one wolf was trampled to death while hunting).

If Raspail had been a real facet at heart, he would have led these hunts. But his ambition -- even though it required a complex and unwieldy strategy -- was modest; he wanted to be with Kileo. He wanted to play with her, to mate again, and to rest side by side with no worries of being interrupted. Poitu occasionally visited them, but like the wind and the sun, her company was natural, welcome, and untroublesome.

They sprawled on the hill that they'd tumbled down as pups. Their bodies were pressed close together and Raspail enjoyed the intimacy that he had both yearned for and shunned from his thoughts thinking he was destined to never have it. Kileo drifted towards sleep herself, but sleep was thwarted by the recurring sensation that something was spying on her.

Siksak was prone in the grass staring and drooling at Kileo from about fifty lengths. He imagined how the food from her stomach would taste doubly sweet, since it would nourish not just his master, but his hunger for revenge against Raspail.

Seeing that Kileo was agitated by his presence, Siksak distanced himself and secreted through the timbers till he found a dead recruit sprawled in the snow and untouched yet by scavengers. He carefully opened its stomach. Out spilled the steaming, chymus meat. Siksak licked the stomach lining clean, then slipped invisibly back to Draguignon.

***

Revisiting Poitu's Cache

Kileo, unable to rest where she lay, nudged the sleeping Raspail awake.

"Sleep," he mumbled

"I can't. Not here. Let's run somewhere."

"I've done enough running."

"I've done enough staying in place, I was imprisoned on that mountain." She stood. He gently took her leg in his mouth and gnawed it.

"I'm never letting you out of my sight again."

"So I'm destined to be a prisoner then? I don't think so."

She ran off, inviting him to chase her. He rose and stretched at a leisurely pace, kicking his legs out one by one as he yawned contentedly, then pursued her, Poitu flying overhead. After a while they reached the area where Raspail played and hunted with Poitu when he was mute. He saw Poitu break away and fly askew, moving in a zig zag pattern from tree to tree. He knew exactly where she was headed and changed course so that he would beat her there.

Because of the raven's fastidious security rituals, Raspail and Kileo arrived at the stand of spruce trees first.

"Where are we?" Kileo asked.

"Shh. Stay hidden and watch."

Poitu arrived a moment later, landing on the conifer's peak, working her way down, surveying the area as she did. She finally hopped to the ground, faced north, hopped forward counting her steps -- eight north and four east -- brushed the pine needles away with her flapping wings, swept the dirt with her talons, and exposed a life's worth of souvenirs.

Raspail jumped out at her, infuriating her. Once her anger abated, she stood back from the cache and proudly let the two wolves peer in the hole.

Raspail poked his nose in the glass shards, moving them around, remembering that the strange crystals' scent provoked a wondrous feeling in him once. With the passage of time, the scent had mostly disappeared.

"Why does she do this?"

"She's a raven."

Poitu hopped over to the hole and delicately swept aside the glass with her claws. There, Raspail and Kileo saw the real treasure. Raspail was immediately drawn to an old black claw, still attached to its large leathery pad, and moved it with his tongue. Poitu snatched it up in her bill, vigorously shook the dirt off, then laid it down on the snow in front of Raspail.

Raspail swabbed the pad with his tongue. As his warm saliva lubricated the dry flesh, he could taste what he remembered smelling. Kileo licked it too, and said the thoughts that were in Raspail's head.

"That is the foot of a wolf -- a very large wolf, one foreign to warmpools."

"My mother, perhaps." Raspail said. He looked at Poitu, trying to fathom their first experience together. It seemed like there was never a time he didn't know her.

"Do you remember that dream I had, the one where a raven was chasing me, hopping on the ground, fanning its wings?"

"Yes."

"I believe that was Poitu. She must have been protecting me somehow -- she only does that when there's danger." He licked the pad again. "Poitu was there when my mother died." He looked into the raven's black eyes with renewed appreciation. "Why would a raven help me when there was nothing for her to gain? I was a pup, I couldn't hunt yet. It makes no sense."

They flopped by the cache. Raspail quietly thought to himself while Kileo finally felt secure enough to fall asleep.

Raspail laid his head across Kileo's chest, staring into Poitu's eyes while Kileo slept. He'd always assumed their relationship started as an alliance between two outcasts, each exploiting the other in a way that benefited them equally. At some point their bond was tested enough times that wolf and raven knew they had something more than a temporary pact. They started to care about each other, even growing anxious when the other went missing for too long.

But now, through the revelation gleaned from the old severed toe of his mother, he realized that the raven had been watching over him since the beginning.

***

The Pact of the Shahn

Early that evening, while the ramblefoots explored the perimeter of their new province and drenched scent posts with their own piss, Hagi gathered Repetto, Aratus, Raspail, and Kileo and brought them to a clearing in the trees where they could speak uninterrupted. Upon seeing just the four of them laying in the clearing in good cheer, Hagi moaned with deep satisfaction. He regarded Kileo with a melancholy smile, one that suggested a familiarity beyond that which he seemed entitled to for the scant days he had known her. Nevertheless, she received his odd stare confidently.

"You look at me as though you know me," she said. "Which doesn't surprise me, for I feel I know you as well."

Aratus was relieved that another of them shared this uncanny feeling.

"You are excused for not remembering how or why you know me, Kileo. That goes for all of you." Hagi sighed, then said, "I'm quite used to it by now."

"You remember us and yet we do not remember you. I for one do not like this disadvantage. End this mystery." Aratus demanded.

"Do not call what I have an advantage, my friend," Hagi bellowed back at him, "It is a *curse,* a burden that I've carried on my shoulders alone for thousands of years!"

Repetto cried out for the sanity of Hagi, "He is gone, the great Hagi! Gone to the scatters! Mercy!" He then looked up at the eye of the ancestors and howled for their pity.

"Repetto, there is no need to look up at the sky to peer into the eye of the ancestors. You need only to look at each of us, and us at you."

Hagi paused for emphasis, then said:

"*We* are the ancestors."

The statement stunned them. Repetto howled even louder, fearing that his blasphemy would bring misfortune upon them.

"Explain how that can be true, Hagi, before I believe like Repetto that you have the scatters."

"Fathom, if you're able, death. It happens not once but many times. When you die, your experiences and memories disappear just as your flesh does. When you come back -- as Kileo, as Raspail, as Repetto, as Aratus -- you have no memory of your previous life or lives before that one. You are free to seek new dreams, new alliances, new grudges."

He paused and let them contemplate this.

"Well, for me it is different. When I die, my flesh disappears like yours... but my memories survive. And they go very far back, farther than you could possibly imagine."

Again he paused.

"There was a pack that settled this valley which is now called Cob Ash and Draguignon. That pack was the Shan. We are that pack. We are the *Shahn.*"

The name, and how he let it flow from his mouth caused a rumbling in the murky depths of their memories.

"We came from different, faraway provinces, so long ago that you can't go to these places any more. We'd each splintered from packs that rambled for survival. The north, the west, the south and the east were each represented. Out of necessity we formed a pack. We bore children and these children made our bond strong. We swore to always stay together, and we kept our word. Only death, it turned out, could tear us apart. Look around you. This is where the first of the Shahn died."

Kileo didn't need to look around the clearing to see if it evoked something in her heart like the others. She'd always avoided this part of Cob Ash.

"On that day, we swore that even death would not keep us apart. We swore to keep the Shahn intact wherever it was we went in death." Hagi looked solemnly at Kileo. "That was the pact we made over you, Kileo. That was the pact of the Shahn.

"Today is the first time all of us have been reunited since that day."

The noble Aratus could not accept that he was a wolf of such high provenance, that he was an *Ancestor*. He had failed so many trials and disappointed so many loved ones, that Hagi had to be lying.

Aratus raised his head and spoke resolutely, but without hostility or aggression, for part of him felt an undeniable kinship with Hagi.

"I would like to believe this unusual story, for it is flattering and would mean I am a wolf of great provenance. But I know in my heart I am not. And when I look at you I hear a voice saying not to trust you."

Hagi grew irritable at his stubborn old friend. "Of course you do. And you'll never be convinced otherwise, for we have had our broils in the past and that's sadly all you remember of our friendship."

"If this is a deceit and you are using us for some grander scheme, you will get no mercy from me when the time comes."

Aratus stood up and strode back to camp. Hagi sighed.

"Hagi, I will be honest: It troubles me that Aratus distrusts you," Raspail said, "for Aratus is wiser than all of us. Assuage this worry and I will let the awe that wants to grow in me blossom."

"Many generations ago, Aratus lived in a province east of here that now lies vacant like so many wolf provinces. He had a daughter named Sotsy. Sotsy was one of the original seven Shahn. She was also my mate. We tussled and he killed me. Whenever he encounters me, he remembers to distrust me. And that is why he usually ends up killing me."

"Aratus has killed you before?"

"So many times it is almost comical."

"Is this Sotsy among us?" Kileo asked.

"No. I never saw Sotsy again after that." Hagi said mournfully. "The beautiful white wolf, elegant and lithe, always eludes me. Why, I do not know. But since the easy meat arrived, I grew less diligent in my search. My woes were dark. And the darker my woes grew, the harder it was to leave the meatdrunk splendors of Ramblefoot. Raspail, I want you to fathom spending endless winters searching for your Kileo."

"I cannot, Hagi."

Hagi whimpered cries of sorrow and regret, and the others whimpered with him in sympathy for a long moment.

Waiting till he was sure that Hagi was done with his amazing disclosure, Raspail led them silently back to camp, his thoughts spinning in every direction.

Along the way back, Repetto walked closely to Hagi and asked in a quiet, serious tone that showed a hint of worry:

"Hagi? Am I always, y'know... like *this?*"

Hagi let the others continue ahead and stayed back with the little wolf. "Yes, you are always a brave and loyal friend, an unconventional fighter, and a source of good humor and happiness to all who are lucky to be in your company."

The answer was pleasant on Repetto's ears but did not satisfy his worry. Hagi saw that he had not satisfied Repetto's curiosity, and continued:

"But if you are inquiring about your physical stature -- I have never seen you much bigger than you are now."

Repetto had clearly hoped for a different answer, but smiled regardless. Hagi licked his ear then said quietly in it: "I will tell you a story that is only for your ears. There was a wolf I knew who engaged two others, myself included, in a challenge to see who could eat the most meat."

Repetto interrupted him. "Hagi, I love this story, it's your greatest story ever -- but I've heard it many times before!"

"Yes, but I never told you that the wolf who ate so much meat he died -- that wolf was *you,* Repetto."

Hearing that he was a Shahn -- an ancestor -- was one thing. But hearing that he was the star of Hagi's greatest story ever was an honor that made him feel ten times his size.

Raspail climbed on to a high promontory that jutted out above where his pack was resting and looked at the content faces of these wolves, freshly fed and faithfully waiting for his command. If Hagi was right, these wolves and all wolves in Warmpools were descendents of them, the original Shahn. As they waited for his first howl in the home he'd promised and delivered them to, he looked at them staring up at him with the same adoration and respect they stared up at the eye with. He closed his eyes and felt a vibration, not unlike the electrical feeling transmitted through his foot pads when earth was trampled. This vibration came from the collective power of his huge pack, and from the love of Kileo, which would pulse strong by his side forever.

But also it came from the dead-eyed ghosts who haunted him since escaping the man's prison. He saw them again, staring at him from behind their hollow masks. Then they violently shook their heads and pawed at their masks until the lifeless visages were cast off. He could see the faces now, and they looked like him, a thousand times, him.

Possessed by this vision, he keened a mournful howl with complex overtones that could only come from a throat that had been wrecked and then restored. And as Raspail conducted the power of the pack back through them, they added their droning voices by degrees to form an astonishingly beautiful song. Hagi recognized it with a shiver.

It was the song of the Shahn.

***

Balfort's Ruse

The howling of these bloodthirsty ruffians drove terror into the hearts of the surviving border recruits billeted on the outside of Draguignon camp, recovering from wounds and mourning the death of friends.

Moorea, herself badly maimed, knew it was time to leave. She made inviting gestures with her perfumed haunches to a big wolf she'd fought side by side with, and soon the two were deserting south. Polwin was alerted. He caught up with them and herded them back to the billet where he executed Moorea in front of the eleven remaining border recruits.

"That is what I do to my sister. Imagine what I will do to you."

Polwin, who had previously roamed the border keeping these wolves out, now patrolled to keep them inside.

Past these bloody ranks Hesser walked with Balfort, Maddocq and their three wards. Maddocq, distracted by a familiar smell, stopped and followed the trail to a wolf bleeding from bites to her neck who looked either dead or near dead. Maddocq smelled the fur on her back and shoulders where the wolf's attacker had clamped on tightly enough to leave a clear imprint of his perfume. Balfort looked at Maddocq impatiently.

"I smell Aratus. Aratus fought her."

Balfort leaned over and smelled the wolf. Lacking Maddocq's sensitive nose, he needed to taste the fur, his licks startling the wounded wolf awake. The wolf was a border recruit, like them, and they recognized each other.

"You appeared dead."

"I perhaps should be," she said weakly.

"Were you fighting above your league?"

"He was slender and not huge of stature, so I assumed no. But his quickness surpassed mine. It was as if he was fathoming my thoughts and one step ahead of me."

"What color was this wolf?"

"Gray and orange with a blackish ruff. Avoid him if you like to live."

They bade her goodbye and caught up with Hesser. Balfort spoke quietly so he could not hear:

"That is indeed Aratus's scent, his fighting style, his color and ruff. Which means we are fighting on the wrong side. Oh, this is troubling. What do we do?"

"We do what Aratus would do." Maddocq said.

"And what would Aratus do?"

"He would do the opposite of what you would do."

Balfort looked aghast. "He would never! He always asks my counsel."

"Yes -- so he knows what to do the opposite of."

Balfort reflected on this. Indeed, Aratus often asked his advice and then did the opposite. His pride was wounded, but he could not deny the truth.

"Well? What would you do here?" Maddocq asked

"I..." And he hesitated, for it was easier to suggest a plan of action when he thought it would be taken seriously. "I would try and run, get out, flee to the east as far from those hideous ruffians as possible."

"So if we were to do what Aratus would do, we would flee to the west and engage them."

Balfort huffed. "Well -- I like my plan better even if Aratus would see it as a reverse template for his own."

Hesser snarled sharply at them to move. They walked together till they reached Draguignon, who was lying beside Sarassin where she was grooming her father. Behind him sat the white yearlings on one side and his six sons -- the strongest sons from his two oldest litters -- on the other. Balfort and Maddocq immediately recognized the white bitch, her father and his sons from past broils. It was not clear whether Draguignon recognized them, but the white bitch's scrutinizing suggested she did. Maddocq muttered nervously to Balfort:

"It would be good if she did not recognize us."

"You recognized *her*, didn't you?"

"She's memorable. She's white and fine-looking."

"You haven't a fang longer than a molar, you smell like scat because you roll in it all day, and your left ear is ripped and hangs like a leaf. You're not unmemorable yourself, Maddocq."

"Ah." Maddocq sighed resignedly. "Well, I lost my foot since the last time she saw me. Maybe that will throw her off."

"We shall see." Balfort said.

Balfort, diverting his gaze so as not to provoke her memory, made the mistake of staring at one of the beautiful white yearlings instead. Immediately the young wolf thrust at him and flashed fang threateningly. Balfort stood his ground confidently.

Sarassin walked closer and sniffed him. When the prolonged interrogation was over, she said. "This border recruit is a former Cob Ash wolf. I remember him."

Balfort, though scared out of his wits, was able to glance at Maddocq as if to say, "See!"

"They rambled, my dear one." Hesser said, "They rambled because they disagreed with their facet and returned when they heard he was gone. They should be judged for their loyalty to their province and hatred of their former facet!"

Balfort and Maddocq looked ashamed to have to go along with the wretched lie, and their hearts weighed heavily under the eye of the ancestor's bright and penetrating gaze.

"And their loyalty is to us?" she asked.

"So long as they are given some land once Cob Ash is taken back from those hoodlums."

Draguignon grumbled, then looked up at Hesser.

"You and your wolves will fight next."

Hesser, his shoulders thrust out and his head held high, could do nothing to stop his shaking. From his teeth, clenched tightly and chattering wildly, down to his hind paws, which skittered sideways in the snow, he shook, because he'd watched the enemy fight, and the enemy was a mob of angry, disfigured, well-fed drunks who were experienced and carefree at killing.

Draguignon spoke menacingly under a curling lip. "You are the facet of Cob Ash, aren't you?"

Hesser shrank back from his persecuting glare, anticipating a lashing. Draguignon opened his jaws and drew back his lips to show off the long white fangs in his arsenal. With his eyes blazing insanely over this deadly contraption he cried:

"Then fight like Cob Ash!"

Hesser crumbled in fear, squirming on the ground, peeing where he lay. Every wolf looked at the pathetic actor stripped bare of his costume.

Balfort saw in the moment an opportunity, and in that opportunity a plan that would make Aratus proud.

"We five will fight." Balfort said mightily, drawing the attention to him. "We will take on as many as they throw at us."

"Really," said Draguignon dubiously.

"Yes. However, we will need to borrow some of your wolves, fresh ones unscarred by battle."

"The only fresh wolves I have are my six sons. I am saving them to fight by my side at the final stage of this battle. You will fight alone."

"Yes, we will. And though we are five we can fight like three times that number. However, in battle appearance is everything as you know, and we do not want our enemy to think that such poor numbers are all you can afford on the battlefield."

"And why not?"

"They will run around us, insignificant as we may look against their vast numbers, and leave us in their dust as they continue on to take out the heart of the beast, so to speak."

Balfort's colorful prophecy generated foreboding in the large wolf.

"Lend me your pedigreed sons, my liege. Just to give us the *illusion* of numbers. They will not be asked to fight, just to stand tall, look strong and be counted. They will not receive a scratch."

Draguignon thought quietly, then gestured for his sons to join them. Before they left he said, "You will feel an urge to fight when you see these Cob Ash wolves engage invading wolves at the border of your province. Promise me you will save your fighting for when we need it most."

Indeed, his sons looked eager to do battle.

"Whatever you ask, father." They responded in unison.

While the father spoke to his sons, Balfort whispered urgently to Maddocq and their three wards. "They will march behind us. As we get to the border of Cob Ash, I will signal and we will split into two flanks and kloot in the timbers. When they reach our position, we will ambush from either side and waste the sons of Draguignon."

He could see they did not quite understand so he elaborated. "The fighting will draw forth those rampaging hoodlums that Aratus has found himself sided with. It will advertise our loyalties to them and insure we are not torn to shreds while waiting for the laconic Aratus to confess he knows us."

Maddocq understood and liked the plan. They were joined by the six sons of Draguignon, all gruff and aloof, trailing behind them by many lengths as Balfort hoped. As they got nearer to the border of Cob Ash, Balfort split left with Lucien, and Maddocq went to the right with Horus and Ferier. They klooted in the trees until the six sons of Draguignon passed, then sprang out from behind them, surprising the unsuspecting wolves.

Now, as these sons had promised their father they would not fight, they were reserving their energy by maintaining a calm mood. The same cannot be said for Balfort and Maddocq, whose hearts were pumping in preparation. They worked fast in those first moments of the skirmish, exploiting their advantage for as long as they could, killing two of the enemy early in the confrontation. But Maddocq was not the invincible fighter he was when he had four feet, and this protracted the fight to a point where both sides were evenly matched.

The skirmish attracted ramblefoots from the other side of the border in Cob Ash as they had hoped. Repetto led nine wolves to the battle, then made them stop as he watched with confusion at what looked like Draguignon wolves fighting amongst themselves.

"Join us in arms!" Balfort barked to the ramblefoots, "Our loyalty is with you!"

"Kill 'em all!" Cried Repetto, and the Ramblefoots entered the fray and attacked both parties.

Well this is going as planned! thought Balfort sarcastically as he fought a ramblefoot from one side and a son of Draguignon from the other. There was such confusion, such mismatched alliances -- like Maddocq and a Draguignon son taking on three ramblefoots -- that Balfort stepped outside of the whirlwind of blood and fur for a breath of clarity.

"Pull out!" Balfort barked. By degrees the three wards and Maddocq stepped out of the fight, leaving the ramblefoots to finish off the sons of Draguignon, which they did quickly. The mob of ramblefoots then turned threateningly on Balfort, Maddocq, Lucien, Horus, and Ferier.

Balfort studied Repetto, the tiny wolf leading rowdy wolves twice his size and thought: *So they let a tiny child lead the pack. How strange. It is a good thing I have experience with youth.*

"Young lad, I have never seen a child fight like you. You have a natural born gift! With proper training, you would grow up to be a great fighter indeed."

Repetto laughed. Boonbrekker and the others laughed with him.

"But you will need a reliable father figure, someone to raise you. I beg you, look no further." Balfort bowed his head proudly.

Repetto, despite his instinct to kill any wolf who maligned his size, felt amused by the wolf and not inclined to kill him.

"No wolf never want to be my father before," Repetto said with false gratitude in his gravelly, mature voice, surprising Balfort. Then Repetto smiled, showing off his bizarre teeth.

"My apologies if I have offended you thinking you were an infant. But before you kill me little wolf, let me at least plead my case to you: we were killing those Draguignon wolves in order to benefit you. We have no loyalties to them. We wish to fight for you."

"Hmmm." Repetto said. "We play a game."

"What sort of game?"

The nine ramblefoots laughed again, because they all knew that no wolf ever beat Repetto at his game. Repetto demonstrated the game, darting under Boonbrekker's body and weaving through his legs, then said to Balfort, "If you can catch me, I let you live."

"How many chances do I get?"

"Uh..." Repetto thought for a moment. "One."

Balfort looked nervously to Maddocq, who shrugged his shoulders and said nothing. Balfort tentatively assumed a spread-legged position.

"Good lucky," said Repetto as he licked Balfort's eye. Repetto warmed up, running a few laps around Balfort, then dove under his body and weaved between his limbs.

Watching the demented little dwarf dance around and under him made Balfort dizzy and sick. He thought to himself, *He can only do that so long before he exhausts himself, so I will wait and use my one chance when he is spent.*

Repetto stopped and barked angrily at Balfort, "What you waiting for! You got to drop on me! Come on! Squash me you big fat ass!"

"Don't rush me! I'll squash you when I'm ready!"

"You ready *now!*"

"I'm ready when I'm ready!"

Repetto dove and weaved while Balfort waited, observing his opponent wearing himself down. His erratic movements were becoming more predictable, and Balfort was about ready to take his one chance when he saw wolves arriving in the distance. The company of fifteen or so ramblefoots descended the sloped valley to meet up with their dwarf leader. Balfort scanned their faces and saw Aratus at the front.

"Aratus!" Balfort howled as loud as he could

"Balfort?!" Aratus howled from the company he was leading.

Repetto, panting with exhaustion, heard the name "Balfort" and recalled how Raspail spoke lovingly of him, especially Balfort's special gift for song.

"Balfort!?" Repetto said excitedly, "You're Balfort?!"

"That is me," said Balfort looking confused.

Repetto did one final dive under Balfort, rolled to his feet and broke into song, repeating word for word, note for note, one of Balfort's famous howls:

All along this path I pee,
it smells of my brothers and mee,
but if you put some 'yours in it,
you'll find yourself coyote shit.

Balfort watched stupefied as the little wolf sang a song he had composed. And as if his mind weren't besieged by enough confounding wonders, he soon found himself surrounded by an unbelievably large mob of frightening wolves. The pack went wild as their huge black facet stepped forward.

Balfort lowered his head submissively, avoiding the massive beast's golden eyes, sighing and muttering to himself, *"First Draguignon, then the insane dwarf, and now this terrifying giant. How many times must I lower my head and beg for mercy in one day?"*

"Mercy, I am Balfort, brother of Aratus who fights in your ranks!"

"Hoy! If you are a brother of Aratus, then you must be a brother of mine!"

Balfort looked up. Immediately he recognized the grinning beast as Raspail.

"Raspail!" Balfort shouted with joy as he leaped on Raspail, embracing him. Maddocq charged at Raspail, and the three wrestled on the ground for a moment.

"You were always the portrait of brute strength in my youth, Maddocq. Three feet and you only look more fierce"

Aratus also stepped forward, with Kileo next to him, and the reunion was heartwarming to all who watched, for as we have said, these wolves had all left something behind, something they would never recapture, and seeing that it was at least possible for Raspail was inspiring to them and they shared the powerful moment with him shamelessly.

When the greetings were finished, Balfort and Maddocq explained how they tricked and slayed the sons of Draguignon. They reported that the border recruits, wounded, demoralized and eager to desert, were terrorized into staying to fight by Polwin and his patrol. Raspail asked Repetto to spread this information around camp -- the border recruits would be spared, but no Draguignon wolf was to be left alive, and that included yearlings.

Aratus took Raspail aside and said, "We have something to negotiate. We must decide who executes Draguignon, and who executes Hesser."

"Let us negotiate then."

"Draguignon killed my facet and first brother. I am responsible for his execution."

"By all means, it is your obligation and right to kill him, Aratus."

"But you are facet. You are expected by your pack to kill their facet."

"I will tell them, 'I am passing this great privilege over to my broken-hearted brother, who will hopefully shed some of his woes as he sheds the blood of the wolf who slayed his brother.'"

Aratus smiled and spoke sincerely, "And they will love you even more."

"Now as for Hesser--"

"He is my first brother," Aratus said. "I am responsible for him too. I must execute him as well."

"Greedy Aratus! You are not the only wolf who wishes to shed some woes!"

"True," Aratus sighed.

"Furthermore, you would kill Hesser out of obligation, but I would kill out of revenge. You could be talked out of the job, whereas I could not."

"You were fooled by Hesser once, weren't you?"

"True," Raspail sighed. "My potential for mercy is greater ever since that wretched prison. I'm haunted by those sad, hollow visages whenever I'm compelled to waste a wolf. I'm not fit for the job of executioner, and yet he must be killed."

Both wise wolves put their minds to finding a solution, but neither arrived at one. Instead, Aratus' worry shifted to something else that plagued him.

"Remembering how you were fooled once by Hesser, I worry now about this Hagi."

"You must trust me about Hagi. I agree, the Shahn is a tall story and most likely the fantasy of an aging mind and wishful heart. But he has no other motives. He is a true brother."

Aratus gestured with his head affirmatively, but Raspail knew that Aratus never let another wolf's judgment supersede his own.

***

The Duel

Repetto ran around the pack, jeering manically at them, pumping them up for the siege that would eliminate Draguignon forever.

At the Draguignon camp, Sarassin suspected things had turned rotten when her brothers did not return. Then she heard the avalanche of wolves rolling in to Draguignon, and her worries were confirmed.

Her father looked at her and said, "Take the children and flee."

"We have lost. Flee with me and one day we can return and take our province back."

"I cannot run. They killed my sons."

She saw that his mind was set for battle. She turned, gathered the yearlings and led them at a quick pace out of her homeland and towards the mountains.

Hearing the thunderous approach of the ramblefoots, the wounded recruits billeted outside camp were suddenly miraculously cured of their ailments as they shot up and ran like they were in the prime of their health, heading for the northern border. Polwin was almost trampled by them and had no choice but to let them desert. Without their numbers, Polwin knew the battle was lost. It was time to flee himself.

Draguignon sat with his great ruff fanned out, his crest proudly pronounced, watching Raspail lead the enemy (and what an enemy they were) to where he sat. The two massive wolves faced each other.

"I am facet of Draguignon."

"I am facet of Ramblefoot!" Raspail said with a flourish. He watched Draguignon's eyes fall to the exotic shackles on his ankles and squint in puzzlement.

Raspail spoke calmly, "You killed my facet and plotted the downfall of my province. For that you will die."

"You have your chance to fight me! Take it!" And Draguignon looked every bit the cornered animal ready to go down with a good fight.

"I pass that right to a wolf who is thirstier for your blood than a newborn pup is for his mother's milk."

Aratus launched out of the mob and on to Draguignon's back where he clamped his jaws on to his spine and wrenched it side to side, trying to crack the bone.

The bigger Draguignon stood and flipped Aratus on to his back, crushing him beneath him. Still, Aratus did not withdraw his fangs from his back. But with each twist of his powerful neck he felt the strengthening counter-force of his opponent who, knowing he was doomed to death, was determined to doom his enemy with him.

Aratus felt that dreaded feeling of self-doubt that happens when the balance of power suddenly shifts to one's opponent, and the pain, which has been held back by the dam of confidence, begins to flood through the fissures in that dam. He was not just fighting Draguignon anymore, but the fatigue in his neck and the stiffness in his rear legs which had not yet recovered from his long imprisonment.

The din of wolves around him -- droning in excitement and anticipation, casting their hopes towards Aratus, cheering for his victory -- was truly amazing. Every wolf at this point knew that the uncle of Raspail was of such noble character that he'd let himself be captured rather than leave the side of his dead mate. The story resonated meaningfully with them and so they rooted Aratus on as one of them. He felt the power surge through him as their howling reached a crescendo, reviving his spirit.

With this jolt to his wary muscles he flipped Draguignon with a force that was greater than when he was fresh in the fight. He ground his molars on the facet's backbone while his fangs pierced the joints of the spine until finally Draguignon shrieked in mortal agony, lost control of his muscles and died in Aratus' jaws. Aratus released the dead wolf and the mob roared their approval.

Aratus' children, old enough to appreciate their father's heroic feat, jumped on him proudly. Ipsy came to him to lick his wounds. He thought, as he looked down at that delicate beauty born of wolf and coyote, *Woes, you will always be with me, but you will not weigh me down, for I am here to live, and live I will.*

Raspail and Kileo led the pack through Draguignon, flushing out enemies from the nooks and crevices of the rugged province that was now theirs.

    ***

Hagi's Gullible Heart Gambles Poorly

Sarassin heard the influx of invading wolves fanning out around Draguignon and adjusted her heading to avoid them. At one point she attracted the attention of Aratus, but, knowing the province better than him, she quickly lost him.

The stream that formed the southern border was in her sight. Running with the yearlings behind her at a lightning-fast clip, she saw something to her left, the movement of a klooting wolf's fur bristling as a gust of wind hit it.

She slammed her front paws into the snow and halted, scanning the trees and snow-covered rocks. The wolf emerged from hiding as if drawn out by some invisible force. He was old and missing one of his feet, but looked imposing and well-fed. He looked at her not with the visage of a predator, but with the wide-eyed daze of a stupefied deer. She froze as she stared into his eyes.

To her children she barked, "Go! Cross the border and wait for me!"

Without hesitation they sprinted for the stream. But being curious students, they circled back and spied on their mother's conversation.

As Hagi looked at her he felt energy conduct from the pads in his feet through the earth and into hers and back again. Dappled sun shined on her gleaming white fur, and he knew it was that ancient love of his, that wolf who had eluded him for centuries.

"Sotsy!" the name rumbled uncontrollably from his throat. He saw her look of confusion, but continued undaunted. "Sotsy. You were lost for so long and now we have found each other!"

The three-legged ramblefoot inched towards her. Fearful of the crazed derelict, she stepped back and flashed fang.

"Stay where you are!"

Hagi pleaded pathetically, "It's okay. You will remember me soon. You will remember your Hagi."

Sarassin cocked her head and seemed to understand suddenly, to feel this connection that Hagi was seeking. Her eyes moistened as she stared forlornly at him. "Hagi? It's you?"

"You remember?!" he said, astonished.

"I remember!" she said, sharing his excitement.

Hagi had so much to tell her.

Far off in the timbers, Aratus ran with preternatural quietness until he finally caught up with his quarry, Sarassin, who was involved in some intrigue with another wolf that he soon realized was Hagi. Watching Hagi negotiate with the daughter of Draguignon, and unable to hear their conversation, he was sure his suspicions about the old wolf being duplicitous were true. He surged with anger as he prepared to attack Hagi the traitor then kill the white bitch. But then a voice in his head nagged him, *He is a friend of your friend, so before you kill him you must be absolutely sure he is a traitor.*

He klooted closer until he could hear their voices clearly.

Hagi bowed his head reverently before his old love, his tired eyes shutting. "I have searched for you forever, I never stopped. I failed, wandering alone without you, Sotsy."

Sarassin stepped forward and peered down at him compassionately, saying, "You found me and that is all that matters. Shut your eyes and rest now."

The moment he closed his tired eyes, she whipped off her mask of compassion and exposed a monster with enormous, harrowing eyes and gaping jaws stretched so wide open it would make a snake blush.

Aratus, seeing he had misconstrued the liaison, charged out of hiding and barked, "Hagi -- *Beware!*"

But as the old wolf turned to see Aratus running to his aid, he felt her fangs puncture his throat. Unable to breath, his old body became limp. She held him up by his punctured neck and shook him side to side. With his head slumped over he was able to peer closely into the white bitch's stone-cold eyes. In his desperation to reunite with his old mate, his gullible heart let him be deceived.

Aratus slammed into her side and knocked her down. The two rolled together, gnashing and jabbing. Out of the snow sprang her five precious yearlings. Aratus, already wounded from the fight with her father, wisely knew he could not take on all six and live. But he also knew that he had to kill to show his willingness to fight. He struck at the smallest yearling and killed him quickly. The others retreated snarling till they were by their mother's side again.

"You killed my brother," She cried dramatically at Aratus, "You killed my father. And now you kill my son."

Aratus' noble heart was not moved by her woes. He was calculating his attack when Hagi spoke:

"No. Mercy."

She turned and bolted for the border. Aratus heeded Hagi's request and stayed by his side.

Sarassin led the four surviving yearlings across the border to safety. To her surprise, she was haunted the entire trip by the odd name the old wolf called her. Her yearlings saw that she was nagged by something.

"What is it, mother? You are worried."

"I was just thinking."

"About what?"

"It's of no importance!" she snapped at them.

She kept them running at a good pace.

"Sotsy."

Sarassin stopped short and looked at her brood, her stress palpable.

"Who said that?!"

They looked at each other confused.

"Said what?"

The yearlings continued running. Sarassin trailed behind them this time, unable to see they were laughing.

They paused to drink from a stream. Sarassin lapped at the cold water, hoping to never hear the name again.

"Sotsy."

"Sotsy!"

Sarassin looked up at them to find the culprit, but all pretended they were drinking. Then, every time she bent her head down to take water in the stream, she heard the voice again:

"Sotsy."

And then they looked boldly at her, barking the dreaded name, over and over, driving her mad. Sarassin had no idea that they'd eavesdropped on her conversation and were merely playing an infantile game with her, teasing her with the name that the crazy old three-footed wolf gave her.

They had no sense that the name, inexplicably, resonated painfully with her.

"Sotsy."

Sarassin lashed out at her children in that playful moment, killing two of them, and sending the other two running for their lives.

When clarity returned, she tasted the blood on her muzzle and looked at her dead yearlings shocked, as if something had possessed her to make her kill them, as if something else had orchestrated the tragedy. She cried for her two last children, but they were already running as far from her as they could go.

Hagi Tells his Last Story

Hagi, with Aratus supporting his listing body, was able to limp back to Cob Ash, and knowing that it would be his last travel, he made Aratus walk especially slowly.

When they reached the place where he told them about the Shahn, Hagi said, "Hoy. This'll do."

That night, every ramblefoot bade farewell to the great Hagi Shahn, who lay on the snow breathing slowly with his eyes barely open. Hagi, who had difficulty speaking, asked Raspail to tell them it was a time to celebrate, not mourn.

After everyone bid their farewells to Hagi, it was just Raspail, Kileo, Aratus, and Repetto who remained, keeping Hagi warm by huddling around him.

"I would like to tell one last story..." Hagi said, surprising them. And then he paused.

They waited silently. He said nothing.

So gone looking was he that some in his audience thought that his last words would be "I would like to tell one last story..." and that would be it for old Hagi. But Hagi was taking his time, summoning the details in his foggy head, for this story needed to be told right.

"There were two wolves," he began. "Together, they were hunting an elk. But when the elk fell, the two friends suddenly turned enemies competing over the meat. While they fought, a bear strolled over, stole their elk and ate it."

He studied their innocent expressions. They listened like captivated children, registering the injustice and irony exactly as he'd hoped

"Well, the two wolves who were fighting a moment earlier became united as friends again because of their hatred of the bear, and together they kill him. Not only did they eat him, but the meat that he'd stolen too. Soon they were meatdrunk, laughing about the earlier broil, over which there were no hard feelings. Then one wolf turned to the other and asked, "Why ever *did* we fight? There was plenty food for both of us. And we have real enemies, like the bear.""

At this point, everyone was so captivated by the story that they forgot about Hagi's condition.

"So what he say? Why did they fight?" Repetto asked anxiously.

Hagi said nothing, and Repetto pouted like a disappointed child.

"That's the end of the story?" he whined. Raspail growled at Repetto, stifling him.

Hagi continued: "Now that the Shahn owns these two rich provinces again, keep routes open. Let wolves ramble across your borders if they need to. It's the only way we will survive. We face a scourge to the south that will send many more wolves northward looking for safety. And it will get worse. You must let them ramble through. Tell your children to let them ramble through. Because..."

He shuddered in pain, waited for it to pass.

"Because one day, when the metal jaws appear in Cob Ash, it may be you rambling North, *you* begging for mercy at your neighbor's border, har."

He made a noise like a laugh that may not have actually been a laugh, then drifted in and out of life and death for an eternity of excruciating sadness for his friends. They moved even closer to him, clinging to every incomprehensible utterance he made. But it made no sense, none of what he said, until he finally muttered angrily, *"Where's the damn raven..."*

Just as they were comprehending these four garbled words, a huge sheet of black flashed before them, startling them back from Hagi. It was Poitu, plummeting from the sky like a meteorite, landing on the dying wolf. She croaked harshly at them, urging them back, then proceeded to do something very strange. She strutted back and forth on Hagi's prone body as if she were counting the steps to her cache. Finding the spot she was looking for, she opened her wings and lay flat over Hagi's chest and made a low gurgling sound as her head vibrated. She did this for a long moment then strutted up his neck towards his head, and lay down again with her wings spread open as before, this time covering his face and eyes. She made the same strange noise, which the wolves found mesmerizing, then pushed off of Hagi's muzzle and flew into the sky cackling.

When they looked back down at Hagi they could see immediately that the light was gone from his eyes.

***

The Shameless Hesser

Raspail delayed the parceling of territory until the next full moon and told his pack to spend the next few weeks basking in their victory and being merry without the stress of laying down territorial claims. He urged them to remember the faces of their co-celebrants so that in the weeks to come, when negotiations started, they would remember they were all brothers. This was to honor Hagi, but it was also so Raspail could put off business and be lazy with Kileo, who he was enchanted by more than ever.

The ramblefoots, who adored and respected Raspail, reveled and caroused as they were ordered to do. But behind the masks of carefreeness each wolf took to growing anxious, secretly wondering what hierarchies were already forming and who to ally with, because they were, after all, wolves.

Raspail became more private as Kileo's pregnancy advanced, staying with her while she renovated her mother's old den. Raspail's constant presence grew annoying to Kileo, for she had grown very self-reliant in her time away from him. Inside the chamber she worked hard, scratching the dirt on the walls to reveal the fresh, moist earth. When she stepped out of the den for air, Raspail was always there waiting for her, sleeping.

This is where Raspail was when, on the second week after the taking back of Cob Ash, Repetto ran breathlessly up to him.

"That wolf that took your voice, he come back! He come back and he squiggle on the ground like something funny! You gotta see!"

Raspail and Kileo ran so quickly back to camp that Repetto could not keep up.

Hesser, unable to survive on his own and terrified of what lay outside his known world, had come back to Cob Ash hoping for mercy from his brothers. He did this with a display of submission that was so pathetic and ignoble that Raspail, who had once dreamed of the day when he would kill Hesser, found no desire to do so on the day that opportunity arrived.

"Brothers, mercy on me!" he whimpered. "Cob Ash is my home. I made mistakes, terrible mistakes that were influenced by evil, scheming wolves. I am not a bad wolf. Mercy, let me live in Cob Ash!"

Wolves around camp laughed and ridiculed him. Aratus looked at Raspail. "We never did settle on who gets to kill him. And now I have lost the desire entirely."

"As have I, Aratus. As have I. Hmm."

Raspail stepped forward and looked down at Hesser, curved like a fetus on the ground.

"Stand."

"I am not worthy of standing, for all the terrible things I have done to you, poor boy. But I can see you are a good and merciful facet." And he licked Raspail's foot.

"Hesser, Cob Ash is your home, and it shall always be your home."

Everyone looked surprised, but none more so than Hesser. He looked quizzically up at Raspail.

"Stand," Raspail commanded him with no anger in his voice.

Hesser stood with that shrinking posture of a kickaround dog. Raspail addressed the pack:

"I want every wolf to hear this! There will always be a place for the wolf Hesser in Cob Ash!"

"You are a good wolf. No -- you are a *grand* wolf!"

"Thank you. Walk with me."

Raspail walked with Hesser, playing with him in such a way that Hesser felt he was being pardoned. Behind them trailed Kileo and the others, eager to see what would happen.

"You have a special place in this pack, Hesser."

"I do?" He said with false humility.

"Yes, you do. And that place is right there."

Raspail stopped in front of Hesser's old perch, that nasty sliver of granite which cantilevered over a vast moat of bramble. In the time since Hesser spent his last sleep in this private domain, the thorned bramble had overgrown threefold. His secret route was no longer a viable passage.

The cowardly Hesser looked at the bramble with trepidation.

"But...the thorns-- it's impossible!"

"Nothing is impossible, my beloved uncle. All you need do is look at me for example -- me, muted by *you,* and now able to speak -- me, banished from Cob Ash by *you,* and now *facet. "*

Raspail curled his lip just enough to show a glint of fang to the despicable fiend. Hesser trembled terribly as Raspail forced him forward to the thick stump threshold. He stepped on the stump where thorns impaled his sensitive pads.

"Yes. If there is one thing I have learned, anything is possible."

Hesser extended his other trembling foot, placing his weight on the springy branches that intertwined into a thick braid, and took his next step, standing on this unstable bridge. He panted with a sickening grimace.

"Take the leap of faith," Raspail said, "Or life will not reveal to you its many wonders."

Hesser shut his eyes and stepped forward. He plunged into the swirling canals of thorns and swam for his life, thrashing and tangling himself in the lacerating web while he shrieked in pain. Soon he was trapped and suspended like a fly in a spider's web. He made several efforts to free himself, but these only cost him more blood.

Throughout the day people came and amused themselves watching the villain's protracted death, and as with the joy that blossoms when well-liked wolves have large healthy litters, seeing this fiend die and leave their world brought them immense good cheer.

Since large scavengers dared not enter the thorny net, meat rotted off his bones so gingerly that to this day one can still see the actor's skeleton tangled deep inside the web of bramble, preserved in the same anguished pose it had died in.

***

Freedom

On one of those days when Raspail went to flop outside
the den where Kileo was working, he slept so soundly to the
music of her scratching that he did not hear her leave. Kileo used
this time to visit the low mountain where she had been prisoner.
She ran without stopping to Carel's perch. From there she looked
out at all of Cob Ash as she had done when she was hiding there
and not free to leave.

*This is actually a lovely place when one is free to come
and go*, she thought, *This will be my refuge from my big
handsome annoying mate.*

In the sky she saw a raven rolling and tumbling in the air
and Kileo wondered if it were Poitu. Poitu had still not returned
after the strange ritual she performed on Hagi.

Kileo howled to the bird, causing it to glide over and circle
above her. Then it moved on, passing over the mountains to the
west, out of sight.

Kileo returned to her den. When she arrived, she saw
Raspail with his head in the mouth of the den. She quietly ran up
and bit his tail hard and heard him hit his head on the ceiling of
the tunnel. He came out and they played roughly with each other
as they liked to do when they were young.

Raspail chased her and she chased him, and before they
knew it they were at the northern-most border of Cob Ash. Kileo
lay down and rested.

"Let's keep going," he said.

"I can't, I'm tired, you're not -- you are not pregnant. Play
with Repetto. He's not pregnant either."

"I meant, let's *ramble*. North."

She laughed. "You assemble a pack larger than any wolf
has ever seen. You reclaim Cob Ash and reunite your uncles.
And now you want to walk away from all that?"

"I could walk away from everything so long as you are
walking with me."

"You can't abandon your pack!"

"I built that pack for one purpose -- to rescue you."

Kileo looked astounded, realizing for the first time: *That massive force of wolves was assembled for my benefit. That is how strong this wolf's love is for me.*

"Soon we will have children," He said. "It is our last chance to be truly alone."

"We can't," She said.

"Don't ever say we can't," He said sternly.

"I want my children to be born in Cobb Ash. To know Aratus, and Balfort and Maddocq. And Repetto. And Carel and..." she stared at him angrily. "You could walk across that border right now and leave all this?"

"Right now."

She felt disgusted by him. She turned and headed back to camp. He bounded by her side and stopped her.

"I want to ramble somewhere with you, somewhere far from the terrors of the south."

"Stay and protect your borders from this enemy."

"This enemy is too scary to face again. You haven't seen it."

She gazed at his ankle bracelet. It remained a mystery to her, one he never spoke of.

"Come. Let's ramble. Now, so we have time to find a new home."

"No. We can ramble when the children are yearlings if you still want to."

"All this power!" Raspail bellowed in frustration at the trees. "And my legs might as well be shackled again!"

He stomped on the snow and kicked it up with his feet.

"I'm going back to camp now," She said.

"I am rambling! And you are coming with me!"

In that instant, with their two stubborn personalities at odds, Kileo hated Raspail as much as she had adored him a moment ago when she learned that he'd waged a war to free her. She turned away from Raspail and trotted briskly back to camp.

Raspail huffed in exasperation, then turned and headed for the border, not trotting like Kileo, but walking ponderously, hoping she would change her mind and follow. He crossed the narrow crevice that formed the northern border, and rested in a cove of trees hoping that he would see Kileo coming to join him.

She didn't come. Raspail, being wise in so many areas, was not wise in the ways of the opposite sex. And so with another huff he muttered to himself, *I'll wait here all night and let her miss me, then I will surprise her at the den in the morning and we will love each other again.*

"All night", as it turned out, was a little ambitious for our hero, in love as he was. He lay down with his head resting between his arms and tried to make himself comfortable, got up and circled, then tried several other equally uncomfortable poses until finally he lost his resolve and was trotting back to Kileo.

From the periphery of his vision he saw a sliver of eyeshine from a wolf klooting twenty lengths to his right. He slowed and faced the direction where the wolf was lurking. In that brief moment, the klooting wolf had already moved to another hiding spot. Raspail froze in place and scanned the horizon, waiting without breathing until he saw a twinkle of light escape from the klooting wolf's eyes as it spied on him.

Raspail locked on the animal as it lost its ability to cloak its presence. The animal slowly stepped back, and now Raspail could see that it was Polwin.

As Polwin slowly retreated, Raspail stalked him, the gap between them not expanding or shrinking, their eyes locked together. Neither enemy spoke provoking words or flashed fang to the other; nothing needed to be said -- this rendezvous, arranged by Fate, was inevitable.

In the crater-shaped valley that was to be the arena for their duel, giant corridors of spruce forced frigid air into the sunny inverted dome. And since these corridors were counter-opposed, rivers of air collided and accelerated until cyclonic winds spiraled at its center, birthing a great plume of snow that rose up and spun dancing at its center. The sun dazzled this crystalline vortex, and it was a blinding distraction that Raspail, unlike his opponent, had the bad fortune to be staring into.

Polwin stepped back into the swirling tower of snow and vanished. Raspail charged in after him, passing through the violent clash of winds, and when he emerged on the other side of the cyclone he saw not just Polwin, but fourteen other wolves flanking him. They quickly fanned out in a circle around Raspail.

He had stupidly followed Polwin into a trap. Hopelessness was not a state of mind that Raspail liked to indulge, but the direness of the situation was so complete that he was forced to confront the mounting fear and doubt in his heart.

Raspail looked down at the shackles on his ankles and recalled that freedom will swing its gate open to you if you want it badly enough. He looked at the enemy wolves as they tightened their circle around him and silently begged, *Freedom, open your gate for me again.*

With the cyclone raging at his back and the gap closing between him and Polwin's pack, he saw no gates swing open, he only saw them close.

And then he noticed one of the wolves jerk its head back and lick at something nagging it, something that had just struck its back from above. A white stain was splattered across its fur. Raspail inhaled hard to extract the scent out of the swirling windstorm and confirmed that Poitu had indeed dropped its scat on this wolf, marking it as she would prey. There was no ambiguity to the signal; Poitu had determined that this wolf was incapacitated somehow, making it the weakest wolf in the ring of assassins who encircled him. Freedom, using a raven as its instrument, had opened a gate for him once again.

Raspail lurched back into the vortex of spinning snow, vanishing for a moment, then charging out of it at the marked wolf. In a heartbeat he was trampling over the surprised wolf and continuing on at delirious speeds towards Cob Ash with the feet of fifteen wolves pummeling the snow close behind him. Again he was leading an enormous pack of wolves towards Cob Ash, only this time the common goal of that entity was to tear him asunder.

He saw her shadow appear in front of him and followed it without question as he had a thousand times before. Looking up as he fled the horde of murderers pursuing him, he saw Poitu, who he hadn't seen since Hagi's death, gliding above him. Seeing her made his legs longer, his strides more powerful, and his momentum unstoppable.

And as the two flew across the border and back into the realm where Raspail was facet, he heard the wolves stopping behind him at the warning line inscribed by him and his pack, not daring to cross it.

Freedom, Raspail sighed with the euphoric relief that comes from cheating death -- *freedom.*